Heroines Behind the Lines

CIVIL WAR
Book 4

SPY *of*
RICHMOND

JOCELYN GREEN

MOODY PUBLISHERS
CHICAGO

Published in association with the literary agency of Credo Communications, LLC, Grand Rapids, Michigan, www.credocommunications.net.

This is a work of fiction. Names, characters, places, and incidents either are the product of the author's imagination or are used fictitiously, and any resemblance to actual persons, living or dead, businesses, companies, events, or locales is entirely coincidental.

Edited by Pam Pugh
Interior Design: Ragont Design
Cover Design: Left Coast Design
Cover photo of woman's face copyright © by domi79/Shutterstock 79244173. All rights reserved.
Cover photo of dress provided by The Museum at FIT.
Author Photo: Paul Kestel of Catchlight Imaging
Map of Richmond: Rob Green Design

Library of Congress Cataloging-in-Publication Data

Green, Jocelyn.
Spy of Richmond / Jocelyn Green.
    pages ; cm. -- (Heroines Behind the Lines: Civil War ; Book 4)
"River North fiction."
Includes bibliographical references (pages   ).
    Summary: "Trust none. Risk all. Richmond, Virginia, 1863. Compelled to atone for the sins of her slaveholding father, Union loyalist Sophie Kent risks everything to help end the war from within the Confederate capital and abolish slavery forever. But she can't do it alone. Former slave Bella Jamison sacrifices her freedom to come to Richmond, where her Union soldier husband is imprisoned, and her twin sister still lives in bondage in Sophie's home. Though it may cost them their lives, they work with Sophie to betray Rebel authorities. Harrison Caldwell, a Northern freelance journalist who escorts Bella to Richmond, infiltrates the War Department as a clerk, but is conscripted to defend the city's fortifications. As Sophie's spy network grows, she walks a tightrope of deception, using her father's position as newspaper editor and a suitor's position in the ordnance bureau for the advantage of the Union. One misstep could land her in prison, or worse. Suspicion hounds her until she barely even trusts herself. When her espionage endangers the people she loves, she makes a life-and-death gamble. Will she follow her convictions even though it costs her everything-and everyone-she holds dear?"-- Provided by publisher.
    ISBN 978-0-8024-0579-1 (softcover)
    1. Abolitionists--Virginia--Richmond--Fiction. 2. Slaves--Virginia--Richmond--Fiction. 3. United States--History--Civil War, 1861-1865--Women--Fiction. I. Title.
PS3607.R4329255S69 2015
813'.6--dc23
                        2014031519

We hope you enjoy this book from River North Fiction by Moody Publishers. Our goal is to provide high-quality, thought provoking books and products that connect truth to your real needs and challenges. For more information on other books and products written and produced from a biblical perspective, go to www.moodypublishers.com or write to:

River North Fiction
Imprint of Moody Publishers
820 N. LaSalle Boulevard
Chicago, IL 60610

1 3 5 7 9 10 8 6 4 2

Printed in the United States of America

Praise for *Spy of Richmond*

Spy of Richmond is meticulously researched historical fiction that shares the struggles, courage, fears, and faith of ordinary citizens who lived in extraordinary times. Jocelyn is a master at weaving historical facts into her novels so the reader is simultaneously educated and entertained. A captivating story that brings history to life.

—**JESSICA JAMES**, author of *Noble Cause* and two-time winner of the John Esten Cooke Award for Southern Fiction

A spellbinding story, told with historical veracity, about loyal Unionists who risk everything for their country in the heart of the Confederacy. Once begun, *Spy of Richmond* is nearly impossible to put down.

—**JOSEPH WHEELAN**, author of *Libby Prison Breakout: The Daring Escape from the Notorious Civil War Prison*

The Spy of Richmond is richly peppered with descriptions and details of Confederate Richmond as it feels the strains of the last two years of the Civil War. Tensions in the city come to life through characters, both Northern and Southern, grasping for hope and survival. Sophie's desire to do what is right and morally humane in the face of the terrors of war is applaudable. It's inspiring to see how one woman's sacrifice could impact the freedom of so many.

—**KAREN A. CHASE**, Church Hill Association, Richmond, Virginia

Praise for *Wedded to War* (Book 1)*

*2013 Christy Award Finalist (Historical Fiction and First Novel categories)

With stirring detail and a firm grasp of the historical background, this novel totally engages the reader and shows the difficulties women encounter as they strive to serve the Union and make unconventional choices.

—**CAROL KAMMEN**, editorial writer for *History News* and Tompkins County (N.Y.) historian

The research behind this shines. Green's descriptions of the first hospitals, the horrors of battlefield medicine, and the extraordinary courage and vision of the women who took on this challenge carry the whole book. For this alone it's worth the read.

—**HISTORICAL NOVEL SOCIETY**

Praise for *Widow of Gettysburg* (Book 2)

With equal amounts history, romance, and mystery, Jocelyn Green writes with heart-stopping detail, crafting a story that resonates on every page. Highly recommended!

—**LAURA FRANTZ**, author of *Love's Reckoning*

Amazing . . . Green gives a voice to the women and children of the Civil War and skillfully shares their struggles.

—*RT REVIEWS,* 4.5 out of 4.5 stars and named a TOP PICK

Jocelyn Green does a masterful job juggling the different storylines that parallel Liberty's life experiences, creating an urgent desire to continue reading from one cover to the other . . . A compelling, realistic rendition of a woman's life during the Civil War.

—*CBA RETAILERS + RESOURCES*

Praise for *Yankee in Atlanta* (Book 3)

Green has written a rare Civil War novel that hits no false historical notes. In a cruel and violent time that divided loyalties, families, and hearts, Green's heroines' enduring courage, compassion, and mercy show the wellspring from which a renewed nation could emerge from the fires of war.

—**MARC WORTMAN**, PhD, author, *The Bonfire: The Siege and Burning of Atlanta*

Rarely have I read a novel that so envelops you into the excitement and intrigue of 1864 Atlanta. With passion, courage, and accuracy, *Yankee in Atlanta* hits the mark. A must-read for all historians and romantics alike!

—**AMY REED**, curator of Exhibits and Educational Programming, Marietta Museum of History, Marietta, Georgia

Move over, Scarlett O'Hara. *Yankee in Atlanta* mixes grit and grace in ways that transcend stereotypes and tug at your heart. A terrific must-read.

—**JANE HAMPTON COOK**, historian and author of Pulitzer-nominated *American Phoenix*

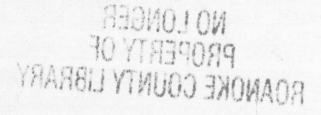

For Deb, who inspires me.

*Be of good courage, and he shall strengthen
your heart, all yet that hope in the Lord.*
—Psalm 31:24

Map of Richmond

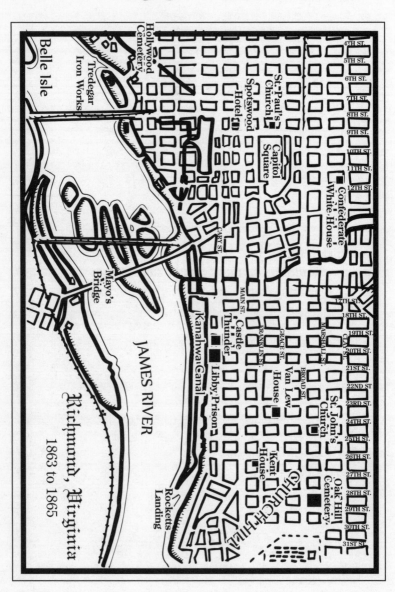

Belle Isle

Hollywood Cemetery

Tredegar Iron Works

St. Paul's Church

Spotswood Hotel

Capitol Square

Confederate White House

4TH ST.
5TH ST.
6TH ST.
7TH ST.
8TH ST.
9TH ST.
10TH ST.
11TH ST.
12TH ST.

Mayo's Bridge

CARY ST.

17TH ST.
18TH ST.
19TH ST.
20TH ST.
21ST ST.
22ND ST.
23RD ST.
24TH ST.
25TH ST.
26TH ST.
27TH ST.
28TH ST.
29TH ST.
30TH ST.
31ST ST.

JAMES RIVER

Kanahwa Canal

MAIN ST.

Castle Thunder

FRANKLIN ST.

GRACE ST.

Van Lew House

MARSHALL ST.

BROAD ST.

St. John's Church

Libby Prison

Kent House

CHURCH HILL

Oak Hill Cemetery

Rocketts Landing

Richmond, Virginia
1863 to 1865

Contents

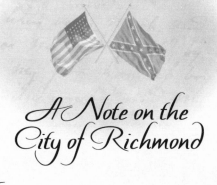

A Note on the City of Richmond

Virginia was the cradle of democracy. Not only could it claim the settlement of Jamestown, but the leaders the state produced—George Washington, Thomas Jefferson, Patrick Henry, and James Madison—guided the new nation through its earliest perils.

So when the Southern states seceded from the country Virginia helped birth, the Old Dominion hesitated. In fact, as late as April 12, 1861, Richmond was a Union town. The diverse, urban area had little in common with the agrarian sector of the Cotton South. But the action at Fort Sumter, South Carolina, changed everything. When Lincoln called for his 75,000 volunteers, Richmond and Virginia felt the choice was made for them. In the face of an invading army, Virginia was the last state to secede. Weeks later, the Confederate capital moved to Richmond. The city of 38,000 would balloon to more than 100,000 souls. It seethed with government officials, refugees, speculators, prisoners, soldiers, criminals, and wounded. No other American city endured what Richmond did during this war: four years of periodic attack, frequent raids, siege, famine, capitulation, and partial destruction by fire.

A small band remained loyal to the Union—and to the cause of freedom, especially after Lincoln's Emancipation Proclamation—even in this feverishly patriotic capital. The Richmond Underground comprised native Virginians as well as immigrants, white and black, slave and free, men and women. *Spy of Richmond* tells a tale of commitment to conviction no matter the cost.

Prologue

Outside Savannah, Georgia
Thursday, March 3, 1859

It is madness.

Rain hissing to the earth behind her, Sophie Kent shivered and craned her neck toward the platform, half expecting lightning to strike the Ten Broeck Race Course any moment. It was the second day of the auction selling more than 420 slaves, and the second day of boiling, weeping storms. Gripping her pencil and papers beneath the folds of her wrap, Sophie trained her eyes and ears to the drama around her.

Humiliation tightened her throat as she watched a woman on the stage made to jump, bend, twist, and turn. Her smooth complexion was the color of tea with milk and honey, a bright contrast to the cocoa and coffee bean shades of the others. Her almond-shaped eyes were cast downward as a man tugged off her shawl and head rag before pinching her arm and pulling her lips apart to display her teeth. Modesty told Sophie to avert her gaze from the indignity, but she resisted. For years, she'd been blind to the horrors of slavery. This time, she would not look away. *Neither will I stay silent. Not any longer.*

The man spun the woman around and exposed her back to the audience. "No scars from the disciplining lash—no trace of rebellion in her spirit," he said. The woman covered herself once more.

As the bidding began from within the two hundred buyers in attendance, Sophie withdrew her auction catalogue from her wrap, her pencil poised to take notes. Humidity curled the pages, and the list of souls for sale drooped in her gloved hand.

116—Rina, 18; rice, prime woman.
117—Lena, 1.
118—Pompey, 31; rice—lame in one foot.
256—Daphne, 32; house servant.
257—Judy, aged; rice hand.
342—Cassander, 35; cotton hand—has fits.

Murmuring voices pricked Sophie's ears. "Well, Smith, I saw you inspecting this chattel yesterday. Going to buy her?"

"I think not. No. 256 looks healthy enough, and can do a heap of work. But it's been years since she had any children, she told me. Done breeding, I reckon."

Heat scorched Sophie's cheeks as she furiously recorded the exchange in the margin of her catalogue. *Do they not hear themselves? Do they not understand these are people not livestock?*

In front of her, rough-looking young men with knives in their belts and tobacco in their cheeks spoke of managing refractory slaves. Joining them were white-haired gentlemen with silk cloths at their necks. These advocates of severe whipping and branding were silenced by a booming voice: "I'm a driver, myself, and I've had some experience, and I ought to know. You can manage ordinary slaves by lickin' 'em, and givin' 'em a taste of the hot iron once in a while when they're extra ugly; but if a brute really sets himself up against me, I can't never have any patience with him. I just get my pistol and shoot him right down, and that's the best way."

Sophie looked up to see more than one man nod in agreement.

"Sold!" The gavel struck, and Daphne, chattel no. 256, twisted her bright yellow head scarf back into place over her hair. Her face settled into tense lines as a family of four replaced her on the platform.

Thunder snarled, and wind wailed through the pines surrounding the race course. The crowd shifted closer to the platform, away from the spitting rain. All except for Sophie, who remained rooted in place.

"Pardon me, Miss." A man in gold-rimmed spectacles tipped his broad-brimmed hat to her. "Tedious doings, eh?"

"I can think of another word for it," she muttered without looking up from her catalogue, waiting for him to pass.

He didn't. "Sophie?"

She turned in time to see lightning's flash brighten his twinkling brown eyes. "I thought you were in—" *New York.*

But the sharpness of his gaze penetrated her surprise. Harrison Caldwell was here for the same reason she was, which was why he wore spectacles he didn't need, and a mustache too full to be his own.

"Shhhh," he said beneath his breath. "You can do this. Write it." He bent, kissed her hand, and whispered, "Four years to go," then stood tall and stepped away from her, his eyes focused on the platform.

Heart hammering, Sophie clenched her papers, careless of the ink and lead smearing her gloves. Aware that he would disappear into the crowd any moment, she stared at his broad back while she could. Memories kindled until her face burned.

A hand squeezed her shoulder, and she nearly jumped out of her kid leather boots.

"Daddy!" Sophie gasped. "You startled me."

"Our business is finished here." Head and shoulders above Sophie, Preston Kent's silver-striped suit gleamed with the light of the storm, as if he were Zeus himself.

"Do you mean—"

"We've secured a new maid for your mother. Rachel's been doing her best since Matilda died, but she's no maidservant. I don't blame her, of course, a housekeeper isn't trained to wait on the personal needs of a mistress the way your mother has been accustomed. We simply must have a proper replacement. A marvel I was able to get this chattel no. 256—calls herself Daphne—alone, with most slaves being sold in families."

"Has she none, then?"

"Not anymore." Mr. Kent puffed on his cigar, the wind stripping the sweet blue-grey smoke from his lips. "No. 257—apparently, her aged mother—died of consumption in the sheds just after the catalogues were printed. Fortuitous, yes?"

She looked away. "Not for Daphne," she murmured. "Not for her mother."

"It's good business. For instance, why buy two horses—especially when one of them is infirm—for a one-horse carriage?"

"No. 257? Her name was Judy, Daddy, and she most certainly was n-not a h-horse!"

Preston's gaze pounced around them until landing on Harrison, who had never strayed far from Sophie, and watched her still. Lips forged into an iron smile, Mr. Kent caught his daughter's wrist and cut his voice low as he led her away from the crowd. "You're making a scene. Don't embarrass me." His blue eyes slanted into glittering slits. "Is this what I can expect from you from now on? Blatant, public defiance?"

"I'm capable of walking without you dragging me." Sophie pulled away from him, but he only twisted harder. "You're treating me like a child. I'm nineteen years old, Da—"

"So was—" He dropped the thought like hot coal, but Sophie could hear the unspoken. *So was Susan.*

"I'm nothing like her." Sophie was Daddy's little girl from the first.

Mr. Kent jerked her farther from any listening ears, wrenching her wrist harder, until her catalogue dropped from her weakened clutch.

As her father scooped it up, the draft of the story she'd been working on last night peeked from between the pages. She reached for it, but he turned her notes toward the watery light of the rain-drenched sky.

"What's this now?" He squinted at her script as ash dripped from his cigar. "A story? You were writing a story about the auction?"

"A newspaper article about the largest slave auction in history. I—I want to be a writer. Like you were, before you became editor."

The lines around his eyes softened as looked down at her. "I still write, you know. But to be published—that is not a ladylike enterprise. There's a reason all the writers for the *Richmond Enquirer* are men."

"Not all." The words slipped from her lips like oil through her fingers. "Daddy." Her smile trembled as she gathered courage. "I have a surprise for you. Those columns you've been printing these last several months from a writer who goes by the name John Thornton . . ."

"Yes? With his anti-secession views it's no wonder he uses a pseudonym. Still, his arguments are sound and well-stated. What is it? You don't mean to say you want to write by a pseudonym, too?"

Sophie shook her head. "I've already done it." For a moment, she wondered if he'd heard her. "*I'm John Thornton.* You've already been printing me. Don't you see? You've already decided my words are as good as any man's."

Mr. Kent looked through her draft again. Winced. "What is the meaning of this?" He jabbed his finger at her words, a storm gathering in his eyes.

"I—I told you. I want to be a writer, like you."

But he was already stalking from beneath the shelter of the Grand Stand and into the driving rain. Sophie followed him, shoulders hunched, her boots sinking in mud.

"No." His voice matched the rolling thunder as he threw his cigar down and ground it beneath his heel. "Not like me. Like Harriet Beecher Stowe."

Sophie's spine straightened at the name of her secret heroine. With a single book, the woman had influenced millions. *Uncle Tom's*

Cabin infuriated her father. "She wasn't wrong."

"And I suppose I am?"

Raw, wet wind swirled in the silence between them, knifing through Sophie's wrap as though it were made of lace.

"I never should have sent you to that boarding school in Philadelphia."

"Mother's old school—"

He held up his hand to stop her, as if he couldn't bear to be reminded that Eleanor Kent, the woman he'd married after his first wife died, was born and raised in Philadelphia and not in his native, beloved Virginia. "Yes, your mother. I blame myself for bowing to her demand that she nurse and raise you herself. You should have had a mammy from infancy, like every other child in the civilized South. You should have learned from the cradle that white people command the lives of colored. These are the proper roles for our races, Sophia Virginia! It is madness to suppose otherwise."

He paused for breath, and looked at her as though searching for the daughter he wanted to see. If he only knew their Richmond home had served as a stop along the Underground Railroad right beneath his nose . . . "Just how many abolitionist rallies did you attend for you to write such fanatical nonsense about a simple slave auction?"

She set her jaw and lifted her chin as the voices of Frederick Douglass, Sojourner Truth, and the Grimke sisters washed over her.

"It ends now." Mr. Kent shredded her article draft, as well as the auction catalogue in which she had taken notes. "The writing must stop."

"Oh no, don't!" Sophie lunged for the remnants, her bonnet slipping off her head and bouncing against her back. Rain sprayed her face as mud puddles swallowed the crumpled remains of her story.

"Have I lost you, too?" Mr. Kent's face twisted. "After I've given you everything a father could possibly lavish on his child—you would turn your back on me now?" He lurched one step toward her, then grimaced, his fist to his chest.

"A disagreement is not a personal betrayal." Blonde ringlets, teased free by the wind, clung to her face and neck.

"It is to me. This time." Blanching, he dropped to his knees in the spongy earth.

"Not your heart!" *Not again!* Wrapping her arms around his shoulders, Sophie knelt in the mud beside him. "I never wanted to hurt you!"

"Some things have been too painful—for me to speak of—" He collapsed onto his heels and leaned into her for support. Terror seized her breath.

Her father's eyes closed. "But you need to know this."

Still mute with fear, Sophie nodded, barely noticing the water dripping down the back of her neck, or the cold seeping into her from the ground as she leaned in close to hear him.

"My parents didn't just die years ago as I told you . . . After I moved to Richmond to be a reporter, they—and my younger sisters—were killed in their beds. By slaves."

Sophie's stomach roiled.

"Nat Turner's Rebellion. Did you learn about that—in Philadelphia? The slave said he'd been called—by God—to murder white people. So he—and dozens of other slaves—killed sixty good citizens in Southampton County. My—entire—family. I was twenty-two—when I lost them all. When you choose—to crusade for the slave—you reject me."

"No, Daddy, I—"

His groan stopped her. "You're all I have left."

Sophie wanted to deny it, to say he had Mother still. But he didn't, not really, and they both knew it.

"The one thing I want—and the one thing it seems I cannot have—is family. Truly," her father whispered, "you are breaking my heart." His lips pulled back as he clutched at his lapels once more.

"Let me go for a doctor."

"Say it first. Say you'll not betray me."

17

All the speeches she'd rehearsed retreated behind her fear for her father. She'd planned on telling him she would always love him, but she was a grown woman now with a fine education, and that her conscience demanded she follow her own convictions. She was going to be strong.

Instead, she leaned over and planted a kiss on her father's clammy brow. "I'll always be your girl."

"FROM THE TIME I knew right from wrong, it was my sad privilege to differ in many things from the perceived opinions of my locality. This has made my life intensely sad and earnest . . . [I became] quick in feeling and ready to resent what seemed to me wrong."

—ELIZABETH VAN LEW, Union loyalist in Richmond

Act One

THE PRIVILEGE TO DIFFER

Chapter One

Oakwood Cemetery, Richmond, Virginia
Thursday, September 24, 1863

*T*ell no one how it ended. Please," Sophie murmured to
Daphne, her gaze flicking over the precious few mourners receding
from the graveside. A sticky breeze whispered through her black net
veil as she bowed her head, praying she did not look as relieved as she
felt to finally lay the past to rest. A thin ribbon of scar tissue itched
beneath her wristband.

Questions swimming in their eyes, neighbors paid their respects
to Sophie and took their leave until only the household staff and the
family lawyer remained.

"My deepest condolences, Miss Kent." Mr. Whittaker doffed his
hat and smoothed his grey hair back from his brow. "You have sent
word to your father, of course."

She hadn't. Part of her wanted to tell her father every detail, to
make sure he knew how much his wife and daughter had both suffered.

She wanted to heap guilt upon him for joining the army and leaving home just when home became unbearable. It was easier to serve the Confederacy, she supposed, than to stay and serve what was left of his family.

"He receives mail at the prison camp?" Whittaker prodded.

"He does." *He also gets cold, I imagine, and weak, and sick. He is forty-seven years old. What if I tell him about Mother and—it kills him?* Sophie balled her black-edged handkerchief in her hand. "Thank you for being here. If I might have a moment of your time, there is a matter I wish to discuss with you."

"Regarding your mother's property, I presume," said Whittaker.

Sun flashed on spectacles as Otto Fischer, the Kents' German immigrant steward, looked up. If the slaves had heard, however, none of them showed any sign of it.

"That's right."

"I have the documents with me." His tone was hushed as he glanced at the fresh mound of earth. "Shall we?"

While Daphne waited, Mr. Whittaker and Sophie put a respectful distance between themselves and the grave.

"Now, the only 'property' Mother personally owned, was Daphne," Sophie began. "When my father purchased her four years ago, she was to be my mother's maid, and freed upon Mother's death. My father said he'd secured this with you." He had also stipulated that Daphne not be informed of the arrangement, lest she have motive to end Eleanor's life herself.

"I remember."

Sophie's breath suspended while Whittaker slipped an envelope from inside his jacket. Then his frown sent dread trickling down her spine.

"Did Mr. Kent not inform you of the change?" He unsheathed the document. "The ownership of the property has been transferred."

Sophie blinked, unable to process the word. "Transferred?"

"Bequeathed. To you."

She gasped. "There must be some mistake. I don't own slaves."

"You do now, my dear."

No. No.

"You don't already have a maid, do you?" he continued. "It isn't fitting for a twenty-three-year-old woman to be without one. Besides, you know how folks would talk."

"No!" She reined in her voice. "No. I free her. I manumit her myself."

"I'm afraid that has not been left to your discretion. There is a codicil on the will. You may not sell or free her. She is to be yours for life. Daphne will be freed upon your death."

Or hers. Sophie's throat burned as she turned to look at Daphne. Though it was illegal for both of them, Sophie had taught her how to read and write for this day, so she'd be equipped for freedom. "She's thirty-six years old and has never lived according to her own wishes."

Mr. Whittaker held up his hand to stop her. "There is wisdom in this, Miss Kent. I know of your abolitionist leanings, and for your sake, I keep quiet about them." He sighed. "Couldn't be helped, I suppose, with your mother being from the North, and you going to school in Philadelphia. But you are no longer a child. It's time to leave childish thoughts behind you, and accept that this is the way things are. It is the way things *should* be."

She shook her head. But her lips refused to move.

"Accept this, my dear. It's what your parents wanted. Your father wrote you this letter to help explain. Again, my deepest regrets on your loss." His message delivered, he tipped his hat to her and left. By degrees, she absorbed the news, as her black mourning dress absorbed the sun.

Nearby, warping lids of unburied green pine coffins popped loose, cracking through the air like gunshots, exposing the dead from Chimborazo Hospital to the glaring light of day. Sophie pressed her handkerchief to her nose and returned to Daphne without the news she had longed to bring. Nothing had changed, after all. Daphne was a slave before Eleanor Kent's death, and she was a slave still. *My slave.* Sophie's chest squeezed. *Are the sins of my father now mine?*

Alone in her bed chamber, Sophie's hands shook like linden leaves. Her father's words blurred on the page. *The Negro's happiest condition is that of bondage. Your mother and I could not punish Daphne with freedom.* Since when had Eleanor Kent believed that slaves should not be freed? It smacked of deception. Eleanor most likely had no idea her will had been changed.

The rest of the letter was a repeat of his farewell speech. He was sorry if his absence caused her pain, but after Lincoln announced his Emancipation Proclamation in September 1862, the war brazenly attacked slavery in a way it hadn't before. *But slavery is God-ordained,* he'd said, *and without it, the South cannot survive.* This was why he'd decided to fight. So that white Southerners could keep Negroes in bondage.

White Southerners like me. Her friends in Philadelphia would never believe it. *If Harrison could see me now . . .*

A sigh slipped from her. With Eleanor's body now removed from the house, Sophie withdrew the black crepe draping her mirror. The bright green eyes in the face that stared back at her were wiped of their former bright, inquisitive look. There was no sign in that reflection that its owner had once been the favorite child of her parents, and as protected from unpleasantness as any Southern girl could be. Those lips, which had been slow to speak but quick to smile, now lay flat. The face in the mirror was symmetrical but blank, vacant, so like her mother's at the end, it chilled her. *Make a difference,* her mother had told her years ago. *You'll find a way.*

Sophie thought she had. But her father had cut her writing career short, and now it was too late. To even hint at the opinions she had formerly published as John Thornton would be her ticket to Castle Thunder, the prison for political enemies, deserters, and citizens suspected of treason. *I have no voice at all.* She had failed her mother, and she had failed herself.

Sweeping out onto her second-story balcony, Sophie watched a flock of geese recede into the blue-and-gold edged sky, then let her gaze drift down Church Hill. From her house at the corner of Twenty-seventh and Franklin Streets, the James River was a gilded, wrinkled ribbon. Though Confederate ship masts at Rocketts Landing and the Navy Yard bristled along the banks, Sophie's mind's eye saw the Delaware River instead, and the island within it teeming with men. Since the stunning Confederate defeat at Gettysburg, her father was one of them. Still he controlled her, even from inside a Federal prison camp.

As she gripped the balustrade, her mourning gown stark against the weathered white railings, Sophie mourned indeed. The war had killed her mother and taken her father. Nearly every family in her neighborhood had a husband, father, brother, or son in the army. The widow Madeline Blair, the only neighbor who had called on the Kents since the war started, had sent three of her four sons. Two of them had already been killed.

While Sophie had been ensconced in her home tending Eleanor, the war had turned her beloved, provincial Richmond into an over-crowded metropolis. The city was bursting with both living and dead, the way unburied corpses burst their coffins. Danger lapped at Richmond so often the tocsin in Capitol Square sounded with the regu-larity of a grandfather clock. The stakes could not be higher, and yet Sophie had barely even been a spectator, so entrenched had she been with Eleanor.

Marching footsteps grew louder, and Sophie turned toward the dipping sun. Dusty columns of soldiers—hundreds of them, maybe thousands—tramped toward her on Franklin Street. They wore blue. Prisoners from the dazzling Rebel victory at Chickamauga, no doubt. On either side of the street, windows opened, and women and children leaned out to watch. As the prisoners came closer, the jeers that fol-lowed them grew louder, too.

Well, you've come to Richmond at last, now where's your arms?

Oh, is these the kind of brutes that has come down here to kill our noble sons?

"Miss Sophie?" Daphne's rich voice drifted out to the balcony. "You hungry for supper? You need anything?"

Sophie beckoned her out on the porch with her. "I need these prisoners to be soldiers again." Her words tasted of treason. "And so do you."

Daphne cocked her eyebrow. "You sound just like your mama, God rest her."

Her throat burned. She wanted Daphne to be free, along with the rest of the Kent slaves. But, "My father says you're to be my maidservant now."

She bowed. "I'm grateful to stay."

Sophie nodded, mustering her own gratitude that at least her father had not decided to sell Daphne outright. Still, "Do you ever imagine living your life for yourself?"

A short laugh popped from Daphne's lips. "Now what good could come of such a notion? It ain't fitting to dwell on what can't be."

"Look." Sophie pointed at the prisoners now snaking south and east. Some of them may have fought against her father. But they also fought against slavery. "Those men don't think it 'can't be.' If the North wins, you're free. Immediately and forever. If the South wins, slavery will go on just as it has for centuries."

Daphne's shoulders squared. "Well, then. Let the white men fight. Ain't nothing we can do about it."

But as Sophie watched the prisoners pack into the waterfront warehouse that was now Libby Prison, she wondered if Daphne was wrong.

Chapter Two

Capitol Square, Richmond, Virginia
Friday, September 25, 1863

"I want to help. Surely you agree with me that a Christian nation such as ours should exhibit charity to those who cannot help themselves . . ." Head down, Sophie Kent weaved between clusters of people strolling through Capitol Square and quietly rehearsed her speech. Gravel crunched beneath her feet on the cobblestone-lined walkways dissecting the grassy lawn.

Stopping on the west side of the George Washington statue's granite pedestal, she shielded her eyes to gaze upon the bronze form of the nation's first president astride his horse. Behind him, the massive white columns of the classical Virginia Capitol gleamed in the morning sun. "The wounded Confederate have nurses enough," she practiced aloud, as if she were addressing the statue before her. "I want only to serve where the need is greatest . . . Surely *you'd* understand, Mr. President," she added, musing that though Washington was a Virginian and a revolutionary, he was also the founding father of the United States and would certainly wish for its preservation.

"Look! That's Eleanor Kent's daughter!" The whisper froze Sophie in place. "Did you see her talking to herself just now?"

"Or is she talking to Mr. Washington?"

"Either way, she's going the way of her mother!"

A chill swept over Sophie as she fought for composure. She had hoped she had buried the past last week at Oakwood Cemetery. But wagging tongues were slow to stop.

"Nonsense."

Sophie turned just as Madeline Blair looped her arm around Sophie's waist. "Don't you listen to any of that talk now, dear. It's all nonsense." Madeline darted a sharp gaze over her shoulder, and the whispers fell silent.

"Thank you," Sophie breathed. "How are you, Mrs. Blair?"

"Happy to see you out and about, that's for sure. Fresh air is always an excellent choice." She smiled, and kindness filled her hazel eyes.

"Have you heard from Asher lately?" At age twenty-seven, he was the eldest brother and had been the man of the house since his father had died several years ago. The middle boys, Thomas and Solomon, had both been killed at Antietam, a year ago.

"It's been sixty-three days since the last letter. The house seems awful lonesome now."

"I imagine that's so," Sophie murmured. She and Susan had grown up listening to the Blair boys scramble up their mother's garden trellises and chase each other with firecrackers. They had teased the Kent girls mercilessly with lizard tails and frogs, but eventually learned more gentlemanly ways to capture female attention. "I suppose Joel misses his brothers something fierce, as well."

Mrs. Blair pressed a crooked smile from her lips. "It's no wonder you haven't heard, considering." Her gaze skimmed Sophie's black dress. "Joey joined up, too. Left a fortnight ago."

Joey. The baby. He couldn't be more than fourteen years old.

"Oh, Mrs. Blair," Sophie whispered. "However do you manage?"

"I'm proud of my boys, Sophie. Our cause is worth the sacrifice. Independence. Isn't that what the first Revolution was all about? Breaking away from a tyrannical government? Joel's young, but he knows what he's about. Who can fault him for wanting to protect our rights and our homes?" Sniffing, she pulled a lace-edged handkerchief from her sleeve and dabbed her leaking eyes. "And who can fault me, for wearing holes in my floor with my knees?"

"May God protect him," Sophie said. Images of Joel as a chubby toddler stumbling after his brothers scrolled through her mind. "And Asher."

"And your father. I pray for him, too, dear, and you can tell him so."

Sophie nodded. "May He bring them all home."

"Amen. In the meantime, do come see me sometimes, won't you? I would dearly love some company."

Sophie promised she would visit, and they parted ways.

Drawing a steadying breath, she turned north, thoughts swaying like the hoops beneath her skirts. She was overcome by Mrs. Blair's sacrifice and genuinely concerned for her sons. All she could do for them was pray.

She could do more than that for the sons of Northern mothers. Resolutely, Sophie marched to the corner of Tenth and Broad, just outside Capitol Square. With the spire of St. Paul's Church impaling the sky behind it, the frame building serving as the provost marshal's headquarters seemed a shanty in comparison.

Once inside, she found the provost marshal and two busy clerks writing at a table. Thick waves of frosty hair crowned General John Winder's bullish head. His piercing eyes and Roman nose reminded Sophie of her father. Nervous-looking people seemed to have sprouted in his office like mushrooms, some in clumps, a few by themselves. Passport seekers, Sophie guessed. The news from Chickamauga was favorable for the South, but the defeats at Vicksburg and Gettysburg cast long shadows of poverty and despair over the Confederate capital. Those with less hope of victory than most chose to go North.

Finally, it was her turn. Winder spared her but a glance. "Speak," he barked, glancing at his pocket watch before steepling his fingers.

Sophie sucked in her breath. "My name is Sophie Kent. I've come to request your permission to do my part in the war."

"You need no permission to sew, knit, roll bandages, donate food to the hospitals."

"If you please, sir, I'd like to help our prisoners."

"Fine. Packages may be received at the Northern prison camps, and I'm sure our boys will be glad of whatever you can spare." He waved his hand toward the door in dismissal.

"Forgive me, I haven't been clear. I want to help the prisoners among us. Libby Prison is just blocks from my home. I would like to bring the prisoners there small comforts. Food, blankets, reading material. As I have my own resources, this would not burden the government at all."

His eyebrows pinched together. "Better to use your resources for our own wounded soldiers. There are dozens of hospitals in Richmond. Chimborazo alone has three thousand patients on any given day—I'd say that's ample enough outlet for your benevolent instinct." With more than 120 buildings, the hospital complex was the largest in the South, perhaps in the North as well. In truth, it was just as close to her home as Libby was, but in the opposite direction.

Yet, "The women of Richmond are already pouring themselves out to meet those needs. But as you likely know, the gospel of Matthew says we are to love our enemies, and do good to those who persecute us. To minister to the hungry, the sick, those in prison—the least of these. Are not Yankee prisoners the very least of these?"

He grunted.

"If we wish our cause to succeed, and believe in the Christianizing influence of our nation, certainly we must begin with charity to the unworthy. I am not speaking of military policy, but of personal, individual kindness to those already captured."

31

General Winder's chest swelled. "Your views—"

"Forgive me, General. They are Christ's views."

His eyes narrowed, chin jutting forward, and Sophie held her breath. "If you show sympathy for the Yankees, you will generate talk."

People are already talking. "I am less concerned with what people say than with what my heart is telling me to do. I just lost my mother, and I need something meaningful to fill the time."

"What does your father say of this?"

She swallowed. "He is a prisoner of war himself. Fort Delaware, Pennsylvania. Isn't it true that our treatment of Northern prisoners often produces treatment in kind of our own soldiers in Union captivity?"

Winder guffawed. "Do you expect better treatment for your father because of your good deeds here in Richmond?"

She bristled at his condescending tone. "I pray that women in the North feel the same pity toward our Rebel prisoners that I do for the men now languishing in my very neighborhood!"

By now, the two clerks were staring at her, nibs of their pens suspended above their papers.

Winder's chair scraped the plain pine floor as he stood and walked to the window. After a moment's hesitation, Sophie joined him there. At length, he spoke. "My job is to keep the city safe."

"I understand."

"Your Unionist sympathies are suspicious. Dangerous."

Sophie's eyes widened. "Dangerous?"

"Spies, like roaches, skitter throughout the city. Until we destroy them." With a jerk, he consulted his watch again. "I must be off."

Sophie took a half step backward. "Are you suggesting I'm a spy because I want to visit the prisoners? I assure you, my motive is to relieve suffering!"

He rounded on her, fire burning behind his coal black eyes. "Join me on my—errand. I'll consider my answer by the time we return."

Sophie's gaze darted about the room. The clerks had already gone. "Where are we going?"

"Camp Lee."

Sophie blinked. *The garrison and hospital grounds?*

"And it is imperative that we not be late."

———

A little more than two miles outside the city, Camp Lee writhed with people. Men in top hats and women in their threadbare gowns spilled out of carriages and omnibuses while still others arrived on foot. Old men leaned on canes, while small boys made guns of sticks. Nearly every conversation, whether shrill or hushed, was punctuated with *Yankee* and *spy*. Goosebumps raised on Sophie's flesh. There could only be one reason for this vast congregation.

A rhythmic rattle grew louder until drum taps penetrated the din of the crowd. Soon voices dimmed, and the people ebbed from the Broad Street gate. The marching footsteps and steady drumbeats thudded on Sophie's chest as they drew closer to Camp Lee.

All around her, necks craned and toes tipped toward the empty gate until the drum corps filled the space. Behind them, with the slow crush of a tide, came two companies of worn and faded militia, and then a hack, closely guarded by mounted men. At this, shouts erupted from the tittering mass of onlookers. Insults exploded until the hack was obscured from view, swallowed up by two companies of infantry bringing up the rear.

Sophie thought she was going to be sick.

With razor sharp tone and West Point bearing, General Winder parted the crowd. Sophie followed in his wake, breath squeezing against her corset to keep up with his spit-polished strides. The throng pressed around and between them.

Winder grabbed her by the elbow and pulled her to his side. "Pay attention." He pointed up at the wooden gallows. "Do not turn away."

A man in captain's uniform stood beneath the gallows. In booming voice, he read the charges against the accused, a man named Spencer

Kellogg Brown, and the sentence of the court-martial: "Hanged by the neck until dead."

Winder bent his head toward Sophie. "This is what we do to spies, Miss Kent. Observe."

Her eyes and throat stung. Just as horrifying as the impending hanging was the multitude who had come to glut their hatred on the morbid spectacle. As the condemned man climbed the scaffold, however, he gave no impression of horror himself. Though his skin was pale from months of confinement, his blue eyes were clear and bright.

"He attained his twenty-first year while in Castle Thunder," Winder said. "Leaves behind mother, father, sister, and a bride. A personal favorite of Captain Alexander's, given a spacious room, reading material. Even ate at the captain's table. The prison chaplain tells me he is a most devout young man, firm in his faith."

Sophie's gut twisted. By now his arms were pinioned and his ankles tied together, but no shadow cast over his face, even as he watched a Negro climb a ladder and tie the rope to the upper beam. Wonder filled Sophie as Brown examined the rope, declared it too long to do the job, and politely requested they shorten it.

"But you see, Miss Kent, it matters not. Spies hang. We do not spare for love, youth, charm, or religion. Take heed."

The rope now shortened, the black cap was placed over Brown's head of rich brown hair. After bowing for mere seconds, he stood perfectly erect, and proclaimed himself, "All ready!"

Sophie squeezed shut her eyes. A sickening bang as the floor dropped away. The squeak of stretching, jerking rope. Finally, the silence of a soul departed.

At length, Sophie exhaled. The death achieved, the crowd turned its back and receded.

General Winder pinned Sophie with his gaze. "Now tell me, Miss Kent. Do you still want to play this game?"

"It's not a game." Tears bathed her cheeks, when she wanted to be stoic. Furiously, she wiped them away.

He sneered. "Contact with Yankees in the Confederate capital is a game, indeed. A deadly one. You play by my rules, and know that if there is ever a question, I always win."

Sophie tucked her fear behind her indignation, and still she could form no response.

"I grant you no pass to Libby Prison. Simply and absolutely out of the question. But if you choose to visit the hospital room on the first floor of the east side of the building, you may be of some use to the medical staff there. I make no objection. Your pass."

With trembling hands, Sophie took it, and turned to leave before he could ridicule her for that as well.

"Remember," Winder called after her. "Play by the rules. And I always—always—win."

Chapter Three

Kent House, Richmond, Virginia
Saturday, September 26, 1863

Sophie's head pounded as she stared at the dingy brown page of newsprint before her. *Crude stationery, indeed.* But with Richmond's paper shortage, it couldn't be helped. Around the notice of runaway slaves being held at Castle Thunder for their owners, and the report of Spencer Kellogg Brown's execution, she would have to pen the news she was loath to deliver.

Dear Daddy,
Mrs. Blair sends her greeting and prays for you.

She stopped, overcome with the news she must write next. If she closed her eyes, she could imagine he was here in the library with her even now, so strongly threaded was his cigar smoke in the red brocade draperies and in the carpet blooming giant peonies beneath her feet. Head bent over the tea table, a silken curl of sunshine bobbed against Sophie's cheek. Once upon a time, he used to call her Goldilocks. *But our tale has no happy ending.* She dipped her pen back into the inkwell.

I have the burden of informing you that Mother has gone to her eternal home. Do not mourn overmuch. She is at peace and at rest, God bless her. You will want to know, of course, that she died well.

Sophie examined the lie, curving gracefully among the boxy newsprint. Truly, it was merciful. Beautiful, like Preston and Eleanor in years gone by. He may have resembled a Greek god to Sophie, but there was no doubt that Eleanor had been his Aphrodite. Preston would want to picture her like this, even on her deathbed. It was charity for Sophie to let him.

Her body rests at Oakwood Cemetery and the place will be marked by a tasteful marble headstone.

He did not need to know her mourners were so few. Nor did he need to know the bodies of unburied soldiers poisoned the air during her interment.

Tantalizing aromas stilled her pen. Daphne and Pearl entered the library, heavy-laden with baskets over their arms, and Sophie jumped up to greet them.

"Pearl outdone herself." Daphne smiled at the cook, whose face beamed with a gap-toothed grin and shone with the heat of the kitchen's fires.

"Thank you!" Just as she had requested, there were loaves of soft bread, covered dishes of chicken soup and corn gruel, and for the surgeon in charge of Libby's hospital, a special gift of buttermilk and ginger cake the very color of Pearl's skin. Finally, they had a tangible way to serve.

"Daphne, we'll go in a moment."

As Pearl and Daphne swished out of the room, Sophie scribbled one more line before leaving. *We fare well despite our grief, and are doing what we can for the soldiers.*

He did not need to know they wore blue.

———

Mosquitoes buzzing in her ears as she walked, Sophie tried not to pine after the horses and carriage the Confederate government had impressed from her household. Daphne hummed a tune beside her as if the baskets she carried were no burden at all. As the Indian summer sun baked their backs, their shadows glided over the brown-stained sidewalk along Cary Street. Once a lucrative tobacco district, the Union blockade rendered it obsolete. The warehouses and factories were emptied by the Rebel government and refilled with Yankee soldiers.

Composed of three warehouses connected together, Libby Prison loomed large as they approached it. Sentinels paced in stark relief to the lower half of the building, which was whitewashed to expose prisoners trying to escape. With every footstep that brought Sophie and Daphne closer, the smell of the James River one block south bowed to the odor of illness and confinement.

"Good morning," Sophie said to the first guard she came to, and produced her pass. "We've come to visit the hospital, by the permission of General Winder." The guard's gaze skipped over the small paper and speared the basket instead.

"Would you like some?" Sophie nodded to Daphne, who broke off a piece of ginger cake and extended it to him.

He snatched it from her, inhaled its aroma, and shamelessly devoured it. "If you please, sir." Sophie tried again. "Is this the door to the hospital room?"

Nodding, he wiped his mouth with the back of his hand. "You coming back?"

"I certainly plan to." She smiled into his hollow eyes, and she and Daphne stepped inside the door.

As soon as the door shut behind them, Sophie's eyes stung with the smell. In moments, a surgeon in grey was at her side, his brow already etched in apparent confusion. "I'm John Wilkes, surgeon-in-charge here. May I ask how you came to be here, and why?"

"I have a pass from General Winder," she began, and handed it to him.

He held the paper in the dust-flecked light pouring through the window. "Sophie Kent? And you desire to visit for the purpose of . . ."

"Bringing food and drink to the men."

Daphne handed her the plate of ginger cakes and bottle of cold buttermilk, and Sophie offered them to Dr. Wilkes.

His eyes widened. "Smells heavenly, but these are much too rich for the men here. I'm afraid their reduced condition would never be able to digest them."

Sophie shook her head. "They are for you, sir. A gift, for allowing us the privilege of serving these men. For the ill, we've brought soft bread, corn gruel, and chicken soup."

"Truly?"

Daphne lifted the linen on her basket, and he peered inside.

"Manna from heaven. Yes, yes, we need all you can spare, and I thank you on their behalf. Dr. Lansing," he called, then turned back to Sophie. "Dr. Caleb Lansing is an assistant surgeon captured at Chickamauga."

"He's a prisoner?"

"By night. By day, he works here in the hospital room. I'm spread quite thin, you see, and—ah yes, Dr. Lansing." He turned to the Union doctor. "This is Sophie Kent, and she's brought some food for the patients. I'd like you to oversee proper distribution, taking special diet considerations into account."

A smile creased Dr. Lansing's face as he bowed to her. "Pleased to meet you, Miss Kent. And you are?" He turned to Daphne.

Dr. Wilkes waved his hand. "A servant, clearly."

"I'm quite sure servants—even slaves—have names, too. And I'd sincerely like to know yours."

Daphne shifted her weight before sliding a glance to Sophie and back to the floor. "Daphne."

He bowed to her, and Sophie's breath caught at the gesture. "So pleased to make your acquaintances, ladies. Now let's see what you've brought."

Dr. Wilkes sighed. "I take my leave of you then, Dr. Lansing. Other hospitals await my services."

Dr. Lansing knelt by the baskets to inspect their contents. "Wonderful." He stood, swatting mosquitoes and flies from in front of his face. "Ladies, these men suffer from diarrhea, dysentery, typho-malaria, and simple, but fierce, hunger. They are absolutely wasting away. The quicker they eat, the bett—"

"Then let us feed them." Sophie had not meant to interrupt.

He nodded, his grey eyes glinting like steel. "Did you happen to bring any spoons? Cups? It seems the Confederacy is plumb out of them."

Daphne pulled a handful from the bottom of her basket.

"Voila!" Dr. Lansing cheered. "Now, small doses of food, very small, even if they say they are ravenously hungry and could eat a horse." The rest of his instructions drilled into Sophie with a sense of urgency. If she could just help these men get well again, they could return to their regiments, or at least to their families one day.

But the men she fed looked more dead than alive. Large eyes, sunken cheeks, limbs so thin they appeared as fragile as spun glass, bones poking sharply beneath almost translucent skin. Some tugged feebly at the remnants of their clothing to better cover themselves in a lady's presence. Most of them didn't bother.

The last patient Sophie came to expelled his dying breath as she tipped the first spoonful of gruel past his lips. With trembling fingers, she wiped the food from his face, then wrung her hands in her apron.

"Dr. Lansing." Her voice was hoarse as she called for him. She stood, and the room swayed. Not trusting herself to speak, she simply pointed to the shell of the man who expired beneath her touch.

"Ah. I see." He closed the body's eyelids, and returned to Sophie, lines framing his careworn eyes.

"What's going on?" she whispered. "I had no—no idea!"

Lansing nodded. "The worst cases are soldiers from Belle Isle, which has insufficient clothing, food, and shelter. The officers held here in Libby are better off, although still so hungry many are in a state of semi-starvation. By the time the poor fellows are brought to us, particularly from Belle Isle, they're already past saving. Eighteen were brought to us last night. Ten of them were dead this morning. Sims here—" He motioned to the soldier she'd failed to feed in time. "He makes the eleventh, just out of that batch. Fifty Union soldiers die per day here in Richmond."

"Fifty? You're sure?" Sophie asked.

"Quite." He jabbed his finger toward the west wall. "There are five hundred men out there who should be in the hospital, but there simply isn't room enough. The number of those who yet live but are becoming permanently broken down in their constitutions must be reckoned by thousands." He shook his head, then offered a smile as Daphne came near. "Thank you both. I must get back. You still have the two loaves of bread I asked you to save?"

Daphne picked up the two baskets left on the floor. "Yessir."

"Good. Break each of them into sections small enough to fit between prison bars. Wrap in this newsprint. Fold the paper so no bread shows through. Now. From which direction did you come?"

Confusion pulled Sophie's brows together. "The east."

"When you leave, go west on Cary Street and amble down the length of the prison before turning right on Twentieth and going home. Time your steps so the sentinel has his back to you by the time you reach the western third of Libby. Be sure no one is watching you. Walk close to the building, and let the paper-wrapped bread fall to the ground just outside the cellar window bars. Kick them in through the bars. Do not bend down. Walk at the pace of leisure, so your pace is not as noticeably altered. Do you understand?"

Sophie's mind whirred as she searched his earnest, sun-browned face.

A patient's groan claimed his attention. "You will," he said over his shoulder, and returned to his patient's side.

"What kind of sense does that make?" Daphne hissed. "You trust him, Miss Sophie?"

"There could be only one reason Dr. Lansing would ask us to kick bread into the cellar."

Daphne shook her head. "Secrets spell trouble, and don't we got enough of that already? Your pass says you can be here in this room. It don't say nothin' else."

"I'm forbidden from entering the prison, yes. But General Winder didn't say a word against kicking rubbish from the sidewalk alongside it."

With nimble fingers, the women divided and wrapped the bread in paper until each small bundle resembled nothing more than crumpled wads of old news. News, ironically, which declared that whatever the Yankee prisoners got to eat was "more than they deserved."

Outside, the few people on the street didn't seem to notice yet another woman in mourning and a servant with market baskets. The sentinel neared, and Sophie nodded politely while Daphne tucked her head until their paths crossed and then separated. In ten more paces, they'd be at the barred cellar window.

"I'll roll 'em down my skirt. You help me kick 'em in," Daphne whispered, and Sophie nodded. Once they covered the bundles with their hems, no one would be able to see what their feet were doing anyway.

Still, Sophie's middle fluttered. If they were caught, she might be able to talk her way out of it. If Daphne were caught, the punishment would be stripes. *And it would be my fault, completely.*

Five more paces.

Three.

Two.

"Halt!"

Sophie's breath seized in her throat.

"That is—pardon me, Miss!"

"We've done nothing," Sophie whispered to Daphne before facing her accuser.

"I believe you may have dropped something." A Confederate officer doffed his kepi. Sunlight glanced off his chestnut hair.

Her back still toward the officer, Daphne whispered, "Go stall him."

"Wait here, Daphne." Sophie spoke loudly enough for all to hear as she leisurely strolled away, toward the man whose attention was fixed on her like a bead on his prey.

He was of average height, and his uniform, if it once fit him properly, bore evidence that he'd dropped ten pounds, perhaps, since he began service. His neatly trimmed beard and mustache disguised the angles of his face only slightly.

"Please do pardon me, Miss. I should not have shouted for your attention."

Sophie smiled and swirled around him, so that as he turned to face her, his back was to Daphne. "It's quite all right, I'm sure."

"I'm rather used to barking orders, to being barked at myself. My manners are out of practice, I'm afraid, yet another casualty of war." He cleared his throat. "This belongs to you, I presume?"

His lake blue eyes sought hers as he extended the black-edged handkerchief she must have dropped. Suppressing a sigh of relief, she inspected the ribbon trim and embroidery as much as she dared, to give Daphne more time at her task. "It does," she said at length, and pressed it to her eyes, though they were as dry as the Sahara. "I'm sorry, the grief is very fresh."

"Oh." Clearly, the officer was ill at ease.

"But thank you just the same, Captain . . . is that right? I'm afraid I read Homer much better than I read shoulder straps."

"Oh yes! Do forgive me. Captain Lawrence Russell, Ordnance Bureau. I had some business at the James River Towing Company concerning a shipment of ore for Tredegar Iron Works."

"And I am Sophie Kent. Charmed." She curtsied, low and long, before lifting her face to his gaze once more.

"The pleasure is all mine, I'm sure. Only, I'm so sorry to not have met you under less trying circumstances. Your husband's death—was it for Dixie?"

"What? Oh no, I have no husband. I mean, I never have. It was my mother who passed."

Something flickered in his eyes. "My deepest condolences. If she was anything like you, your father must be devastated."

The compliment swirled in her middle, like indigestion. Despite being well past marrying age, Sophie had never played this game. Nor did she want to, not when more important matters begged for her attention.

Bending her lips in a smile, she stole another glance past him and found Daphne facing her now, her baskets resting on the sidewalk. "Please excuse me."

A line formed between his eyebrows. "Are you quite well?"

"Yes, quite, thank you. Good day, Captain Russell."

She felt his eyes on her back as she skirted him and strode down the sidewalk toward Daphne. The baskets were empty, save for the covered dishes, and not a newspaper in sight.

"Well done," she told Daphne, and peeked at the cellar window. A colored man stood at the bars, one eye swollen shut, the other eye wide, his bread unwrapped and uneaten in his hand. He was looking at Daphne. "Do you know that man?"

Head bowed, Daphne shook her head. "Ain't never seen that Negro in my life." But as they turned the corner onto Twentieth Street, he still clutched the prison bar with one hand, and the bread in the other, unblinking.

Chapter Four

Libby Prison, Richmond, Virginia
Saturday, September 26, 1863

*F*lies droned and mosquitoes hummed in the cellar of
Libby Prison, undulating between the growing stack of mottled-white
corpses, and the bread in the filthy brown hands of those still alive.
Abraham Jamison barely noticed. Not until the woman who kicked
the bread through the bars rounded the corner, a white lady by her
side. Her face—that honeyed tea complexion, those almond-shaped
eyes, those smooth, broad cheeks, full lips—he knew that face.

It's the hunger. I'm seeing things. Turning his back to the outside
world, he slid to the floor and devoured his bread. It wasn't much,
but it was enough to keep them alive another day, if the Rebel guards
didn't shoot them for sport first. His body still ached from the butt of
the rifle that had hammered him for saying aloud that he was a freeman. Though they came like rain, the blows failed to produce a retrac-
tion. *I am free,* he told himself again, though the shadow of the prison

bars lay on the floor at his feet, mocking him. Though his left eyelid still pulsed with pain and his ribs protested every breath, his soul, at least, was not in chains.

But I'm living on borrowed time. Truth be told, Abraham was surprised he hadn't been killed the moment he was captured. He'd been on his way from Florida to Pennsylvania for furlough, making his way to Bella, wearing his 54th Massachusetts regimental uniform. He was clearly a colored Union soldier, and Jefferson Davis had stated that captured Negro soldiers would be treated as runaway slaves, and their white officers executed. Yet here he festered, along with twenty other colored Union troops.

Yesterday, there had been twenty-one of them. Last week, there had been twenty-five. Where the others had gone, no one knew for sure. They just—disappeared. If Davis's word held true, they'd been sold into permanent slavery. *If they were lucky,* Abraham thought, *they were already dead.* Some of these men had been former slaves before fighting for the Union and knew the fate that awaited just beyond the auction block. Others, like Abraham, had been born free. Were it not for the war, he never would have set his big toe south of the Mason-Dixon line. And now here he was, in captivity in the Confederate capital, wondering if this was mere purgatory to the hell of slavery that awaited.

The guards certainly treated them like slaves already. The black prisoners performed every menial task for the prison, from swabbing floors to emptying chamber pots to loading putrefied bodies onto a dead cart when it was time for them to go to the cemetery. For the most trivial breach—an insolent word, shuffling feet, a question—they were at risk of being stripped, tied to a barrel, and filleted open with a horsewhip or cat-o'-nine-tails. The screams were loud enough to wake the entire prison.

Leaning his head back against the wall, Abraham closed his eyes. His baritone voice reverberated through his chest as it rumbled from his lips. "Oh freedom, oh freedom, oh freedom over me." Another voice joined his, then another. "And before I'll be a slave, I'll be buried in my grave, and go home to my Lord and be free."

Soon, each man matched his voice to the chorus, either with words, or with the groans of spirits in the deepest distress. *And before I'll be a slave, I'll be buried in my grave, and go home to my Lord and be free.* Urgency seeped from the words. The prospect of death, of meeting Jesus in eternal paradise, seemed far preferable, indeed, to bondage beneath a master's lash.

But if I die here, how will Bella get along? Thoughts of his wife crowded Abraham's consciousness as he let his forehead drop to his knees. The squeak of the cellar rats faded beneath the memory of her rich, alto voice. The woman who had kicked the bread in through the bars today had done so while humming a haunting tune. It was her voice he heard now, her skirts he saw swaying on the backs of his eyelids. *Who was she?* The question nagged, even in his sleep. In his dream, Abraham followed her, somehow drawn to her tragic posture. Head bowed, shoulders hunched, feet shuffling. Careful to never make eye contact with a white person. Obviously a slave.

Suddenly, she turned and looked him full in the eyes, and Abraham wrenched awake, gasping for air. Beneath that yellow head scarf was the face of his wife.

St. John's Church, Richmond, Virginia
Sunday, September 27, 1863

In a rustle of black crepe, Sophie slipped into the pew box at St. John's Church and greeted Mrs. Blair, who sat in front of her. This was not just where her family had worshiped ever since her father, Preston, moved to Richmond as a bachelor. This was Patrick Henry's stage as he delivered his famous speech during the Second Virginia Convention, prior to the signing of the Declaration of Independence. She had learned the words well in grammar school, and never had forgotten the stirring conclusion.

Is life so dear, or peace so sweet, as to be purchased at the price of chains and slavery? Forbid it, Almighty God! I know not what course others may take; but as for me, give me liberty or give me death!

"Miss Kent?" A woman's voice, unfamiliar, whispered from behind her. "Don't turn around. Just listen." Palms sticking to her gloves, Sophie itched to turn around.

"My servant saw you leaving Libby Prison yesterday. My heart is true, as well. We are watched. Continue your work. Trust no one."

Sophie gave no sign that she heard the words. Her blood turned to ice in her veins as she realized perhaps even this disembodied voice was not a friend.

"Deflect suspicion. We are watched. Do not greet me."

Where the woman's voice had just been, a chorus of whispers now filled Sophie's ears. The ladies across the aisle may have been hard of hearing, but Sophie certainly wasn't. They remarked on her presence after such a long absence, and set sail to the rumor that she had entered the "vile Yankee prison" yesterday. Heat bloomed in Sophie's cheeks just as a retort formed on the tip of her tongue. But there it would stay.

After the closing prayer, Sophie exited through the church's back door, grateful that her bonnet eclipsed most parishioners from her view. As ever, she preferred to remain as anonymous as possible. *Am I watched even now by unfriendly eyes?* Her grip tightened on her Bible.

Stepping into the sunshine, Sophie inhaled deeply, but humidity had thickened the air. A hot wind sloughed through treetops that bent as though sharing secrets among themselves. Her face tight with unease, Sophie could not get home fast enough.

"Miss Kent? Miss Sophie Kent?"

Surprise plucked her nerves, and she whirled toward the voice to find Captain Lawrence Russell striding over to greet her.

"Lawrence Russell. We met yesterday."

Heads turned toward his commanding presence. Young belles in

48

made-over gowns peeped up at him while their mothers nudged them closer. It was attention Sophie did not want, yet she could not break away.

"Forgive me. I'm sure you meet dozens of officers in Richmond every day. We met on Cary Street, next to Libby Prison. Remember?"

All around her, eyebrows raised at the mention of the prison. All except for those belonging to Elizabeth Van Lew, a known Union sympathizer. When Elizabeth and her mother brought aid to prisoners at Ligon's tobacco factory during the first summer of the war, they'd been virtually thrown into the stocks in the local paper. Elizabeth caught Sophie's eye now and steadied her.

She fixed a smile on her face. "Of course I remember. You had business at the towing company. Checking on a delayed shipment of ore for Tredegar, correct?"

Faint lines fanned from his eyes. "So you were listening after all. I confess you did seem a bit—distracted—and I was afraid I had bored you to no end. I hoped I'd see you again, but did not dare to dream it would be so soon. Is your father here this morning?"

A sigh escaped Sophie. She was as eager to leave as the captain seemed to detain her. "He worships elsewhere."

"Ah. St. Paul's?"

"Fort Delaware."

He blanched. "How very hard." Captain Russell's voice dropped, his blue eyes softened in his chiseled face.

His sympathy touched something raw and painful, an abscess on her spirit she rather preferred to ignore. "Everyone has suffered in this war. Not just me." Her gaze slid toward Mrs. Blair, who had paused to watch, as well.

The captain studied Sophie a heartbeat too long. "That does not erase your own pain, Miss Kent."

She turned her head, furious that her eyes misted without her permission. *I am only tired,* she told herself. "Good day to you."

"Please, allow me to escort you home."

Sophie had nothing more to say to a Confederate officer, especially one whose words brought tears to her eyes. She certainly didn't feel compelled to lead him to her house. But, standing just to his side, Elizabeth Van Lew cocked one eyebrow, just slightly, and barely nodded. Whispers filled Sophie's hesitation. *Deflect suspicion,* she heard again, and realized the voice had belonged to Elizabeth.

Sophie met Captain Russell's gaze. With Elizabeth, Mrs. Blair, and a handful of the church's most prolific busybodies watching, her excuses dissolved. "Fine, thank you, if you're sure it's no trouble."

"On the contrary, nothing would give me more pleasure."

Sophie nodded, and noticed the ghost of a smile on Elizabeth's thin lips. Even Mrs. Blair nodded slightly. Captain Russell guided her out of the churchyard, and stares fell away while women resumed their conversations.

As they descended from the church's bluff down the hill, horses stepped to the ringing of church bells, and carriages rumbled down Church Hill's considerable grade. Finials and lampposts pointed to clouds tufting the sky, like cotton ready to be spun. Negroes in threadbare Sunday finery dipped into the street, yielding the sidewalk to Sophie and Captain Russell until they passed.

Beside her, Captain Russell bridled his strides to match her pace. From the tightness in his face, she sensed that wasn't all he held back. At length, he spoke. "I do wish there was something I could do." A humid gust from the South brought the brackish smell of the James wafting over them.

"I cannot think why you'd feel an obligation. I'm a stranger."

"A wrong that must be righted." His eyes sparkled. "And you are a woman in need, and I am a gentleman, or so I'd like to think."

A laugh broke from her lips. "There are needy women enough in Richmond, Captain, if that is what you seek."

"Not exactly." He laughed with her. "Tell me, what is it that *you* seek?"

"Pardon me?"

"You have a habit of looking everywhere but in my eyes. It's as though you're on picket duty."

A nervous smile parted her lips as she snapped her attention back to him, until she could bear his penetrating gaze no longer. Whether he was teasing or in earnest, his eyes sent a charge down her spine. "Let's turn here, shall we? My house isn't far."

They turned east onto Franklin at Twenty-fifth, where the road slanted uphill once more. Sunlight streamed through the linden trees and live oaks and landed in lacework on the ground. In just two more exhausting blocks, she'd be home.

"What are you looking for?" he prodded.

Something uncurled inside her. Resolution, perhaps, or— "Purpose. I'm looking for my purpose, my place in this miserable mess of a war." In truth, she'd found it already.

Captain Russell frowned. "The woman's place is in the home. There is purpose in that, Miss Kent, even—and especially, I would say—in times of war."

"My home is a shell. An empty tomb, save for our slaves. Those walls hold nothing for me but memories now."

"But do you knit? Sew? Spin or weave?"

"I can knit, but never learned to sew, spin, or weave. Daddy wouldn't hear of it, that sort of work being 'slave labor.' I can embroider, but of what use is decoration now?"

"'A thing of beauty is a joy forever.' More important now than ever, to my thinking."

She shook her head at his teasing tone. "I will not be useless anymore."

"Is your purpose really so elusive?"

A wry smile tilting her lips, she fixed her gaze straight ahead. "I do believe I'm gaining on it." At the bottom of the hill lay the James River and its surrounding factories, where sea gulls squawked, and the air smelled of canal water and tobacco dust. Where prisoners languished for want of human kindness.

"Libby? The prison where—" His gait hitched. Eyes flashed. "The prison where we met."

"I was in the prison's hospital room only," she corrected.

Slowly, he released a long breath. "Of course, I understand your feminine impulse to help those in need."

"Doing to others as you'd have them do unto you is a tenet of the Christian faith, and one that I desperately hope the women of the North feel as compelled to follow as I do."

Comprehension lit his eyes. "For your father's sake." Dappled sunlight danced across his shoulders.

"Yes." She had not meant for it to sound so much like a hiss. "For humanity's sake."

"And does your instinct to aid your fellow man extend to the patients in grey as well?"

"I want no man to suffer. But I go where the need is the greatest. Tell me, how many women do you suppose already tend the Rebel wounded? And how much help do you suppose the Union wounded receive here in the Confederate capital?"

Their footsteps marked time in the silence that dropped dully between them. It occurred to Sophie that as an officer in the Ordnance Bureau, Captain Russell oversaw the production of weapons that reduced so many soldiers into patients—or corpses—in the first place. Relief expanded in her chest as they neared Franklin Street. In mere moments, their sparring would end.

"That's my home." She nodded toward the corner, and hoped he would take his leave graciously.

His eyes narrowed. "Say, do you know that fellow?"

A man's lanky shadow flitted from between the columns of her porch. In the same instant Sophie saw him, he was already gone, a mirage in broad daylight. She felt the color leech from her face as she shook her head, speechless.

"Halt!" Captain Russell barked, and took off after the man's trail, dust rising from the dirt road in his wake. The gate to her property, left open by the intruder, creaked on its hinges as the captain barreled through it after him.

Sophie crossed the street and slipped through the gate, as well, then latched it firmly behind her before crossing the short distance to her porch. Stuck in the front door, flapping erratically in the wind, was a brown scrap of paper. With trembling hands, she caught it. The words scrawled inside stole her breath.

Her thoughts still tangling in the dreadful script, Sophie stuffed the note up her sleeve as Captain Russell bounded up the porch. She could barely hear his voice between the drumbeats of her heart.

No sign, she watched him say. *Shall I tarry with you?* The words curled off his lips and dangled in the space between them, waiting. *Miss Kent?* But her thoughts were absorbed by the note now branding the inside of her wrist. "Miss Kent?"

She shook her head to clear it, and ringlets swirled against her cheeks and neck, teasing her back to the present moment. The captain's eyes probed hers as he leaned toward her, and she suddenly worried he would take her hand if she remained silent. "No, thank you," burst from her. Slowing her speech to a more gracious drawl, she managed to dismiss him with assurances that she'd have Fischer keep a sharp lookout, and that Captain Russell may call on her again. He bowed and took his leave.

With barely a tremor, Sophie let herself into her house and locked the door. Her heels clicked on the hardwood floor of the entrance hall as she passed between the classical bronze statues depicting Venus and Mars. Each echoing footstep magnified the emptiness yawning around her. Drawn by warm voices and the smell of hot bean soup, Sophie swept out the rear door, all the way to the detached kitchen.

Rachel and Emiline, the head housekeeper's daughters, sat on the stoop, shelling peas into their aprons. "Miss Sophie? You needin' anything?"

She told them she didn't, and stepped into the dark, stuffy kitchen. "Smells wonderful, Pearl," she heard herself say, and strode directly to the stone fireplace. With the slightest flick of her wrist, she sent the stranger's note into the fire licking at the pot. The edges blackened and crumbled, but the words stayed with her, like the eye's long memory of flame.

Yankee lover, all alone
You're still made of flesh and bone.
Daddy's gone and Mommy's dead,
Turn your aid to Rebs instead.

Beneath the rhyming lines was written: *Big houses still burn. Watch yours!*

Sophie was not under the authority of a husband, or a suitor, or her father. She would not be bullied by an unsigned note when she had done no wrong.

Chapter Five

Philadelphia, Pennsylvania
Monday, September 28, 1863

*T*he staccato clicks of the telegraph echoing within the *Philadelphia Inquirer* building became the rattle of musket fire in Harrison Caldwell's ears. Energy—far more than he needed—surged through his veins in response as he rapped his knuckles on the doorframe of Boris Trent's office.

Boris jerked his head up. "Thought I got rid of you," he grunted through his cigar.

Harrison stepped forward. "I'm not here for my old job." Truly, he did not want to be a war correspondent any longer, not since Gettysburg. But he still wrote his own stories—and every once in a while, he even got paid for them. "I've got an exclusive for your paper." *Only because all the other papers in the city already said no.*

With a puff on his cigar, Boris leaned back and crossed his ankles on his mahogany desk. His beady eyes skewered Harrison from behind his spectacles. "Don't tell me you want to write about women and children again. That sort of article doesn't get me readers, and you know it."

Harrison clamped down on the frustration swelling in his chest. After the battle of Gettysburg, he'd written a story about the townspeople who had been caught in the crosshairs. Boris wouldn't print it. Not nearly ghastly enough for his taste.

"No, nothing so decent as that, after all. There's a story right under our noses, practically. Fort Delaware."

"The prison camp? On the island in the river?"

"The very same."

Boris folded his legs beneath the desk once more and leaned forward on his elbows, tapped ash into a walnut tray. "All right. Let's hear it."

"We complain of the South's prisons for Yankee soldiers, but Fort Delaware holds twelve thousand Rebel prisoners when it should only hold four. The island is situated on the same level as the river, and at high tide it is submerged up to six feet. Twenty die each day of dysentery brought on by the poor conditions of the prison, and—"

"No," Boris growled. "No one is going to pay good money to feel guilty about the prison camp in our own backyard."

"Let me finish. There have also been escape attempts, if it's excitement you're after. The ones who failed have lots of stories to tell, not just about their daring but about what's waiting for them at home. Human interest stories, you know? A glimpse into the Southern home front through the eyes of the loved ones risking life and limb to get back home to them." *Or perhaps, back to their regiments . . .*

"Exactly whose flag are you flying, Caldwell?" Blue wisps puffed from his mouth, drying Harrison's eyes, tickling his throat.

"This isn't about patriotism. It's about people." Harrison needed to sell a story. True, this wasn't the most compelling idea he'd ever had, but he had to try. He was hungry. Boris's disapproval cloyed with his cigar smoke, upsetting Harrison's empty stomach. Sweat prickled his scalp, though the weather was mild. Turning to hide his anger he crossed to the window and opened it. A gust of wind slammed the door, and his body, already tense, jolted.

"Still jumpy, I see." Boris's chuckle was vinegar on Harrison's frayed nerves.

His knuckles whitened on the windowsill as he struggled to master himself. Six stories below, carriages clattered over cobblestones as business downtown went on as usual. Stockbrokers hustled to the Merchant Exchange and ladies to their shopping. Beyond the Greek edifice of the National Bank, the spire of Independence Hall stood sentinel over the city. Newsboys leaned on gaslights and called out their headlines, and for one fleeting moment, he saw his former self among them. Thirteen years old, fresh without a father, and only too happy to be shouting headlines to drown out the grief that constantly whispered his name.

"You would do well to listen, Caldwell. Those are the headlines that sell. You used to know that. Here." The familiar rustle of newsprint turned Harrison's head. "Today's issue. Take it. Tell me what you see."

Tossing his hat onto the desk, Harrison dropped into the chair opposite Boris. "Spencer Kellogg Brown was hanged last Friday at Camp Lee, outside Richmond."

"Yes. Espionage, death, a martyr to the Union. Very good. Go on."

"Three hundred Union prisoners were released."

"Aha. Our own boys, with their own tales to tell of the horrors of Richmond's prisons. Stokes the fire of public sentiment. What else?"

"A bread riot took place in Mobile, Alabama. This is the third bread riot we've heard of this year, isn't it?" Both Atlanta and Richmond had their own in the spring.

"The third in six months' time. What does that tell you about the Confederacy?" Boris drew the ghost of a circle in the air with his diminishing cigar. "Empty bellies. If the home front is hungry, so is the army, and hungry men can't fight for long. *These* are front page stories, Caldwell, mark it well. Spies. Union soldiers in captivity. Desperation in Dixie."

Harrison's own stomach gnawed on itself. "I still think a story on our own Fort Delaware—"

Boris slammed his fist down on his desk again, and Harrison started. "Quit wasting my time! I will not print a self-righteous sermon of Northern atrocities against Rebel prisoners. Now leave. Some of us still have deadlines to meet."

Harrison grabbed his hat and stalked out, smarting as though he'd just been taken to the woodshed. Before covering battles for two years had unhinged him, he had been Boris's best correspondent. Now he was begging for crumbs of work—and still rejected.

Libby Prison, Richmond, Virginia
Friday, October 2, 1863

Wind chilled the sweat trickling from Abraham's brow to the bandana tied over his nose and mouth. The thin layer of cotton kept the flies and mosquitoes off his face, but was no barrier from the eye-watering, gut-twisting stench. "Ready?"

Henry, the colored prisoner assigned to share the task, nodded, and lifted the corpse under the knees and Abraham scooped beneath the armpits. Together, they hoisted the body off the stack in the dead-house and staggered through leaden air toward a pile of empty green pine coffins. Though Abraham did not look directly at the dead man's face, the movement of vermin over the ridges and valleys of his face swam in the corners of his vision. This Union officer had melted away while living at Libby, but in death he had swelled enough to strain the few buttons he had left. The remains thudded dully in the box.

Raindrops began to fall on Abraham's bare head as he and Henry loaded the coffin onto the wagon and ducked back into Libby's cellar for the next corpse. There were twenty more bodies to load. *Tomorrow it will be someone else's turn,* he reminded himself.

In the meantime, Abraham scanned Canal Street and the vacant lot east of the prison with every trip outside. Since he'd first seen the woman wearing Bella's face, he'd glimpsed her twice more, but only through the prison bars. If only he could see her today, he might get some answers. White folks—including the guards and sentinels—always gave the Negro prisoners a wide berth when they were loading the dead. But some slaves dared approach, knowing they'd not be over-heard if they spoke.

Pain seared Abraham's burning ribs as he lifted another body, reminding him that though he was outside the prison walls for the moment, he was never far from the warden's blows. He held his head high as he carried his decomposing burden to its narrow box, though his stomach retched and his muscles hardened beneath the rain.

With a grunt, Abraham and Henry shoved the coffin onto the wagon, then turned back toward Libby to fetch another from the cellar.

And there she was. The woman masquerading as his wife stepped around puddles as she made her way toward him. "My mistress thought you'd be hungry." Her nose wrinkled as she spoke, and no wonder. The odor of spoiling meat sharpened in the wet air. "Seems like no one's got stomach enough to watch us now, if you'd want to just take a few loaves . . ."

Abraham tugged his kerchief down to his neck, smiled his thanks, and accepted the welcome gift without a word. Her voice, if not her words, belonged to Bella, too. *After all this time, can she possibly be—*

"I best be going. We pray for you." She spun on her heel to leave.

"Daphne."

She whirled to face him. "What you say?"

"Is your name Daphne?" He looked around.

She nodded.

"You have a twin sister? Bella?"

She flinched. "Who told you that?"

He held out his hands as he would to steady a skittish horse.

She took a step back, shaking her head. "I don't know who you been

59

talking to around here but I ain't seen Bella in sixteen years. Don't even know if she's dead or alive, let alone where she is." Her eyes flickered over him, clearly suspicious. Alarmed, even.

"I don't mean to startle you. But Bella is your sister?"

A short nod, more like a twitch. "I had a sister named Bella once, but it's not such an uncommon name."

"But she's your twin. You are nearly her looking-glass double. You were raised on the Pierce Butler plantation on St. Simons Island, Georgia, your mother's name was Judy, and you had no other siblings besides Bella. Correct?"

Daphne covered her mouth with her hand. "Don't you tease me about that."

"I have no reason to." Rain dripped from his hair into his eyes as he pinned her with his gaze. "Bella worked in the rice fields and you were a servant in the big house, a reward for your beauty and compliant behavior. You had babies starting at age fifteen, but—"

"Stop," she begged him, lunging forward. "Stop talking!" Her knees gave way, and he caught her before she fell.

"Your sister says that too."

"You know her? Is she safe?"

"She is well, and free, in Gettysburg." Even as Abraham said it, the contrast between the twin sisters struck him.

Daphne pulled back. "Who are you?"

"Abraham Jamison. Your brother-in-law. Your sister, Bella, is my wife."

Chapter Six

Kent House, Richmond, Virginia
Tuesday, October 6, 1863

Please God, not Daphne too. Dread lodged in her throat, Sophie pulled her skirts between her legs and tucked them securely in her belt, affording free movement of her legs. With a cup of tea made from boiled dogwood bark in one hand, she climbed the rough-hewn ladder up to the loft above the kitchen. Rachel was right behind her, carrying a kettle of hot water. Pearl stood at the bottom, concern etched on her weathered face, a long wooden spoon spiking from the fist propped on her ample hip.

"Let's get this in her." Sophie knelt beside Daphne's pallet on the floor.

Lois, the head housekeeper, dropped next to Daphne and scooped her head into her lap. "Fever sure is fierce today."

"Much worse than yesterday?" Sophie noted the grooves in the older woman's ebony face.

"'Fraid so, Missy." With her thumb on Daphne's chin, she pressed down enough for Sophie to tip a spoonful of tepid tea between her cracked lips.

Rachel poured her kettle into a bucket, her lips pressed together just like her mother Lois's, then bent Daphne's knees and guided her feet to rest in it.

"Good." Sophie nodded approvingly at the young woman three years her junior. "Perhaps we can draw the fever down from her head." She hoped her voice carried a tone of confidence she did not feel. The last time Sophie was a nurse on this property, the patient had died.

By the light of the dusty sunbeams falling in through smeared windows, Sophie spooned another dose of tea into Daphne's mouth, then another, and another. Every time her hand neared her face to feed her, she was astonished by the heat radiating from her yellowing skin. "It's going to be all right," she said, and wondered if it was a sin to say such a thing when really, there was no such guarantee.

It had started with violent chills last night, Lois had told her. Guilt still niggled at Sophie that when she was dining with the relentless Captain Russell, Daphne was bundled up with all the winter blankets they had, before the fire, and still chattering with cold. Then as suddenly as the chills had begun, a raging fever took hold. By this morning, however, it had passed. Daphne had been tired, but coherent and, they had all hoped, recovering.

Mutterings bubbled from Daphne's lips now, and Sophie leaned in closely to catch them. "What is she saying? Sounds like 'bell, bell.' What can she mean?"

Lois shrugged. "It maybe don't mean a thing, Missy. That's the fever talkin', I guess."

With a start, Daphne's eyes popped open. "My baby cryin'? That my baby cryin'?"

Chills cascaded over Sophie as Daphne kicked in an effort to push herself up to her elbows. Frantically, she looked about the room, evidently unaware that she had upset the bucket of water her feet had been in. Pearl's muffled cry from below announced that the spilled water was bleeding through the floorboards and leaking into the kitchen.

"Shhhh, it's all right, there's no baby here, Daphne." Sophie hoped her tone was gentle, rather than terrified, as she had been when Eleanor had been slipping. *Susan! Is that Susan at the door?* She had cried, looking wildly about her in the sickroom. *Has she come back? Preston, for pity's sake let her in, she's your daughter!* "Shhh, shhh," Sophie said again, as much to the haunting memory as to Daphne.

"Don't you shush me, woman! You bring me my baby! Where he at? Can't you hear he want his mama now? Why won't you bring him to me?"

Stunned, Sophie sat back on her heels, vaguely registered that Lois and her daughter Rachel both covered their gasps with calloused hands.

Daphne flopped back, flat once more on her pallet, but her face twisted with a pain known only to her. "Hush little baby, don't you cry . . ." Her voice warbled pitifully as she sang. Tears traced her broad cheeks.

"Did she have children?" Sophie whispered through tightened throat.

Lois spread her hands in a gesture of baffled ignorance. Rachel only shook her head as she mopped the floor with her apron.

Every moment that Daphne writhed in delirium on her pallet was a moment lost, possibly with irreparable damage to the brain. Sophie ticked off her options in her mind.

"Here. Keep trying, if you can." She thrust the cup of tea and spoon into Lois's hands. "I'm going for a doctor."

Lois clucked her tongue, wagging her head. "Now, Missy. With all these thousands of soldier patients here, you think a single solitary doctor gonna come up this ladder to see bout a sick slave? Uh uh. Ain't happenin', honey."

"True," Sophie admitted. "But maybe one of them will talk to me."

Lois raised an eyebrow. "You going to Libby's hospital, ain't you?"

"I have to try."

"Better take Rachel with you. Wouldn't look fittin' for you to go alone. And grab some bread for those boys, too."

As soon as the words left Lois's mouth, Sophie was backing down the ladder. Rachel was right behind her.

Breathless, Sophie Kent swatted through a cloud of mosquitoes and burst into Libby's hospital room, brimming with impatience as her eyes adjusted to the gloom. "Dr. Lansing? Dr. Wilkes?" Rachel shrank back, and Sophie realized she should have prepared her scrub maid for the scene more thoroughly.

"Miss Kent?" Dr. Lansing looked paler than he had a week ago, his radiant energy dimmed. Still, he smiled at Rachel and introduced himself before he accepted three loaves of bread from her.

"This is Rachel," Sophie breathed. "Daphne's ill."

His eyes softened. "Can you describe the symptoms?"

Sophie told him everything she could, right up to the moment before they left her. "She was searching for a baby she was certain was hidden in the loft somewhere. She was—she was—"

"Perhaps a little bit—like that?" Dr. Lansing nodded toward a groaning, thrashing patient. His eyes looked as if they'd been lit from within, his skin looked thin against his bones, and stained yellow with dandelions. His moans were peppered with snippets of a one-sided conversation.

"Who is he talking to?" Sophie asked.

"A loved one only he can see. Sound familiar?" Dr. Lansing asked a few more questions of her, then rubbed a hand over his stubbled jaw. "It sounds to me like she is in the throes of typho-malaria. We see it here every day, I'm afraid."

The lump Sophie swallowed grated her throat. *Malaria.* People died from it. "Is there nothing we can do for her?"

"If we were about a hundred miles north, I'd give her quinine."

Sophie blinked, waiting. "But?"

He shook his head, casting a long gaze at his own patients. "Quinine, chloroform, morphine. All of these are in desperate demand in the South. That which can be had goes directly to the Rebel army."

She searched his eyes for any glimmer of hope. "Is there really no quinine to be had?"

"Quinine? No, none," said Dr. Wilkes, joining their small huddle. "There's barely any for our own soldiers, as it is. You'd be lucky to get an ounce for four hundred dollars if you find it. And the price will only keep rising."

Rachel twitched beside Sophie at the mention of the impossible sum. Dr. Wilkes nodded, his face a perfect storm. "You can thank the blasted Union blockade for that, my dear." He cursed under his breath as he hustled along. Dr. Lansing did not contradict him.

"The dogwood bark we boiled into tea—will that not help her?"

"There is no effective substitute for quinine." He looked over his shoulder at his patients, his body taut. "Just keep her as comfortable as possible. If you're lucky, after three or four weeks, she may pass the worst of it. But the convalescence is tedious in the extreme. I'm sorry it's not what you wanted to hear. Now, if you'll excuse me."

If you're lucky . . . Sophie could not tell how long she stood there, watching Dr. Lansing's back, willing him to turn around with some bright new recollection that could help Daphne, and the rest of his patients, after all. It was Rachel who finally broke the spell.

"He didn't take these," she whispered. Two loaves of bread trembled in her arms, and Sophie chided herself for lingering when clearly, Rachel was distraught.

"Come, you can help." Shoving thoughts of Daphne's illness to the corner of her mind, Sophie led Rachel outside for one last task before returning home.

In the vacant lot east of Libby, between Cary and Canal Street, a few Negro prisoners were unloading a supply wagon and carrying the packages into the prison. One of them paused long enough to notice

Sophie and Rachel watching. "Take the bread to them, please. You'll attract no attention. I'll talk to the sentinels if I need to. Hurry back." She was anxious to return to Daphne.

———

They call that food? Abraham Jamison could scarcely go near his own rations, let alone eat them—which made the recent reduction to half rations per man more tolerable. The corn bread was railroad iron hard, the bacon was maggoty, and the black-and-blue meat announced its presence in the dark by its rank odor alone. Worst, perhaps, was the soup, so full of black bugs that had gorged on the inside of the beans that they died and floated on the surface. Had it not been for the soft bread Rachel had brought a few hours ago, Abraham would not have eaten a bite all day.

Of course, even that had soured in his mouth when he learned of Daphne's illness. Typho-malaria, Rachel had said, and not a drop of quinine to be had. He wondered if he would ever see her again.

Henry had disappeared. Without warning, without cause, he was just—gone. There was no record that he'd ever been here, no way of writing to his wife. It was an ominous presence that never left, this constant question of who would be next. Whether Abraham would starve to death or discover for himself where the vanishing Negroes ended up, he could not guess. He only knew his days were numbered, and that his regiment had no idea he was even here.

Neither did his wife.

He should have listened to her when she came to visit him in Beaufort last summer after he was wounded in the leg. He should have kissed her better. Had he even told her he loved her? A frown creased his face as he racked his memory. He'd been so offended that she spoke of being hungry when the honor of black soldiers was at stake. Well, now he understood a thing or two about hunger, himself. Closing his eyes, he prayed she had enough to eat now, and that if he died in this godforsaken hole, she would one day learn to forgive him, even though it was impossible for him to beg it of her. He prayed that Daphne would live, and that the war would end, and that they could find each other and be happy. For without Abraham, Bella would be all alone.

Abraham's eyes popped open. The voices on the other side of the room simmered with energy. Pushing himself off the floor, he joined the dark knot of men. Their eyes gleamed in the twilight spilling through the prison bars.

"Tomorrow you say?"

Lewis, who walked through the upper floors every morning with a pan of burning tar, nodded. The fumigation was of questionable value, judging by the thriving population of vermin upstairs, but the opportunity to communicate with the imprisoned officers was priceless.

"What's tomorrow?" Abraham asked.

"Chaplains are being released. Seven of them. Said they'd take out letters with them."

"Won't they be searched?" Abraham asked. Surely the guards wouldn't send incriminating evidence through the lines if they could help it.

"They've got a plan." He paused, eyes twinkling. "Did you know that with a pen knife, you can split a uniform button in half, and fit inside it one small sheet of paper folded up very, very small? Snap the button back in place, the letter disappears. They promised to mail them for us once they're at Fortress Monroe. They'll find the stamps and envelopes themselves. You want in, get your letters to me before first light. I'll pass them right along for you when I burn the tar upstairs."

It was a chance to write Bella, to explain what happened, to tell her he wanted her to move on if—rather, when—he died. A dim hope flared, then sputtered like a drowning wick. "Where we going to get our stationery and quills?"

Lewis smiled, his teeth flashing white. "Courtesy of the boys upstairs."

Abraham felt a nudge in his aching ribs, and looked down to find paper and a pencil.

"Be quick about it." Lewis motioned to the others who would surely want to use the pencil next. "Light's almost gone."

Promising he would, Abraham shifted into the stream of fading light, and stitched his heart with lead onto the paper in his hands.

Chapter Seven

Richmond, Virginia
Wednesday, October 21, 1863

*T*he James River blinked beneath the ruddy October sky as Sophie marched out of Libby's hospital and past the sentinels, alone. Her empty basket dangled from her elbow and bounced against her leg with every step. The doctors hadn't said it, but they didn't need to. The truth was obvious. It was her fault Daphne was ill. Sophie would not risk the health of another slave in her care.

If she hadn't asked Daphne to accompany her to the hospital, she likely wouldn't have caught typho-malaria, would not be lying, sweaty and insensible, on the bed even now. Sophie had moved her from her pallet above the kitchen to the spare bedroom at the rear of the house two weeks ago, but her condition had not significantly improved, even with the better ventilation and Sophie's daily caregiving. Lois and Rachel took turns helping, but their own work kept them busy enough without adding nursemaid to their list of regular duties.

Besides, Sophie was used to the role. *And I am to blame for exposing her to the disease in the first place.* The thought wore a weary circuit in her brain. With each plodding footstep that carried her toward home, guilt drilled deeper. Perhaps, if Daphne were sleeping when she arrived, Sophie could slip in a visit to Mrs. Blair. The older woman's companionship steadied her.

Voices raised behind Sophie, and she glanced backward, just in time to see someone duck behind a lamppost. The hair raised on her neck as the intruder from last month flitted through her memory. A tendril of fear curled around her. She shook her head, but suspicion clung to her like ivy to brick. As she faced forward again, the warehouses and merchant stalls of Cary Street dimmed in her vision. The seagulls' squawks dulled beneath the alarm clamoring throughout her spirit. She turned north on Twenty-second Street.

Footsteps followed, but every time she turned, she saw no hunter. *Is he hiding behind a tree? Am I only imagining it?* In one block, she turned east on Main Street then north on Twenty-fifth, and still she felt she was being trailed. Sycamore branches swayed with the wind that hissed through them.

By the time she turned east on Franklin, hoofbeats and carriage wheels sounded far away, though they stomped and whirled right beside her as they passed. A mere two blocks from home, her footsteps broke from their measured gait and she glided over the sidewalk double-time. Dried leaves caught in her hem, scraping the dusty ground in her wake. Were the footsteps behind her matching her pace?

Sophie's breath whooshed in her ears. *I've done no wrong,* she reminded herself. *I have nothing to fear.* But her throat clamped tight with it. If this man was mad enough to threaten her with burning her home, what would he do with her in person?

Behind her, footsteps pummeled the earth. Any second, he would overtake her.

"Miss Kent!"

Her stride hitched.

"Miss Kent?" Captain Lawrence Russell drew rein and dismounted his horse, holding the bridle with one buckskin-gloved hand. Relief poured through Sophie, and she fought the urge to link her arm with his. Her gaze darted behind him, around him, looking for the shadow that had followed her.

"You look—hunted. You're being followed?" His voice was low. "Is it that sly devil who was lurking about your gardens?"

"I think so." She swallowed. "But I couldn't tell you who or where he is."

He wrapped his arm about her waist, drawing her close. "I'll bet you my last pound of coffee he's watching you still."

The breath whisked from her chest at the captain's nearness.

He dropped a glance on her basket and clucked his tongue. "Just coming from Libby again? You're asking for trouble. You look disloyal to the Confederacy. There are laws against that, you know."

Sophie opened her mouth to argue.

"Shh. Don't be cross with me, you'll only convince him further that you'd rather be with dying Yankees than with a Rebel officer with a bare fourth finger on the left hand. Don't you know I'm helping you here? Play along." He brought her hand to his lips and pressed a kiss to it. His mustache sent shivers down her spine. "And you're alone? What did you do this morning, wake up and decide to be an easy target for that man's foul designs?"

"You know I can't let any of my slaves come with me after Daphne has fallen ill from that place!"

"Why do you continue to go yourself, when you know you're putting yourself at risk? You could cut the miasma hovering around that place with a saber."

She glowered as he brushed a strand of hair from her cheek.

"Be sweet, now. We're throwing him off your scent. You can't be disloyal if you're being courted by an officer in the Ordnance Bureau, now can you?" He winked. "I'll walk you home."

With the reins in one hand, Captain Russell offered Sophie his arm, and she looped her hand through his elbow. "Don't look back. It's more effective if he thinks we've forgotten about him altogether."

She nodded, suddenly aware of how she must look to him. The shadows beneath her eyes had deepened with her vigils by Daphne's side. Her mourning gown was stiff and dull. It had not mattered to her earlier today. It should not matter to her now.

A pang of disloyalty sliced through her. She was beginning to forget Harrison Caldwell. His eyes, his touch, the way he pushed her to follow her dreams. *Five years,* he'd said when she completed her courses at the Philadelphia boarding school where his mother taught. He couldn't support a wife on his reporter's wages yet, and she wasn't ready to settle down in the family way, either. Both of them had work to do. *We'll meet back here at the five-year reunion of your class. In the meantime, you set the South on fire with your writing, and I'll do the same with the North.* The five-year reunion came and went last spring, and Sophie, of course, remained in Richmond. She hadn't seen Harrison since the Weeping Time. Little wonder his image was a fading tintype in her mind compared to the flesh-and-blood man warming her hand.

"I do believe some recreational distraction would do you good, Miss Kent. To take your mind off things, and show you're not the recluse some folks say you are."

"Recluse?" she snapped.

"I know you've been tending Daphne, and from what you've told me, you were nursemaid to your mother for months—years?—before she died. Now you only leave the house for church and to visit *enemy* prisoners. Do you go anywhere else? Does anyone enter your home?"

Moments seeped by, and his words stayed with her like molasses. Other than a few visits to Mrs. Blair, which attracted no attention from anyone, she kept to herself. She could see how it looked. *Deflect suspicion,* Elizabeth Van Lew had warned, but Sophie drew gossip like a magnet, just like Susan, and just like Eleanor. *Perhaps,* she thought, *I could also draw a crowd.* The idea sparked, then flared.

Sophie's mind cleared as they reached the gate of her residence. She had work to do, still. "You're right," she said quietly, and suppressed a smile at the startled look on his face. "A change of pace would be good for me. Our house is large—and empty. How would you and several of your friends like to have a party?"

"Here?" He nodded to her columned house, the cupola's trim almost pink in the setting sun. "You do realize that if I came to such an event you'd have to actually let me in. Are you saying you're willing to do that?" An easy grin softened his war-weary face.

She laughed in spite of herself, and her cheeks warmed as he placed his hand on hers. "I'll ask Pearl to make some of her famous ginger cakes and lemon tarts, and real coffee to drink, of course. Guests will be invited to bring something we can send to the Confederate prisoners at Fort Delaware. A pillowcase, article of clothing, a needle or length of thread . . . anything would be welcome, for everything is needed, Father says. You'll bring your friends from the war department?"

"Indeed. I can think of nothing better."

A genuine smile spread on her face. "Then we are agreed, for once." With a houseful of uniformed men, Sophie's shadow just might leave her alone.

———

Philadelphia, Pennsylvania
Monday, October 26, 1863

Harrison Caldwell's mouth nearly watered from the tantalizing aromas still thick in the air. Inside the Union Volunteer Refreshment Saloon, hundreds of soldiers had filed through the line while women loaded their plates with beef, potatoes, bread, and pie. Whether they were soldiers on their way to the front, veterans returning home, or prisoners en route to or from Fort Delaware, the Southwark neighborhood women made sure they had a hot meal, no matter the time of day or night. When Harrison found himself between stories, he usually came here to hunt for leads. Lately, he'd been here quite a bit.

The lunch crowd funneled back outside to catch their trains, and Harrison remained at one of the tables, rubbing his eyes with the heels of his hands. The clatter of a plate hitting the table jolted through him, yet another reminder that his nerves had not yet healed from two years of constant battle reporting.

"Beg pardon, Mr. Caldwell." It was Amelia Sanger, one of the volunteers who worked the line. "You looked as if you could use a bite to eat, and we have plenty." She slid the plate closer to him, and he nodded, uncomfortably aware of her scrutinizing gaze.

Harrison tore the bread apart and watched the steam rise, curling, from its center. He'd met Amelia at Gettysburg last July at the home of her son's widow, Liberty Holloway. Liberty's husband had died fighting the Rebels in the first battle of Bull Run, and then, two years later, her farm had been overrun with fifteen hundred wounded Rebel soldiers during and after the battle at Gettysburg. Liberty had stayed and nursed the soldiers in grey—she had even fallen in love with one of them, a Rebel scout by the name of Silas Ford. Silas had taken an oath to the Union and been released from Fort Delaware about six weeks ago.

"What do you hear from Liberty these days?" he asked.

"Not a word. But Silas keeps me informed." Her eyes sparkled, as they always did, when she spoke of other people's business.

"That's right, the two of you were hatching a plan to help Liberty get back on her feet, weren't you?" Her property had been all but ruined by the battle and its bloody aftermath, just as she was turning the place into an inn.

She nodded. "Silas tells me he's got a crew of students from Gettysburg's Lutheran seminary willing to help him rebuild. All he needs is materials."

"Has he seen her yet?"

Amelia shook her head. "No, she pitched a tent at Camp Letterman where all the remaining wounded have been gathered, and she hasn't been home since. Silas and Bella want to have everything ready for

74

her before she does, anyway. Bella and some of her church friends are making quilts and curtains for Liberty Inn, and you know that takes time."

"Indeed." Bella's face surged in his mind. The former slave's complexion was nearly the same shade as the cream-lightened coffee in his cup. When her last owner died, his will stipulated that her daughter Liberty be raised by his sister as white, though she was one-fourth Negro. Bella had stayed in her daughter's life as the hired hand. Only when Harrison discovered the true relationship last summer did Liberty learn of it as well. It was a shock to Liberty, to be sure—but a fabulous story, one which simply begged to be written. It would have rivaled the one Harrison had written about the Weeping Time, only this time he'd be famous under his own name rather than a pseudonym.

He hadn't, though, because Bella had convinced him not to publish it. But in a moment of drunken candor at a local bar, Harrison spilled the story, unwittingly, to a ruthless New York reporter. The other man was the one who got the story printed. And Harrison was fired from the *Inquirer* because of it. It was the story that got away. It was the story that wreaked havoc in Liberty's life, and Bella's, and he was solely to blame.

Harrison cleared his throat and took a drink of water, but the faint taste of guilt remained. "Rebuilding the farmhouse as an inn, you say? Won't it be a challenge to get all the lumber he needs with so much wood going to build coffins? Gettysburg is such a small town, with limited resources. I hear the work of reinterring the bodies into the National Cemetery will take months yet."

She waved a hand. "No matter. He gave me a list of what he needs and I purchased it in Philadelphia myself."

Harrison raised his eyebrows. "Did you, now? And how will these supplies be finding their way to Silas?"

"On the train, of course."

He put down his fork. "On their own?"

"Why—yes. It would be an exhausting round-trip errand for an old lady such as myself. Besides, I plan to see Liberty next month anyway, when President Lincoln comes to dedicate the National Cemetery."

Kneading his napkin in his hands, Harrison formed a plan of his own. "What if—what if I offered to escort your shipment myself? And stayed to help Silas with the work? Nothing is tying me here, at present. These hands can wield more than just a pen, after all."

She cocked her head at him. "What's your angle this time?"

Harrison spread his hands in a gesture of innocence. "No angle. Stories are slow right now, anyway. Maybe it's time I help clean up a mess, rather than just leave them in my wake, as Bella so justly accused me of doing."

Pursing her lips, she squinted at him for a moment before slapping the table with her blue-veined hand. "Mr. Caldwell, if you're willing to work on Liberty Inn, I'll pay for your train ticket myself."

Richmond, Virginia
Friday, October 30, 1863

Her father was in prison. Her mother was in the grave. Her maidservant suffered with a deadly disease upstairs. And Sophie Kent was throwing a party. *Smile,* she had told herself as she received every guest, but guilt tugged at the corners of her mouth.

"It is the right thing to do," Captain Russell whispered to her, as though he could read her mind. He nodded toward Fischer, who was stacking more donations against the parlor wall. The simple necessities were a stark contrast against opulent crimson flocked wallpaper: slippers, socks, nightshirts, pillowcases, old newspapers. "The prisoners at Fort Delaware will rejoice to have them. Your father will be proud."

A tentative smile bloomed at the thought. Her father would also be pleased to hear that his house was filled with life again, like the old days. Some of the guests were neighbors, a few were familiar faces from St. John's Church, but most were strangers to her. Captain Russell had invited some fellow government workers, who had invited women who worked at the Treasury, signing and cutting Confederate notes. Yes, Preston would be pleased. Fischer clearly enjoyed welcoming guests into the house once more, as well.

Still, the shrill laughter of people desperate to enjoy themselves put Sophie on edge. She only hoped her agitation was not present on her face. Nervously, her hands busied themselves patting her hair back into her chignon and smoothing the wrinkles from her rusty black skirt.

"You look fine," said Captain Russell.

"I look like a mud puddle, but thank you just the same." A self-deprecating smile quirked her lips.

His eyes were as the sun-sparked sea. "Let's join the party, shall we?" His hand warmed the small of her back as he guided her through the parlor's open pocket doors and into the drawing room. George Washington's portrait looked out from over the white marble fireplace, and huge gilded mirrors doubled the crowd.

With her starched white apron bright against her black serving dress, Emiline, Lois's daughter of sixteen years, wove between guests with her tray of refreshments: warm, moist ginger cakes, delicate lemon custard, and classic rice pudding. Rachel carried a silver platter of steaming cups of coffee, while Lois discreetly plucked dirty dishes from marble-topped walnut tables and carried them away.

Captain Russell steered Sophie toward two gentleman admiring a hunting painting on the wall. "You remember Trevor Hayes, clerk for Secretary of War James Seddon."

"Haven't had coffee—real coffee—in months." Mr. Hayes raised his cup to her, and Sophie started at the thinness of his wrist. "I thank you."

"Hear, hear," chimed in a short, swarthy man who filled his outdated suit better than most.

Captain Russell jabbed him with his elbow. "Come now Graham, you're not saying you haven't had coffee in months, either, are you?"

"Well, I—" He pushed his spectacles up the bridge of his nose. "It's not an everyday occurrence, even for those of us working for Northrop in the Commissary Department."

Music tinkled above the buzz of conversation, turning all heads to the other side of the room where one of the women from St. John's had made herself at home with the piano. When the first measures of "Bonnie Blue Flag" rang out, men and women wafted toward the strains. On the fringe of guests clustered at the piano, Sophie couldn't help but hear the snippets of conversation that fell between the lines.

Substitutes selling for six thousand dollars . . . flour at seventy dollars a barrel . . . General Lee wrote to Seddon . . . enemy informed of his movements . . . doubtful plan to remove iron from the Aquia Creek railroad . . . endless trouble at Tredegar.

The song ended, and Sophie stole a glance at Captain Russell. Gaslight glinted on his russet hair, but shadows sagged beneath his eyes. She edged close enough to hear him speak, close enough to smell the coffee and ginger cake on his breath. "They cannot get adequate supply of good firebrick. The furnaces go out after a few days when they should last many months. Now they buy corn to feed the furnaces as well as to feed their two thousand workers."

"And can they get it? Enough corn?" Mr. Graham asked quietly, almost as though he were afraid to hear the answer.

Captain Russell took a drink of his coffee. "It's never enough. The furnaces between Lynchburg and the West Virginia border have suffered from cavalry raids."

"Union?" asked Mr. Hayes, his hazel eyes glowing above cheekbones that looked painfully sharp.

"Rebel. Our cavalry units have been given specific orders not to impress grain from any of Tredegar's facilities, for without their iron products, how can we win a war, let alone fight it? But they sweep in and eat everything that looks like food. General Stuart says the horses are starving, though, and must be fed."

"And the soldiers are just as hungry," put in Mr. Hayes.

Mr. Graham shifted his weight, rather awkwardly, Sophie thought, though she could see why he was uncomfortable. His expression simmered until she was afraid he would erupt. "Northrop is a political office seeker who is more concerned about being right than he is about men having enough to eat. But you didn't hear that from me." Smirking darkly, he met the gazes of Mr. Hayes and Captain Russell, and skipped completely over Sophie. No matter. She was used to being overlooked. She was also used to listening behind a blank mask of feminine indifference to politics.

Mr. Hayes snorted. "I didn't have to. I see enough correspondence between Northrop and Seddon to come to my own conclusions. They match yours, by the way. We have thirteen thousand Union prisoners in Richmond and General Winder has written to Seddon that Northrop won't let him have meat for them. Spittin' mad about it, too, Winder is. Says he cannot be answerable for their safekeeping without it." He drained his coffee cup and placed it on Lois's tray as she passed.

"Northrop says it's the quartermaster who ought to feed them," said Mr. Graham, wiping lemon custard from his mouth.

"And the quartermaster says the job falls to Commissary General Northrop."

And in the meantime, thirteen thousand men go hungry. Sophie knew better than to say it aloud, and only hoped her eyes did not radiate the fire burning her belly. Indeed, she was sure her face was flushed with it. She pressed the backs of her hands to her cheeks to cool them.

"Enough talking, yes?" Mr. Hayes said, turning his gaze on her. "More dancing. I've just the thing." He threaded his way to the piano, disappearing into the knot of people still gathered there. When he emerged, it was with a gleaming, honey-colored violin on one shoulder, and a contagious grin on his face.

Clear, lilting tones soared in three-quarter time. Even before Sophie had time to be nervous, Captain Russell took her hand. "Dance with me."

"I'm in mourning."

"But not for a husband," he countered. "Come now, it will boost Confederate morale to have you dance. No one here will fault you for it, I assure you. Besides, it's far too depressing to have the walls spotted with women in black."

"Go on, dear," urged Mrs. Blair, now beside her. "Never refuse a soldier in wartime. If my boys were home, I'd want you to take a turn about the room with each of them, as well." She winked.

"Quite right. Thank you, Mrs. Blair." Captain Russell grinned broadly before turning back to Sophie. And then she was in his arms, growing warm inside his touch. The room spun in a blur of scarlet and white and gold. He drew her closer. His blue eyes penetrated hers as a ring of guests looked on.

"People are watching," she breathed.

"Isn't that the idea?"

Sophie's gaze drifted to the smile curving his lips before returning to his eyes once more. Yes, that was the idea. To deflect suspicion of disloyalty by proving her attachment to the cause—or at least to Captain Russell.

He steered their steps to dance in front of the floor-to-ceiling windows, and she knew he had her shadow in mind. For once, Sophie prayed the mysterious man was watching, so she could be free of his surveillance for good.

At the end of the night, when the parlor and drawing room had been set back to rights, and the lamps were all extinguished, Captain Russell was the last guest to leave. Sophie stood with him on the front porch. Below Church Hill, Richmond twinkled with gaslights, and the river shimmered beneath the moon. Darkness caressed them as they stood listening for the snapping of twigs or crunching of leaves in the garden. Only the subtle hoot of an owl greeted their ears.

Captain Russell took her hands in his and brought them to his lips, sending ripples through Sophie's middle. "Maybe that rascal wasn't watching, after all," he whispered, eyes gleaming. "It would be prudent to give him another opportunity—perhaps several more, in fact—to see the two of us together."

Sophie did not object.

Chapter Eight

Gettysburg, Pennsylvania
Thursday, November 19, 1863

A smile struggled on Bella Jamison's face as she realized her years of watching over Liberty were hastening to an abrupt end. She was a grown woman, and as any fool could see, she belonged with Silas Ford. There were twenty thousand people gathered here at the cemetery to hear its dedication. But the way Silas held Liberty close had little to do with the crowd, and Bella knew it. So did Amelia Sanger, standing at Bella's side.

Bella tossed a glance over her shoulder, and Silas caught it with a smile. The handsome young man had made it easy to forgive him for being the son of a slave owner when he had set out to rebuild Liberty's life—even before he knew Pennsylvania law would allow their marriage despite Liberty's Negro heritage. The fact that he'd lost a leg in the battle of Gettysburg had not slowed his pursuit of her.

Applause broke Bella's reverie, and she realized that after droning on for two hours, the honorable statesman Edward Everett was now yielding the platform to President Lincoln. She craned her neck to see the tall, awkward-looking man in the stovepipe hat, and was struck by the sorrow lining his face. His words were simple, humble, profound.

And then, almost as quickly as he began, he was finished. A moment later, cheers erupted for the people's commander in chief, or perhaps for the dead they had all come here to honor.

As the applause receded, Harrison Caldwell jostled his way to Silas, Liberty, Amelia, and Bella. He had surprised Bella by arriving with Amelia's building supplies last month, but he had shocked her outright with his decision to stay. He'd spent every day helping Silas refurbish Liberty's house, raze the old barn to the ground, and build a new carriage house.

"How did you rate our speakers?" Silas asked him.

Harrison straightened the slouch hat on his head. "I preferred Lincoln."

"A newsman would. Shorter is better, right?"

The reporter chuckled. "Usually, yes. But a little clarification would have been appropriate. Lincoln said that the men who died here gave their last full measure of devotion in doing so. But I believe the fullest measure of our devotion to the cause is not just dying for it, but living for it. From where I'm standing, each one of you is giving your full measure of devotion in your own way."

"Let me guess," said Bella, barely suppressing a smirk. "You want to write a story about it."

"It's a great story." A smile brightened his face. "But you should be the ones to tell it. Write your story. The world needs to hear your voice, not just the voices of the reporters."

"Women don't publish," said Amelia. "It isn't ladylike."

Harrison shook his head and pulled from his knapsack the package of licorice wafers Bella had given him yesterday. "I'm telling you, just write it." He popped a wafer in his mouth and tucked it in his cheek. "If you don't, no one else is going to do it for you."

"And what will you do?" Liberty asked, clearly still content to remain in Silas's arms.

"Me? Oh, I'll keep writing stories, but my battle days are behind me."

Bella nodded. At thirty years old, he was six years her junior. Above the freckles dusting his nose, his eyes were deep, dark pools of stories she suspected he would never want to pen.

Harrison tilted his head toward the platform. "I should at least try to get an interview with the President." He shook hands with Silas, Amelia, Liberty, and Bella. The brightness gone from his voice, he added, "I deeply regret any sorrow or pain I may have caused you all."

Liberty reached out and squeezed his hand. "God used it for good, Mr. Caldwell." The child was right. If Harrison hadn't dug up their story—and leaked it to the *New York Times*—Liberty may have lived her entire life without knowing Bella was her mother.

Smiling, Harrison nodded, tipped his hat, and melted into the crowd encircling the president.

Amelia's voice registered vaguely in Bella's ears, but she did not turn to face her. Instead, Bella stood watching the throng of people who had come for this momentous day. For one glorious, irrational instant, she thought she saw her own Abraham among them, but immediately dismissed the idea, ashamed of her desperation.

Truth was, Bella missed her husband, and the way they had left things, she had no idea if he missed her or if he even thought of her. She'd had no word from him since August and still no paycheck. The uncertainty wore her down, like pebbles in her shoes. One look at her daughter, however, left no doubt that she was as certain about Silas as he was about her. When the wind teased a curl of her ebony hair from its pin, he brushed it from her face, and her cheeks bloomed pink in response.

Bella cleared her throat. "We'll see you back at the inn, Liberty, Silas." With a gentle nudge to Amelia, they left the young couple alone.

By the time Liberty and Silas made their way back home, Bella was not at all surprised at the sunlight glinting on her daughter's ring finger. Meeting her on the pumpkin-lined porch, Liberty hugged her fiercely around the neck and whispered, "I've finally found where I belong." Tears fell from her sapphire blue eyes, and Bella wiped them away, though her own face was wet as well. After everything she had gone through, from being a widowed bride two years ago to being steeped in the ghastly field hospital that had become her home, Liberty more than deserved this happiness. This was what Bella wanted for her.

Yet, even as she congratulated Liberty and Silas on their engagement, she felt her world shift beneath her feet. With Liberty taken care of and Abraham gone, she could not help but feel untethered. For the first time in her life, Bella did not know her place.

———

"I figured I'd find you in the kitchen."

Bella smiled as she sprinkled cloves and nutmeg into the pumpkin pie filling she stirred. With nothing else pressing for her attention and no one waiting for her at home, baking a pie at Liberty's house-turned-inn just seemed like the right thing to do. "And I figured you wouldn't be out taking battlefield tours with the rest of the group."

"You figured right. I've seen enough of those fields. Still do, almost every night . . ." he trailed off, and Bella did not draw him back. If he wanted to talk about his nightmares, he would do it on his own. But he didn't.

"Don't step on the dog." Bella pointed to Liberty's Newfoundland, Major, sprawled on the floor across a fading patch of day's last light.

Harrison chuckled as he knelt and stroked the dog's fur like so many wounded soldiers had done here just a few months ago. Then, straightening, he inhaled. "Smells divine."

Nodding, Bella poured the batter into the waiting crust. "Sure was good of you to help fix this place up. I feel a weight lifted to know it will bring Liberty income now."

"I consider it an honor to be among the first paying customers. I admit it will feel strange to leave after being here for the last few weeks."

"I bet you're eager to get home to Philadelphia tomorrow. Amelia, too."

"Will you miss me?" he teased, and she could not help but smile at his boyish grin.

"Well, I've grown accustomed to you being around Liberty Inn, just like I've grown accustomed to that clock on the wall. When you leave, I'll notice you're gone, but I'll sure enough get by."

"Ah well, we can't all be heroes, can we?" His words were playful, but his eyes were distant. "Say, did you see the mail on the hall table for you?"

Bella frowned. "Now why would I be getting mail here when my house is on Washington Street?"

"Apparently a letter for you was mixed in with your neighbor's mail. Aunt Hester, I think it was. She stopped by to see the Liberty Inn in all its shining glory, and dropped that off for you while she was here. I'll fetch it."

Heat flashed on Bella's face as she opened the cast-iron door and slid the pie in the oven to bake. Closing the door again, she wiped her hands on her apron and met Harrison in the hall. Taking the envelope from him, she turned it over, inspecting the unfamiliar handwriting and return address.

"Someone you know?" Harrison asked, ever the nosy reporter.

"I don't think so." She slit the envelope, and pulled a small, terribly creased and smudged paper from inside. "What on earth?" She glanced at Harrison.

"Come to the parlor, there's better light."

She did so, and was grateful to find it empty. Easing into the armchair, she slanted the paper into the kerosene light. Suddenly, the tiny script loomed like dusk's lengthening shadows. "It's Abraham." Her breath suddenly burned her lungs. *And Daphne?* "It can't be," she whispered. Her twin sister had become a chalky memory already half rubbed away. Shock descended upon Bella like a curtain. Numbness allowed her to continue functioning as if she hadn't just learned her husband was in the cellar of a Richmond prison, as if she hadn't just learned he'd found her sister.

"Mrs. Jamison?"

She met his earnest eyes. "He's in prison. In Richmond."

He blanched. "But how? After South Carolina, the 54th Massachusetts went to Florida, did they not?"

"Abraham was on his way home on furlough." *To me.* "The ship wrecked. He was captured by a Southern blockade runner."

Harrison jumped to his feet and began to pace the braided rug. "And yet still alive. Astonishing!"

She glared at him. "Why astonishing?"

Harrison raked his hand through his hair. "The Confederacy's policy is to treat colored Union troops as runaway slaves."

Bella's stomach roiled as the meaning filtered through her consciousness. They could put him in bondage, though he was born free. Or they could put him to death.

"But you say they're holding him in prison?"

Bella looked at the slip of paper again. "Yes. Libby, I think it says. Libby? Can that be right?" *Libby. Libbie. Liberty.* Prison, her daughter, freedom. The words clanged madly together in her mind.

Harrison grimaced. "It is notorious. What else does he say?"

"That he expects to die there." She blinked as she spoke, and noticed that the corners of her vision were veiled in white, as though she were seeing things through a thin gauze frame. "That he is starving and beaten and that colored prisoners disappear every week. But is there no hope for exchange?"

"I'm afraid not," he replied gently. "The Confederacy refuses to acknowledge black men as soldiers, so they cannot be exchanged as prisoners of war."

Her cheek twitched, even as Harrison drew near. "There's more." She handed him the letter and watched his brow furrow as he deciphered the tiny print.

"Daphne!" His head jerked up. "Your twin sister." When Harrison met Bella last summer, her face had reminded him of Daphne, who he'd seen on the auction block in Georgia. It was why he so doggedly investigated Bella's identity. "She's in Richmond!"

"But not well." Bella's voice was wooden. Harrison ran his finger along the text, then stopped. "Typho-malaria . . . And no quinine." Light glinted in his eyes as he looked into Bella's. "Blast the blockade," he growled. "Blast this insufferable war!"

"You think she'll die." An observation, not a question.

Harrison set his jaw. "I pray not. But I'll not mince words, Mrs. Jamison. Others—countless others—have died when quinine could have saved them."

Daphne could be dead already. The truth neither one would voice. And yet, "Abraham, at least, still lives."

His eyes narrowed as he regarded her. "What makes you think so?"

"If he died, I would have felt it." Their last meeting had been tense enough, but that did not erase the union they shared. "Surely his soul cannot depart this earth without my own feeling its void." She shook her head. "No. No. He lives, I know it." Her nostrils flared with conviction. "But for how long I cannot say."

Gettysburg, Pennsylvania
Friday, November 20, 1863

The clock in the hall chimed twice, but for once, Harrison Caldwell did not mind his insomnia. *I can do this.* Just how many miles he had paced inside his room at Liberty Inn that night, he did not know, nor did he care. His thoughts, at least, were finally getting somewhere.

I can do this, he told himself again. *I can do something worthwhile.* He would talk to Dr. O'Leary back in Philadelphia as soon as he could.

As a delegate of the Christian Commission, the doctor had tended the patients here in this very house right after July's battle. He knew Bella and Liberty—surely he would give Harrison some quinine to take to Richmond. Of this, he had no doubt. If he could reach Daphne in time to save her life, it would be worth the risk.

After all, it was a risk he had taken before. Posing as a Southern slave trader at the Weeping Time had gone off without a hitch. No one had detected that the man in the straw hat and gold-rimmed spectacles was a Northern reporter. If they had, he'd surely be hanged from the nearest tree, or perhaps merely tarred and feathered.

It had taken no small dose of repugnance for him to play the part of a bidder and inspect the slaves up for auction. Never one to forget a face, he saw many of these slaves still, when their images weren't crowded from his subconscious by the cadre of dead parading through his nightmares. Bull Run, Antietam, Fredericksburg, Shiloh, Seven Pines, Gettysburg. Harrison had been at all of these battles, seen boys and men torn apart by war. He never forgot their faces, whether they were blank with tedium, tight with terror, or bloated with death. It was his curse, the reason insomnia was a relief, and why he refused to cover another battle. He simply was not strong enough to carry more ghosts.

Harrison paused at the window and pressed his palm to the pane, allowing the cold to jar him back to the present moment and away from the hot sulfurous breath of battlefields. An owl gurgled, and Harrison picked up his detailed train of thought and set it chugging back in motion. *This is about Daphne.*

It was also about Sophie, if he were honest with himself. Abraham's letter had said Daphne's mistress, a Miss Kent, routinely brought food to Libby. Could it be anyone other than Sophie Kent? He'd seen her at the Weeping Time, where her father had purchased Daphne four years ago. Hornets swarmed his middle at the idea of seeing her again, even after all this time—and this war—had separated them. Of course it had been impossible for her to meet him in Philadelphia last spring. *But had she wanted to? Did she think of me?*

Harrison Caldwell had considered himself immune to feminine wiles long before and long since meeting Sophie Kent. But Sophie had been guileless. Harrison's mother had been a friend of Sophie's mother, when they'd both been students at the boarding school, themselves. So when Sophie enrolled, Christine Caldwell rejoiced to have her nearby and asked Harrison to go out of his way to make the shy young woman from Richmond feel welcome. He had.

Harrison drummed his fingertips on the sill. Sophie could be trusted not to turn him over to the authorities when he arrived with medicine for Daphne. He wouldn't stop there, either. Somehow—he would weigh his options once he knew them—he would get a letter from Bella to Abraham. Surely she would jump at the chance. If he could only find a Confederate uniform, perhaps he could pose as a newly detailed guard and get it to him himself.

Anticipation thrummed through Harrison. If he could pull this off and infiltrate Libby Prison, he would see for himself the conditions for both the white officers and the Negro soldiers in the cellar. *Imagine!* He could interview the prisoners directly. Experience the truth for himself rather than relying on the rumors that so often passed for news these days. Just possibly he could manage to befriend an unsuspecting young guard and question him—casually, of course—as well. The main priority in Richmond would be Daphne and Abraham. But as long as he was there, if he could produce an investigative report of the Confederacy's most notorious prison, all the major city papers of New York, Philadelphia, and Washington would be bidding top dollar for exclusive rights to print it.

"It could work," Harrison whispered to the haggard face in the window. "It could work!" Louder this time, before he realized the other guests might hear him through the walls. Slapping his thigh in a burst of excitement, he spun on his heel and began pacing again. There were a few challenges to overcome, such as getting through the picket lines—but challenges had never stopped Harrison Caldwell before. A grim smile stole over his face as he stared, unseeing, at the door.

The sooner he could leave, the better.

———

Long before dawn's pale fingers poked through the scalloped curtains of her house on Washington Street, Bella had given up on slumber completely. She had no appetite for breakfast, not when she knew Abraham was hungry, and Daphne was at death's door. She had brewed some coffee, purely from habit, and now the cup sat untouched on the table, and cold.

Bella stared at the empty chair across from her, and could barely remember what it felt like to have it occupied by her husband. To have his strong hands ease the tension from her neck and shoulders while he told her about his day at the blacksmith shop. "I bent more iron to my will today," he would say, chest puffed up, just to make her laugh. The house barely felt like home without him in it.

Yet the distance between them was more than time and space. Since he'd become a soldier, he hadn't yet been paid. He had fought, he had been wounded, and he had done it for free, rather than accept a salary less than the white soldier's. On their last reunion, in Beaufort, South Carolina, this had been their conversation. *Did I even tell him I loved him? That he was brave and courageous?* Bella pressed her fingertips to her temples, but could not remember.

"Just what am I supposed to do now?" she questioned the emptiness that surrounded her. "Just sit and wait for this all to play out?" That was Daphne's way. It had never been Bella's, not ever. "No," she said aloud, and the force of her voice startled her.

Bella was a fighter, and she had the scars to prove it. Even when there had been no hope of success, she had stood up to her foes—and to the foes of her family. Whether it was an overseer bent on bedding her mother or a relentless reporter threatening to expose her daughter to scandal, Bella had stood staunchly in the way. Defending her family was in her blood. And now her family was in peril again.

Something uncurled inside Bella and lifted her from the inside.

Rise up, she had so often told Liberty. Now Bella was on her feet, too, her spine ramrod straight, her shoulders squared. She could not be at ease now, not when her family was in danger.

A knock on the door spun her around. Opening the door, she was immediately struck by the fire lighting Harrison Caldwell's brown eyes. She had seen that fire before. The last time Harrison had been in Bella's house, it had been to tell her that though Liberty didn't know she was Bella's daughter, Harrison did. And that he was going to tell the world.

"May I?" And in he came, bringing a damp gust of November wind along with him. He hung his hat on the peg behind the door but did not sit. "Do I smell coffee?"

"It's cold, but I haven't touched it." She pointed to the lonely cup, then raised an eyebrow at him. They'd said their goodbyes last night at Liberty Inn. "Well?"

"I've got a plan." His step-by-step description burst from him like a geyser, until he was nearly out of breath.

"You're going to Richmond." Bella sat, and motioned for him to do the same. "For people you don't know?"

He dropped into a chair. "You are hardly a stranger to me, Mrs. Jamison."

In truth, he knew her better than anyone, outside Abraham and Liberty.

"I'm going to do this," he continued. "Write a letter, and I'll bring it to Abraham."

Bella tilted her head and studied him. In his face was all the determination she had ever seen in one man. But, "Your plan has holes."

"I have time to fine-tune it."

She shook her head, and something unlocked inside her chest. "Gaping holes. And there is *no* time." Her heart thumped as if it had just now been jolted awake.

He squinted at her. "Do you have a solution, or do you just like pointing out—"

"Underground Railroad goes both ways." She watched the light come back to his eyes as he realized what she was suggesting. It was the best of their options. "They keep travelers safe if their lives depend on it. If you try to travel through the mainstream channels, you'll have to fib your way through the journey, dodging suspicion the whole way. Too dangerous."

"Good." He rubbed his jaw. "That's good. I can get right into Richmond that way?"

Bella nodded. "And then what?"

"I'll find Daphne and give her the medicine, of course. And deliver your letter to Abraham if you'll but write one."

"A strange white man's going to visit the Negroes in Libby's cellar?"

"I could dress like a Confederate guard. I caught Amelia this morning, and she says she can sew me a uniform straightaway, as soon as we get back to Philadelphia. I can feign a Southern accent, I've done it before."

"You'll stand out, Mr. Caldwell, and be caught before you ever reach the prison."

"I'll be careful. I've gone undercover before."

"You need a Negro to deliver it, someone who can blend in."

"Then I'll find one."

"No, no." They were talking over each other now in a heated crescendo, until Bella put up her hands to silence him. She cut her voice low, spoke slowly. "You can't trust just anyone. And not everyone on the Underground Railroad is going to trust a solitary white man enough to guide you to the next station. Besides, a new face shows up around Libby's cellar, even a new colored face, could be enough to arouse suspicion. You need to use someone the guards are already accustomed to seeing. Only a familiar face will do. A face like Daphne's." She paused. "Mine."

Harrison blanched. "You?"

"No one will suspect me."

At length, he rested his elbows on the red-and-white checked tablecloth and stared at his clasped hands. "It's too big a risk for you to

93

deliver a letter. If you were discovered, you could be re-enslaved."

"In their eyes, I'm a slave already, as Daphne. I'll pose as Miss Kent's slave while my sister regains her strength with the quinine. I'm sure Miss Kent would let me stay with her." At least, Bella hoped she would.

"I can do this errand for you." Storms swirled in his eyes.

"It's not just quinine Daphne needs. She needs her family now. I have to see her before she dies—that is, if the quinine cannot save her. She's been sick for weeks. And Abraham—maybe we can do more than give him a letter. Maybe we can give him a way out."

Harrison's chair rasped over the floor as he jumped up. "I want you to remember for one moment just exactly how you felt last summer when this place was crawling with Confederate soldiers. Remember what it cost you to stay at Liberty's farm and help her nurse the Rebel wounded. I could smell the fear on your skin, Mrs. Jamison, and I'm not saying you weren't justified, because you were. And now you're telling me you want to go to Richmond, the very capital of the Confederacy, and, in essence, become a slave again after nearly twenty years of freedom."

"Just so," she managed to say. The trembling of her hands, the tightening of her chest—it meant nothing.

"Are you not scared?"

Bella swallowed as she stood. "'Scared' won't stop me. I'll not stand idle when I can help my family. Liberty is taken care of now. Silas can stay in my house while I'm gone. I'm going."

Harrison exhaled a long breath. "We'll go together. I'll do my utmost to protect you, should you need it . . ."

She nodded triumphantly, even as she gripped the back of the chair for support.

"PERIL AND FATIGUE she courted now so they might escape their prisons."

—ELIZABETH VAN LEW, referring to Unionist Lucy Rice

Act Two

COURTING PERIL

Chapter Nine

Blair House, Richmond, Virginia
Monday, November 23, 1863

Afternoon sun threw golden stripes across Madeline Blair's parlor, warming the cobalt blue carpet and bouncing off the gilded mirror. As Sophie listened to all the words Mrs. Blair had obviously saved up for her, she could not help but smile at the sleek white cat watching the yarn dance from their needles.

"You work yourself too hard, and I don't mind being the one to say so," Mrs. Blair was saying, her voice silky smooth above the staccato clicks of their knitting.

Sophie glanced up to measure her neighbor's face, pale against the coffee brown hair that framed it. "I've never known you to be idle, either." With two sons in the army, she was never without something to knit or sew, even with company present.

"But the work you do will waste you clean away."

Sophie shook her head. "Daphne is wasting away. Not me." Aside from visiting Mrs. Blair and Libby's hospital, much of her time was spent in the sickroom at her own house, warding off chill with a mixture of red pepper, tea, and table salt. When fever was present, she tipped dogwood bark tea past Daphne's lips—just in case Dr. Lansing had been wrong about its being useless.

Mrs. Blair sighed. "I worry it's taking a toll on you, spending so much time with the ill. Not just Daphne. I know you visit the Yankees down at Libby's hospital room, as well. Talk flies faster than even your needles, you know."

Sophie's hands slowed for a moment. "Yes, I do."

"Well, it's right Christian of you to love your enemies that way." She laid her work in her brown silk lap and stretched her fingers. "And there aren't many of us who dare to follow suit, it being quite an unpopular form of the Golden Rule at the moment. But if any of my boys were captured, I'd want some compassionate soul to do the same for them. I suspect thoughts of your father may have steered you that way, too, am I right?"

Sophie nodded. "Precisely."

"I completely understand. They are in need, no one can deny that. It's charity to try to help. Even though they're on the wrong side of this war. But enough of that. I've noticed Captain Russell has been calling on you routinely. Things must be going well." Her voice tilted up, questioningly, an obvious invitation for more details.

"Just fine." A smile tugged at her lips at the merriment on Mrs. Blair's face. Sophie had grown to look forward to the captain's reassuring presence, his manners and charm a reminder that she was still a lady, despite the unending work of war. And he had learned to accept that she would not abandon her instinct to help the prisoners in need. *You realize this only means I must spend more time with you, in order to offset your actions,* he'd said with a twinkle in his eye, *on the chance that anyone is still watching you, of course.* But certainly no one watched her more than Lawrence Russell himself, whenever he had the chance.

"He does appear smitten with you, dear, and I can't say I blame him. I always hoped one of my boys would end up with you or your sister. But then—"

"Susan married Noah Becker." Sophie finished for her before it was necessary to say that Thomas and Solomon were dead.

"Yes. Broke poor Asher's heart clean in two."

She broke more hearts than that, her father's being one of them. But all Sophie said was, "Poor Asher," and picked up her knitting again.

After five more rows around the sock, Sophie bundled her knitting into her basket and bid her kind neighbor goodbye. "You're another day closer to Asher and Joel coming home," she offered, and prayed again they would be preserved.

Mrs. Blair smiled wistfully as she walked Sophie to the door. "God bless them and keep them. And you come again soon."

———

With one step inside Libby Prison's hospital room, Sophie's thoughts were yanked from Daphne, Captain Russell, and Madeline Blair. Dread drizzled coldly over her as she noted how large Dr. Lansing's eyes were in his face, the growing gap between his neck and his collar. Even in the dusty beam of sunlight, his straw-colored hair was lifeless and dull. His skin had faded from the sun-browned hue of a soldier in camp, to the pasty shade of captivity.

His stethoscope clattered to the floor as it slipped from his hand. He bent to retrieve it, then stood, and swayed. Fearing he was about to faint, Sophie reached out and steadied him. The doctor shook his head, eyes shut tight.

"Take a break, Dr. Lansing," Dr. Wilkes called from three beds away. "Five minutes."

A tense nod, and Dr. Lansing extracted himself from between the rows of patients. On the perimeter of the room, he leaned against the wall and settled his gaze on the window.

"You're unwell." Sophie kept her voice low.

A moment's pause. "No worse than most." He held his hand up, and it shook. "We are starving, Miss Kent."

"The patients?"

"And the prisoners. All of us."

No.

"Even the ones you don't see, the ones who are not ill enough to get a bed. I've shed thirty pounds in less than two months."

Thirteen thousand prisoners and no one wants to feed them. Mr. Hayes's words echoed in her mind then. But that was weeks ago. "Is there still so very little beef? Has the situation not improved in the last month?"

"Improved? Heavens, no." His voice was so quiet, Sophie leaned in to catch every word. She flicked a glance toward Dr. Wilkes on the other side of the room before studying Dr. Lansing's face once more.

"It used to be we went ten days or so without meat," he went on. "Our rations have been nine ounces of corn bread and a cup of water per day—although Dr. Wilkes has given me more water than that, but it's pumped directly from the James and not altogether potable. These days, we're lucky to see two ounces of beef every four weeks. And from what we hear from the cellar, our colored comrades fare even worse." Cringing, he covered one ear with his large-knuckled fingers.

"What? What is it?"

"My ears are ringing." A hoarse chuckle broke from his lips as he dropped his hand. "Everyone's ears are ringing, unless they've only just arrived. Everyone gets dizzy when they stand up too quickly—like I just did. We all get headaches when we concentrate, whether our focus is tending the sick, or on an improvised chessboard on the floor. Some men faint before they finish the game. Checkmate."

Tears pooled in Sophie's eyes. The need was so great! Flour was $120 a barrel in the market right now, and meat becoming so dear that possums were now hung in butchers' windows. It would take a king's ransom to feed these men adequately. "My help has been—" She spread her hands.

"An extraordinary gesture," Dr. Lansing finished for her, his eyes sparking. "The very thread between life and death for so many of these men. We cannot save them all, Miss Kent. As a physician, that's been a hard truth to reconcile. You can have no idea how many patients I've lost in this war, even in this building alone. But remember this: we must work as hard as we can at what we've been called to do and leave the outcome up to God. If we don't, we'll lose hope. And that is one thing we must not do."

The doctor looked out over his patients, for whom there was very little hope indeed. They had told Sophie of their homes and loved ones whenever she was near, their fond memories their only comfort. With a start, she realized she'd never heard the doctor speak of anything but his work. *Perhaps . . .* "Would you like to tell me about home?"

A sad smile bent his lips. "I lived in Connecticut before the war. Beautiful place. But my heart is in Rhode Island."

"You have a sweetheart there?"

He nodded. "Charlotte, a nurse—co-director, actually—in a military hospital. We will marry, if we can only survive this war." His eyes misted uncharacteristically, and Sophie wondered if bringing up home had been a mistake.

A lump shifted in his throat before he turned back to her. "Do you believe in a sovereign God?"

She nodded.

"Then you understand me when I say He is the Alpha and the Omega, the Beginning and the End. We may not see how all of this ends in His master plan. But we are to be faithful in the middle just the same." He cleared his throat, rubbed his eyes. "Now if you'll excuse me."

Sophie watched him go. His movements were stiff and slow, as though he were walking under water. Then, before she realized what was happening, his knees buckled, and he collapsed to the floor.

"Doctor!" she heard herself cry out and in an instant Dr. Wilkes was on the floor with Dr. Lansing.

"Just a fainting spell, that's all." Dr. Wilkes's words were nonchalant, but his eyes betrayed him.

Sophie stared at the young doctor crumpled on the floor, and at the older doctor pretending not to be troubled, and at the hollow-eyed patients all around her who, mere months ago, had been hearty and hale. She thought of the Negroes suffering in the cellar, and the rest of Richmond's prisoners wasting away for want of food.

Then she stared at her basket, sitting empty by the door. Her pathetic, pitiful basket. What good had she done, really? With so little food for so many men, it was like spitting on the Sahara and expecting it to bring forth fruit.

Libby Prison, Richmond, Virginia
Wednesday, November 25, 1863

Abraham Jamison covered his nose and mouth with his handkerchief and knotted the ends tightly at the back of his head. "Would you believe I hoped I'd get used to this smell?"

Peter Colson slanted a glance at him as he adjusted his own kerchief on the bridge of his nose. "Boy, were you wrong."

"Dead wrong," Abraham said, and Peter's eyes crinkled. Dark as it seemed, they took their humor where they could get it.

Especially on days like today, when forty-five corpses waited to be loaded into the dead-cart. The Rebels had dispensed with using coffins altogether, which made the job a sight quicker, but far more disagreeable. It was an impossible stink of which to rid oneself.

Though the loads were lighter without the wooden boxes, Abraham still tired alarmingly quickly. The muscles he'd built as a blacksmith in Gettysburg were withering away for lack of fuel. Worse than the regular reminder of his sapping strength, however, was the starker reminder of his own mortality.

He shuddered, and prayed for the thousandth time that Bella had received his letter. She deserved to know what happened to her husband. So very many wives would never know. *Lord,* he prayed, *help them find peace.* A supernatural feat if ever there was one.

Hoofbeats and footsteps plodded in the alley. Merciful distraction. It was Robert Ford, a Negro who'd been a Union army teamster until he was captured in May 1862, and was now pressed into service as the hostler for Dick Turner, Libby Prison's despised warden. His nose wrinkled as he approached, but his eyes shone with intelligence—the kind Abraham was only too eager to hear. The stomach-turning stench gave them a wide perimeter from other would-be listening ears as Robert passed along information he'd gleaned from the Unionist slave and free black population of Richmond.

"Well, what's it been, Ford? A week?" Abraham lost track of the days. "You look like the fox who got the hen."

Robert's smile flashed brightly in response. "Sure did taste good going down, too!" He rubbed his belly, chuckling.

"Save us any?" Peter asked.

"Oh, I got plenty of morsels for you today."

Cary Street's clattering merchant district seemed to hush as Abraham focused on the words falling from Robert's lips as if they were crumbs, and Abraham were a begging dog. *If only words were food, indeed.* His head ached with the effort to hear past the ringing in his ears.

"Believe it or not, Turner still requests meat for us prisoners," Ford began, "and still Northrop refuses. The Commissary General is terrified that if we are strong enough, we'll break free and attack our captors, or the whole city of Richmond."

Not likely. They were far too weak to revolt. Especially the poor souls on Belle Isle, whose skeletal forms all but disappeared in the stacks of corpses they handled. *Going mad with hunger,* Robert had said earlier. They hunted the guard dogs for meat.

"Northrop is so paranoid," Ford continued, "that when the U.S. steamer *Convoy* arrived from Fortress Monroe last week, bearing clothing and forty thousand rations for Union prisoners, the ship was turned away. They refused one hundred tons of food though it would have cost them nothing to distribute it. Could have fed all of us for three days."

Enough food for three days! Abraham could scarcely suppress the groan pushing up from the pit of his cavernous belly. Surely it would not have been the fried chicken, boiled ham, baked potatoes, roast beef and gravy they dreamed about, but to come so close to quelling hunger—and then to be refused—it was almost more than Abraham could bear. The look of despair in Peter's eyes told Abraham he felt the same.

"Northrop isn't the only one concerned about a breakout. Being so close to Washington to the north, and Union-held Williamsburg to the southeast, General Winder says it's a constant temptation to prisoners, and that he'll be forever hassled with Union raids to free us, like a puppy nipping at his heels."

Abraham frowned. "The provost marshal compared the Union army to a puppy? The man must not be facing reality." The Yankees outnumbered the Rebels in every way.

"Yesterday he dispatched his son to canvass the deep South, looking for a place to build a new war prison."

Deep South. Dread rippled hotly through Abraham's veins. "For future prisoners?"

"And current. They mean to move us further from temptation, and away from that giant nipping puppy. Puppies have sharp teeth, you know, and Winder has had enough."

Abraham felt light-headed. "What about the prisoner exchange program?"

"Suspended. Because the Rebs refuse to exchange colored souls for white ones."

A muffled groan came from behind Peter's kerchief. He'd been here months longer than Abraham. "This war just plain got to end."

"Only if we win it." Abraham's voice was hoarse and distant, but his conviction was much stronger. He had not become a soldier, been wounded and captured, all without pay, for a losing cause. The North would win. It had to. "What do you think, Ford? Are we close?"

"Don't know that, but I know this." Robert's eyes glowed as he spoke. "We're not the only ones going hungry. Even the guards would blow away in a slight wind."

Abraham nodded. "Yeah, they're hungry. They steal from our ration supply when our rations are barely fit to be eaten."

"Just so. Lee's soldiers in the field are hard-pressed to get their vittles, too." Robert cut his voice low. "But this Reb government is so mismanaged that forty thousand bushels of impressed sweet potatoes are now rotting at depots between Wilmington and Richmond."

"Hard to fight hungry." Peter's tone seemed laced with hope.

"Sure is. Also hard to fight without gunpowder."

Abraham's eyes popped open wide. "What?"

"Colonel Gorgas of the Ordnance Bureau says their supply of saltpeter will be completely exhausted by January if they don't find a large quantity of it soon."

Peter's brow furrowed, and Abraham guessed the former butler didn't understand.

"Saltpeter, when mixed with sulfur and charcoal, makes gunpowder. Can't have bullets, or grapeshot, or cannons, or torpedoes without it."

"One more thing." Robert looked casually over his shoulder. "Our source in Seddon's office says Bragg sent a brief dispatch saying he had a prolonged contest with the Yankees for Lookout Mountain. He didn't say who won, but all who read it assume Bragg is retreating into Georgia. So how'd I do this week? Food for thought?" He grinned.

"Oh, you definitely gave us something to chew on," parried Abraham.

"Pass it along, then. These white boys upstairs could use the encouragement, I'm sure."

Abraham agreed. The officers hung on every word of news that came through Robert Ford. Abraham felt a twinge of pity for them, all cooped up in that stinking building, never allowed outside even to exercise their limbs. They were shot at if they came within three feet of a window. *More or less.* They'd been shot at for coming within twelve feet. *And the only way they ever get outside is as a corpse.*

Richmond, Virginia
Thursday, November 26, 1863

Sophie stirred the logs in Daphne's fireplace and watched the copper and gold flames leap higher before turning back to listen to her maidservant's heart. Though it was weak, the rapid-fire pulse had begun to slow toward a more normal pace in the last week, which Sophie grasped at as a positive sign. Yet she could not deny that Daphne's body seemed to melt away beneath her skin until her bones pronounced themselves sharply. Her cough now sounded suspiciously like bronchitis, the presence of which made sleep next to impossible. Sophie began dreaming of medicine the way the prisoners said they dreamed of banquet tables groaning beneath the weight of food. But of course, neither were likely to appear.

Flipping her braid behind her shoulder, Sophie wiped her hands on the apron covering her pink and brown gingham work dress. She'd learned to save wear on her mourning gowns by only wearing them when she left the house or when she was expecting visitors—neither of which was on the agenda today.

Quietly now, she left Daphne to her fitful slumber, closed the door behind her, and leaned against the hall beside it. *Thank God that at least the fits of hysteria have ceased,* she thought with a shudder. Daphne no longer seemed to be hearing babies crying in the shadows of the room. In fact, she no longer seemed to hear much of anything. Whether it was simple dullness of hearing brought on by the disease, or a more sinister cerebral inflammation, Sophie could only guess. And pray.

Rain bounced on the back porch like silver needles dropping from the sky. But it was another sound that made her squint into the storm.

Hoofbeats. Carriage wheels. *At this early hour?*

Throwing a shawl around her shoulders, Sophie stepped outside in time to watch a delivery carriage pull up. The horses slowed to a halt, steam rising from their hulking bodies, and a man emerged with a tray. It was Thomas McNiven, the local baker who catered to all the fine houses on Church Hill.

"Special delivery for you, Miss Kent." Under the portico, he offered her a platter of small cakes.

"I beg your pardon? I—I didn't order these," she sputtered.

"Take them," he said through a smile which barely moved. "Or it will make my presence at your home very suspicious, indeed."

At once, she was wide awake. Her spine tingled as she received the delivery, absolutely at a loss as to what was happening.

"Come, now. Why don't you put those inside your house, and then come back out. I have some other delicacies you may be interested in for those parties you sometimes give."

The hair on her neck stood at attention. After the first party went so well, she'd given one more, last week. More guests had come than to the first one, but she did not know her social activities were common knowledge.

"The longer we stand here, the more likely we are to be noticed," he muttered. "The rain and the darkness are fair cloaks for now, but we are not invisible."

Curiosity bested prudence. Sophie took the tray inside, then returned to Mr. McNiven and followed him to his carriage. When he invited her inside to get out of the rain, she did so. The carriage lurched into motion, and her tongue cleaved to the roof of her mouth. Had anyone seen her get in? Would anyone see where they went?

The rain drummed atop the enclosed carriage. Three blocks passed, and they turned north on Twenty-fourth, then west on Grace.

Sophie's chest tightened, but she finally found her voice. "Whatever we're doing, Mr. McNiven, I'm not properly dressed for it. I'm in mourning."

His bushy eyebrows bounced. "Always wear black, then, do you?"

"Outside my home, yes." Not to mention the fact that her blonde hair was still plaited in a braid from the night before, rather than piled on her head as usual. "Why, I look like a working-class girl!"

He nodded. "If anyone is looking for you, they'll be looking for a woman darkly draped and formally groomed. Your appearance is perfect, trust me."

But he did not seem sinister, this man she had known by sight for years, a man who smelled of yeast and sorghum. Still, here she was, having been spirited from her home in predawn darkness, and taken to—

The Van Lew mansion? Confusion fogged her brain as they turned into the drive and circled to the rear entrance of the most well-known Union sympathizer in Richmond. Hadn't Elizabeth said not to be seen together? Or had Sophie misconstrued the message?

Wordlessly, Mr. McNiven peered through rain's silvery veil. Then, "Take this, delivery girl." He handed her a baker's box, and he took another.

Bare head bowed beneath the showers, Sophie followed Mr. McNiven's footsteps until they brought her into the kitchen behind the main house. She did not hear what he said as he placed his box on the table and left her, dripping, in the presence of Elizabeth Van Lew.

"It is safe to speak here," Elizabeth said, her voice much softer than her eyes. "My servant Caroline will not repeat what we say." Behind her, a Negro woman fried bacon in a cast-iron skillet. "Please, sit."

Stiffly, Sophie moved to the kitchen table and sat across from Elizabeth.

"My heart is true," the spinster said, "to the true government, and to our true president." Sophie had a feeling she was not referring to the Confederacy and Jefferson Davis. Elizabeth did not bat an eye. "I would not invite you here if I did not suspect the same is true of you, given your work for the patients of Libby Prison."

My interests are charitable, not political. But Sophie knew better than to say it aloud. If Elizabeth Van Lew had been born male, she would very likely be mayor of Richmond or the boldest member in Virginia's legislature. Her grandfather, Hilary Baker, had participated in Pennsylvania's constitutional convention, and served three terms as Philadelphia's mayor. Government, it seemed, ran in Elizabeth's blood.

Sophie marshaled her thoughts. "It's slavery I abhor."

"As do I. The slaves we have on our estate would be free were it not for the codicil my father attached to his will, preventing my mother from emancipating them." Elizabeth's face darkened. "Silly, isn't it? They are emancipated already, according to Lincoln's proclamation. Unfortunately for them, they live about one hundred miles too far south. For now." Her eyes burned, and Sophie read them easily.

"I knew your mother," she went on. "I know you went to school in Philadelphia—my alma mater—and came home with a loathing for slavery, as I did. I know you have had rows with your father about it, as I did with mine. I know you feel compelled to aid the Union prisoners."

None of this was untrue. "Does this brand me disloyal?"

"Your father's captivity at Fort Delaware protects you to some degree. So does the fact that you're being courted by an officer in the Ordnance Bureau—the very same bureau that creates the weapons being used against the Union. Well done."

Sophie's face flamed. She had not intended to use Captain Russell as a shield indefinitely, but their relationship had flared into something brighter than either had expected. But neither was she at peace with herself for growing attached to a man who upheld slavery with his job and personal convictions.

"I'm doing what I can for the prisoners here."

"It is chaff."

Sophie blinked, stunned. "I beg your pardon?"

"What you've done, what I've done, what Lucy Rice and Abby

Green and others have done, is but chaff compared to the need that exists. Don't misunderstand. Your sacrifice is noted, as is the risk you've taken to visit them. But can you not see they are dying just the same? These men are dying via systematic starvation, a fate never before doled out to the worst criminals. Their treatment goes against the articles of war, and it goes against humanity. It would be more merciful to put them in front of a line of cannon and blow them all to pieces."

"Yes," Sophie whispered, unable to hear any more. Frustration boiled in her veins. Daphne was dying on account of Libby Prison, and Sophie had spent a tidy sum of her father's money feeding Union prisoners while they yet died in droves. "I don't know what else to do."

"Come now. I had it on good authority you had a sight more imagination than that. Think, Mr. Thornton." A thin smile curled on Elizabeth's face as she used Sophie's old pseudonym. "You're smart as a whip, Miss Kent, and far more daring than you realize. Now think."

Sophie's spine straightened. A cold ember in her chest slowly warmed. She met Elizabeth's frank gaze as her own convictions, once hidden, broke loose from her lips. "Our larders won't save them. Their only hope—" she glanced again at Caroline. "Their only hope is to be free." Surely merely forming the words was bravery. *Or treason.*

"Would you help them?"

Sophie flinched. Help them? It was tantamount to sedition. A sentence to Castle Thunder if caught.

In her hesitation, Elizabeth spoke again. "We can't fight slavery ourselves. But they can."

Dr. Caleb Lansing surged in Sophie's mind. He was just one man, but as a surgeon, if he were free, he could help heal countless bodies and send them back to their regiments. And he could give a true account of the condition of the prisoners to U.S. authorities. Here, in Libby's hospital, he was only going through the motions without proper tools or medicine. Yes, he was able to make diagnoses, but beyond that, his work could be done by Sophie or any other compassionate soul. He was wasting away himself—and to lose a doctor was to lose many more who were desperate for his help.

"I'll help Caleb Lansing." *You'll be breaking the law,* her conscience hissed. But she blew the thought away like thistle down.

Elizabeth nodded. "I have a plan, and you will be the linchpin."

Chapter Ten

Eastville, Virginia
Thursday, November 26, 1863

*B*ella's feet plunged through the scrubby coastline hugging the Chesapeake Bay. The night was scarcely dark enough for safety, but she and Harrison could wait no longer for chance of a moonless sky. A raw wind swirled around them as they followed the sable guide who had secreted them in his cabin last night. At last, Cherrystone Lighthouse came into view, and they were one step closer to Richmond.

Faithful souls had led them from station to station along the Underground Railroad, burrowing through the border state of Delaware, then through copperhead Maryland, until they were here, in the county seat of Virginia's Northampton County.

"You see that figure there?" Their guide, Randolph, said. "That's Marshall. He smuggles passengers and mail through the lines in his canoe. Best pilot I ever saw. Just keep a low profile as you get in. Safety awaits on the other side. You'll be fine."

But they were not fine yet. Bella's breathing sounded loud in her ears. Still in Rebel country, her body was tense and ready to fight or run at the first sign of a slave catcher. Her ears were tuned, straining to hear the baying of bloodhounds. She had hidden among sand and brush in the dark before. But then, there had been no escape, for she had been trapped on an island off the coast of Georgia. Still, at the age of sixteen, she had waited for days in the swampy quagmire, waiting for a miracle that never came. By the time she had returned to the plantation, she was half starved and more than half mad. Though it was twenty years ago, the fear, the anger, and the pain all came rushing back to her in vivid color. Once her path had led her to the North, she swore she'd never go south again.

"Looks clear—go now," Randolph said, but her limbs would not obey. Bella's mind said *Go!* But her heels dug deeper into the sand.

Harrison grabbed her hand, and jerked her into action. Together they ran, half crouching, to the canoe, and fairly leapt inside the dugout. Once Marshall had collected his fee from Harrison—coffee and greenbacks—he pushed off into the water's inky expanse.

No one spoke. A short distance into the bay, Marshall rested on his oars, scanning the water for signs of hostile craft. The clouds were thin and scattered, the stars peeping dangerously through the dark, ragged curtain overhead. Wind blew strongly from the east, chopping the water that rocked them.

Bella saw nothing unusual, and apparently neither did Marshall, for he hoisted his sails. As they rapidly filled, the little vessel sprang forward like an arrow from the string. Skimming over the waves, the sharp prow cut into the water, dashing clouds of salted spray onto the passengers. Bella turned up the collar of her cloak, and tightened the green scarf around her head. They sped due west like this for fourteen miles.

"We'll find them, Bella. It will all be worth it when we do." The wind snatched greedily at his words, but the conviction in his voice was clear. Though she could barely distinguish his features, she imagined his lips pressed together as they so often did when he was set on a course he'd determined to see through. Truth be told, Bella was grateful to have him on her side this time. Harrison Caldwell was as relentless at pursuing as Bella was at escaping, and with the added advantage of being a white male.

A comfortable quiet settled on them as Marshall turned the boat southwest by west for ten or twelve more miles, then due west again to their destination. By the time they reached Gloucester Point three and a half hours after leaving Eastville, they'd sailed thirty miles in three and a half hours—and crossed the Rubicon.

The boat slowed as it neared the landing, and Bella shuddered before the cold unknown.

"Who comes there?" a sentinel hailed.

"Marshall—mail boat!"

"Stand, Marshall, and give the countersign!"

"No countersign," was the reply, and Bella's stomach flipped. Would they be turned away because Marshall didn't know the countersign? *But Randolph said we'd be safe!*

The sentinel called out: "Sergeant of the Guard, Post No. 1!" Bella caught Harrison's gleaming eyes.

Another voice, farther away, cried: "Who's there?"

"Marshall," said the first sentinel, "with mail boat and passengers."

"Sentinel, let them pass."

Quietly, Bella gave vent to her relief, exhaling slowly. Before she could rally her nerves, Harrison cupped her elbow and helped her out of the rocking craft.

"We're safe," he told her.

Safe. Safe. She chanted the word in her mind until she actually believed it. They slept in their clothes in a rude cabin, surrounded by Union soldiers just outside. Truly, she had never been safer.

The next day, Harrison and Bella sailed a short distance to Yorktown, and from there set out by foot across the peninsula. If she had to cover every mile one step at a time to reach her family, she would

115

do it without complaint. But time mocked her as it dragged on. Bella could only pray they would make it to Daphne and Abraham in time.

Ten miles later, they reached Grove Wharf only to learn the next steam packet would not depart for Richmond until Monday. It was all Bella could do not to cry.

———

Richmond, Virginia
Monday, November 30, 1863

Eyes squeezed shut, Sophie Kent tried to focus on her silver locket, cool and still against her pounding heart. The faces of her mother and father inside were smooth, clean, and bright with life. But she could barely breathe. She could not shut out the image of dead Union officers surrounding her, their swollen lips pulled back in deathly grimace. *How long has it been? Is he coming?* She twisted her hands together, then immediately dropped them. That wringing of the hands had been her mother's fretful habit. And Sophie was not her mother.

She measured the scant rays of light falling in through the chinks in the walls of the morgue as she waited. Last Friday she had handed Dr. Lansing a bag of tobacco and told him it was a special gift meant for him alone. In the bottom of the pouch was a note: *Would you be free? Then be prepared to act. Meet me Monday at 8 in the morgue.* Had he seen the note? Or had another? That bag of tobacco could have been confiscated by a guard or the warden himself. Slowly, she blew out a breath to calm herself. *He is only waiting for the right moment.*

Moments here in the dead-house lay as still and prostrate as the corpses within it, as if time had expired when they had. Sophie's skirt swished as a rat scuttled just beneath the hem. She could barely contain her horror as she heard—for she could not look—that it had found its food. She made a jail of her teeth to keep from crying out loud.

Lord, help!

The door squeaked on its hinges, and Sophie looked out from the shadows at the wedge of light spreading on the uneven dirt floor. The figure was a black silhouette against the sharp morning sun.

Then he spoke, and she stepped forward, her knees threatening to buckle as relief streamed through her. "Tell me." Dr. Lansing's voice was hoarse, distant.

Sophie whispered the plan Elizabeth Van Lew had devised. On Thursday, he was to be laid out as a corpse before the morning roll call, covered with a blanket, and conveyed here, to the dead-house. "You'll have to stay here until dusk, without moving a muscle." She watched for a flinch or cringe. *If I were tasked with this assignment, I fear I would go*— Sophie dropped the thought as if it had burned her. She focused on the doctor instead. "Can you do it?"

His eyes were as flint as he nodded. "And then?"

"You'll have to arrange for a few friends to distract the guards with a sham fight. Then, with their attention fixed elsewhere, you will pass out of the hospital and head east on Cary Street. It will be nearly dark, but you'll see my white handkerchief, bordered with black ribbon." Fishing it from her pocket, she showed it to him. "Keep it in sight and follow me."

"To a safe house?"

She nodded. "Mine."

Suddenly, he grabbed her hand and kissed it before recovering his usual decorum. "God bless you," he whispered, and a rare smile brightened his thin face. "I'll see you Thursday. I'll be a dead man, no matter what."

If it was a joke, Sophie found no humor in it. Her stomach cramped violently as he slipped out through the door. With a jolt, she whipped her skirts to one side, doubled over, and retched.

Chapter Eleven

Spotswood Hotel, Richmond, Virginia
Monday, November 30, 1863

And so it begins, Harrison thought. More than a week of traveling, including all day today rocking and swaying on the steam packet from Grove Wharf to Rocketts Landing, was only a prelude to the real adventure now unfolding before him. As he entered the boisterous Spotswood Hotel, Bella following closely behind with downcast gaze, a smile slanted on his face.

So this is Richmond. Or at least, it might as well be. It was commonly known that the five-story Spotswood was to the Confederate capital what Willard's famous hotel was to Washington. It was its own miniature world, the place where politicians, generals, profiteers, spies, and the gentry communed. The air was thick with gossip and a smell of bourbon so strong Harrison could taste it. Jefferson and Varina Davis had stayed here early in the war, while their house on Clay Street was being prepared for them, and the place still hummed with import. This was where Harrison would stay.

Jostling through the crowd, he rested his hands confidently on the brass railing circling the reception desk and reserved his room. "I assume you accept greenbacks." Confederate currency was crumbling. The last Harrison had heard, right before they'd left Philadelphia, it took eighteen Confederate dollars to buy one dollar in gold. Greenbacks—U.S. dollars—were the next best value.

"Of course, sir."

"Good."

Eagerness shone in the receptionist's eyes as he took Harrison's money. "You'll be in Room 321, but it's being cleaned right now. Come back in an hour and I'll give you the key. And—" He craned his neck to look past Harrison. "She yours? She can stay in the underground cells."

"Pardon me?"

"Your slave. We keep our patrons' slaves locked up safely for them so you can be free to enjoy your time here. We have our own parlors and public rooms here, but there are also other fine restaurants, the Richmond Theater . . ." He lowered his voice. "And, I might add, seeing as you're as spry as they come around here these days, gambling and, er—companionship can also be found in abundance." He winked. "So just take your wench downstairs and we'll hold her tight. The cells are quite roomy, and if somehow she manages to escape, the hotel guarantees the full price of her value will be paid to you. That's just how sure we are she'll be there when you need her."

Harrison swallowed. "I see. Have you a map of the city?"

The man spread one on the desk. "You're here." He pointed with the tip of his pencil to the corner of Eighth and Main Streets. "This here is Capitol Square. Anywhere else you'd like to go?"

"Provost marshal's office."

"That'll be here, at Broad and Tenth. Just north of the Square. But it'll be closed until morning. What else?"

Harrison assessed the fellow in front of him. Was he the sort to be suspicious? Or was he only the sort to curry favors with a patron who paid in greenbacks? Judging him to be the latter, he asked quietly for one more address. If he and Sophie had written letters since they'd last seen each other, he wouldn't have to ask. But her father had forbidden any correspondence with her Northern friends after she returned from boarding school, so concerned was he about lingering abolitionist influence. "The Kent residence," Harrison said. "Do you know it?"

"Mr. Kent, the editor? Newspaper man?"

"The very same."

"Last I heard he was at Fort Delaware."

Harrison's eyebrows raised. He wondered if he had seen him there. But, "He has a daughter. And I have a letter from him to deliver." He put his hand over his pocket, though it held no such thing. "I imagine she's anxious for word from him."

"Do you now? So you've been to the prison, have you?" He folded his arms, tilted his head, poised to call a bluff. "What's it like?"

Harrison described the Confederate prison camp in detail, putting to use the notes he'd taken for a story he'd never sold. "Now, I'd like to deliver his letter to her. Can you help me or not?" Fire crackled in his voice, and he was well repaid with a dark lead circle on his map.

"Corner of Franklin and Twenty-seventh."

Harrison nodded his thanks, feeling flush with his victory. Now that seeing Sophie again was within reach, uncertainty swirled in his gut. Would she be happy to see him? *Frivolous, trifling concern compared to saving Daphne's life.* With map in hand, he turned and led Bella away from the receptionist's stare, all the way back out onto Main Street.

Evening had dropped its filmy veil on Richmond, and the gaslights sputtered and flared at intervals. The street was alive with people, both black and white, government and civilian. It was not a place to speak freely. "Did you hear what he said?" he managed to ask, and Bella shook her head no, eyes still cast down in submission. With her hair bound in a green head scarf, and her posture almost curled in on itself,

120

Harrison caught a glimpse of her life before Gettysburg. He could not lock her in an underground cell for the night. And she would not stand for it, either, which would be even more dangerous.

"Let me think for a minute," he muttered, his gaze drifting with the flow of traffic toward Capitol Square, if he remembered the map correctly. And just north of that, was the provost marshal's office, but closed. A sigh brushed his lips. He needed a pass to move freely in the city. Sitting in the hotel and just waiting, when their time was so short already, grated on him.

As carriages, wagons, horses, and pedestrians crossed in front of the hotel on Main Street, Harrison noted that no one was stopped and made to show their pass. These people were moving freely already. Surely, if Harrison and Bella hired a cab, they would be hidden on their journey to the Kent house. Bella could give her sister the quinine, and Harrison would be back at the Spotswood soaking up all the booze-flavored gossip he could. *If Sophie seems agreeable to catching up for old times' sake, perhaps I could work that in, too.* As though he could fool himself into a comfortable apathy. The pounding in his chest said otherwise. Harrison opened the map once more, and measured the distance between Spotswood and the Kent house. Twenty blocks. *We can do this.*

"Let's go find your sister."

<hr />

As if guests were not already filling the parlor behind them, Captain Lawrence Russell leaned in and planted a kiss on Sophie's hair. She wondered if he detected the smell of the dead on her, or perhaps, the scent of a secret. After her meeting in the morgue this morning, she'd soaked and soaped and scrubbed, yet still she felt marked.

It was not that she regretted her actions, but that she felt so drastically altered by them. Sophie marveled that the captain, at least, seemed not to notice the change. For the woman he held near was entirely different from the one he'd first set out to protect. His hand curved around her tightly cinched waist, and his beard bristled against her cheek as he whispered a compliment in her ear. She barely heard him.

"Please." She smiled into his blue eyes. "There are guests to greet."

The party was three times larger than the first one Sophie had hosted. Mrs. Blair wasn't here yet, but guests were still trickling in. This in spite of the fact that they'd stopped serving refreshments, per Fischer's strong suggestion. No matter. Starvation parties were the fashion now, anyway. With water to drink, and music and dancing for food, the guests went home more than satisfied.

"Hello, Mr. Hayes, Mr. Graham." Sophie flashed her most charming smile. The two clerks handed their hats and cloaks to Fischer, whose high forehead shone as he bowed to each guest.

Captain Russell pumped Mr. Graham's hand and clapped Mr. Hayes on the shoulder. "I see you brought your violin! Splendid!"

"Wouldn't come to a party without it! Let the dancing begin!" Hazel eyes gleaming, he held his instrument aloft and fairly waltzed into the parlor with it. Approving murmurs punctuated the room as the first few bars of music sounded.

Sophie watched from the doorway between entrance hall and parlor as the guests paired off, smiles wreathing their faces. It felt like a dream to her, so stark was the contrast between her morning's errand and this evening's determined merrymaking.

"Miss Kent, the coat rack is full." Fischer pushed his spectacles up the thin bridge of his nose, his black mustache all but hiding his lips as he spoke. "I do apologize. I'll fetch another and return in a moment."

"Go ahead, Fischer," said Captain Russell, and Sophie chafed that he'd answered for her. "I'll open the door if anyone else arrives. Sophie, go enjoy yourself. Just not too much until I can dance with you myself." He winked, and Sophie forced a smile before joining the guests in the parlor.

———

"Wait here." Harrison paid the cab driver extra to hold him, and helped Bella down at the corner of Franklin and Twenty-seventh. Wasting no time, he opened the wrought iron gate and waited for Bella to pass through it before closing it behind them both. Light and music spilled from the windows. *Somebody's home, at least.* They marched up the stairs to the white-columned front porch.

"Courage," he whispered to Bella, and she nodded. He knocked on the door and stood back, praying they'd be admitted at once.

The door opened, and Harrison's stomach clenched. A Confederate officer gazed curiously between Harrison and Bella. He could almost hear him demand Harrison's nonexistent pass.

"Is this the Kent house?" Harrison asked.

"Yes, it is." He looked again at Bella. Frowned. "Why, Daphne!"

So Daphne is still alive. Thank God, Harrison thought as Bella looked up for an instant before lowering her gaze again.

The officer turned to Harrison. "Yes, yes, this is where Daphne's mistress lives. I confess I had no idea she was well enough to be up and moving around. But Daphne, breaking curfew? It doesn't seem like you. I assume you at least brought your pass with you?"

Bella shook her head, said nothing.

"Well then. Thank you sir, for returning her directly to us. To Miss Kent, I mean. Daphne is fortunate. Another would have just put her in the slave pen for the night. Come in, both of you, Sophie will want to speak with you, I'm sure."

Hearing Sophie's Christian name on the officer's lips did not sit well with Harrison. He schooled his features into a display of indifference.

"I'm Captain Lawrence Russell, by the way." The captain shook Harrison's hand heartily as he stepped over the threshold and into a houseful of strangers. Laughter and Southern drawls floated on strains of music.

The door clicked shut. "Oliver Shaw," Harrison said, determined to ride the wave of this new development.

Just then, Sophie swept into the entrance hall. Awkwardly, Harrison spun the brim of his hat in his hands.

"Sophie, dear, this is Mr. Oliver Shaw."

Harrison flinched at the intimate term, gauged Sophie's reaction to it. The roses in her cheeks faded. Her bright green eyes arrested Harrison as they had the first time he met her. They were the color of new grass and budding leaves, of all things fresh and tender and vulnerable. A striking contrast to the mourning that draped her from collar to hem. Though he had no idea who she lost, the longing to comfort her ached in his chest. He suspected Captain Russell was taking care of that himself. A jealousy he had no right to feel licked through his veins. *But I waited for her,* he thought coldly. He had hoped she had waited for him.

"He found Daphne out on the streets and came here to return her to you," Captain Russell continued, and Sophie's wide eyes took in Bella. "You're a big one for secrets—I didn't even know she'd recovered from her illness!"

The Confederate officer looked at her like he owned her. Something curdled in Harrison's stomach.

Her gaze hit him like a blow to his chest. Her lips parted slightly, but still she didn't speak. *I'm Oliver Shaw,* he told himself fiercely, recovering his alias. *And I've never seen this woman before in my life.*

Sophie studied Daphne's face, and yet knew it was not Daphne. Confusion rippled through her. She turned to Mr. Shaw, and he held her with his deep brown eyes. Eyes that knew her. She clasped her hands to keep them from flying up to cover her mouth. A five-year-old ache burned in her chest as memory intruded. No, not memory. Harrison was here, now, fairly drinking her in with eyes that told her he hadn't forgotten their pledge.

But she was being watched, even now. Especially now. Sophie must play the part she had chosen.

"Thank you, Mr. Shaw." She extended her hand, and he took it.

"I'm most grateful to have her back. Daphne, come with me, please. Captain Russell, you'll see to the guests?"

"Of course."

The woman with Daphne's face followed Sophie down the hall and into the vacant dining room. She closed the door but did not bother to sit before turning and facing her visitor.

"You're not Daphne. Speak freely." *And quickly.*

"I'm her twin sister, Bella. From the North. I've brought quinine for her." She opened her cloak and withdrew the precious medicine.

Sophie's jaw dropped. Daphne had never mentioned a sister. But then, Sophie never mentioned her own sister. But, "From the North? How did you hear . . ."

"My husband wrote me. From Libby Prison."

Sophie's memory flashed. The Negro prisoner who had studied Daphne so intently every time they were there with bread. It must have been he, and little wonder.

"Please. My sister?"

"Follow me." Sophie led her to the doorway of the sickroom but did not go in. "She's in there. I must go. Please stay here until I can introduce you to the rest of the servants properly."

Before she'd finished her sentence, Bella had already nodded and slipped inside. Sophie prayed the quinine would prove effective as she returned to her guests, hoops swaying with every stride.

When she reached to the parlor, smile pasted on her face, she found Harrison still there, with Captain Russell and Mr. Graham as his audience. Hiding her trembling hands in the pleats of her skirt, she joined them.

"Sophie, darling." Captain Russell drew her closer, and she fought the urge to pull away. She flicked an apologetic glance to Harrison, willing him to divine the truth, but how could he? The smile on his face grew thin and cold, if one knew how to read it. Which Sophie did. "Mr. Shaw here was just telling us he's a correspondent for the *Southern Examiner*. He covered Baltimore for a few years but the

Yankees harassed him South, lucky for us. He's hoping to be assigned here in Richmond now."

Sophie's eyes popped wide. *He hopes to stay?* "Welcome to Richmond," was all she said.

"Thank you. I only just arrived tonight and already I'm impressed with your famous Southern hospitality."

"Virginia, especially Richmond, has grown accustomed to hosting guests," Sophie remarked.

"And do your hostess responsibilities extend to the dance floor?"

Sophie's breath skittered across her lips.

"By all means," Captain Russell said with a graceful flourish. Obviously, he wasn't threatened by an orange-haired Marylander.

Before Sophie knew what had happened, she was in the arms of Harrison Caldwell once again, moving in time to a waltz, and the five years that stood between them dropped away.

"Are we in time for Daphne?"

"What? Yes, I mean, I hope so. Thank you." Words, so inadequate, so trifling.

"Good." His gaze caressed her as it moved from the corn silk tendrils framing her face to her eyes, to her lips. The hollow of her throat. Her hand in his. She squeezed his fingers, just barely, and he met her eyes again. "Missed you at the reunion." His smile cracked her heart.

"Wished I could go," she whispered through tightened throat.

His grip on her strengthened as he twirled her around the floor, and she warmed with fond memories. Years ago, his mother had made him dance with all the girls in her class to help them practice their steps.

"I see you haven't forgotten anything," she remarked.

"Have you?" Suddenly they weren't talking about dancing anymore. "Did I hear Russell say you're Daphne's mistress? You *own* her?"

Sophie blinked back the burn in her eyes, her throat. There was so much to explain within the scant measures of the waltz. "My mother bequeathed her to me. I can't manumit her!" The whisper choked her, and suddenly Harrison's eyes grew soft again.

"You lost your mother. So did I."

Grief flooded her then, in this place of safety. They had lost so much in the missing years. "I'm so sorry," she whispered. *I missed you. I miss you still. Please don't let go.* But the words were barricaded behind an indestructible dam. Her chin trembled, and Harrison pulled her close, far too close for a couple pretending they'd never met before this evening. But not close enough by half for the couple they could have been.

His shoulder grew taut beneath her hand. "I forget myself," Harrison muttered into her hair, his chin grazing her temple. "Your captain is going to throw me out for this."

"He's not *my* captain."

"Isn't he?" His eyes searched hers, and Sophie's pulse outpaced the slowing music.

"Things are not always what they seem."

"Song's ending. I'm coming back for Bella in three days. She is a free woman, here at great personal risk. Will you keep her safe?"

"Yes," she whispered.

"She wants to see her husband, a prisoner at Libby. Please advise her against it if you think it dangerous."

Sophie nodded.

"Three days." He released her, bowed, and returned her to Captain Russell. "Much obliged," he said. "Now if you'll excuse me, it's been a very long day. The arms of Morpheus await."

Captain Russell took her hand, but her eyes were on Harrison as he left. "Did he make you uncomfortable, darling? Your cheeks are flaming red."

Bella stooped over Daphne's sunken form, a dose of quinine quivering in the cup in her hand. Even if Daphne had been healthy, seeing her again on this earth would have been a shock. But seeing her like this, ravaged by disease, Bella could not recognize herself in her twin.

"Wake up, Daph. Wake up and drink this."

Daphne stirred, eyelids fluttering. "Why?"

"It'll make you well again, now drink it."

Silence. Then, "What if I supposed to cross the Jordan River now?"

Dr. O'Leary said this might happen, Bella reminded herself, though dread bloomed in her chest. *Malaria often breeds depression. It's the disease talking.* "That's enough of that. You're going to take this whether you like it or not." She held the cup to her sister's lips and tipped it up.

"You sound like my mother," Daphne complained.

"You need mothering." Bella turned on the gas lamp on the nightstand. "Always did."

Gradually, recognition lit Daphne's eyes.

"Surprise." Bella's smile wobbled as she held her sister's bony hand. "You're going to be fine now. I'll take care of you, if you'll just let me."

Not that she had done such a wonderful job taking care of Daphne in the past, though with their mother in the rice fields all day when they were children, Bella had felt some responsibility toward her from a very early age. After all, Bella had been born first, by three minutes. That responsibility dissolved, however, when Daphne moved into the Big House to train as a house servant.

"Shame about your Abraham being in prison." Daphne shifted on the mattress. "Do you two have children together?"

"No, none with Abraham," Bella said awkwardly. It was surreal, talking this way. They were twins, but nearly strangers now.

"The child you carried when you were sold to that man in Virginia. Did it live?"

"Yes. She lives in Gettysburg, too." Which meant that Liberty, too, was free. So Daphne was Bella's only family member still in bondage, though Lincoln's Emancipation Proclamation had set her free already. *A fact Miss Kent conveniently ignores.*

"You see her often?"

128

Bella nodded. "But it will be less soon enough. She's engaged to be married." That he was white, and the son of a slaveholder, did not need to be said. "And your babies?" She knew better than to ask after their freedom. Daphne's children had not been born out of love.

"Dead."

The word thudded in Bella's ears. "Moses? Miriam?" They were only a year old when Bella saw them last.

"My boy tumbled into a fire at eighteen months. Miriam died of fever before her second summer. Then there was Lena, born dead. Two more miscarried after her. All my children are dead."

The parade of names stalled the air in Bella's lungs. She could scarcely breathe, let alone offer some appropriate condolences to her sister, the childless mother. Tears streamed down her face.

Daphne closed her eyes. "I'm going to see them again soon. They callin' for me, Bell. Wonderin' what's takin' me so long to hold 'em. They got their grandma, but babies just need their mama."

Bella bit her lip at the mention of her mother. So she was dead, too. "That's fever talk." Her nostrils flared. "We'll get you better."

"I'll be better when I'm with my family."

"I'm your family. You could come back to Gettysburg with me."

"No. Your family is Abraham, and your girl." Daphne's lips slanted. "You know where to find me, Bell." She lifted a shaky finger, pointed to the mirror above the washstand. "I'll always be with you no matter what."

Nonsense. Bella wiped her tears fiercely away. "I can make you well again. Don't tell me I'm too late for you."

Coughing racked Daphne's wasted body, lifting her off the pillows until she sank back down, breathless. "You just in time," she whispered. "For Sophie."

Bella frowned. "What, Daph?" But her sister had fallen asleep.

Fever talk, Bella decided as she watched the slight rise and fall of Daphne's chest.

By the time Harrison left the Kent house, the cab he'd paid to tarry was gone. Cursing beneath his breath, he shoved his hat on his head, turned his collar up against the wind, and marched down the front steps to Franklin Street.

Actually, he could use a brisk walk in the cold. Dancing with Sophie Kent had lit a fire under his skin—a fire he'd been trying to tamp down for five years. *Three days.* That was all he had before he'd be escorting Bella back North. What could he do in three days' time? And what had Sophie meant when she said Russell wasn't hers?

Focus, Caldwell. You're here to work. Chagrined with his weakness for Sophie, he remembered now how hard it was to part with her before—and why he absolutely had to do it. If she was his, he'd never muster the strength required to leave her in pursuit of his stories. Important stories. Surely, it had been the right decision, for both of them. She'd wanted time to write on her own, as well. *And now what do you want?* He lengthened his strides but could not run from the question.

"Going somewhere?" A wiry man snaked out from behind a lamp-post and planted himself in Harrison's path. A burly man smoking a cigar joined him, leaning so close to Harrison he choked on his smoke.

"Had a mind to, yes." Harrison stood his ground, tried not to appear as jarred as he felt.

"Coming from Miss Kent's house? Never seen you around before."

"And I suppose you've got eyes on the place round the clock, have you?"

"In fact, we do."

Harrison bristled. If Wiry wasn't bluffing, Sophie was under suspicion already. *In danger, perhaps?* Heat crawled up his neck.

"What were you doing here? If you were here for the party, looks like you sure didn't have a good time. Arriving late, leaving early . . ." Burly clucked his tongue. "So whadja do?"

"Returned a slave I found on the streets after curfew. Surely that's no crime. Miss Kent and Captain Russell can verify this."

Wiry shrugged, then spewed a single word: "Pass." He held out his hand.

"Look, I arrived tonight, only after the provost marshal's office closed. Ask the Spotswood. They'll confirm the hour I arrived was too late to secure a pass."

"So you have no pass."

Harrison blinked. "Because the provost marshal was not there to give me one." His voice was rising.

"So it's Winder's fault then, is it?" Burly threw his fist against Harrison's jaw, and the metallic taste of blood filled his mouth. Wiry yanked his wrists behind him, and bound them with a length of rope so tightly his hands went numb.

Chapter Twelve

Libby Prison, Richmond, Virginia
Monday, November 30, 1863

*W*ith a kick to his backside, Harrison stumbled into the second floor room of Libby Prison feeling considerably lighter than when he'd arrived in Richmond. The welcome committee searched him and robbed him of both his cloak and the greenbacks that were to get him and Bella home. Harrison's lip was numb and swollen, and his eye now black, courtesy of Warden Dick Turner.

Beware of what you wish for. Less than three hours after landing in Richmond, Harrison Caldwell had managed to get into Libby Prison. But being admitted as a prisoner was not what he had in mind. Still, he would commit his experience to memory and record it at his next opportunity. What he would give for a pencil and foolscap now! Tomorrow he would see if there was a bartering or exchange program among the prisoners. There certainly was at Fort Delaware.

"Fresh fish!" a prisoner shouted. Then another, and another, until the room reverberated with the chant. "Fresh fish! Fresh fish!" Spoons beat on tin cups, punctuating the prisoners' cries as they came rushing to surround him, like a teeming school of fish themselves.

"I did have a reservation at the Spotswood for tonight, gentlemen, but when I saw there was a vacancy at the Libby Hotel, I simply couldn't resist."

They roared with laughter before prodding him with questions. "Where'd you come from? What's the news? What's happening on the outside?"

Harrison smiled. There was nothing he liked more than sharing the news, especially with those hungry to know it. "Well, men, I've been traveling for the last ten days, but here's the news from Philadelphia as I left it." He told them everything he could remember, especially of military movements, predictions, and reports.

But then, "Can you tell us what you ate? Before you came down South?" Murmurs of approval rippled around the room, which suddenly fell silent again. "Yes," came another voice. "Tell us."

Their eyes gleamed in the scant starlight filtering through the windows. He knew how brave these men were. He'd seen them fight in almost every major battle up until Gettysburg. And now they were reduced to this.

Nevertheless, he cleared his throat and described the food at the Union Volunteer Refreshment Saloon to what seemed like a spellbound audience. By the end, tears glistened on strong men's gaunt faces, and Harrison again saw firsthand the horrors of war.

"Do they remember us up North?" one man asked. "Do they remember that we fought for them, and that we'd do it again if we could just get free?"

"That, my good fellow, is what I intend to tell them. And I'll do it in such a way they'll never forget." Maybe it was a rare case of bravado that kept his tongue wagging, or perhaps a sincere desire to inspire courage and hope in these officers who had sacrificed so much. "Did anyone read that story of the Weeping Time in the *New York Tribune* four years ago? It was reprinted as a pamphlet and distributed all over the country. I wrote that. Under a pseudonym, but I wrote it. Some say it had more impact on public opinion than *Uncle Tom's Cabin*. I'll shine the light on your plight next, soldiers, mark my words."

Their eyes gleamed, but they did not seem remarkably impressed. "Except for, how do you plan to get published in anything but the *Libby Chronicle* from here?"

"I'm a civilian, they can't keep me long. But I'm keen to stay as long as it takes to fully understand the depth and breadth of your misery here."

The prisoners laughed again, as though he had made another joke, before receding to their personal patches of spittle-flecked floor. Suddenly without an audience, Harrison hunted for his own space, careful not to step on the tightly packed men. Some, he noticed, used books for pillows, others preferred knapsacks. Having none of those, Harrison simply stretched his limbs out on the bare floor—and kicked a man in the head.

"Beg pardon!" He would need to sleep with knees bent all night long. Sleep, however, was more of a dream than a reality for Harrison Caldwell. Whether he was flat on his back or lay on his side, his bones seemed to poke into the filthy wood floor. That his hips and shoulders ached with the mere effort to rest did not bode well.

Even if he had a pillow, he likely would have used it over his face rather than beneath his head, both to dull the smell of the latrine along the wall, and to dim the sounds that peppered the night. Six hundred men in this room, plus another six hundred on the floor above produced enough coughing, snoring, and groaning to drown out a military band. One clown apparently thought it was funny to imitate a crying baby. *And they made that guy an officer?*

If he ever did fall asleep that night—for he really couldn't tell— he was jolted awake every half hour with guards hollering out their reports:

"Post number 1, all's well!"

"Post number 2, all's well!"

"Post number 3, all's well!"

Harrison groaned. *All's well, indeed.*

———

After what felt like hours of restless turning, Sophie abandoned her warm bed. Tying a flannel wrapper snugly about her waist, she fed wood to her dying fire, then crossed to her bureau and turned the knob on her lamp. She opened the top drawer, felt beneath the lining, and extracted a thin stack of papers. The words blurred together as she dipped it into the shallow pool of light. Sophie's flowing script tangled with Harrison's terse block letters on the page. Her early journalistic efforts. His frank edits pushing her toward excellence.

"I'm a writer, too," she'd told Harrison the first time they met. They were dancing at a boarding school function and he'd just made it clear he was only there to please his mother, the instructor. He was a serious journalist with more important things to do. He'd been unimpressed with her penchant for fiction.

"Why make it up, when there are stories all around you just begging to be told?"

She'd thought him cross and argumentative. If Mrs. Caldwell hadn't been watching the two of them dancing, she'd have broken free of him then and there. But he held her fast.

"Why do you want to write? What drives you?"

"I like writing," she'd answered, when what she meant to say was that she liked having a voice. Wanted to be heard.

"Not good enough," he'd said, and her face flamed with indignation. "Writing is important, and your interest in it does you credit. But there is danger in writing when you have nothing to say."

Sophie dropped her lashes to her cheeks, concentrated on her steps. Harrison was twenty-four years old to her seventeen. The fact that their mothers had gone to school together here, and been fast friends, made him only somewhat less intimidating. Susan knew how to talk to men, especially older men. Sophie didn't.

"So tell me, Miss Kent, what is it that you want to say?"

She looked up, locked her gaze upon him. "That slavery is wrong." Her Southern drawl was smooth as silk.

"But you—you're—"

"In a position to see it every day. When I'm home, that is."

"And you believe fiction is the right vehicle for your message?"

She bristled. "Didn't Mrs. Stowe?"

"Yes, and many discount her work as mere exaggeration, abolitionist propaganda. Why not simply report the truth instead, without cheapening it with artificial varnish?" The intensity in his eyes sparked something inside her. "Listen, I'm going to hear Frederick Douglass speak tomorrow night. Come with me."

She did. From that point on, she accompanied Harrison to the abolitionist rallies her father abhorred. But that wasn't all he'd led her to.

The boarding school taught literature and composition, but not journalism. Harrison did, though—just for Sophie. He taught her how to write like a newsman. The first stories she'd attempted were almost illegible by the time Harrison finished editing them, so covered was the page with his marks.

"It's the only way to get better," he'd told her, and she knew it was true.

After two years of tutoring, he'd dubbed her a "writer," and she had nearly floated away on the compliment. Were it not for Harrison, she would never have published her first article as John Thornton in the *Richmond Examiner*. Far more than her own father had ever been, Harrison was her inspiration and mentor.

He was almost—almost—more.

Sophie's face grew warm now as she slid her old stories, peppered with Harrison's edits, back beneath the lining of her drawer with as much tenderness as another woman might hide away her love letters. The fire danced and swayed behind its grate, and she felt the burn of

Harrison's hand at her waist once more.

Grabbing a blanket from her bed, she padded out upon her second-story porch and tucked herself snugly into her rocking chair. Stars studded the sky like saber points, and she craned her neck to find the constellations. When a star fell from the sky, Sophie realized that one wish had already come true. She had seen Harrison again. *Not at all, however, the way we'd planned.*

Libby Prison, Richmond, Virginia
Tuesday, December 1, 1863

By dawn, Harrison could not remember ever being more exhausted. His eyelids refused to open, but his ears magnified every sound.

"Great news in de papers! Great news from de battle o' Missionary Ridge!"

One eye popped open to see an elderly colored man stepping between the prisoners, Richmond newspapers rattling in his hands.

"That's Old Ben," said a man yawning beside Harrison. He pushed himself up to sit, then ran his hand through his dark, curly hair before attempting to smooth down his bushy beard, both of which were tinged with grey, though his face was yet unlined. "Charges twenty-five cents a paper—five times the price on the streets—but he finds plenty of customers here, as you can imagine." He extended his hand to Harrison. "I'm Colonel Thomas Rose, 77th Pennsylvania."

"Very pleased to meet you. Harrison Caldwell, noncombatant. Philadelphia." Nosy by trade, Harrison interviewed his new acquaintance and learned Colonel Rose was a schoolteacher and principal from Pittsburgh before the war. He'd been captured in September at Chickamauga. The thirty-three-year-old officer had a wife, a keen eye for observation, and a bright hope that his days at Libby were numbered. Harrison liked him immediately.

"And who's that?" He nodded to another colored man ambling

through the room waving a skillet of burning tar. The smoke burned Harrison's throat and stung his eyes.

"Here is your nice smoke, without money and without price!" The man chanted, his voice competing with Old Ben's over the stirring of waking prisoners.

Colonel Rose yawned again and rubbed the heels of his hands to his eyes. "That's The General. Comes here every morning, but the smoke only bothers us, and not the bugs."

"You mean that's supposed to help us?"

Rose chuckled. "The General does. He passes messages between us and the colored prisoners below when there's anything worth passing. But the smoke itself is useless. In fact, it's time you learned how to skirmish before roll call."

Harrison watched as Rose pulled his shirt off and meticulously picked through it like a chimpanzee. As his gaze drifted around the room, he saw one prisoner after another disrobe to varying degrees— including full nudity—to do the same.

"Hunting for lice," he said. "You'd do well to do the same."

"And you call this skirmishing?"

Rose nodded.

Clever. Harrison would have to remember this for the story he'd write about life in Libby Prison. He removed his own shirt and began inspecting it.

"We're like jealous husbands, yes?" Rose smiled. "Searching for evidence we hope we do not find."

Harrison laughed and hoped he'd remember that line as well.

"So Caldwell. Did I hear you right last night—you're a Northern journalist?" Rose's eyes remained intent on his work.

"Yes, that's right."

"So were Junius Browne and Albert Richardson."

Harrison rifled through his mental files. "Should I know them?"

"Northern reporters. Captured in the Mississippi outside Vicksburg in May. Came here holding paroles from the regular

Confederate Agent of Parole at Vicksburg, certifying that they were at full liberty to return to the U.S. They're still imprisoned here in Richmond, even though the Union soldiers who'd been scooped out of the river along with them were sent north via flag-of-truce boat. There was even another reporter, Colburn, of the *World*, who was captured at the same time, but he was released with the soldiers. Yet Junius and Albert are still here. In Libby for several months, and now in Castle Thunder."

Harrison's fingers froze on his tunic's seam. "On what charge?"

"No explanation was given. But we all think they're being punished for the crime of writing for the *New York Tribune*—the most famous abolitionist paper in the United States."

Dread clamped over Harrison's chest.

"Say, didn't you say you wrote that all-famous story for the *Tribune*? The one about the Weeping Time?" Rose looked up when Harrison did not respond right away.

Then, "I did."

"Well, that'll get to the guards by noon, I'm afraid. You would do better to 'set a watch before thy mouth.' The Rebels deliberately plant spies among us, to ferret out who is planning an escape, when, how, that sort of thing. But what you shared last night was pretty big news, I'd say."

Harrison grimaced. *Pride goeth before destruction, and an arrogant spirit before a fall.* "But how do you know I'm not a spy myself?"

Rose laughed again. "Oh, I can tell." He pointed to Harrison's shirt. "There's one. Dispatch him!"

Harrison squeezed the tiny vermin with all the vexation he harbored toward his own flapping jaws.

"Sorry, old chap, truly. I'm afraid you're here for keeps."

Foreboding spread coldly through Harrison's limbs. He'd survived battle after battle before. Surely he could find a way to do the same in prison. But how would Bella get home again? And had he directed even more suspicion toward—

Sophie. He stared at the shirt in his hands, a realization chilling his veins. His cloak. The map was still in it, and only one location marked: Sophie's house. *Maybe Turner won't find it,* he thought desperately. *Maybe he won't investigate, and Sophie and Bella will be fine.* But sweat beaded on his brow. If they were in danger, it would be because of him.

Chapter Thirteen

Richmond, Virginia
Wednesday, December 2, 1863

A sharp wind stung Bella's face as she trudged along Canal Street, a fake pass from her fake mistress burning her leg through her apron pocket. Time was running out and going nowhere, all at the same time.

Yesterday morning, she had come here with Sophie, but no Negro prisoners had been out of doors. This morning, they came again, and were met with the same failure. *Please, Lord, I need to see him.* Tomorrow Harrison would take her home.

A black curl bobbed against her face until she tucked it back up under Daphne's yellow head scarf. Hugging her shawl tightly around her shoulders, she bowed her head and shuffled toward the two Negro prisoners chopping wood in the alley. Perhaps they could fetch Abraham, somehow.

Though the wind was keen, one of the men was shirtless as he worked. As she neared, she understood why. His back had been ripped open with a cat-o'-nine-tails, it looked like. Even a thin layer of cotton would feel like needles in the open wounds. A homespun shirt would be shards of glass.

Within a few yards of him now, she wondered how he could even raise the axe. She could count the ribs through his back, not to mention the stripes well laid on.

After waiting until his axe had hit its target, Bella spoke. "Pardon me."

Both men turned, one with a curious stare, the beaten man with eyes open wide. "Daphne?"

His face was so thin, his eyes and teeth so large, his hair so untidy. His voice was but a thin shade of Abraham's, but then, so was his body. The air trapped in her lungs. Instinctively, she reached out her hand to touch his face. "Is it really you?"

The axe head still stuck in the block of wood, Abraham let the handle swing to the ground. "I must be dreaming," he whispered, his gaze raking over her.

"You're not dreaming."

"I'm seeing things." He shook his head. "Hearing things."

Fleetingly, Bella noticed the other man frown as he watched the exchange between husband and wife.

"Abe." His name caught in her throat. "I got your letter."

He blinked, eyes bright beneath his furrowed brow, then turned to his fellow prisoner. "Peter." He jerked his head to the guard standing some distance away, and the man he'd called Peter nodded, his lips in a straight line, before trudging over to the armed man to distract him.

Light and shadow fought within Abraham's eyes, and he breathed in deeply. Bella could almost see the wheels in his mind grinding, laboriously. Until finally, "I didn't ask you to come."

Bella tried not to stiffen. "I got things I need to say to you."

He picked up his axe, scanned the perimeter, but did not look at her directly. Nodded, and she understood that she was to speak, and quickly, for Peter's ruse could end at any moment.

Bella wanted to be smooth and eloquent, when her nature was to be practical and straightforward. Perhaps a little too sharp. She wanted her words to sing to him, draw a smile from his lips. She wanted them to be a tender caress, a balm to his wounds of both body and spirit. But they were standing in an alley outside a Confederate prison, with the clatter of horses and merchants and shoppers rattling the very air about them. As the guard's voice raised itself over Peter's, Bella's speech was chopped to bits by Abraham's swinging axe, and he did not look at her as she, dressed as the slave she had once been, dripped pieces of her heart from her lips. But she did it. It was as splintered as the wood scattered at her feet, but she had told him what he needed to hear.

"Thank you. I know you love me. It's good to hear you're proud. But you have got to go. Now." With a slam, another block of wood splintered on the stump.

"I leave tonight. Unless . . ." She didn't know why she said it. Her mind held no other plan. But everything in her railed against leaving her husband here to die. Her gaze darted furtively around her. Could he not escape? He was already outside, after all. The guard assigned to watch him was still distracted by Peter. *What if—*

"There is no 'unless.'" He raised the axe again and swung it down hard. "You go on home to Liberty."

"She's engaged."

"You're her mother, even if she doesn't know it."

"She knows."

His grip slipped on his axe, and he looked at her then, eyebrows high in his forehead.

"It's all fine," she said.

"Then think how she'd feel to lose you now, her only blood relative. You get on home, and leave me be." His voice shook. Abraham plowed his axe into the stump of wood, looked around, then pulled her close. "I love you." His lips met hers, and she closed her eyes, aching to throw her arms around his neck. A thousand memories from sixteen years of marriage exploded inside her, and all she could think was that for all her strength and fire, she would have been lost without him. Far too soon, he pulled away, his eyes slick. Flinching with silent pain, Abraham scooped up his firewood. The bright grooves on his back blurred in her vision as her husband returned to prison.

———

Kent House, Richmond, Virginia
Wednesday, December 2, 1863

Back aching with years of bending in the rice fields, Bella bent over Daphne, bathing her face. "You won't get better without the medicine, you know." The precious bottle of quinine, now worth at least six hundred dollars an ounce in the South, remained tucked inside the bureau where the sun could not dilute its value. It was almost as full as the day Bella had arrived with it.

A fragile smile cracked Daphne's lips. Her eyelids fluttered open, then closed again. "I won't get better. Period." She turned her head toward the wall and coughed, the fluid gurgling in her lungs.

Bella straightened, swallowing the bile backing up in her throat. If it was only the fever, only malaria, she would have told her sister she was wrong. But pneumonia had taken hold and refused to release its prey.

Light seeped between the shutters in thin yellow stripes, but the room still felt like a tomb.

"I'm dying, Bella." Daphne's featherlight voice sat on Bella's shoulders like a vulture. The words, piercing talons.

Her moments of clarity, like this one, were as painful as her fitful mutterings about Moses and Miriam, plus her stillborn child and the ones she miscarried. "Will you not try?" Bella's voice cracked as she eased into the hardback chair beside the bed.

"My babies in heaven been waitin' on me. I'll be free, Bella, and with all the ones I love. Except for you. But your work here ain't done."

"My work—"

Another fit of coughing interrupted.

"My work is to keep you alive." But the quinine wasn't working. Daphne was slipping.

"I need you—to do something for me."

Bella leaned in close.

"Take care of Miss Sophie."

Confusion throbbed at Bella's temples. "It's you I came to take care of, not a slave owner courted by a Rebel officer!" Her own words pricked her conscience. Wasn't her own daughter engaged to a former Rebel scout? *This is different. Lawrence Russell is no Silas Ford.*

"There's more to it than you see."

"She's holding you in bondage. That's all I need to know." She pressed her lips into a firm, thin line.

Though the effort clearly cost her, Daphne shook her head slightly on the pillow, lines creasing her brow. "When her mama died, her daddy gave me to her, but without power to free me. She's more . . . abolitionist . . . than me."

Bella frowned, struggling to net the words swimming back to her now. Harrison's words. *I knew her in Philadelphia. Father from the South, Mother from the North. Unless she's changed since I saw her last, she can be trusted.* Only it seemed to Bella that if Sophie owned Daphne, she must have changed.

"Why you think . . . she riskin' so much . . . to help those Yankee prisoners?"

Lord, help me see the truth of it. Bella was quick to judge, she knew that about herself. Usually, she was right about folks. But she hadn't been right about Silas, when she had lumped him in with his slaveholding father, much to Liberty's dismay. *Is my instinct to protect Daphne dimming my view of Sophie, too?*

"So. You want me to take your place as Sophie's maidservant?" The idea chafed even more than the rough clothing she'd worn as a field hand. *I cannot go back to bondage, I can't even pretend it!*

"Not as a slave . . . but as a friend. Her equal." Daphne's thin chest rose and fell with every labored breath. "She needs you now . . . more than she ever needed me."

Bella grasped her twin's hand and squeezed it. Her skin was cool. Waxy.

"Miss Sophie taught me . . . my letters."

"I thought that was illegal, for both you and her!"

Daphne smiled. "You thought right." Her lips fell flat once more. "She been through so much with her mama . . . and now she tryin' to do so much more . . ." Daphne's eyes were opaque. "She gonna blame herself for me dyin'. Tell her not to. My helpin' at Libby . . . brought you back to Abraham . . . Now. Stay with her, or I fear she gonna end up . . . like her mama . . ." Her lashes fluttered against her hollow cheeks.

"What happened—?"

Daphne pressed Bella's hand, ever so slightly. "Promise . . . to stay . . . until she fine." She wheezed as she drew in another breath. "If you love me . . . pour it out . . . on her."

"I do love you," Bella gasped.

"Love you . . ."

Tears spilled down Bella's cheeks. "I'm sorry I didn't take better care of you, on the island, and here. If I had come sooner . . ." Her voice trailed to a whisper, as regret and sorrow choked her. "I missed you," she squeezed past the lump in her throat. She hadn't realized how much until she said it.

Eyes suddenly flaring open, Daphne sucked at the air, mouthed, "My babies," and exhaled her last, long breath.

Every ragged breath Bella drew was a chain of broken glass shredding through her lungs. She bowed her forehead over Daphne's hand, whispered, "I miss you," and wept. Her throat ached so intensely, her stomach turned in sympathy.

"Bella?" Sophie.

Sluicing the tears from her cheeks, Bella turned. Caught Sophie's anguished gaze. Her complexion snowy white, Sophie covered her face

146

with her hands and sank to the floor in a pool of faded black mourning. Rocking back and forth on her knees, Sophie's sobs racked her shoulders and stabbed into every corner of the shadow-laced sickroom. "I'm sorry!" she gasped. "I'm so s-s-sorry, forgive me, B-Bella, G-God forgive m-me!"

Bella's heart burned. Could she handle Sophie's pain, as well? *Lord!* she prayed. *Help me love that girl like Daphne did. Help me love her like You do.*

Releasing her sister's cold hand, Bella crossed to Sophie, and knelt upon the black skirt that radiated from her like grief. *It's not your fault,* Bella should have said, but couldn't. Instead, she laid her hand on Sophie's shuddering back, and the young woman leaned into Bella's shoulder, sobbing. "She's where she wants to be now," Bella managed to say, to herself as much as to Sophie. "She's free."

At this, Sophie began to quiet, but did not move away. As she rubbed the tears from her face, her shirtsleeve pulled down from her wrist, revealing a razor-sharp scar. A barb of alarm shot through Bella. *Take care of Miss Sophie.* Daphne's dying words echoed in her mind.

"Lord, be the light in the valley of these shadows," Bella prayed as her tears dampened the blonde curls of the woman who had owned her sister. *And help me know what to do.*

Chapter Fourteen

Richmond, Virginia
Thursday, December 3, 1863

*D*usk. Water sloshing below Canal Street. The faint smell of sewer in the air. Shouts. Pounding footsteps. The echoes of a fight bouncing off the river. Sophie's handkerchief, growing damp in her grip, white against the darkness that cloaked her. Daphne's lifeless form in the hastily dug grave surged in her mind, and she shoved it from her. Grief frayed the edges of her composure. But war did not pause for a woman to collect herself, but forged ahead, relentlessly. So must Sophie. *Lord, help.*

The door of the dead-house opened ever so slowly, and suspense wrung Sophie's chest. Then Dr. Lansing emerged like Lazarus from his tomb, his face nearly as white as her kerchief.

Slowly, she waved the small square of fabric like a flag in front of her skirt, until his head stopped turning and fixed upon it. Sophie swiveled, clasped her hands behind her back and let her kerchief trail down. *A man's heart deviseth his way: but the Lord directeth his steps.* The ancient proverb reverberated in her mind as she prayed that God would direct their steps tonight, indeed.

Only eight blocks stood between Libby and Sophie's house, but their hills reared up and dipped and reared again beneath her trembling legs. Every lamppost looked like a sentinel, every bare tree limb, a reaching arm. Her feet itched to run. But she must not attract attention, and she must keep a pace that Dr. Lansing, unused to such exertion, could match.

At long last, her home came into view. Fighting the urge to look over her shoulder, Sophie walked through her gate, left it ajar, and skirted the house. After stopping at the kitchen house for a moment, lest any observer wonder why she did not use her own front door, she crossed to the main house, entered through the rear, and waited.

By the time Dr. Lansing, too, stumbled through it, she felt as breathless as he was, panting from the uphill climb.

"Thank God!" She locked the door quietly behind him. "Were you followed?"

"Not that I could tell," he wheezed, and she pressed a tumbler of water into his hands.

The smell lifting off his clothing was enough to turn her stomach. "How could you stand it? Hiding with the dead all that time?"

"I tried to think of them just as my former patients. As they were not menacing in life, neither were they in death. But I confess it gave me ample time to regret losing them." His grey eyes shone like polished silver. "And courage to make it North, where I'll have the tools and medicine to do my job properly. I'll forever be grateful to you, you know."

And so will Charlotte, Sophie thought with a smile, remembering that he was engaged to be married. "Come with me." She had waited as long as she dared to let him catch his breath.

Sophie led him up the stairs and into the spare bedroom until they were standing in front of a closet. She unlatched the knob from its hook and swung the double doors wide. After removing the bottom shelf, she pushed on the false back until it opened.

Dr. Lansing bent to peer inside the small, squat room with sloping ceiling. "Underground Railroad?"

"My mother's idea." Eleanor had secretly arranged for this space to be built into the house in the early years of her marriage, and had put it to use when Sophie's father was out of town to follow the news, which was often. To this day, he still didn't know it existed. Neither did Fischer. Like so many other immigrants, he was pro-slavery, if only because it meant the immigrants were not the lowest class of society. "There is food and water, a lantern, and pallet inside. Try to rest. A farmer named William Rowley will come for you at midnight. You'll stay with him until he deems it safe to move from there. He's gotten you a pass to allow you out of the city." She did not mention it had cost the Unionists three thousand Confederate dollars and the help of a colored railroad superintendent, Samuel Ruth, to get it. "Here is a suit for you to change into. You'll be free soon enough." Fischer would never hear the soft tread of Rowley and Dr. Lansing from his quarters in the basement. "Thank you," the doctor breathed, and Sophie nodded.

"Now, once you are inside and I replace the shelf and latch the doors closed, you'll not be able to get out."

"I'll be content to stay hidden."

"Good." Sophie motioned to the door, and the doctor crawled through the small opening toward the glow of the kerosene lamp.

Dr. Lansing pushed the false door closed behind him, effectively blocking the light—but not his voice. "Thou art my hiding place," she could hear him say, though just barely. "Thou shalt preserve me from trouble; thou shalt compass me about with songs of deliverance." Then, silence.

Hands trembling from anxiety and fatigue, she replaced the shelf into the closet, redistributed old clothes on top of it, and latched the double doors securely. By the time Sophie reached the doorway to the hall, his faint snoring turned her head. Should she wake him just to tell him not to snore? She couldn't bring herself to. Just a few hours of slumber would do him good.

Downstairs, Sophie found Bella fidgeting in the parlor. Of course she was ready to leave, especially since Daphne had died. And especially since Fischer, who had shed no tears for Daphne, clearly disapproved of Bella's presence, though he had at least promised not to tell anyone she was here.

"Everything settled up there?" Bella asked, brown eyes intent. She was aware of their secret visitor.

"Yes. I think so, yes." Suddenly exhausted, Sophie eased into the armchair. "He's snoring, though."

"You can hear it through the closet?"

"He's very tired." A giggle bubbled up from Sophie's throat, and she covered her mouth to trap it. It must be the stress, she supposed, that made her want to laugh when there was no joke. "What time is Mr. Caldwell coming?" She still could not believe he was here in Richmond.

Bella glanced at the clock on the wall. "He didn't say."

"I'm glad you decided to go." She could scarcely trust her ears this morning when Bella asked if it might be helpful for her to stay with Sophie. Her place was in the North, the only land of the free. Thankfully, she'd been able to persuade Bella of this truth.

"Well." Bella shifted in her chair, awkwardly, and the clock ticked in the silence between them. "You're sure you'll be all right?"

Sophie nodded. "And there's nothing else you can do for Abraham by staying. Didn't he tell you to go home?"

"He did."

"Then it's settled." Sophie leaned her head back against the chair and closed her eyes. Saw Daphne again, and her eyes popped open. There would be time enough to process her grief tomorrow. *And the next day, and the next* . . . Unseeing, she focused her weary gaze on the fire behind the grate.

When the knock sounded at the door, she jolted. It was not yet midnight. "It must be Mr. Caldwell for you." A lump shifted in her throat. Once upon a time, Mr. Caldwell had come for Sophie.

As she smoothed her hair back into place, the knock became a pounding. Then he rang the doorbell, which chimed downstairs in Fischer's room. She hurried to let him in.

It wasn't Harrison.

"May I help you?"

The man pushed through the door and into the main hall, then turned to face her. "Dick Turner. Warden, Libby Prison."

An electric charge coursed through Sophie. "You're trespassing."

Mr. Fischer burst into the hall then, disheveled from getting dressed so quickly after he'd clearly already gone to bed. "If Miss Kent did not invite you in, sir, then you will kindly vacate the premises."

Turner answered the servant's loyalty with the back of his hand, and Fischer stumbled backward, knocking his head on Mars's pedestal before sinking to the floor, unconscious. Sophie flew to kneel by his side and check for blood.

"Now." Turner growled above her. "Save us both a whole heap of trouble and explain why an inmate at my prison had this hidden away in his cloak." He produced a map of the city, creased every few inches. A dark circle ringed her address.

"I don't understand!"

"Pity. Then I'll have to search myself. If you're a friend to one of my prisoners, you're an enemy of the Confederacy, and I intend to find proof! Unionist!" He spat the word.

A friend to a prisoner? Had he discovered Dr. Lansing's ruse so quickly? Sophie's stomach rolled and china rattled in its cabinet as he stormed through the first floor, ransacking the parlors, dining room, and library. But if he were looking for the doctor, why was he tossing books from their shelves and capsizing Grecian urns barely large enough to hold a cat? *Has he gone mad?*

"There must be some evidence here," he muttered. "A stash of greenbacks. A U.S. flag. A Northern newspaper. A hiding place for escaped prisoners."

When he bounded up the stairs, two at a time, Sophie fisted her skirts and followed him from room to room. Turner rifled through drawers, threw open the French doors to the second-story porch and snarled in rage when he found that empty, too. With each passing moment, his face grew darker. He was beginning to look like a fool for his fruitless theatrics, and by the storm gathering on his countenance, he knew it full well.

Then he came to the spare room where Dr. Lansing hid, and Sophie nearly forgot to breathe. He threw the counterpane off the bed, looked beneath it, then unlatched the closet doors and wiped everything off the shelves.

Finding nothing, he pushed past her into the hall, and in a dark whirl, went up the spiral staircase that led to the cupola, while Sophie waited below, as still as the needle on a sundial. There was nothing up there but glass and wood.

Time halted until Turner thundered back down the stairs. "Think you can hide it from me forever?" She heard his slap on her face before she felt it, then covered the smoldering pain with her hand.

Just how long she stood there after she heard him slam the front door behind him, she couldn't guess. It was Bella who came to her and broke the spell.

"That devil hurt you?" she said, anger edging her tone.

"It just smarts." Her voice was unsteady. "But where did you go?"

"Ran up here to wake up Dr. Lansing, tell him to quit snoring for pity's sake or all would be lost. Then I climbed out onto the porch and shimmied down the railing 'til I could jump. I went to the kitchen house, and found he'd been through there first, so I figured I'd stay out of sight there. He may have seen me talking with Abraham today."

Sophie nodded. "And he definitely has noticed me at Libby."

"You might think twice about going back."

Sophie's chin quivered, but she could not contradict her. "At least

Turner didn't find the doctor, thank God."

"I don't think he was looking for the doctor. Didn't he just say something about hiding 'it'—not 'him'? He was looking for evidence of Union loyalty. Although, an escaped Union prisoner certainly would fit that description, wouldn't you say?"

Sophie shuddered to imagine what may have happened if Turner had found the doctor. "But why did he come here? If it was my visits to Libby's hospital room that aroused his suspicion, why didn't he come before?"

"I saw the map he waved in your face before I took off. It was Mr. Caldwell's. I think he's in trouble." Bella's eyes flashed, and dread snaked through Sophie's middle. When they deemed it safe, they opened the closet and spoke with Dr. Lansing. He confirmed that a new arrival had joined the ranks of Libby prisoners. "Brown eyes, a freckled nose, and shocking orange hair. He's also a journalist," Dr. Lansing said. "From Philadelphia."

Bella groaned, and Sophie stood silently, suspended in disbelief.

———

Libby Prison, Richmond, Virginia
Saturday, December 5, 1863

"That better be Daphne," Abraham muttered to Peter. But as she came closer, he knew it wasn't. He cursed under his breath as he lugged a crate of rations off the supply wagon and carried it into the prison.

"Looks like she's got a piece to speak," Peter said. "I'll carry on."

Abraham grunted. By the time he and Peter returned to the wagon for more, Bella stood waiting between the buckboard and Robert Ford, with Turner's horse, shielding her from view. The wind flirted with a stray curl of her hair, and played with the fringe of her shawl. But her eyes were deadly serious.

So am I. "You were supposed to be gone two days ago." Though frustration buzzed in his veins, he kept his tone even, as though he were merely chatting with Robert as he lifted another crate. As his breath clouded in the chill air in disappearing puffs, ancient words of wisdom scrolled painfully through his mind. *Whereas ye know not what shall be on the morrow. For what is your life? It is even a vapour, that appeareth for a little time, and then vanisheth away.* Abraham wished his wife would vanish from Richmond.

"Harrison Caldwell was arrested. He's in there." She nodded toward Libby.

Abraham's gut twisted in a spasm of dismay. Bella was trapped. Same as him. *I should never have sent that letter!* Anger leapt over his fear for his wife. "Blast him!"

"I don't think arrest was his aim."

He shook his head, too furious to make excuses. While Peter carried his burden away, Abraham's hands flexed uselessly on the edges of a crate. "That boy brought you into the lions' den—and left you here to fend for yourself!"

Canal Street traffic bounced off the river, filling the crackling quiet between them. Then, "He brought me to you, Love. I had to see you. Had to see Daph—" Bella's voice broke on her sister's name. "I couldn't save her." She pressed a fist to her lips.

The fury in Abraham's chest gave way to a crushing ache. So long beleaguered by war and prison, he had grown calloused to his own pain. But not to Bella's. He reached out and touched her face, wiping a tear from her cheek with his thumb. She covered his hand with hers, and, closing her eyes, leaned into it.

"You miss her," he said.

Her eyes opened, drawing him into their warm chocolate depths. "And you."

Abraham nodded impotently, unable to find the words that would make everything better, or at least easier to bear.

Peter returned for another load, and Bella released her husband's hand. Tears clung to her long lashes as she fished small bundles from her basket and passed them to Abraham, Robert, and Peter. "Salt pork." A miracle.

Turner's horse pawed at the ground behind Bella, twitched its tail. "Warden coming," Robert Ford warned, instantly severing Abraham from his wife. As she tucked her head and swished away, Abraham dragged the last crate off the wagon and followed Peter back toward the prison.

"What are you doing?" Turner's voice carried. Abraham did not envy Ford his position, daily subject to the warden's tempers as he was. "What's in that basket?"

Abraham froze. *Basket?* He whipped his head around. *No.*

Turner ripped the basket from Bella's arm, upended it, righted it, smelled it. Cast it on the ground. "You bringing food to my prisoners? Curse you!"

"I meant no harm."

"Harm? I'll show you harm!"

White-hot alarm knifed through Abraham as Turner ordered two guards to his side.

"Steady. . ." Peter, beside him.

But Abraham was not steady. The ground reeled beneath his feet. His crate fell with a thud, and sawdust spilled from between splintered planks. The guards dragged her toward a barrel. *Please God, have mercy!*

One guard subdued her flailing fists while the other grasped her collar and ripped her dress open down to her waist.

"No!" The shout burst from Abraham at the same time Peter dropped his crate and grabbed his arm.

"Can't do nothing about that, now. They'll kill you as soon as look at you if you try and interfere."

Spots darkened his vision. The filthy Rebel guards yanked through the laces of her corset until it loosened enough to be cast off into the dirt. Their ribald comments and gestures about a slave using a ladies' undergarment was the match to Abraham's fuse. He jerked free of

Peter's grip and stumbled forward, only to be toppled again by Peter.

"They will kill you, man! Maybe her too! Let it go, stay alive another day!"

Abraham seethed. He sat on his heels in the dirt and bit his fist to keep from shouting obscenities that had never entered his mind before. His wife was tied over the barrel, naked from the waist up. Head tucked down, her head scarf had fallen off, and her hair tumbled in ribbons to the ground. Her fingers clawed at the metal bands ringing the barrel. Her back rippled with knots and scars.

Turner uncoiled his whip. It flicked like the tongue of Lucifer himself.

"You two! Boys!" Another guard aimed his rifle at Abraham and Peter. "Hoof it back inside with those boxes! Or do I get to drop me some Yankees today?"

"Come on now," Peter said, helping Abraham to his feet. In an agony of helplessness, he turned his back on his wife at the time she needed him most. His every dragging footstep was marked by the snap of leather on flesh, and Bella's sharp cries, until it almost seemed that it was his walking away that caused it. Tears spilled down his face for the first time in memory. The cost of mere survival was becoming too great a price to pay.

———

Fire burned in Bella's back, but it was the soft murmuring at her side that pulled her back to wakefulness.

"We are troubled on every side, yet not distressed; we are perplexed, but not in despair; persecuted, but not forsaken; cast down, but not destroyed . . ."

Bella opened her eyes and found herself on a pallet in the back of the kitchen house. Rachel, the same age as Bella's daughter Liberty, sat reading to her, while Sophie laid a warm cloth soaked with comfrey on her bare back, extinguishing the smoldering itch of her open wounds. She must have lost consciousness before Turner finished filleting her.

157

She had no memory of being brought home by a couple of slaves from a neighboring household. "How many stripes?" she asked.

Tenderly, Sophie laid another towel over Bella's fraying skin. "Many." Her tone was quiet, heavy.

Too many to tell, Bella guessed, wincing. It had been twenty years, maybe more, since she'd born the lash in Georgia. She'd forgotten how it stripped her of both humanity and skin. Humiliation churned in her gut still. She had never, never wanted Abraham to think of her as a slave, and yet today he'd seen her dignity ruthlessly peeled away.

It made her want to fight. Not just in revenge for herself, but for all the colored people who still lived in a place where bondage was normal, even considered God-ordained, and violence was an acceptable if not regular occurrence. For sixteen years, Bella had been free. She married the man she chose, and was able to watch her daughter grow up without fear of any of them being abused or sold away. If she had forgotten what life was like before Gettysburg, it all came rushing back to her now in rivers of scarlet.

"You want me to read some more?" Rachel asked. "Or you maybe want to rest?"

"You can read, thank you."

Bella closed her eyes. Rachel's voice mingled with the snapping fire and Pearl's soft tread, as she rustled about her domain.

Abraham had been right to enlist, Bella decided. For Rachel, Pearl, Emiline, Lois, and every other soul still in captivity, whether they lived in constant fear of the lash or with mistresses who taught them to read. Grudgingly, she realized that even white folks like Sophie were not truly free, when their opinions alone were enough to land them in prison and lose their property. It wasn't right.

"For unto whomsoever much is given, of him shall be much required," Rachel read.

Lord, You've got me stuck in Richmond like a fly in molasses. Now what do You want me to do?

Chapter Fifteen

Libby Prison, Richmond, Virginia
Wednesday, December 9, 1863

*H*arrison's skin was more freckled than ever, and it had nothing to do with the sun. Vermin bites speckled his lean limbs and torso. Scratching, bleeding, and scabbing beneath his clothes was proving to be a cycle without end. It was the same way for every inmate in Libby, and considered not at all uncouth to scratch oneself even while kneeling here, at the evening prayer meeting, where a sense of the holy mingled freely among the lice-ridden captives.

"The whole secret of making it endurable consists in having something to do. Something to do, something to do at stated hours, making one forget where he is, is the secret," a fellow prisoner had told Harrison. But if this was a secret, it seemed that most of Libby's prisoners were in on it. This hour-long prayer service occurred every evening, with singing always following. Chaplains took turns speaking on Sunday mornings, too, but the activities for the prisoners didn't end there.

Using a few textbooks donated by a generous Southern soul, the officers taught and attended classes on arithmetic, algebra, geometry, philosophy, history, theology, medicine, Greek, Latin, Italian, Spanish, French, army tactics, and—by far the most popular—phonography, the system of phonetic shorthand. Just since Harrison had arrived, there also had been a Lawyers Tournament and a Bone Fair, where bones inmates had carved into rings or other trinkets were judged by a committee.

On Tuesdays at ten o'clock, the Lyceum—dubbed the Lice-I-see-'em—Association held lively debates on varied topics. Last week, they had discussed the resolution "that men ought not to shave their faces." Yesterday the debate revolved around the statement, "that the Fear of Punishment has a greater influence upon mankind than the Hope of Reward." At the end of each session, the following week's topic was announced so men had time to prepare their speeches.

"Mr. Caldwell."

Harrison looked up to find the chaplain looking at him intently. "Yes?"

"I asked how we might pray for you tonight."

"Uh—" he laughed nervously. "I'd like to get out of here. Or has that one already been taken?"

Laughter rippled through the crowd, and Harrison joined them, though he was in earnest.

"Of course we continue to pray for deliverance from this place, if it's God's will."

If? Harrison thrust the word from him, even as manners told him to nod his head. *How could it be God's will to stay here?* Ludicrous.

Soon they bowed their heads in prayer, then lifted their voices in an a capella doxology. When the prayer service ended, the group morphed into a singing circle accompanied by split quills, combs, tin plates, and cups. They led off with a stirring rendition of the "Battle Cry of Freedom." Harrison had heard it sung in countless army camps, but never with more passion than when it came from the mouths of prisoners.

The Union forever! Hurrah, boys, hurrah!
Down with the traitors, up with the stars;
While we rally round the flag, boys, rally once again,
Shouting the battle cry of freedom!

Between stanzas, Rebel guards shouted at them to stop, but the prisoners replied with even more boisterous singing than before. Eventually, a cluster of folks on Cary Street shouted up at their windows the Confederate version.

Our Dixie forever! She's never at a loss!
Down with the eagle and up with the cross
We'll rally 'round the bonny flag, we'll rally once again,
Shout, shout the battle cry of Freedom!

By the time the singing circle had exhausted their repertoire, Harrison had barely any voice left.

Apparently, the "all's well" chaplain did. He pulled Harrison aside, and introduced himself as Eli Putnam. "You're a journalist, aren't you?" he prodded.

Not at the moment. "That's right."

"Perfect."

"Why so?"

Eli smiled. "Let's take a turn about the rooms, shall we?"

Harrison agreed, grateful for a chance to exercise his long limbs.

"We used to have our own paper, the *Libby Chronicle*. Various contributions were cut from other papers and pinned to brown sheets that served as the only copy of each edition. The prospectus was based on the idea that 'A little nonsense now and then, Is relished by the best of men.' But it wasn't just nonsense and amusement in those papers."

His interest piqued, Harrison nodded as they passed a man lying motionless on the floor, eyes closed, though at his side was a fellow who whistled loudly a bright, cheerful tune, presumably to keep up his comrade's courage, or his own.

"The *Chronicle* also published news, as well as rumors, poetry, notices and reports of special events, admonitions to induce good behavior, and meditative reflections. Some of the pieces were devotional thoughts written by the editor."

As he spoke, they neared a ring of men engaged in conversation like soldiers around a bivouac fire. Beyond them, a bearded fellow studied a textbook by the pale light of a distant candle. Laughter turned Harrison's attention to a pair of soldiers playing jacks with small bones. "Wait, wait. Did you hear this one: Why is our soup in Libby like the stuff of which dreams are made? Because it is a body without substance!"

Chaplain Putnam laughed. "That joke was printed in the *Chronicle's* first issue last August. As you can guess, the publication of each new edition proved the highlight of the week. Chaplain Louis Beaudry, who served as editor, read the entire edition aloud to a spellbound group of men every Friday. But after only seven issues, Louis was released—thank God—and the paper dissolved. Louis smuggled the issues out with him, and since then, no one has taken up its torch here again."

Harrison pinched something off his neck, then slapped his hands against his trousers. He could see where this was headed. "I'm honored that you'd think of me, but I won't be here long. Just as soon as Meredith gets to my letter, it will be all sorted out, and I'll be released." He'd written to General Meredith, the Union Officer of Exchange at Fortress Monroe last week.

The chaplain smiled at him but did not say what was surely on his mind: *How vain that hope.* After all, the *Tribune* correspondents Browne and Richardson were yet held captive in Richmond, despite their parole papers. Harrison's confidence flagged. "I sound ridiculous, don't I?"

"Have you considered, Mr. Caldwell, that you are not here by accident?" The chaplain smiled.

"I'm not here on purpose, if that's what you mean." A mirthless smile tilted on Harrison's face.

"Not your purpose, perhaps. But God's."

Harrison stiffened. "And what am I being punished for?" Even if his motive to find a rabble-rousing story was a greedy one, his intention to help Bella was sincere.

"You misunderstand. What if He brought you here because you are perfectly suited to encourage the men through the *Libby Chronicle*? Think about it, won't you? Take your time."

Harrison agreed. After all, in Libby Prison, time—and vermin— was all he had.

Chapter Sixteen

Capitol Square, Richmond, Virginia
Thursday, December 10, 1863

A stiff, cold wind stung Sophie's cheeks as she sat on the cold granite steps at the base of the George Washington statue. On his lunch break, Lawrence Russell sat beside her. As he unwrapped a square of fresh, warm gingerbread, the spiced steam curled around the smile on his face.

"Heavenly," he sighed. "Pearl is the best."

Sophie forged a smile from iron lips as he clearly enjoyed his first bite. She missed Daphne dreadfully, her grief compounded both by guilt and the fact that Bella was a constant, living reminder of her twin. If Bella resented Sophie, she'd be justified. Yet she stayed, most likely because she had no other place to go.

Captain Russell knew none of this trauma. He—and Sophie's neighbors—still assumed Bella was Daphne, a mistake better left un-corrected. No doubt the captain would have Bella thrown in the slave pen if he knew she'd infiltrated from the North, and that her husband was a Libby prisoner. He followed the rules of the Confederacy to the letter.

Sophie buried her hands in her muff, and absently grazed the ridge inside her right wrist with her left thumb. The rules were exactly what she wanted to discuss today. "So . . . did you hear anything yet? From your friend, the exchange officer? Mr. Ould, is it?" If there was a way to sound casual while asking a Rebel officer about the fate of a Union spy—for what else would you call a Northern reporter gathering information—Sophie Kent didn't know it.

Captain Russell frowned. "You haven't forgotten about him, I see. I must confess I don't see why you're so concerned about this Mr. Caldwell's plight." That Mr. Caldwell was already known to the captain as Oliver Shaw was completely lost on him, thank goodness.

Sophie raised her eyebrows. "Oh, it's not so very difficult to understand. He's a journalist, just like Father."

"Speaking of, I wonder how Mr. Shaw is getting along. Oliver Shaw? Have you heard anything? I stopped by the *Southern Examiner* office the other day and no one there knew anything about him. Odd. I'd hoped to invite him to dinner with Hayes and Graham."

A bracing breeze ruffled the hem of her skirts, and she hugged them to her ankles, vowing to be less flappable. "N-no, nothing. But this Mr. Caldwell—he's from Philadelphia. In fact, his mother taught at the boarding school I attended there."

Captain Russell took another bite. Lifted his gaze toward the capitol building, gleaming starkly in the sun. "Then he should have stayed there. Whatever his errand, he had no pass. I'm sure he knew the rules as well as the consequences of breaking them."

Sophie tucked her chin into the soft fur collar of her pelisse before looking up again. "He's a civilian. I—I don't understand why he's in a military prison. Wouldn't it serve the purpose just as well to ship him North and be done with it?"

Captain Russell's eyes narrowed into icy blue slits. It was the cold, Sophie hoped, and not anger that reddened his cheeks above his beard. "You do defend him rather fiercely."

She smiled sweetly, forced a tinkling laugh from her lips. "You, of all people, should know that what appears to be treason in me is only simple charity. I d-don't pretend to understand military protocols and strategies, Lawrence." It was the first time she'd called him by his Christian name, and she could tell it affected him.

"Don't upset yourself, dear." His smile warmed his face as he patted her hand magnanimously. "Besides, your charity won't do a lick of good. I've heard from the prisoner exchange officer. He is unmoved."

Her heart sagged. "What did he say?"

"Verbatim?" He sighed and withdrew a letter from his pocket. "I thought you'd prefer that. Here."

The paper crinkled in her hand as she read:

WHEN WAS THE RULE ESTABLISHED THAT NON-COMBATANTS WERE NOT TO BE RETAINED? DON'T THE UNION ARMIES OCCUPY-ING CONFEDERATE TERRITORY IN VIRGINIA AND TENNESSEE HOLD HUNDREDS OF NON-COMBATANTS? WHAT PECULIAR IMMUNITY SHOULD THE CORRESPONDENT OF THE TRIBUNE HAVE OVER AN OLD GRAY-HAIRED GRANDFATHER WHO NEVER SHOULDERED A MUSKET OR FOLLOWED IN THE WAKE OF AN ARMY?

So they knew Harrison was behind the Weeping Time story, for it was printed in the *New York Tribune*. But was there no caveat?

IT SEEMS TO ME THAT IF ANY EXCEPTION BE MADE AS TO ANY NON-COMBATANTS, IT SHOULD BE AGAINST SUCH MEN AS THE TRIBUNE CORRESPONDENT, WHO HAS HAD MORE SHARE EVEN THAN YOUR SOLDIERY IN BRINGING RAPINE, PILLAGE AND DESOLATION TO OUR HOMES. I HAVE NO COMPASSION FOR SUCH, EVEN IF THEIR MISERIES WERE TEN-FOLD GREATER. YOU ASK WHY I WILL NOT RELEASE HIM. 'TIS BECAUSE THIS SORT IS THE WORST AND MOST OBNOXIOUS OF ALL NON-COMBATANTS.

She handed the letter back to Lawrence and glanced at the harsh winter light now stabbing through the clouds. All hope for Harrison's release ebbed silently away.

A carriage rumbled by while the captain wadded his napkin. "It's high time you rein in that runaway sympathy of yours, anyway. It has already taken you where you shouldn't go."

Sophie blinked back the frustration stinging her eyes as Lawrence smiled condescendingly.

"Leave the military matters to the men, will you?" His break over, he stood and helped her to her feet. Turning her hand over, he traced the lines in her palm with his fingertip. An unpleasant shiver rippled over her. "A woman as soft as this was never meant to have a hand in war. Besides, there's nothing you can do."

––––––––

There it was again. *The wind,* Sophie told herself, hugging a pillow over her head. *The trees.* But was the tapping really coming from outside? An intruder would be less frightening than the thought that she was hearing what was not there. That the sounds she heard were all in her mind. That her mind was not sound after all.

Logs crumbled in her hearth, and she jerked in her bed, breathless from the strain of both listening and trying not to hear a sound. On the other side of the wall was the spare room. The tapping grew in strength and urgency, until it rang like a clapper between her ears. *It's them. It's Mother.* With her mind's eye, she could clearly see the closet that led to the hiding place.

Hiding night travelers in the spare room had been the special mission of Eleanor, Sophie, and their slaves, right up until the time Eleanor fell ill. Neither Susan nor their father knew about the room's existence. It was the first important secret Sophie had learned to keep. It was the first time deception, even among family, became a normal aspect of life.

It was also the first time she felt important, despite her halting speech. Her childhood stammer mortified her so much that she preferred filling her mouth with special treats from Pearl, rather than with words. She felt awkward, burdensome, and mute, until she learned to read and write. Then the words flowed through her. She feasted on ideas and language rather than food and found that writing satisfied her craving to have a voice. Eleanor fed her the contraband novel *Uncle Tom's Cabin* even though it was almost too much for her to digest at her age. Then, in spite of the stammer, or perhaps because of it, she drew Sophie into her secret plans with the Underground Railroad. "I need a helper who knows how to be quiet," she'd said. Which Sophie did.

Until she had a reason to speak up.

She was thirteen years old, and while her stammer had all but faded, she was adept at keeping quiet and going unnoticed. It was why Eleanor trusted her to bring food up to the fugitive slave family in the hiding place while she and Sophie's father hosted the party downstairs.

Sophie had already pushed open the false back of the closet when footsteps in the hallway warned of someone's approach. *But I locked the door.* A key scraped inside the hole. Scrambling inside the hiding place, she pushed the false back securely into place behind her and prayed that whoever was bursting into the room right now, sputtering and breathy with laughter, would not notice the mess on the floor and the mysteriously open closet doors.

In the dingy yellow glow of lantern light, Sophie brought her finger to her lips. The husband and wife nodded, their wide eyes gleaming. When the newborn baby opened its mouth and screwed up his tiny face, his mother quickly brought him to her breast to quiet him. From the other side of the closet, a lilting giggle pricked Sophie's ears. *Susan.* If her seventeen-year-old half-sister discovered this space, she'd tell their father, who would send this trembling family back to their owners and board up the hiding place for good.

"Wait, stop!" Susan laughed, and Sophie imagined she was pushing an admirer away with one hand while her other hand held fast his lapel. "What's all this? Such a mess!"

"Your servants need a stronger hand if they rifle through a closet and don't even trouble themselves to pick up again."

Sophie couldn't breathe.

The baby, however, squirmed, clearly unsatisfied with his mother's milk. *The laudanum.* Noiselessly, Sophie plucked up the bottle Eleanor had placed here for this purpose, and dosed the baby before his wail could give them away. It worked. The baby's head lolled back on his mother's elbow, and she rocked him back and forth, though Sophie suspected it was more for the mother's sake now than the baby's.

"Oh, look at this! My mother's wedding dress! No, don't look!" Susan cried. "Turn around, go stand in the corner like a good boy and no peeking until I say so."

Shock coursed through Sophie then as she realized what her sister was doing.

"Blast!" Susan laughed. "Shelby, come back please, I need a hand. Your hands." Another giggle. "Unfasten the buttons down my back, but keep your eyes closed. Are they closed? Oh, I don't trust you! Here, let's tie this on as a blindfold. That's better. Now we're playing Blind Man's Bluff—but don't worry—I want you to find me."

Shame flamed in Sophie's cheeks at the muffled sounds that followed. In moments, Susan had apparently stepped into her mother's wedding gown, for she was asking Shelby to fasten her up so she could remove his blindfold. But Shelby obviously wasn't eager for Susan to be fully clothed. It was a scandal too scorching, almost, to be believed.

Whether Shelby ever buttoned the wedding gown, Sophie couldn't tell. Her ears popped as a bottle of wine uncorked. Goblets clinked as the two drank to each other a sham wedding toast, and then—Sophie covered her ears for the rest.

By the time the couple left, the secret room was still secret, and that was all that mattered. Later that week, however, somehow Mr. Fischer discovered fresh wine stains and a small tear in the wedding gown that had belonged to Mr. Kent's first wife. It even smelled of perfume, a telltale sign that it had been worn. When Sophie's father was told, the roar that ripped from his throat rattled the windows in their panes. He questioned each slave individually, but none confessed, enraging him beyond reason.

Then one day Sophie found Esther, one of the maids, weeping behind the kitchen house. "Massa selling me down South, Missy, only I swear I ain't done nothing wrong. Miss Susan says I messed up that wedding gown, only I ain't done no such thing." She was Lois's younger sister, and aunt to Emiline, Rachel, and Fran—Susan's maidservant. "He gonna sell me away from my family—my whole family!"

And Sophie could stay silent no longer. Confiding in her mother, however, did not solve the problem. "You can't prove Esther's innocence without jeopardizing the hiding place. I know it seems harsh, Sophie, but think what would happen if your father knew what we do," Eleanor had warned. "Think of all the souls who would never be able to find safety here again. I need you to keep quiet, which you are very good at doing. There's nothing more we can do. We shall pray for Esther, yes? We'll pray she finds escape, and that we will meet her again someday. She'll use our hiding place on her journey North. She will forgive us our debts . . ." Her mother's voice quavered. "May they all forgive us. God, forgive us." A mere whisper.

Still, Sophie stubbornly sought an audience with her father, and prayed he would simply believe her when she said she knew for a fact Esther was not to blame.

"How do you know?" Without looking up from his newspaper, he tapped the ash from his cigar into its tray, as casually as if she had said there would be snow.

Sophie dug the toe of her kid leather boot into the Persian carpet. "Sh-she n-never l-lied before, D-Daddy and I b-believe her." Humiliation bled from her eyes as her old stutter, the one she thought she'd outgrown, reared up. She sounded like a blathering child again. Her father would never take her seriously now.

He peered at her above his spectacle rims. "Come now, Goldilocks, you've upset yourself. Esther hasn't had a reason to lie before this. Now she does. She's fooled you. We've taught our servants what the Bible says, to obey their masters, to tell the truth, to respect others' property, and so on. Esther has chosen not to obey those rules, so we can no longer allow her to stay."

"B-but w-what would she w-want with the g-g-gown? It m-makes n-no s-sense," she blubbered.

"Who else, then? The gown did not just wreck itself, after all these years of being safely preserved. Who did this, if not Esther?"

It was Susan! She'd wanted to scream, but Eleanor had begged her not to. Her fists trembled with anger and frustration. "P-please d-don't s-s-s-send her away." Sophie was sobbing now.

Eleanor rustled into the library. "What's this?" The roses in her cheeks faded.

"Sophie insists that Esther is innocent and should not be sent away." He opened his paper and ducked back into it.

Susan swept in next, as porcelain and poised as a china doll. "I thought I heard a baby. Should have known it was Sophie."

"Es-esther d-didn't do it!" Sophie hissed, looking directly at Susan, whose face blanched white before blooming a shade of scarlet to match the draperies.

Susan mimicked Sophie then, and shame nearly crippled her.

"Susan," Preston growled. "Don't."

"But she—"

Eleanor waved her hand as if to diffuse the tension in the air. "Yes, dear, Sophie is making up a story, perhaps, the way she always does. All the reading she does has blessed her with such a fanciful imagination." Her smile was stiff, her eyes pleading as she looked at Sophie, as if to suggest this betrayal was really for the best.

Preston grunted. "She'd do better to stick to the facts. Like a journalist."

Sophie could almost feel herself shrinking as they discussed her in the third person, as if she were not even there. She had lost, and it was over. Esther would be sold away.

But the hiding place was still safe, and fugitive slaves continued to be secreted in the closet on the other side of Sophie's bedroom wall—at least, until Eleanor felt ill. They tapped to Sophie when they needed something, and she made sure they were supplied. Two Kent slaves had fled North, eventually, but they never saw Esther again.

The fire popped in the fireplace, and Sophie's memories released her to the present, but the words, "There's nothing more we can do," reached through time to haunt her still. A fresh wave of regret washed over her for Esther and Daphne both.

———

Van Lew Kitchen House, Richmond, Virginia
Tuesday, December 15, 1863

"There's something more you can do." Firelit shadows flickered over Elizabeth Van Lew and Caroline, behind her, while griddle cakes and bacon hissed in the skillet. Elizabeth looked sharply down her nose at Sophie, as if assessing whether she were up for the task. Sophie was not sure yet herself, although when Mr. McNiven had rolled up to her rear entrance again before dawn today, she had behaved as though she'd ordered him there herself. By the time he dropped her off at the Van Lew kitchen house, suspense strummed her nerves. She had to know—

"Did Dr. Lansing make it through the lines?"

"He did more than that, my dear." A rare smile softened Elizabeth's angular face. "While Libby Prison was busy establishing the new office of 'dead-house keeper' to make sure no more deceased officers resurrect themselves, he arrived safely in Washington City. From there, he reported to General Benjamin Butler at Fortress Monroe. Told him that I was 'true as steel' to the Union cause and described to him our underground network. You, me, McNiven, Lucy Rice, Abby Green,

Samuel Ruth, William Rowley, Robert Ford—not to mention the many slaves who faithfully render aid." Her eyes shone. "Butler desires a correspondent here in Richmond, one who will write to him using a false name and drop the letter by flag of truce in the Post Office, directed to a name at the North."

"General Butler." Bringing her cup of genuine coffee to her lips, Sophie sipped the steamy brew gratefully. She had a feeling she'd need the caffeine to keep up with Elizabeth.

"By a false name, but yes. Military information can be delivered into military hands, perhaps in the same day." She folded her hands in her lap as Caroline set a plate of thick fried bacon next to the box of McNiven's pastries.

"And you will be the correspondent." Sophie broke off a piece of bacon and popped it in her mouth, savoring the smoky flavor.

"Without a doubt. If I were a man, I would have voted against secession, and then I would have taken up arms to put down the Rebellion. Do you know, Miss Kent, that the day before the firing on Fort Sumter, fully two-thirds of the Virginia legislature opposed secession? Then the firing happened, and Lincoln called for his seventy-five thousand volunteers, and Richmond went mad, positively mad. Do you remember April 1861?"

Sophie remembered trying to explain it all to her mother. A mistake. Eleanor didn't need to know the world outside her shuttered windows convulsed with revolution, or that battle lines had been drawn between the home she'd left in Philadelphia and the home she now occupied in Richmond. It baffled her. Driven away by her endless questions and childlike petulance, Preston stopped trying to help her understand. Sophie, however, stayed with Eleanor, to help her gather her thoughts every day. But it was as useless as chasing leaves scattered by the wind. "I remember enough."

"Well. We who were not bullied by the fire-eaters are the loyal ones. Virginia—the home of George Washington and Thomas Jefferson— removing itself from the Union—it's disgraceful! Unthinkable!" With fork and knife, she dissected a piece of sweet potato pie into minuscule bites as she spoke. Sophie imagined she would do the same to the Confederacy given the chance. "If I can aid the cause of the United States of America with information rather than a musket, I do it eagerly, and with a clean conscience. But I can't do it alone." Elizabeth's eyes bore into Sophie's.

By degrees, understanding filtered through Sophie. "You're asking for help? From me?"

Elizabeth speared a piece of pie with her fork, suspended it aloft. "I will be Butler's correspondent, but I need eyes and ears everywhere. You feed me intelligence—I'll tell you how later—and I take the risk of sending it to Butler."

Sophie could barely believe her ears. "Elizabeth, I am already under surveillance. My house was searched by Turner himself, an event my neighbors must have noticed." Surely Madeline Blair was the only one who dismissed it as a blustery show of authority brought on by Sophie's help at Libby's hospital room, and her connection to Philadelphia.

"Turner found nothing. You passed muster already, you see, and you have the rare luxury of being alone in your house."

Strange luxury indeed, thought Sophie, *to have a mother in the grave, a father in prison, and a half sister who disappeared.* Hands suddenly cold, she wrapped them around her cup.

"Your business within your own walls is yours alone, if you can trust your servants. Your father's status as a prisoner of war provides a smokescreen for your sentiments."

Elizabeth's persistence closed in around Sophie. But it wasn't just Dick Turner, or her father she was concerned about. "Captain Russell is—"

"An asset, Sophie. Work him." Elizabeth's voice was soft, but her words and eyes were granite hard. "He has always been an asset, has he not? You've been using him almost since the day you met him. Your relationship is a gesture, a token of your loyalty, just as the dinners I hold for

174

my nephew's regiment, the Richmond Howitzers, are a token of mine. Keep Russell as a shield, but tap him for information at the same time."

Sophie twisted her handkerchief until it was nearly knotted. "How?"

"Listen to him. Listen to those who speak to him in your presence, especially in those parties you hold. It isn't eavesdropping if you're standing right there. Think back to the last party."

It had been November 30. The day Harrison escorted Bella to Sophie's front door.

"What did you hear that night that the Union might find useful? Think now."

Her mind scrolled back. "It's old news now."

"But do you remember?"

Sophie pursed her lips. "A woman from Baltimore arrived on November 19 and handed Secretary of War Seddon a complete drawing of all the defenses of Baltimore."

Elizabeth inhaled sharply, clasped her hands. "Following the examples of Belle Boyd and Rose O'Neal Greenhow and countless other women less famous than they. Information is powerful. Union intelligence is already leaking south. And you, my dear, are in a perfect position to help feed Rebel intelligence to the North."

The fire crackled in the silence that followed. The magnitude of Elizabeth's suggestion thudded like a chunk of ore to the pit of Sophie's stomach. "You're asking me to be a spy."

"I am asking you—and several others—to join me in giving information to people who can use it to end the war. I'm already under suspicion merely for what I think. If I'm going to be imprisoned, then God help me, I will do something useful first to earn those chains."

Sophie wavered. "I don't want to be responsible for hurting my fellow Southerners." Bringing food to Union prisoners at the hospital was unpopular, and helping Dr. Lansing escape was illegal, yes. But these actions didn't bring harm to anyone. Would spying? As much as she abhorred slavery, she was still a Richmonder, whether she agreed with her neighbors on all points or not.

"Look around you, my dear! The South is already hurt! We are ravaged! Ending the war helps everyone. Hunger, death, disease from filthy army camps, loss of limbs—it all stops throughout both North and South when the war stops."

Sophie turned her gaze to the window, and her own reflection stared back as Elizabeth's words burrowed into her. The Yankees kept coming. And the Rebels kept fighting them even when they were hungry, barefoot, sick, too young, too old. Jefferson Davis would never surrender. Every family she knew in Richmond suffered loss of some kind, and she could only imagine it was the same all across the South. It had to stop, before thousands more men were sacrificed for The Cause, before every acre of Virginia was ravaged into barrenness. The carnage—on both sides—had to end.

"The North wins, and our slaves are released from their shackles," Elizabeth continued. "Yours. Mine. Everyone's, plus all future generations." Eyes misting, her voice shook with conviction. "Forever free, at last. Don't you want that?" Her thin lips drew a straight line on her resolute face.

"Of course I do," Sophie whispered.

"I know." Elizabeth grasped Sophie's hands. "I knew it the first time I realized you were the writer behind Thornton's columns in the paper. But you understand now, that it isn't your words that matter anymore. It's theirs. What you hear from Mr. Hayes, or Captain Russell, or any of their friends, or what your servants tell you they overheard in the markets—those are the words that matter. Who knows but that God has placed you to hear them for such a time as this?"

"You're asking me to be a spy," Sophie said again, trying to grasp exactly what this would mean. Surely, a betrayal of her homeland and of her father, who she loved even for all his faults. But was it possible to remain loyal to them and to her convictions both?

Silverware clinked on Elizabeth's plate. "I am asking for your help, if you'd rather think of it that way. The cause of freedom needs your help. How will you answer?"

Sophie could barely hear Elizabeth over the sound of General Winder echoing in her mind. *Spies hang. I win. Take heed.* She closed her eyes and heard the sickening bang of a floor dropping away from the feet of Spencer Kellogg. The squeak of stretching, jerking rope. *Spies hang.*

Then another thought eclipsed the fear. *There's nothing you can do,* Lawrence had told her, and in one bleak moment she had almost believed him. Now here was a chance to do more—to be more—than she ever had before. For this was not just about hiding one fugitive but about setting all of them free at once, and ending the war.

Sophie's eyes opened to meet Elizabeth's unyielding gaze, and her loyalty to Virginia seceded from her loyalty to freedom. With divided conscience, she gave her answer. "Yes."

"OUR TRUE HEARTS grew brave. Love of our country in its trials absorbed our being; enthusiasm lightened gloom. . . . I have known the best of men feel their lives in danger from their partners in business & from their sons-in-law, who felt differently from them. Some aged parents endured much from their children who were disloyal. . . . [I] have turned to speak to a friend and found a detective at my elbow. Strange faces could sometimes be seen peeping around the columns and pillars of the back portico, & I can name gentlemen, some of our oldest and best citizens, who trembled when their door bell rang, fearing arrest."

—ELIZABETH VAN LEW, Union agent in Richmond

Act Three

TRUE HEARTS GROW BRAVE

Chapter Seventeen

Confederate White House, Richmond, Virginia
Friday, January 1, 1864

"Too warm, darling?" Lawrence cocked an eyebrow at the black lace fan Sophie fluttered in front of her chest. Or was he looking at what she was trying to conceal? The expression on his handsome face flashed heat across her cheeks.

"Quite." In fact, Sophie's face felt as though it were on fire. She felt practically naked in front of all these people gathered in the connecting parlors of the Confederate White House. Lawrence had given her this gown as a Christmas gift to wear here, to Jefferson and Varina Davis's New Year's Day reception, since none of her dingy mourning clothes would suit the occasion. It was a personal, extravagant gift she could not refuse without offending. The dress now skimming Sophie's curves before spreading gracefully over her hoops was a respectable, true black silk. But the formal off-the-shoulder neckline dipped dangerously close to the cleft between her breasts. To compensate, she kept her matching fan wide open and as close as possible as they stood in line to greet the president and first lady of the Confederacy.

The line of guests crept forward toward their host and hostess, bringing Sophie near the crackling heat radiating from the marble fireplace. Careful to stand far enough away so sparks would not land on her skirt, she gazed at the gilded portrait of President Davis, which looked sternly down at her from its position above two crossed Confederate flags. On the red velvet-draped mantel below the flags, jewelry, and knickknacks, said to have been made for Varina by Confederate prisoners of war, were proudly on display. The contrast between the crude carvings and the opulence that cushioned them jarred Sophie. She could not help but think of the Libby prisoners in their rags, while here she stood in silk and lace. Nor could she help but think of Harrison.

Lawrence's chuckle pulled her back to him, though his low rumble was almost lost in the drone of the crowd. "I must say it's so refreshing to see you in something that flatters."

Sophie laughed at the backhanded compliment. "Well, for your sake, I hope the change of scenery is worth it. I can't imagine what it must have cost you." She'd seen a man's suit selling for six hundred dollars last week. An imported French gown of silk and lace would be well over one thousand dollars.

"I'm more interested in what it might cost you. Later." He winked, and she pulled the corner of her mouth into a half smile. His eyes sparkled with boyish mischief. But his touch had become almost hungry, lately. Clearly, Lawrence thought her coy, when truly, she didn't love him. She felt wicked. She felt like Susan.

Forgive me, she prayed, and fanned her burning face. Blessedly, someone cracked open a window in the crowded parlor. The breeze scampered across her bare shoulders and breathed a welcome chill down her spine.

By the time Lawrence exchanged introductions with Jefferson and Varina Davis, Sophie had snapped into her role with a commitment that would have made Elizabeth Van Lew proud. All she had to do was adapt the cunning and charm of her sister. Taking Varina's hand, she gestured to the trinkets displayed on the mantel. "I see you have excellent taste in art."

Varina's dark eyes sparked as she nodded, regally. "I keep every item a soldier or prisoner gives me. I believe it's a mark of respect for them, and a reminder to us in the midst of my civilian comforts, that war goes on."

It was easy to agree with her on that score.

Jefferson Davis was thoroughly courteous as he took Sophie's hand, and thoroughly preoccupied. Though tall and straight as a ramrod, all of his fifty-five years seemed etched into his face. And little wonder. Sophie had heard he'd suffered bouts of malaria, neuralgia, and dyspepsia, in addition to the ills of the Confederacy. One of his eyes was apparently blind, but the other, hawklike in its intensity, made up for it.

"Charmed," Mr. Davis said to Sophie, barely looking at her, as if impatient for the entire social affair to be done with. But it was not Jefferson Davis she needed to charm.

Their respects sufficiently paid to the Davises, Lawrence and Sophie lingered in the parlor only long enough to be polite before returning to the Kent house.

"Where's Fischer?" Lawrence asked as Sophie closed the door behind them.

"I gave him and the rest the day off for the New Year." She unpinned her hat from her hair and set it on the hall stand. "Fischer went to visit a friend who works in Court's End, and I could hear the servants laughing in the kitchen house before we came in."

"Ah, alone at last," he teased. "I'm glad you went to the reception. With me." The playfulness stripped from Lawrence's tone. Standing behind her, his breath was hot on the nape of her neck. His fingers brushed her skin as he slipped her cloak from her shoulders—and dropped it to the floor. Startled, she turned, and he caught her cold hands in his. Blew on her fingers to warm them.

"Sophie," he whispered, then kissed her knuckles on both hands. "Please say you're mine, truly, with no one here but the two of us to see or hear a thing. We've been pretending all this time, for show. But I'm not pretending anymore." He pulled her hands behind his waist in an embrace, then cupped her face in his hands. "Are you?"

His lips swayed against hers, warm and soft, and guilt chugged hotly through her veins. His hands slid down her neck to her bare shoulders as he deepened the kiss. One hand released her shoulder and skimmed a fingertip across the quivering lace trim of her neckline. *The rogue.*

Alarm coursed through her, and she jerked her head to the side, pressed her hands against his chest until she broke from his hold. "Enough!" she gasped.

He stood back, nose pink. "I beg your pardon, I—you—you're irresistible."

So this is what it feels like to be Susan, Sophie thought. She didn't fancy it.

"Lawrence, darling," she said, hoping to soothe his ruffled spirit. "Remember what you told me the first day we met? You are a gentleman, and I am a lady. Which means we behave like it, even when no one is watching." Pulse still whooshing in her ears, she offered him a smile, and he returned it.

"In that case, I must take my leave before I forget myself again." He tugged on his cloak to straighten it. "But—have we an understanding? You are mine, and not just for show?"

Her hand covered her pounding heart. "I would have thought it was obvious."

Quickly, he brushed a kiss on her cheek and let himself out, whistling as he went.

God forgive me, she prayed again, and slid to the floor, utterly spent from her charade. Tears welled in her eyes. She had never imagined her first kiss would be a lie.

Neither was she proud of how much she'd been deceiving the

captain. Calling him "darling," returning a kiss she didn't want . . . all for the hope of gaining some intelligence that would aid the cause of freedom. Did that make it acceptable in God's eyes? Or was any lie a sin?

Then the story of Rahab drifted through her weary mind until it pulled her toward the library. Sophie opened the Bible to the Old Testament book of Joshua. And there it was. Rahab, a harlot, had hidden two Israelite spies. She lied to the king of Jericho to keep them safe. Then, when Jericho fell, she and her family were spared. In the New Testament, Rahab was listed in the lineage of Christ, and praised for her actions.

Sophie sighed as she closed the Bible. Rahab's situation was different from hers. And yet, she could not help but hope and pray that if Rahab was justified for her deception, Sophie was as well.

Libby Prison, Richmond, Virginia
Monday, January 4, 1864

Harrison Caldwell walked laps around the second floor of Libby Prison. He'd heard from The General that Abraham was still surviving downstairs, but concern for Bella and Sophie wore a track in his mind. Time, useless time, yawned and stretched before him but went nowhere, ever, just like the circuit he paced around the perimeter of the room. Why, he could have walked all the way to Washington by now, or to Fortress Monroe, if it were not for these confounded walls and guards.

He was surrounded by empty moments. He choked on them, drowned in them, convinced he would die by tedium if starvation or Dick Turner did not claim his life first. Harrison's new friend and fellow prisoner, the wiry-thin Major A. G. Hamilton of the 12th Kentucky Cavalry, said it best when he described the days in Libby as "going by like scarcely moving tears." The nights, he said, passed "like black blots dying out of a dream of horror."

Out of habit, Harrison brought his hand to his head, but there was barely any hair left through which to rake. He'd shaved it all off, and the vermin went with it. He was determined to keep it shorn almost to his scalp while at the Libby Hotel, as he had so glibly named it when he'd thought his stay would be as short as the fuzz on his head. *Fool.* Now he knew the truth.

Last month, Union Gen. Benjamin Butler was named special agent of exchange at Fortress Monroe, with General Meredith his subordinate. His Confederate counterpart, exchange officer Robert Ould, refused to parlay with him.

Early in the war, Butler had declared runaway slaves who made it to Fortress Monroe to be contraband of war, thereby creating asylum for thousands of the South's bondsmen. Known as "Beast Butler" throughout the South, the general was so reviled that Jefferson Davis had ordered him to be hanged on the spot if he was ever captured.

But it was in 1862 in New Orleans when he issued his infamous "Woman Order," that sealed his death warrant. Exasperated by numerous complaints that patriotic Confederate women were spitting on and otherwise abusing Union soldiers who occupied the town—one woman had emptied the contents of a chamber pot from a balcony onto Admiral David Farragut—Butler's order proclaimed that any female who insulted a Union soldier be subjected to the same treatment as a prostitute. Even Harrison had deemed the excessive measure despicable when he covered the story for the *Philadelphia Inquirer.* But for Robert Ould to cease the exchange of prisoners because of the Woman Order seemed equally unfair.

Thankfully, the Confederacy reluctantly came to agree. On Christmas Day, Butler's efforts resulted in a man-for-man exchange of 520 prisoners. But since the Rebels stubbornly refused to exchange Negroes, the exchange cartel once again shut down. Harrison, Abraham, Rose, Hamilton, and tens of thousands languishing in prisons all over the South, were there to stay.

A hand squeezed Harrison's shoulder. "So, how is our fearless editor today?" It was Colonel Thomas Rose, with a smile on his face and dust in his hair, as usual. He fell into step with Harrison as they turned about the room. "Staying busy, I see?"

Harrison laughed darkly. He had accepted the job as editor of the *Libby Chronicle*, and was gratified by the men's reception of it, but the investigative reporting he'd done had only served to discourage him. Last month Ould had announced that boxes sent to the prisoners from the North would no longer be delivered, but would rot in the warehouse next door, or else serve the needs of the Rebels instead. There were now five hundred of these packages. The reason, Harrison discovered, was that the U.S. Sanitary Commission began addressing its boxes to "Our Starving Soldiers in Richmond" or "Our Brave Defenders in Libby Prison." For these offensive words, Ould cancelled all deliveries completely, which meant no hope of supplementing their diet of rice, water, and half a loaf of rock-hard cornbread.

"Slow news day." Harrison's mouth twitched toward half a smile. "I've already reported Turner's throwing George Pratt into the dungeon for missing the spittoon. Nothing else to say on that score until he comes out."

"Which could be awhile," Rose added, nodding.

"And if I read one more poem that pines for home and a waiting wife . . ." Harrison's footsteps slowed to a halt as he stared out the window into the inky black beyond. "Rose," he said, rubbing his hand over his sharpening jaw. "There is no light at the end of this tunnel."

"Then it's time to dig a real one," he whispered. "But strictly off the record, of course. Want to?"

Harrison jerked his gaze to meet Rose's shining eyes.

"After dark. Follow me."

———

Night was thick with the snores of twelve hundred men in Libby Prison as Harrison and several others followed Thomas Rose down the stairs, through the dining room, and into the kitchen, where Major

Hamilton waited by the stoves. Confidence surged in Harrison to see he was leading the operation with Rose. Before the war, Hamilton was a builder of homes. *Surely he knows the best way to tunnel through a building.*

"Behind the stove is a tunnel Rose and I have dug, which leads to the east cellar," Hamilton explained in hushed tones to the thirteen men huddled around him and Rose. "Once we go through it, we work without light, and in absolute silence. A sentinel paces ten feet from our positions."

Rose nodded. "We've begun digging through the east foundation wall. Our plan is to continue down, under the east wall, then turn south toward the six-foot-high sewer, less than twenty feet away, that empties into the canal. Once we breach the pipe, we can travel inside it to the canal and just—"

"Vanish," Harrison finished for him, and subdued murmurs of excitement rippled through the men. His hands already itched to work. "What do we do?"

"What we need are three five-man digging teams," Hamilton said. "Team A will work all night, then rest for two nights and keep lookout for the guards, while Teams B and then C take their turns with the tunnel. Each man on the squad will take a specific task. One man digs and fills the spittoon with the dirt. A spittoon emptier will pull it out and empty it beneath piles of discarded straw from hospital mattresses and relief boxes before sending it back through to the digger. Also required is someone to fan air into the tunnel for the digger, using a rubber blanket stretched over a frame. It won't be much oxygen, but God willing, it's enough for a man to stay alive."

Harrison shifted uncomfortably at the mention of "God willing."

"A fourth man will be the relief spittoon emptier and fanner, and a fifth will serve as the lookout."

Rose cleared his throat. "When you hear the sentinels issue their four o'clock calls, stop immediately, climb back up into the kitchen, replace the bricks over the hole behind the stove—there are between fifty and seventy-five of them—and fling handfuls of soot over them. In places where mortar was removed, carefully insert that back between the bricks as well. Only then is your work here done before you slip back upstairs to sleep."

"You must swear to secrecy." Hamilton's voice was as hard and rough as the bricks that lay on the rubber blanket beside him. "There are spies in our midst."

The thirteen agreed, and with Rose and Hamilton, the men divided themselves into three squads. Harrison volunteered to be Team A's digger. A fleeting memory of his father flashed through him as he climbed down the rope ladder through the fireplace chute and into a darkness so profound he felt as though he'd gone blind.

His nose, unfortunately, still worked. Sharpened by the humidity, the east cellar reeked of sewage, rancid pork fat, wet clay, and the pervasive, thick odor of rats. Harrison's stomach lurched, but he muscled it back into place while groping for the tunnel's entrance.

There you are. With a rope tied around his ankle as a routine precaution, and a broken shovel in one hand, he wormed through the tunnel's two-foot diameter mouth and into its throat, for the first time grateful that he'd shed so many pounds since coming to Libby. As he inched forward, all the frustrations that had gnawed at him since arriving channeled into a singular purpose: *Dig.*

Two glowing red dots bounced toward him, accompanied by the scamper of four not-so-little feet. With a swipe of his shovel, he sent the rat squealing out of his way, but not before he felt the whip of its naked tail against his face. Resolutely, he crept forward like a mole in the tomblike darkness.

Finally, his hand found a wall of dirt. Packed in on three sides, Harrison clawed at it with his hands before scooping the loose dirt into the wooden spittoon fastened to a clothesline. Alternately, he lay on his stomach, then his side, then his back, until each side of his body ached from his contortions. Dirt and clay sprayed his face, and at one point a reef of earth gave way and half buried him. But he did not rescind his post. *If Dad could spend thirteen years in a Pittsburgh coal mine, I can stand one night in a tunnel.*

By four o'clock, he had advanced the tunnel by yards. The spittoon emptier waggled the clothesline, the signal to quit for the night, and he inched backwards until he could take a deep, albeit foul, breath of air once more. After caching their crude tools in the cellar, Harrison's team climbed the rope ladder back up through the fireplace chute, painstakingly replaced the bricks and mortar to hide the hole, and threw soot on the surface to complete the effect before lugging the stove back into place in front of it.

Wearily, he returned to his patch of tobacco-stained floor, and eased down onto it. He was filthy with dirt, clay, soot, and rat feces, and smelled like it, too. Shoulders burning, back aching, hands and knees and elbows skinned and bruised, he fell deeply to sleep.

Thoughts of the tunnel consumed his waking hours, whenever he was not working on the *Libby Chronicle* or reading it to the men. He ate every bite of his skimpy, repulsive rations with one enduring thought—that every ounce of strength he could muster would further the tunnel's progress.

Several nights later, however, the digging came to an abrupt halt when his shovel thudded against wood. Chisels and case knives were no match for it. Sick with disappointment, he backed out and motioned to his team to gather up in the kitchen. Their work in the tunnel was done.

"Timbers," he told them, as soon as it was safe.

Hamilton groaned. "I'll bet they're a foot thick, each one of them. They must be the ones supporting the east warehouse."

Two of the men growled that it was over, but Hamilton stayed them with gentling, downward movements of his hands. "We can remake the knives into miniature saws, with teeth. We will saw our way through. Our work is not yet done."

By the time Harrison's team took its next shift, Major Hamilton had transformed the knives into tiny cutting tools, and Teams B and

C had already spent two nights using them to hack away at the wood. Harrison drew his breath deeply in the kitchen before descending into the cellar, and the tunnel for his turn.

After several hours and what seemed like infinite labor making thousands of cuts in the wood, he was digging in red clay once again. His lungs filled with hope—but not air. Nearly gasping for breath, he inched backward out of the tunnel and let Colonel Rose take his place. Once the rope was secured around the colonel's ankle, Harrison crouched by the mouth of the tunnel and fanned air in after him. Silence pulsing in his ears, his shoulders and biceps burned from the effort, and his thighs ached, yet he would not slow his pace. Rose would suffocate if he did.

Rats skittered across straw and the tops of Harrison's feet. The spittoon whined on the clothesline. Straw rustled as the spittoon was emptied beneath it. These were the only sounds that broke the almost deafening quiet.

But then, something else. A trickle. *Water?* Harrison dropped to all fours and crawled halfway into the tunnel, straining his ears toward the distant echo. A gurgle, a gush, a gasping. He groped for the coil of rope snaking out from the darkness. Grasped it. Felt it jump like a fish in his hands. Snapped his fingers for the others to help, then heaved on the rope as hard and fast as he could. The fibers squeaked and creaked in their hands, and lengths of rope thudded in an invisible pile at their feet. Finally, Rose emerged, coughing and sucking at the air, soaked with icy water.

It was over for the night, again. Only this time, there would be no going back. Later, after Rose was dry and daylight had struggled in and out of Libby's prison bars once more, he and Hamilton held a conference with the three work squads.

"We angled too steeply downward from the cellar to the sewer," said Hamilton. "We dug below the level of the Kanawha Canal."

Harrison blinked, looked around at the other men, reading fatigue and frustration in the lines of their faces. Waited for the verdict from Rose.

"The tunnel is of no further use to us and must be sealed. We must leave no trace of our work."

"And then?" Harrison prodded, for he did not see defeat in Rose's eyes.

"Then we begin again. On Tunnel Two."

Grimly, Harrison thinned his lips and nodded.

Chapter Eighteen

Richmond, Virginia
Tuesday, January 5, 1864

I am not a slave. I am free. But either way, the work was the same for Bella Jamison. Inside the kitchen house, steam rose from her bucket of lye-laced water and filmed her face as she swirled undergarments with the handle of a broomstick.

Not that Sophie Kent had asked her to do it. In fact, she'd made it clear that Bella was a guest. She slept in the main house, and no labor was expected of her. But a three-day visit had stretched to thirty-six, with no end in sight. The sharp edges of her grief for Daphne had dulled to a fading ache. After all, up until recently Bella had lived without her for twenty years. She was used to her absence.

She was not used to living in Richmond, without her freedom. So Bella did what she had always done, in good times and bad. She worked and tried to tie her thoughts to the task at hand. Otherwise, they'd run away with her again. Snow whirled outside the window so thickly it blotted the house from view. Fire licked the pot Pearl had hung above it, and the simmering stew cloyed with the smell of Bella's laundry. While Pearl turned dried apples into a pie, sixteen-year-old Emiline presided over her own bucket of rinse water for the laundry. Rachel, her older sister, scrubbed the dishes Pearl dirtied. Lois was cleaning in the main house.

I am not a slave. But surrounded by women who were, Bella could almost feel the shackles of bondage on her ankles even now. Did they know they could be free? Did they even dream of it, or did they feel, as Daphne had, that slavery was their only path? That having a kind master or mistress was the best they could hope for?

Bella tried to plunge her thoughts into the work before her, squeezing her broomstick as she stirred. But thoughts of her family bobbed stubbornly to the surface of her mind. Liberty, likely wondering where on earth Bella was and possibly upset with her for going at all. Abraham, beside himself that she was still in Richmond, desperate for her to leave. And Daphne, the twin sister she had come to save, now in heaven.

Lord! Tears mingled with the warm mist on her cheeks. *What am I doing here?* Hooking her broom handle under a petticoat, Bella lifted it out of the water and let the excess drip off before dunking it into Emiline's bucket for rinsing.

Just then, the door opened and Sophie blew through it, snowflakes dusting her hair and shoulders. "Bella? You don't have to do that."

"I don't mind. Idle hands never suited me, anyhow."

Sophie nodded. "May I have a moment of your time? You have your cloak?"

Emiline took Bella's broom, and Bella reached for her cloak off the peg on the wall. Wrapping it around her shoulders, she followed Sophie back out to the main house.

Once inside, they hung up their wraps, brushed the snow from their hair, and entered the library. Two armchairs faced the friendly fire, and Sophie motioned for Bella to be seated.

"I need your help." The words burst from her as soon as she sat down. "That is, if you are willing."

Take care of Miss Sophie. She needs you, Daphne had said. But Bella hadn't promised. Still, "What kind of help you need?"

"The kind that sets men—and women—free. Forever."

———

Outside Libby Prison, Richmond, Virginia, Wednesday, January 6, 1864

Abraham's nose wrinkled though he held his breath. Emptying pails of greasy kitchen slop into a giant vat on the back of a wagon on Canal Street was far better than moving corpses around, but it still never failed to turn his stomach. At least the cold subdued the stench. It also chilled him through his tattered, threadbare uniform. Snow piled over the tops of his shoes and seeped between the open seams, burning his feet and ankles.

With a grunt, he lifted his pail and poured it into the waiting vat, turning his face to avoid being splashed.

"Hello, Abraham." Robert Ford tipped his hat in greeting, the reins of Dick Turner's horse in his hand. "Any signs inside to confirm what I told you?"

Abraham lowered his empty pail and rubbed the back of his neck. "Not yet, thank God."

Robert nodded, stroking the horse's broad neck. Small clouds of breath hung in the air in front of the beast's nose. "Only a matter of time."

"Abraham."

He turned. Saw Bella. And his stomach wrenched. Anger boiled in his veins that she now risked being seen by Turner again, and that he, her own husband, was powerless to protect her. The warden could do worse than strip and whip her. "What are you doing here?"

"Something important." Eyes burning, she flicked a glance toward

Robert, but by now she knew it was safe to speak with him near. In an astonishing economy of words, she revealed her new role in Richmond. Though she did not use the word, she might as well have screamed that she was a spy, so loudly did it clang between his ears.

"Miss Kent making you do this?"

"Truth is, she tried for a few weeks to do it on her own. Said she didn't want me to be at risk. But when she invited me to help in ways she can't—like coming here and talking to you and Mr. Ford here—I was glad to say yes. It doesn't suit me to do nothing, you know that."

"You'll be killed if you aren't careful."

"Didn't stop you from enlisting." Her voice was low, but steady. "You wanted to fight. Now so do I. This is how I can. With information." Her staccato-style sentences were like bullets firing into his chest. "I won't stay here idle, when I can help."

Her words jolted through him, an echo of his own argument. Abraham had wanted to join up to have a part in the war that would make men free. But Bella?

"And if I say no?" he said.

"You mean like I said no to your soldiering without pay?" A smile slanted on her lips, and he knew she wouldn't back down, just as he had not. "We're on the same side, Love. Work with me."

"You say you can get information to Butler?" Robert Ford jumped in.

Bella nodded. The wind tugged her hair from beneath her head scarf and twirled it in front of her eyes, yet she didn't seem to notice.

"Then you tell him this." Ford slid his hand over the horse's nose again, smiling as he spoke, as if he was crooning his pet rather than passing intelligence. "Winder's planning to remove to Georgia all the Federal prisoners. Butchers and bakers are to go at once. They are already notified and selected. Rebs are building batteries on the Danville road." Ford clucked to his horse, and led him through the snow, leaving Bella and Abraham alone.

"Georgia?" she asked, tone laced with apprehension. She'd been born a slave in Georgia, and grown up there until sold to a man in Virginia.

"Looks like." Georgia was also the place where Abraham's regiment had joined with Montgomery's for that awful raid on the town of Darien in June 1863. Aside from being too far from Union lines for escape, he'd be a tempting target for anyone in Georgia looking for vengeance for the burned-up town.

A Confederate sentinel neared, and Abraham twitched his head toward the road. *Go on.*

Without another word, Bella ducked her head and walked away. She was a spy, and there was nothing he could do to keep her safe. There was only one way she'd go back to Gettysburg now.

I'll have to take her there myself.

Libby Prison, Richmond, Virginia
Sunday, January 17, 1864

Rebel guards are industriously engaged this week in making Libby a safer place, Harrison had reported in the *Libby Chronicle* on Friday. *Wooden window bars are being replaced with those of iron as a deterrent to would-be burglars and thieves.* The sarcastic story had drawn some chuckles from the prisoners, but the last laugh was on the Rebels. For in seeking to make Libby escape-proof, they had provided the tunnelers with the escape tools they needed most: a hatchet, an auger, and a piece of iron bar. Harrison and Colonel Rose had distracted the Rebel construction workers, while Major Hamilton darted in and out like a shadow to get the tools.

A pale gloom slanted across the chimney bricks behind the kitchen stove. Though his hands were scraped raw from gripping their rough edges to pull them free from the wall, a smile lurked on Harrison's face. It was the smile that would have worried his mother most—and she had been right to worry. Ever since he could remember, Harrison found trouble, and wallowed in it. *But it all comes to rights in the end. Usually.*

Climbing down the rope ladder through the fireplace chute, Harrison braced himself for the night's work. If it wasn't for the choking stench of raw sewage, it would be easier to be grateful for the relative warmth of the east cellar. In the upper rooms, whether the windows were barred with wood or iron, they did nothing to keep out the gusts of wind and snow. Five inches of snow blanketed Richmond the first week of January, and the temperatures hadn't climbed above freezing since. By day, Libby prisoners watched ice skaters glide over the frozen James and thanked God that at least they were not in the prison on Belle Isle in the middle of the river, where thousands had no shelter but tents and ditches, and the skeletal forms of each other. By night, they shivered in their rags.

Unless, of course, they were here, underground. After the first tunnel's failure, Rose remained convinced their best route was still via the sewer. And he'd found a new one to try. A smaller sewer connected to the one large enough to walk through. It was toward this small sewer they dug, from the cellar's southeast corner.

Blindly, Harrison inched his way through Tunnel Two. When he found where last night's workers had stopped, he set to work hacking at the hard, wet clay. He was getting quite good at it. *Like father, like son.* As a child, Harrison thought his coal miner father's skin color was black. He was surprised one day to find it white beneath the soot, but the color never mattered. It was the same dad either way.

Carefully, Harrison scooped the loosened dirt and clay into the spittoon and twanged the clothesline for it to be emptied. Again he clawed at the earth, and though his stomach protested the foul vapors filling the small space, he lasted longer in the tunnel than the rest of his team. Perhaps it was because it felt so good to be getting somewhere, even if it was only an inch at a time. Or perhaps it was because he felt closer to his father this way. When Ian Caldwell had died, Harrison's mother, Christine, had done the only thing she could to survive—packed up Harrison and moved back to Philadelphia where she accepted a job teaching at her alma mater. Room and board were included of course, which made it a miraculous arrangement for her, and a nightmarish one for Harrison. His father and everything familiar had been stripped away almost all at once.

At thirteen years old, all he wanted was his father. But since Ian was gone, male companionship of almost any sort would do. Instead, he found himself living at a female boarding school, surrounded by women. Christine tried to include him in her new teaching life as much as possible, but he'd rebelled against her, and against his own teachers at the public school. A boy needed his father. That was all. Harrison paused for a moment to rest his burning shoulder muscles, and thought of the countless boys, both North and South, who had become fatherless during the war. He rolled onto his back. Chest heaving for breath, he deliberately breathed through his nose to slow his pace. Whoever was working the fan at the tunnel's mouth was doing the best he could. The air was simply scarce.

Suddenly, dirt sprayed Harrison's face from above. Earth shook down around him, filling his nose and mouth. The tunnel was caving. Writhing, thrashing, kicking, punching, he fought to break free of his tomb. *God!* He prayed but did not hope. He was being buried alive. *Just like Dad.* Drowning in dirt, he groped for the clothesline to signal for help.

There. He grasped it. Plucked, pulled, shook, twanged. But spots burst upon his mind's eye. His hand relaxed, and all he felt was dirt in his palm, between his fingers. It filled him and covered him, strangely comforting now, like a warm blanket. His mind unanchored, drifted, like a rudderless craft on a black sea, beneath a moonless, starless sky.

Harrison was on the deck, pitching and rolling but seeing and hearing nothing. Stepped inside a coil of rope. It cinched around his ankle, knocking him off balance. In the next instant he was flat on his back, being dragged toward the edge of the deck. Was he being pulled overboard into a watery void? The fibers bit his skin. Pain flashed across his ankle and burned up his leg as the force of the pull seemed intent upon separating his foot from his limb. Then, nothing. Numbness overtook him completely.

I am dreaming, he told himself, and settled into the soft folds of his slumber.

Then rough hands shook him awake. Choking, retching, Harrison was in the stinking east cellar again.

The next morning, Harrison and Colonel Rose awoke to a cluster of voices below the window. Peering down through the bars, Harrison saw immediately what had happened last night. But so did the Confederate sentinels, whose path skirted the cast-off brick furnace now tipped mysteriously into a hole outside the prison wall.

"We dug directly beneath it!" Rose whispered, forgetting his oath of silence. Harrison quieted him with a stern gaze before daring to look down again. A knot of Rebel officers had joined the sentinels. Stamping their feet and rubbing their hands in the chill air, they discussed what may have caused the collapse beneath the massive weight.

Hornets buzzed in Harrison's stomach, and his limbs prickled with a thousand stings. They'd been found out. He held Rose's horrified gaze as they listened intently to the snatches that filtered up to them.

"Tunneling . . . river . . ."

Harrison braced himself.

"Rats."

"Rats," someone said again. And again. Then once more.

"Tunneling river rats." The verdict.

Colonel Rose wiped his hand over his broad face and down his beard, and Harrison almost laughed aloud in relief.

Rose pointed out the window, then made a slashing motion across his neck. Harrison understood him fully. They'd need to seal off Tunnel Two. It would be far too dangerous to continue.

Then Rose held up three fingers. Harrison nodded. *Third time's a charm.*

Chapter Nineteen

Libby Prison, Richmond, Virginia
Monday, January 18, 1864

*A*braham felt the Rebel guard's eyes on him as he unloaded crates of rations from the wagon on Canal Street. As he carried them into the prison and went back for more, he gave the sentry no reason to lift an eyebrow, let alone his trigger finger. He did what he was told to stay alive for Bella's sake, just as he'd been doing for the last 120 days of captivity. He should be grateful he'd lasted this long.

But that's not enough. Not anymore. Abraham's muscles pulled tight as he hefted another crate from the wagon and trudged through slush and snow, but his mind filled with Bella's beautiful, serious face. And her back, already a latticework of scar tissue. She was twenty years old when they married, and he twenty-five, but in some ways, she had aged far more than he already. *All that's done now, Love,* he'd told her as he kissed every ridge on her skin. *You're free. You'll never know fear and pain again.*

It was a promise Abraham intended to keep, despite her new surge of principled patriotism. If it weren't for him, she'd still be safe in Gettysburg. He would take her home, or die trying. Either way, she'd no longer be compelled to stay here.

But how?

Uncertainty needled him now like the sleet now pelting his face. Of the five white prisoners who had simply walked out the doors recently, four had been recaptured and were now in shackles in the dungeon. Black prisoners who attempted escape were lashed within an inch of their lives. Still, he could not stay here while Bella threw herself into peril.

Forgetting himself for but a moment, he looked up—and straight into the eyes of Libby clerk Erasmus Ross. Inexplicably, the small man offered an odd little half smile and a nod. Confusion grooved Abraham's brow, but he returned the nod before dropping his gaze to his chilled, sodden feet and shuffled back to the wagon for more.

Lord, he prayed, wiping winter's spit from his eyes. *Show me the way.*

Richmond Theater, Richmond, Virginia
Tuesday, January 19, 1864

In the dark, with the actors onstage just as dim as the houselights, Lawrence laid his hand on Sophie's knee. He leaned into her, his musk cologne thickening in her throat. "So the performance was guiltless of talent. At least we are together." When his lips brushed her earlobe, she did not turn away from him. Allowing him to believe her heart was true to him was not as difficult as it had been a month ago.

That worried her. Even if her deception with Lawrence was justified for a greater purpose, the unintended result was the same. Dishonesty had become commonplace. Soon she suspected it would be easy. She only prayed she could stop before lying became as natural as breathing. Sophie wasn't ready to reject Lawrence yet, but neither did she want to grow comfortable with deception. *After all,* she mused, *I'm supposed to repent of sin, not perfect it.*

On the stage before her, the curtains dropped, and the play was over. The lights flared, and the theater erupted in applause that was more than generous. When the clapping died down, however, a thunderous noise continued.

Galloping. Just outside.

Lawrence's face pulled tight as he listened. Then his brow knitted together. Sophie heard it, too. *Alarm bells. The tocsin on Capitol Square.*

"Come." He grasped her hand and pulled her out of the gallery after him. Without stopping at the cloakroom, he hurried her outside.

Mounted policemen and fire engine wagons roared past them, bells clanging. Pedestrians spilled from buildings and leaned from windows and balconies to see the commotion. Smoke peppered the air. Something was burning.

"Clear the way!" cried a fireman en route. "The Davis house has been set ablaze!"

The Confederate White House was only six blocks from the Richmond Theater. No flames leapt into the sky.

Lawrence wrapped his arm around Sophie's shivering shoulders. "Arson, I wager," he said coldly. "May the criminal be caught and hanged." He led her back inside and retrieved their cloaks.

By the time they'd hailed a cab outside the theater, reports had already filtered back to them that the fire had been started in the Davises' basement but discovered and contained before it could do much damage.

"Could have been a slave," Lawrence said over the rumble of the wheels beneath their seats. "I believe two Davis slaves ran away this month already. Perhaps another one decided to leave his calling card before making his escape."

"How dreadful," Sophie murmured, and meant it. Arson, even attempted arson, was a horrifying, inhumane form of persuasion.

"'Course, I wouldn't be surprised if Union loyalists had something to do with it." He slanted his eyes at her. "You're not still delivering food to Libby Prison, are you?"

She shook her head. "There's barely enough food for our own household."

He nodded, apparently satisfied. "Good. I'd hate for you to be lumped in with their lot. Their reputation grows more ominous by the day."

"Oh? How so?"

Moonlight glimmered in his eyes. "Some say the Unionists want to arm the prisoners, although it's an outlandish idea. How could it possibly be done? Where would they get the weapons? Even our own soldiers don't have enough." He shook his head. "Any chance they get to subvert the Confederate government, they'll take. But as for arming the thirteen thousand prisoners into a force to be reckoned with—I have no fear of that. Neither does the Secretary of War, from what Hayes tells me."

She entwined her fingers with his. "He believes we're secure?"

"He must, or at least he hopes so. Hoke's and Kemper's brigades are gone to North Carolina; Pickett's got his in or around Petersburg. Certainly if he thought Richmond were in danger they'd be kept closer."

Hoke, Kemper, North Carolina, Sophie repeated to herself. *Pickett, Petersburg. Easy to remember.*

"Three regiments of cavalry were disbanded by General Lee for want of horses, though," Lawrence continued, and suddenly Sophie wondered why he would share such a thing with her. Unless he suspected she would feed the information to the North. Unless it was false, a tempting trap.

"If you ask me, we've let our guard down. We're more vulnerable to a raid now than we've ever been. Still, if the Yanks should come with anything less than thirty thousand cavalry and fifteen thousand infantry to support them, we'd repel them easily."

203

Thirty thousand cavalry. Fifteen thousand infantry. What was Lawrence thinking, to share these numbers with her?

"Forgive me, darling, I didn't mean to bore you." He pulled her close and kissed her cheek. "A woman like you would have no interest in such matters, now would you?"

A nervous laugh tickled her lips. If she agreed, he may never speak like this again. If she didn't, surely he would wonder. "I'm always interested in whatever you want to tell me, dear." Sophie could only hope that her own performance was far more convincing than what they'd seen on the stage tonight.

Libby Prison, Richmond, Virginia
Friday, January 22, 1864

Five officers escaped from Libby Prison with nothing more than an open door and civilian clothing on their backs. Harrison's most recent article in the *Libby Chronicle* echoed in his mind as he lay on his back and stared bleakly at the cobwebbed rafters overhead. *Speculation as to where the civilian suits of clothing were found will be covered by the Rumor Mill in another section of this paper. The rest of us are rewarded for staying with tightened security. We are told the guards will also routinely bayonet the corpses in the dead-house to discourage shamming.*

Not exactly the news anyone had wanted to hear. Least of all the men who had been digging in the putrid tunnels for more than a month. Hope had dwindled in equal proportion to their strength until both were all but snuffed out. When they had begun work on Tunnel Three, Rose and Hamilton directed the teams to work around the clock so they would reach success all the faster. Those not present for morning and afternoon roll call had been covered by other tunnelers who scurried to the end of the line as soon as Libby clerk Erasmus Ross had counted their heads the first time. Other prisoners oblivious to the tunnelers' true design joined the fun, and confounded the small guard they called Little Ross, when his count exceeded the actual number of prisoners on the roll.

Starving by inches, like the rest of the twelve hundred men at Libby, Harrison did not know how much longer his body would conform to his undying desire to escape. *It doesn't matter anymore, anyway.* Despair landed upon his chest like a vulture, ready to pick his spirit clean.

The day-and-night excavation had sped their digging along until they reached the small sewer. When they discovered the wood-lined pipe was too narrow to admit a man, they dismantled the lining and forged ahead.

In vain. Harrison groaned at the memory. The large sewer, which had been their object all along, was lined with seasoned oak, hard as railroad iron and three inches thick. *We can saw our way in,* Harrison had told his squad, propping up his own hope along with theirs. *We cut through those massive timbers while digging Tunnel One, we can do it again here. We're too close to give up now.*

They assaulted the wood with a vengeance only prisoners of war on the brink of escape can muster. Sewage oozed into the tunnel, filling the small space with the worst stench they'd ever endured. One man fainted from the smell alone.

Their chisels barely dented the oak. Their penknives snapped. Their stolen hatchet, by now, was too dull to be useful. Their candles would not stay lit, despite the fanners' best efforts to keep air in the pipe. The thirteen workers gave up. Only Colonel Rose and Major Hamilton remained convinced escape was within reach.

Kent House, Richmond, Virginia
Friday, January 22, 1864

In the marble fireplace of the library, marigold and saffron tongues of flame leaped and curled around blackening wood. Hands shaking,

Sophie unclasped the locket around her neck. The two-inch sterling silver oval was just large enough to hold the folded-up cipher from Elizabeth Van Lew. She pulled it from between the images of her parents. After gauging Captain Russell's cues for three days to determine whether he was trying to trap her, she could not bear to wait any longer.

Lord, she prayed, *direct us.*

The foolscap whispered as she smoothed it out on her father's desk. She could not imagine how he would react if he knew what she was doing. It was difficult enough to imagine him at all anymore. His short missives told her that he lived, and not much more than that. She prayed for his safe return, even as she willfully aided the army that held him captive.

She bent over the cipher now, and found the letter she wanted within the grid. Each row and column was marked with its own number, like the latitude and longitude markings on a map. With her fingertips, she found the letter she wanted to use, then drew lines to the digits at the left and bottom of the page, and wrote them down as a pair to signify the single letter. It was a tedious process, indeed, but one that lowered their risk of discovery. Without the cipher, Sophie's message would be an insensible string of numbers. With it, Elizabeth Van Lew would be armed with valuable intelligence to deliver to General Butler. *Confirm with other sources,* Sophie had added, just in case Lawrence was testing her.

I don't hate Virginia, I hate slavery, she told herself as she rolled up her message as tightly as possible. She prayed it would bring more good, ultimately, than harm. If Richmond civilians were to suffer from her actions, Sophie would suffer right along with everyone else, and rightly so. *I hate war. God, bring the end. And please,* she added, *bring Joel and Asher Blair home safely.* For their sakes and for their mother's.

With her missive now a tiny rod of paper, she held counsel with Bella.

"Tomorrow I'd like you to go to market with Rachel. Find the Van Lew cook's assistant, Elizabeth Draper. Do you know her?"

Bella did.

"Good. She carries a basket of eggs identical to this one." Sophie pointed to an empty basket on the desk. "Only ours has a small blue mark on the handle, here. In the morning, fill it with three eggs and this false one." She drew an empty eggshell from the basket. The hole in the bottom through which she had drained the yolk was half as large as the diameter of a pencil. Into this opening, she inserted her rolled-up message.

Bella's eyes were bright as she followed Sophie's movements. "And we switch the baskets while we chat."

"Exactly." Sophie pushed a curl back over her ear. "There is some risk involved, you understand."

"Could this help get my Abraham free?"

With cautious hope, Sophie nodded.

"I'll do it." She plucked the egg basket from the desk and swished from the room. As Sophie watched her go, she prayed for her protection, and—one more time—that the information she passed would speed the end of the war with minimal further bloodshed.

Moments later, Fischer appeared at the door, eyes dark behind his spectacles, mustache crooked like a furry caterpillar. "Miss Kent."

"Come in, please. What's on your mind?"

"Well, if I may speak freely, Miss." He bowed. "May I?"

"Of course. Please sit."

He obeyed, but perched on the edge of the armchair with back as straight as a board. "I have held my tongue as long as possible. You know it's not in my nature to interfere. I thought there would be no need, that the problem would pass by on its own. But Bella is still here."

Sophie's brow knitted. "I don't see her as a problem, Fischer."

"I don't trust her. Did I see her with an egg basket in the hallway just now? At night? What on earth could she be doing?" Firelight reflected on his spectacles, and his very eyes appeared to dance with flame.

Sophie smiled coldly. "I gave it to her, just a moment ago. Set your mind at ease."

"But why—"

She raised her eyebrows, looked at him pointedly. During all his years of service, he'd never once questioned her father. Neither should he question her.

He clamped his mouth shut, his mustache concealing his lips once more. Then, "You are a kind and generous young woman."

"Thank you."

"Easily swayed by sentiment. Forgive me, Miss, I would not speak so if Mr. Kent were at home, but in his absence, I do feel some obligation to speak common sense to you, from a male perspective."

Her cheeks burned. "Say your piece, Mr. Fischer."

"Bella is colored."

"Yes, she is. And free, as you are, and as I am."

"She is a Negro." His tone barbed Sophie. "She should not sleep in this house. It has gone to her head and given her airs, as though she were your equal."

"She is. Mrs. Jamison is my guest, here at my pleasure."

Fischer reddened. "You don't know how it looks."

"To whom?" Sophie stood, and so did he. "I thought I made it clear that Bella's presence was not to be discussed outside these walls. Telling anyone that she is here would be a serious breach of my trust in you, Mr. Fischer."

He was shaking his head. "No, no, I never said a word."

"See that you don't. To anyone."

Fischer adjusted the glasses on his nose. "You've changed, Miss Kent. I'm not sure your father would—recognize you."

Sophie nodded curtly. "Thank you for the compliment. Good night."

Chapter Twenty

Libby Prison, Richmond, Virginia
Saturday, January 23, 1864

"This is the one, Caldwell. I can feel it." Colonel Rose's large eyes looked wild between the shaggy hair falling over his brow and the beard growing like a shrub from his face.

Harrison grunted and rolled onto his side, though it was neither morning nor night. Time had ceased to exist. "I've heard that one before, you know."

"So you have, so you have." Rose cleared his throat, hugged his ankles as he sat rocking next to Harrison.

"You make me dizzy." He slapped his hand over his eyes. Truly, he was in no mood for company. If he were, he would have joined the four-man-deep columns marching double-quick together just to keep warm. Instead, he lay here, half-frozen, while the struggling fire ate the wooden partitions from the privy, the firewood supply being spent.

"Caldwell. Why are you here?"

Harrison looked through his parted fingers at the rafters overhead. "Depends on who you ask. Chaplain Putnam says it's by God's design. I'd say it has more to do with my own ambition, for better or worse."

"Ambition to do what?"

"To write." He folded bony hands atop his concave stomach. "An important story."

"Yes. If I recall correctly, your entire aim was to discover and pen an exclusive article on Libby Prison, based on your own eyewitness account, the likes of which had never been read before."

His eyelids drifted closed. "Something like that." He yawned and rubbed his hand over his shorn head, fingers feeling for vermin.

"You're missing it."

Harrison looked at Rose, frowning.

"Your story. It's happening downstairs." He cut his voice low, looked right and left with those wild eyes. "We have a new tunnel that doesn't touch the sewer. This is the one. We're getting a half-inch deeper with every chisel stroke."

A half-inch. Compared to their previous labors, this was quite a lot.

"But Hamilton can't fan air into the tunnel, plus pull out the cuspidor, empty it, and send it back to me simultaneously. We're calling back the work teams. Will you join us, and be part of the story yourself? Or will you stay here and write about the escape afterward in the *Libby Chronicle*?"

Harrison sat up and rolled the kinks from his neck. It was not a difficult decision. "I'm in."

He plunged back into the work with an energy that would have made his mining father proud. Tunnel Four soon grew longer than the previous three, and the sense of suffocation hovered over Harrison as he dug. The new goal, Hamilton had explained, was to dig beneath the empty lot east of the prison, and pop up on the other side of the fence, near the warehouse that stored all those boxes shipped from the North to Libby's inmates.

Though the tunnel was twenty-four inches by eighteen inches at its portal, at one point the width cinched to a mere sixteen inches. Harrison, Rose, and the others wriggled through it face down, flat on their bellies, gagging and choking on the impure air. By the time each digger emerged from the portal after his shift, he was more dead than alive. Rats remained a constant nuisance, but now served a greater purpose. When they made more noise than usual, it signaled the approach of Rebel guards, who now searched every room of the prison since the five had escaped earlier this month. As soon as the south door of the cellar opened, the digging team scattered like roaches to the darkest, foulest smelling corners of the room in the seconds it took for the guards' eyes to adjust to the darkness.

Still, the work continued through day and night, the off-duty tunnelers filling in for the absent ones during the twice daily roll calls. Until one day, Little Ross had come in with his superior officers, and taken the roll call by name. Harrison and a soldier named McDonald had been working below, and their absences were noted.

"You have two choices," Hamilton told them when he came downstairs with the news. "Come back up and talk your way out of the jam with Warden Turner. Or stay here and hope they don't find you while we spread the word you escaped days ago."

McDonald chose to go back upstairs.

Harrison decided to stay.

It proved to be a lonely choice. Save for the Rebel guards, rats, and lice that came to visit, during the day Harrison was alone until the workers came at night, bringing food for his hollow stomach. With the roll calls now being administered by name rather than head count, Hamilton had ceased all daytime digging. Harrison did not blame him.

He did, however, blame himself. If he had exercised more caution his first night in Richmond, if he had only waited until he had a pass, he wouldn't be here in the first place. If he hadn't bragged about penning the Weeping Time story, perhaps he would have been released by now. He and Bella would be safely North.

Ambition is such a two-edged sword, Harrison mused as he sat behind a pile of straw. Without it, one accomplishes nothing and is condemned as lazy and shiftless. Too much of it, and one finds himself alone at the top of the ladder, or with one misstep, falling headlong toward the ground.

Harrison Caldwell was driven. Or at least, he had been until he'd landed here, with nowhere to go but circles or dead-end tunnels. That drive to succeed, to tell stories no one else had written, had been tied to the larger purpose of serving the public. But he'd be lying if he said he didn't also want to be famous.

Now look at me. He could no longer even claim to be editor of a prison newspaper. By day, he sat in a putrefied cellar, pinching lice off his skin and shooing away rats, since it was too dangerous to tunnel alone. But it wasn't just being useless that bothered him.

Being captive in Libby Prison also taught him that he was expendable. No editor in the North missed him, or even knew he was gone. The American press still whirred and clanked without him, and they were none the worse off for his absence.

But Bella was. If he were Abraham, he'd be livid that his wife had been brought down here and was unable to get home safely. If only he could figure out a way to get Abraham to the tunnel they were digging, too. But there were two thick walls between the east cellar and where the colored prisoners were held in the west cellar, two warehouses over. Even Rose and Hamilton had said it couldn't be done. *Another failure.*

Sophie's face surged in his mind, too. If that map he'd left in his cloak had been found, he'd brought danger to her doorstep and was powerless to do anything about that from here.

Groaning, Harrison bent his head into his hands. *Lord,* he prayed, though he hadn't approached the Almighty in some time. *This is not how I'd planned things to go. I'd like to fix things myself, but as You can see, I'm stuck. In more ways than one. Please, don't let my indiscretions bring harm to Bella and Sophie. Keep them safe. I've been seeking my own fame and fortune for years, but right now, all I want is to be free and to protect the ones I've endangered. Please. Get me out of here. Then show me the path You—*

The south door flung open, and Harrison instantly covered himself with straw just as several Rebel guards strode across the cellar, stopping a few yards from the tunnel entrance. Harrison scarcely dared to breathe. Unlike the usual cursory visits, this one reeked of purpose. Peering from his hiding place, he watched as two guards strode back and forth in front of the portal without noticing it.

Then dust tickled the inside of Harrison's nose. Pressure swelled and panic bloomed. He tried in vain to contain his sneeze, but it was useless. With his hand over his nose and mouth, the explosion inside his head was so loud, no doubt the guards had heard it. Harrison braced himself. "Something's going on here," said one of them, kicking at the straw that hid Harrison. "They're up to something. Planning an escape, no doubt."

Another guard exclaimed at the foul smell, while another kicked a rat from his way. "Godforsaken place. Let's go." But minutes fell from the clock in slow-motion before they actually gave up and left.

After the door slammed shut again, Harrison finally allowed himself to breathe, and thanked God he had not been caught. But the guards were close. Too close. It was only a matter of time before all would be lost.

———

Kent House, Richmond, Virginia
Thursday, February 4, 1864

"Gone?" Sophie's knitting needles fell silent.

"That's what Robert Ford said at the market just now." Eyes shimmering, Bella crossed to the parlor fireplace and fed another log to the flames.

"You mean Harrison escaped?"

"Ford said 'gone.' Guards say he escaped more than a week ago.

But I can't imagine him leaving without at least getting word to me."

"Bella." Sophie's needles clattered to the floor. Dread unfurled, filling her chest. "You don't think . . ." She bit her lip to trap the words that beat upon her heart.

Bella turned, and a degree of compassion filtered through her eyes. She looked so much like Daphne at that moment, before she fell ill, it nearly stole Sophie's breath.

"I think the best thing is to put it out of your mind, Sophie-girl. We can't see what's going on behind those walls. God's got him, and us, right where He wants us. And Ford says the white prisoners have been planning something."

"And the colored prisoners?"

Bella swiped the scarf off head and sat in a velvet armchair. "Not part of it, aside from passing information to them on the number of sentries and troops along the roads leading out from Richmond."

"I'm sorry. I wish—"

"Wishing never did a lick of good. But if the officers get free, maybe they can help my Abraham and the others with him. They're going to need safe houses."

"I'm sure Elizabeth Van Lew will offer hers," Sophie said.

"Still, we should be ready. Just in case."

Nodding, Sophie rose from her chair. "I'll get the blankets, pillows, and suits from my father's bureau." They would need to be clothed as civilians, as Dr. Lansing had, if they were to leave the city unnoticed.

"I'll bring in pails of water, tin cups, empty buckets."

They whisked toward their tasks, though surely no fugitives would come before nightfall. Still, with Fischer busy downstairs reconciling January's expenses with the budget, the time to act was now.

Chapter Twenty-one

Libby Prison, Richmond, Virginia
Saturday, February 6, 1864

Bang! The door to the west cellar burst open and little Erasmus Ross blew in, snow spotting his hair and mustache, and melting in droplets on his spectacles.

"Jamison!" he barked, and Abraham bolted to his feet, dropping the cornbread to the floor in his surprise. "Thought you could get away with it, did you?" Ross sneered as he marched toward a completely confounded Abraham.

Get away with it? He hadn't done anything—except pass information from Robert Ford to Bella. Beads of sweat studded his brow. His breath grew short and quick. If he was in trouble for this, was Bella?

Before Abraham knew what was happening, Ross threw his fist into his ribs. Pain stabbed, knife-like, before burning white-hot. If there were a giant red *X* just on the spot where they'd been broken before, Ross could not have placed a more effective blow. Abraham's breath seared.

Ross thrust his knee into Abraham's groin, and Abraham folded in pain only to feel elbows plow between his shoulder blades. He stumbled, gripped his kneecaps to keep from collapsing on the floor.

Lord! Keep Bella safe, wherever she is. If taking this pain would somehow mean less for her, he would endure it without complaint.

"Follow me," Ross growled.

Abraham remained rooted to the ground. Peter had followed Erasmus Ross. So had Elisha, Henry, and Raymond. They'd never been seen again.

A swift punch to his jaw, and Abraham tasted blood.

"I don't say things twice. Now git."

Abraham hazarded a glance at his fellow prisoners as he staggered out the door. Their eyes met his in silent, smoldering farewell. The wind bit through Abraham's rags with a thousand feral teeth as he followed Ross's footsteps around the side of the building and into the clerk's first floor office. Curiously, Ross left the door to the outside slightly ajar. Without a word, he pointed behind his desk. Without looking at Abraham, he left the room.

Palms clammy, Abraham waited, watching the door through which the small clerk had just exited, straining his ears toward the receding footfalls. A robust fire blazed in the hearth a mere yard from him, its crackling heat prickling Abraham's chilled skin. Above him, floorboards creaked and groaned as prisoners scuffed the second floor. Their muted voices rose and fell. But no one came back for Abraham.

In two long strides, he was behind the desk. Shock coursed through him like lightning. There on the chair, was a set of civilian clothing, and a pass for a male slave to be out without his owner before curfew. *The other five escapees. So this was how they had done it. Little Ross sure does have folks fooled,* Abraham thought as he rubbed his sore jaw.

He lifted the trousers and shirt from the chair. Five had escaped this way. Four had been recaptured. A one in five chance is better than none, he decided, and quickly replaced his prisoner's rags with the clothing of a slave. *Some trade.* Pass in hand, he peered from the window and studied the timing of the sentinels. As long as they didn't see him exit the building, once he was on the sidewalk, they'd have no cause to be any more suspicious of him as they were of any other person walking by on the street.

Lord, help.

A pattern emerged. He saw his chance. And took it. Head down, he affected a limp and made his unhurried way north on Twentieth Street on the west side of the prison.

"Halt!" A guard approached. "Pass?"

Abraham gave it to him with a bow, the way he'd seen other slaves behave around white folks here.

"Where you headed, boy?"

Abraham's mind whirred, the setting sun so bright in his eyes it disoriented him. "Why, home to Massa, sah," he said.

"And where you been?"

"Wall, I came down to de docks to see if dar be any work so as I could get some mo pay for Massa. He as like to rent me out, see? But dey ain't no work to be had down dar. Dey neber is, but Massa sends me ebery week jes de same, jes in case der be a change!" He tapped his temple with his middle finger, like a fool.

The guard grunted. Handed his pass back to him. "Then git. Go on with you, now."

Abraham bowed again, then limped north until he was past Cary Street, the northern border of Libby Prison, and to Main Street. Live oaks stretched overhead, their skeletal branches silhouetted against a burning sky. The sun was settling in for a long winter's night.

Curfew was coming. There weren't many black folks still on the street. The ones he found unaccompanied by whites, he stopped and asked with hoarse voice for directions to the home of Sophie Kent. He was close, he had to be. But so far, no one could answer his question.

Trying desperately not to look as aimless as he felt, Abraham walked the streets of the Confederate capital, careful to yield the sidewalk to those whose skin was brighter than his. He must look savage, indeed, with his face unshaven. He was sure he smelled, too, though his own nose had mercifully grown accustomed to it. Still, he searched for his wife the only way he knew how, relying on the Lord and a thin sheet of paper for his protection. But with every wandering footstep, his time was running out.

Where are you, Bella?

In the Kent family kitchen house, Bella Jamison stood with her head held high and looked Otto Fischer straight in the eyes. Pearl busied herself brewing a weak pot of tea. Emiline bent over her ironing, while Lois and Rachel sat at the table, their eyes intent on their mending and knitting. They would not meet Fischer's gaze, but Bella would.

"As the steward, the Kent finances are in my charge," he was saying. "So are the rest of the staff."

"I'm not staff." *And I do not take orders from you.* She kept her voice level though the hour was late, and she was bone-tired.

"Then why are you going to market? Our resources are dwindling in proportion to the Confederate currency. We simply must leave the marketing to Pearl, or Rachel in her stead. They know best how to economize. There is no need for you to go, too."

"I go of my own accord."

"But why?" His eyebrows raised into his forehead.

Bella's jaw bunched at his blatant desire to control her. "Do you censure every guest in this house, Mr. Fischer, or only the ones with brown skin?"

Emiline's gaze flickered over to Bella, her eyebrows arched.

Fischer noticed. His eyes darkened, and storm clouds boiled in her belly. She should use caution. She was in Virginia, after all, where she had once been a slave and given birth to a slave. But she had put all that behind her. Scars itching across her back, Bella's spirit refused to bow again.

"I am not a slave," she said through gritted teeth, and could almost hear the other women suck in their breath. Pearl poked fiercely at the fire, and Lois's knitting needles clicked faster. Emiline's and Rachel's hands grew still. *Good. Let them listen.* They needed to hear a brown-skinned woman with a strong, fearless voice. "I am as free as you are. You are neither my master nor my employer, and I do not answer to you. I seek to please God my maker, Sophie Kent as my hostess, and my own conscience. I do not mean to say I am above you. But don't you dare set yourself over me."

Wildly, Fischer's gaze thrust at each of the other slaves in the kitchen. He grabbed Bella's elbow and yanked her to a corner with a strength that belied his thin frame.

She jerked from his hold, every nerve tingling. "Do not touch me." Her voice smoldered with warning.

"You should be whipped for such uppity talk!"

Outwardly, Bella did not flinch.

"Such talk about being free and *equal*—it gives them ideas."

Bella folded her arms across her chest. "And here I thought ideas were a good thing. Wouldn't you consider it an asset to have your help think, and learn, and learn to think?"

"Amen."

Emiline's voice was gossamer thin, but it startled Bella as much as it seemed to jar Fischer.

"You see!" he hissed at Bella. "She never said a word against me in her life. Never! You see how quickly they begin to forget their place."

In the next instant, he towered over the sixteen-year-old laundress and slapped her. Placed his hand over hers on the handle of the hot iron. Lifted it toward her face.

Lois's knitting needles dropped to the table as she pleaded for her daughter. "Please, sir, she didn't mean nothing by it, she's just a baby."

Bella reached for him as though in slow motion, as though she were swimming through a room full of sand.

A pounding at the door, and Fischer put down the iron. Bella swept over to Emiline and Lois while Fischer opened the door. Brittle air invaded, and the fire ducked beneath its blast.

"Get out of here!" Fischer bellowed. "It's past curfew! If you don't get home to your master—or your shanty, if you call yourself free—I'll take you to the slave pen for the night myself! Ugh! And take your stench with you!"

Fischer slammed the door, and the windows shivered. "Probably crawling with lice," he muttered, inspecting his own sleeves.

The hair on Bella's neck stood on end. "Who was that?" She stepped toward the door.

"Filthy Negro."

"What did he want?"

"Irrelevant. Mr. Kent's policy is that no colored males, for any reason, are ever to be allowed on the premises."

"Because he's afraid of arson?" The newspapers had confirmed that it was Jefferson Davis's slave who had set the fire in the basement before running North last month.

"Because Mr. Kent's entire family was murdered by them in the Nat Turner Rebellion." He stalked over to her. "That is what happens when ideas are planted in minds not equipped to manage them. You court danger, Bella. If any of these women steals, runs away, or brings harm to Miss Kent in any form, I hold you personally responsible."

But Bella was looking out the window, after the man Fischer had turned away. She ran out into the swirling snow, her skirts whipping about her legs, but there was no one in sight.

———

Libby Prison, Richmond, Virginia
Sunday, February 7, 1864, 1:00 a.m.

"Break through the surface, Caldwell." Colonel Thomas Rose handed Harrison the chisel. "It's time."

If he hadn't dropped to the floor immediately, Harrison's knees would have given way beneath the wave of relief that now flooded him. Truly, if he did not breathe fresh air soon, he feared he would die of asphyxiation.

It will be over soon enough, Harrison thought as he wiggled through the tunnel. They'd advanced an average of five feet per night, which should put them on the other side of the empty lot, safely behind the fence by now, according to Captain John Gallagher's calculations. The charming Irishman of the 2nd Ohio had cultivated enough goodwill with his captors that they allowed him to walk across the lot a few nights ago and check the warehouse for a box he felt sure had been sent to him. Of course, no such box existed, but by walking at a precise gait—as close to three feet as possible—he had measured the distance the tunnelers would have to cross. Fifty-two to fifty-three feet.

Right about . . . Harrison wormed forward another few yards as the tunnel slanted upward. *Here.* With a kiss to the chisel, and a prayer for God's favor, he chipped away at the ice-encrusted earth above him. Dirt crumbled and fell on his face as he worked until heavenly, clean air poured into the tunnel. *We did it.* Harrison gulped in the cold, fresh air as a man in the desert would lap at a spring. Opening his eyes, he focused on the fence dividing the empty lot from the warehouse full of neglected relief boxes. And nearly lost his cornbread.

The fence was still in front of him. By almost ten feet.

Footsteps sounded on the ground near the hole, yet Harrison remained frozen in place by a horror stronger and colder than ice. The guard stopped within sight of Harrison and leaned on the fence, peering into the darkness on the other side. *Don't turn around. Don't turn around. . . .* The rushing of his blood in his ears drowned out every other sound. Sweat beaded and chilled his face as the guard stood there, listening. Only after what seemed like an eternity, did he walk away.

Harrison slipped back down the tunnel and wormed backwards until he was back in Rat Hell. "All is lost!" he gasped, still shaking from both exertion and mortification. "We came up too short!"

Kent House, Richmond, Virginia
Sunday, February 7, 1864, 2:30 a.m.

Sophie barely noticed the thunder's rumble as she stabbed at her fire. After Bella told her what Fischer had done, she'd dismissed him. It was the right thing to do, of course. Even Mrs. Blair had said on their last visit that a servant who bullies another cannot be tolerated. Still, it soured her stomach. He'd served the Kent family faithfully for as long as she could remember. His volatility, however, was not acceptable. He'd become a liability. She'd given him a week to find new housing but had discharged him from his role as steward and head of the staff immediately. *Besides, if money is as tight as he says, dropping a servant from the payroll is as reasonable a solution as any.* Dully, she sat on her heels and watched the flames leap back to life.

Her windows rattled. *Strange,* she thought, frowning. *The thunder never stopped rolling.* Tossing her braid over her shoulder, she went to her second-story window just in time to hear a church bell frantically peal. Then another church joined in, and another, then more. The tocsin in Capitol Square added to the discordant noise, until it seemed that all the bells in Richmond were competing for heaven's attention. She stepped out onto her balcony in her slippers. *That's not thunder. It's artillery.* She should have recognized the sound immediately, from all they had endured during Union General McClellan's failed Peninsula Campaign in the summer of 1862.

Sophie's gut cinched. *My missive to Elizabeth Van Lew. The recommendation for a raid.* Had Elizabeth confirmed the intelligence with others? If this was a raid, it wasn't going well. The fighting sounded as if it were as far away as Williamsburg, fully fifty miles distant.

Sophie hurried back inside the house and climbed up to the cupola for a better view. From her perch atop Church Hill, she could see lights winking throughout the city. People mobbing the streets in pandemonium. Two bony, sway-backed mules pulling mountain howitzers down the street toward the river. Small boys and old men running to join veterans and raw militia.

She turned toward Libby Prison, her breath fogging the glass. Wiping the condensation from her view, she squinted. Howitzers had appeared on the surrounding streets, aimed at the warehouse prisons and the James River bridges. Captain Russell's words came rushing back at her then. The Rebels were terrified of a raid, and of the arming of the prisoners. *So terrified they would kill the captives rather than risk their release?*

Sophie whirled around in the cupola, taking in every view, grasping for comprehension but fearing she already understood. Her message had gotten to the Union general Butler. The raid was failing. But the prisoners would all be killed. *Because of me.*

Lord, be merciful!

———

Bella stood at the window, grateful for the glass and brick separating her from the throngs on Franklin Street. Bedlam spread like a pox, and the streets boiled over with panic. As clanging bells shook her spirit, and firing guns exploded in her mind, she wondered if the man Fischer had turned away was among them. They were so densely packed, it was impossible to tell.

"Come back," she whispered, her fingertips on the window, and winced when some fool in the street fired his revolver from within the crowd, triggering screams from women who should have stayed inside.

By the time the frothing mob receded, Sophie was at Bella's side, trembling. "Thank God none of the howitzers was fired." But whatever the Union forces had intended to do, they'd failed.

"It's over." Bella squeezed Sophie's shaking hand.

Sighing, Sophie cast one more gaze out the window. Then, "Oh no. Not for that fellow."

Bella looked, too, and found a Negro still lying on the sidewalk. Either he was very foolish or . . . *very drunk*? He pushed himself up on his elbows, grabbed his thigh, then held his hand up to inspect it. As he turned it in the moonlight, something shimmered on his fingers. He turned to the Kent house then, as if gauging the distance between.

"He's hurt," Bella decided, and fled the room, Sophie right behind her.

Cold slapped at the soles of Bella's bare feet as she hurried down the stairs and out into the street. "Well, Brother, and just what were you doing out here this time of night anyhow?" She knelt by his side, her gaze fixed upon the dark red blood oozing ominously from his homespun trousers.

"Looking for you," he rasped, grimacing in obvious pain. "Bella."

Recognition sliced through her. "Abe!" Sorrow and relief churned through her veins as Sophie appeared on his other side. Tears coursed down her cheeks before she swiped them away. "Sophie Kent, meet my husband, Abraham. Abe, this is Sophie. And you're going to be fine."

Without another word, Bella and Sophie helped Abraham to his feet, and supported his weight as they led him into the house. As she closed and locked the door behind them, a shadow fleeted in the periphery of Bella's vision. Otto Fischer had seen it all. She pushed it firmly out of her mind.

"I need light," Bella said as they laid him on the floor, and Sophie scurried to bring a kerosene lamp to his side. A torrent of memories unleashed, and images from tending the Confederate wounded at Liberty's Gettysburg farm surged. This time, she did not thrust those grisly flashes away. She needed them, in all their heart-rending clarity.

As Sophie tore strips from the hem of her nightgown for a tourniquet, Bella rushed to collect the surgical tools she'd need. A leather belt rather than chloroform or opium. Sewing scissors. Lois's narrowest knitting needles rather than a probe. A small sugar spoon, a pickle fork with tiny prongs rather than a forceps to remove the ball. A ghastly collection on a silver tea service tray. But if she didn't extract the bullet, it would turn her husband's body septic.

"Pray," Bella muttered to Sophie, returning to his side, and cut the trousers off his leg.

Chapter Twenty-two

Libby Prison, Richmond, Virginia
Tuesday, February 9, 1864, 3:00 a.m.

*H*arrison's lean shoulders and biceps burned as he fanned air into Tunnel Four. The only sound in Rat Hell was the occasional scrape of the cuspidor being dragged through the tunnel by Hamilton and the intermittent squeals of rodents in a vicious fight. *Lord,* Harrison prayed, but his thoughts could dig no further along that track. He was bone-weary, sore, and secretly frightened that Rose had gone mad.

After the tunnel had come to the surface too soon, Rose had engineered its repair, and vowed they would all be free—and soon. Since that time, he had never handed the chisel to another, but dug with the energy of one possessed. He was convinced that the time to escape was now or never. Harrison agreed.

A rat scampered over Harrison's splayed open shoe, and he kicked it into a heap of straw. He strained to hear some sign from Rose. His forehead ached with worry for his friend, the warrior schoolteacher

226

from Pittsburgh. Last time he'd emerged from the portal, gulping for air, hair standing on end from his head and face, he was slick with sweat, and a visible tremor warned of imminent collapse. "The hour is at hand," he had wheezed, eyes glassy. "I will break free or die trying." Then he disappeared again into his narrow grave.

Please Lord, bring him back. And bring us home. Perhaps it was the crushing isolation of Rat Hell during the last several days, but Harrison had started talking to the Almighty much more frequently. It felt a whole lot better than talking to himself, or to the rats or lice that kept him company.

"He's coming," Hamilton whispered.

Harrison dropped his fan and reached inside the tunnel, pulling Rose out by his sinewy arm. The colonel stood, his face practically alight, as if he were Moses and had seen God at Mount Sinai.

"We've done it!" he whispered.

Shock coursed through Harrison. He blinked, almost afraid to believe.

"We come up under the tobacco shed, where the high fence shields us. I've been for a walk around Libby."

Harrison's jaw nearly hit the floor. "How was it?"

Rose grinned. "Heavenly."

"Come then! Alert the other tunnelers, let's go!" Hamilton said, his voice low but intense. Rose nodded.

"Wait—" Harrison held out his hands. "It's three in the morning. How far do you want to get?" He paused. "Why not rest a little, trade and pack some extra food for your journey, and leave shortly after nightfall tonight." The sun set at seven, which would give them fully eight more hours of darkness to get safely away than if they were to leave right now.

At length, Rose and Hamilton reluctantly agreed. They would return upstairs and Harrison would stay in Rat Hell for one more day.

The longest day of their lives.

Kent House, Richmond, Virginia
Tuesday, February 9, 1864, 7 p.m.

"She did what? Why?" Lawrence Russell studied Mr. Fischer's weary form as the steward hung his cloak and hat.

"Dismissed me. For taking the upper hand with the slaves." His brows slanted downward.

"Why Fischer! Isn't that your job?"

"Used to be." A scowl slashed on his face. "You watch her, Captain. She has secrets."

Footsteps whispered in the hall.

"From me?"

"Especially from you, sir," he whispered. Fischer threw a glance over his shoulder then scurried away, leaving Lawrence, stunned, in his wake.

"Oh!" Sophie said as she stepped into the main entrance hall. "Fischer must have let you in. I didn't expect him to."

Lawrence bussed her cheek. "Yes, he told me you dismissed him."

Her shoulders sagged. "It's true. But I'm allowing him to stay while he secures new housing arrangements."

"Good luck to him. There's nary an inch of carpet to be spared in Richmond." He wrapped his arm around her waist, and told himself for the thousandth time to be patient with her dowdy mourning garb. What was beneath the layers of clothing was worth waiting for. He allowed his hand to stroke up the curve of her waist and back down again, felt the cords of her corset beneath the crepe before they sat on the parlor sofa.

"Well, I hope he finds something, and soon. He cannot stay here much longer, I simply won't have it."

Rachel—or was that one Emiline?—came forward with the tea service, and poured steaming brew for each of them before receding from view. Sophie brought her cup to her rosebud lips, and blew across the rim to cool it.

He smiled at the adorable pucker of her mouth, then forced himself to look instead at her eyes. "What was his offense?"

"He questioned my authority, first of all, but then he slapped Emiline! For an imagined slight!"

"Were you there?" He sipped his own tea. "Did you see it?"

"I saw his handprint on her face, Lawrence. And I will not have violence in this house." A golden curl shook next to her face as she spoke.

"But you were not there to hear what she said to cause the incident."

Sophie rattled her cup back onto its saucer. "Whatever the 'cause,' Fischer should have controlled his impulses!"

"Yes, quite, darling. There now, don't get upset." He placed his hand on her knee to calm her. "And, I suppose, if he questioned your authority, that had to be dealt with decisively. Bravo. Only, what will you do without a man in the house?" He cocked his eyebrow, controlling his own impulses to an impressive degree.

She slanted him a playful gaze. "I'll manage." Her green eyes flashed, not altogether innocently, Lawrence thought. Being the one and only man around her suited him just fine.

She has secrets. Especially from you, sir. Fischer's words froze the smile on Lawrence's face. He drank his tea, considering.

"You weren't frightened Sunday morning, were you? With the artillery and the chaos in the streets? I do hope you stayed tucked in bed like a good little girl."

"It was madness, wasn't it? But no, I didn't venture out of doors. I could see plenty from the cupola. What happened? Do you know?"

Lawrence leaned back, draped his arm over the back of the sofa. Twirled one of Sophie's curls around his finger. "It'll be in the papers tomorrow. A Union detachment tried to make a raid on Richmond."

"Oh?" Her eyes widened before she ducked back into her porcelain cup.

Suddenly, his own words to her filtered back into his consciousness. *If you ask me, we've let our guard down,* he'd told her. *We're more vulnerable to a raid now than we've ever been.* His fingers stilled for moment, her silken tresses caught between his thumb and forefinger.

"Funny, isn't it? Didn't I just say now would be a good time for a raid?"

"Did you, darling? Uncanny." She looked at him, unblinking. Her face a blank slate.

"Well, as it turns out, it wasn't good for the Yankees after all. When they reached Bottom's Bridge they had quite a surprise. The bridge was destroyed, and Rebel troops were already dug into defensive positions on the opposite riverbank. Trains were already bringing reinforcements from Richmond."

"Really? That's remarkable! But how did they know they'd be needed?"

He smiled. "Yankee deserter tipped us off."

Sophie's eyebrows arched. "And just in time. My." Were her hands shaking? She gripped her cup.

"Indeed. But even if he hadn't, we'd have given them a good wallop just the same. They came with only six thousand men." He watched her closely. "Do you remember how many I told you they would have needed to make a go of it?"

"I believe you said more than that, by far." She smiled, inhaled deeply, as though relieved.

"That's right. Thirty thousand cavalry and fifteen thousand infantry. And they made a dash with only six thousand!"

"Ill-advised." Sophie's lashes fluttered against her flushed cheeks as she smoothed down the pleats in her skirt.

Lawrence grasped her hand and found it cold. "Are you unwell?"

"Forgive me, Lawrence. I am only tired." But no shadows ringed her eyes.

Doubt flickered in Lawrence's chest as she wrapped her slender fingers around his hand. Lawrence had been lied to before, manipulated by a woman not half so beautiful as Sophie Kent. He did not enjoy playing the fool.

His smile grew stiff and cool.

She has secrets, Fischer had warned. *Especially from you.*

———

Libby Prison, Richmond, Virginia
Tuesday, February 9, 1864, 7:00 p.m.

At last, night fell, and darkness swaddled the city. Sweat filmed Harrison's skin as he ran a hand over his stubbled jaw. *This is it.*

Above him, the floor shook with the stomping, dancing feet of prisoners carousing in the kitchen. They were doing more than venting their pent-up energy. While the first half of escapees made their exit through the tunnel, the remaining tunnelers struck up some revelry, a farewell serenade of sorts, which doubled as a distraction for the guards.

Here in Rat Hell, the stench, the rodents, the tomblike suffocation would soon be merely black blots on Harrison's memory. Colonel Thomas Rose lined the men up to the tunnel entrance in order of rank, then shook each man's hand before taking his place at the front, just ahead of Major Hamilton. With no rank at all, Harrison fell to the end of the line. He was grateful to be included in the first batch of escapees at all.

Rose grasped his hand, pumping it heartily. "Thank you, soldier."

Harrison's eyes misted at the warmth in Rose's voice.

"You've proven yourself to be one of us—an observer no more." Rose continued, "Now onward, to finish the race set before us, yes? Godspeed and farewell." He returned to the tunnel's mouth and disappeared inside its throat.

Harrison's limbs twitched in anticipation of his turn. One by one, the men were swallowed up by the damp hole in the wall, until he found himself next in line. Muscles taut, his body propelled him blindly along the narrow path toward freedom. *This is not a grave,* he told himself. *It is a rebirth.*

After worming and wriggling for three minutes through more

than fifty feet of dead air, Harrison emerged on the heels of the man before him, under the roof of the tobacco shed. *Free.* At least, for the moment.

Slipping outside, Harrison and three others skirted the brick building where the Rebels had stored the five thousand undelivered prisoner boxes. The two-day-old moon was barely a sliver in the sky, making conditions near perfect for escape. After reaching the arched wagonway through which deliveries were made to the prison, Harrison quietly opened the gate and peered into Canal Street, searching for the sentinels. When the way was clear, he stepped into the street, and the others followed suit by intervals. Blood rushing in his ears, Harrison adopted a purposeful stride, as did Major B. B. McDonald, beside him. They knew exactly where they were headed.

The black prisoners who scrubbed the officers' floors and emptied their chamber pots had told them about Elizabeth Van Lew and had given directions to her house. One could easily see it from Libby, sitting atop Church Hill as it did. *She will be a friend to you, if ever you need one.* As much as Harrison wanted to see Sophie and Bella—if she was still in Richmond—he was reluctant to endanger them with his presence. If they could get to Miss Van Lew's house, a message could easily be sent. Perhaps Sophie and Bella could come to the Van Lew home or some other meeting place without arousing suspicion.

Harrison drank in the cool night air as he clipped along the sidewalk. He was anxious to know how Bella fared. But it was Sophie's face that lingered in his mind. Quiet pulsed between Harrison and McDonald for the rest of the way to the Van Lew house on Grace Street.

Upon arriving, Harrison rapped the brass knocker against its plate on the door. A Negro man opened it.

"Good evening," McDonald said. "Is Miss Van Lew at home?"

"No sir." He shook his head, and began to close the door.

Harrison thrust out his hand. "Pardon me. We don't wish to intrude, but we were told we'd have a friend in Miss Van Lew. And we need one now, desperately." His gaze shifted left and right before he leaned in, dropping his voice low. "We've just come from Libby. We need help."

"I don't know what you heard, but we is faithful Confederates here." The butler's nostrils flared. "I'll not turn you in, on account of your business not being any of mine, but you best take it on with you. Leave Miss Van Lew and her mother out of it."

"Please, you don't understand, we have no other place to go!" McDonald's quiet voice was full of fire. "We wouldn't stay long, but we need food for the journey, some socks perhaps!"

The butler's eyebrows plowed downward. "Get yourself on outta here. Miss Lizzie didn't tell me nothin' bout you folks. So git!" He slammed the door.

Harrison stared at the door and heard the click as it locked.

"Plan B?" McDonald jerked his head toward the sidewalk, and the pair strolled back down to the street.

"I know a place. Not far from here." Harrison winced as he said it, loath to bring trouble to Sophie. But he did not have a Plan C.

From the Van Lew mansion on Grace Street, Harrison led McDonald downhill for one block to Franklin Street, then uphill two blocks to Twenty-seventh. By the time they reached Sophie's corner, both men were panting for breath.

"Pitiful, aren't we?" McDonald joked, but their condition was deadly serious. Union-held Williamsburg was fifty miles away. Getting there by foot in the winter would be a daunting task for the healthiest of men.

"Kitchen house," Harrison said, remembering the party he and Bella had walked in on last time.

His spine tingled as he knocked on the door. It cracked open, and light and warmth spilled out.

"Can I help—Get in here!" Bella pulled him in by his tattered collar, and McDonald after him before closing the door and locking it. For a long moment, she covered her mouth with her hand, with her other fist propped on her hip. Her eyes glistened, and Harrison wondered what he must look like after months in prison, denied the sun as well as food. Finally, she dropped her hand from her face. Pressed her lips together and inhaled. "You're late." A small, sad smile tilted on her face as she shook her head.

"I'm sorry," Harrison bowed to her, though he felt like pulling her into a fierce embrace. "You'll never know how much."

McDonald cleared his throat. "B. B. McDonald, 101st Ohio." He thrust out his hand, and Bella took it, introducing herself as well.

"Land sakes, Bella, those two gentlemen gonna blow over with the next draft that comes whistling through here! Sit them down!" A ginger brown woman clucked her tongue.

"Thank you, ma'am."

"Ma'am nothin'. Call me Pearl." Her gap-toothed grin drew a smile from Harrison.

Knees suddenly shaking, he gratefully slid onto the bench at the table across from McDonald. "Bella." He caught her hand. "Is Daphne—"

Bella shook her head, her piercing eyes deflating his hope.

"I'm so very sorry. When?"

"December."

Harrison suppressed a groan. All this time, she'd been here in Richmond without even her sister. *Useless risk!*

"Abraham's here."

"What?"

She pointed to the far corner of the room, where he lay sleeping on a pallet, his leg wrapped in bandages. Bella told him the extraordinary story of his escape, and Harrison could not have been more astonished.

"Just like that? He just walked out?"

She nodded. "But he's not walking anymore for I don't know how long." Firelight glinted in her eyes. "Harrison. You'll have to leave without us."

As much as he wanted to, he could not, would not contradict her to ease his conscience. She was right. The guards would be combing the area for fugitives soon enough. A man needed the use of both his legs for any hope of evasion.

Pearl slid tumblers of water and plates of cold ham and cornbread to Harrison and McDonald. With their stomachs so unused to real food, they would have to eat slowly.

"We've got a safe hiding place for you in the main house." Bella sat across from them as they ate, folding her hands on the table. "You can rest in there. We'll pack you some food, give you better clothes. Then we'll send for help to get you outside the city."

Harrison nodded as she spoke, eyes closed as he enjoyed the glorious sensation of food filling his belly.

"Only we can't go just yet. Captain Russell is inside with Sophie."

Harrison's eyes popped open. The ham soured in his mouth, and he swallowed it. "Captain Russell, eh?"

"Her suitor."

"Does she love him?" Harrison felt McDonald's eyes on him.

Bella's brown eyes sparkled. "You got a stake in that claim?"

Harrison shrugged. Suddenly he didn't feel like talking about it.

"Mm-hmm." She nodded, smiling. "Well then. In the meantime, there's clean water and soap for you both to wash up. I'd offer a razor if I had one, but it seems you already found one." She flicked a glance to the fuzz on his head.

Self-consciously, he ran his hand over it. "Does it look that bad?"

Bella folded her arms across her waist, tilted her head and squinted. "It looks lighter. You must have shaved all the orange off. Grew back auburn. Get a little meat back on your bones and you just might look handsome." Her smile flashed brightly. It was being near Abraham again, Harrison decided, that brought out this teasing side she'd kept hidden before.

He swung his long legs over the back of the bench and crossed to the wash basin. Laving the water over his face and neck, he rejoiced that it did not smell of sewage or taste like the James River. He spied a tin of tooth powder on the edge of the stand, sprinkled some on his finger and did the best he could to clean his teeth.

"We gotta burn your clothes, men, before you pass your vermin to the rest of us."

Harrison flinched, embarrassed by his unclean state. "Have you got anything other than petticoats for us to put on?"

She tossed a suit of clothes to each of the men, and Harrison caught it at his chest in wonder.

"Like I said. You're late. We had time to prepare." She pointed to the ladder, and Harrison and McDonald climbed up creaking rungs into the sleeping quarters to change.

When they returned downstairs, Harrison joined Bella at the window while McDonald struck up a conversation with Pearl.

"Looks like Sophie's getting rid of him early tonight," she murmured.

Sophie and Captain Russell stood framed in the doorway to the back porch. Harrison's gut curled inward as he watched the captain pull her close, one hand behind her waist, the other plunged into her curly blonde hair. Russell bent and took her lips, their silhouettes melting together into one indistinguishable form.

Unable to watch, Harrison turned away. He could almost smell the roses in Sophie's hair, the violets on her skin.

"Uh-oh," Bella said, jerking Harrison's attention to her.

"What happened?"

"Let's just say it looks like he's not ready to say good night. Mmmm, for shame! Oh—she slapped him! Good girl."

Scorching heat rushed to Harrison's head and licked through his veins. He was at the window again, desperate to make sense of the scene. Russell held her fast at the waist. She arched her back, pressed her hands to his chest, turned her face away. "Is she being coy?" Sophie had never played games with Harrison.

"Captain seems to think so." Bella grunted.

Sophie struggled against him until finally, he let her go.

"Wait another minute now." Then Bella turned to him. "He's

236

gone. I'll take Major McDonald over first. I want to tell her you're here before you show up like a ghost and shock her out of her wits, Mr. Caldwell."

Harrison nodded.

Pearl wiped her hands on her apron. "I'll find Lois and the girls. They can make sure Fischer don't get in the way tonight." Straightening the blue headscarf above her determined brow, she hustled away on her errand.

Bella motioned to McDonald, and he slipped out the door behind her, crossed the yard, and disappeared into Sophie's house.

Sophie smoothed her hair back into place with shaking hands. Maybe she shouldn't have slapped Lawrence. It was instinct, not a calculated risk. He'd been getting bolder lately, and without a chaperone, she had no idea how far he'd let his passions take him. *And me.*

The back door creaked open, and she whirled around to see Bella. A tall, thin, broad-shouldered man was right behind her.

"Sophie, this is Major McDonald, 101st Ohio." Bella's words sent a charge right through her.

"The prison break," she whispered. "We're ready for you. Follow me."

Bella stayed her with a hand on her arm. "Harrison's back." She jerked her head toward the rear door.

Sophie looked from Bella to McDonald and back again. Both of them nodded. "But—but Captain Russell said he escaped weeks ago!"

McDonald grinned. "A ruse. He missed roll call one day while digging our escape tunnel. We spread the word he'd lit out of there days ago, and he stayed in the cellar ever since. Until this very night."

"I fed them in the kitchen," Bella added. "Take McDonald up, and I'll send Harrison over. I expect there will be more to come."

As in a dream, Sophie swept up the walnut staircase to the spare room, heard herself explaining the hiding space to McDonald, watched her finger point to the pallets, the pails of water, the chamber pots, the kerosene lamps. His thanks were muffled by the voice in her head. *Harrison's alive! He's here!*

She barely felt the stairs beneath her feet as she glided back down. For there, at the bottom of them, stood Harrison, in her father's suit. His hair cut short, and far lighter than it had been. His cheekbones sharp above his shadowed jaw. Freckles gone without the sun to bring them out. His eyes, haunted, holding hers fast. He had seen too much of this dreadful war.

Without thinking, she placed her hand on the scruff of his jaw, and he covered it with his own.

"I'm sorry I'm late," he whispered, and a crushing ache consumed her heart. "Too late?" Gaslight glinted on the flecks of caramel in his brown eyes, and she knew. He had seen her with Lawrence on the porch.

Blinking back the moisture glazing her eyes, she shook her head, and locks of hair Lawrence had loosened came tumbling down again. *No, not too late.* But tears locked the words in her throat.

Footfalls thudded on the back porch, and Sophie stepped back from Harrison. The door groaned on its hinge.

And Lawrence stepped inside. "Forgot my hat—oh. You've company. And so soon after I left. And here I thought you were tired, darling."

Sophie's tongue thickened in her mouth, utterly useless.

His back to the door, Harrison's features hardened into carved stone. Then, he winked at her, so solemnly she almost didn't catch it. He spun around to face Lawrence. "Captain Russell!" He extended his hand, and, miraculously, Lawrence shook it.

"Shaw? Oliver Shaw?" Lawrence's brow relaxed as a broad grin stole over his face.

"I was hoping there'd be a party here tonight. Forgive me, I've been away, and was eager for company. How splendid to see you here."

"Yes, quite, but I daresay I wouldn't have recognized you on the street. You look like one of Lee's boys now!"

"Ah!" Harrison somehow beamed, as if it were a compliment. "Yes, I've been out with General Lee's army these past several weeks as a correspondent."

"And from the looks of it, Northrop hasn't been feeding you very well. I'll have to harp at Mr. Graham to see if we can't do something about that."

"Well, when a reporter joins the army, his fare is the same as that of the soldier. I wouldn't have it any other way. Unless there was a way for all of us to be fed, of course." He laughed, and Sophie struggled to match his nonchalance. If Harrison Caldwell hadn't been reported to have escaped weeks ago, surely Lawrence would suspect the subterfuge.

"Say, I called on you at the *Southern Examiner* office and they didn't know a thing about you. Did I have the wrong office?"

Harrison rocked back on his heels, folded his arms. "They didn't have room for one more staff correspondent. As it turns out, I'm not the only one who has come to Richmond in search of work." He chuckled again. "So I've been working independently, writing the stories I want to, and then just hoping and praying some paper buys them."

Lawrence nodded. "That explains it."

Sophie watched the exchange in awed silence. *And I thought Harrison had no use for fiction!* He was better at lying than she was, by far.

"Love to stay and chat, Shaw, especially about how Lee's artillery is holding up. We've had nothing but trouble at Tredegar trying to get him what he asks for. But I've got somewhere else to be right now."

Sophie fetched his hat.

Lawrence took it from her without thanks. "Will you be in town much longer? We'll get Sophie to throw another soiree. How does that suit you?"

"Excellent. Only I expect to leave again as soon as I find a buyer for my stories. So if all goes well, it will be some time before I see you next." He flashed a grin and shook Lawrence's hand in parting.

"Next time, then. Good luck." Lawrence turned to Sophie. "Don't stay up too late. You're tired, remember?" And he pulled her fiercely to him, kissed her right in front of Harrison. Her pulse shot through her as he lingered on her lips.

She broke away, mortified, and tucked her chin to hide the shame now trickling down her cheeks.

Lawrence left, and the silence throbbed between Sophie and Harrison. She could not bear to meet his gaze. Imagining the hurt or anger—or even worse, apathy—was quite enough.

Chapter Twenty-three

Come," Sophie whispered, wiping the tears from her face, and Harrison followed her up the stairs. The sconces in the hallway barely illuminated their path. But he was used to seeing in the dark. "The hiding place is in the spare room, this way." She led him forward as if another man had not just kissed her in front of him. As if she didn't realize how much self-restraint he'd employed not to take her first kiss in Philadelphia.

"Sophie." He touched her hand, and she turned toward him. He would not grab and pull her, like Lawrence had. "I can't hide away without knowing the truth first. About you and Russell. Please, tell me what's going on." His forefinger traced the side of her palm down to the tip of her little finger. He willed her to respond.

Tears shimmered in her green eyes. "It's not what it looks like."

"Really? Because it looks like you belong to him. Has he captured your heart? Or just your lips?" His words lashed from him, snapping like whip.

She gasped. "Harrison, I have to let him love me."

"What? Why?" Confusion and frustration boiled in his chest. "From where I'm standing, he doesn't love you at all. Can't you see that? Taking liberties until you slap him and still not letting you go. Kissing you right in front of a near stranger, for that's all I am to him. Those are not acts of love and respect! Those are the actions of a man marking his territory for both you and me to see."

"Please, you don't understand. Let me ex—"

"Truly, Sophie, if I had known a kiss was all it took to seal you as my own, I would have kissed you in Philadelphia." For he never had. He'd done the honorable thing, and hadn't tasted her lips at all because he hadn't asked her father's permission yet. There would be time for that later, he'd reasoned. "Was he your first kiss, then, or were there others in between?" *How many nights did I dream of kissing Sophie Kent? And how many of those nights was she busy kissing other men?*

She shook her head. "He was the first."

Anger exploded in his head. "So precious a gift, and you gave it to a Confederate officer? A man bent on warring against the principles you once held dear?"

"I still hold them dear!" Sophie's voice shook. "I still hold *you* dear."

Her conflicting messages disoriented him until he barely knew which way was up. "Then why, *why* do you give yourself to him?" And then a single thought snaked through him as the sound of her slap shuddered through him. Perhaps she didn't give to him as much as he took from her.

"He—I—I'm—"

The suspense ignited his imagination.

"I'm a spy!"

Like a punch, the word knocked the air from his lungs. His forehead already ached with his frown. "What?" *What was she thinking to play such a dangerous game?*

"He has information that may be useful to the Union. But I can only hear it if I continue my relationship with him!" Her breath hitched as she gripped his biceps. "I don't love him," she whispered, wide eyes gleaming in the shadowy hallway. "Please believe me, I don't love him."

It was the "Please believe me," that caused his hope to flare. That made him hold his tongue, and wait for more.

"I thought you were gone. Or dead." Her hands tented over her lips.

Harrison opened his aching arms, and she accepted his invitation, resting her forehead against his shoulder. He wrapped her in his embrace. "I'm sorry," he whispered, and kissed her hair, the delicate rose oil scent stirring his senses. "I never meant to stay away so long. But I'm here now."

She shook her head, her silken curls snagging in the stubble of his chin. She slid her hands from her face and leaned them on his chest. "You're leaving again. And soon. You must." He could barely hear her over the roaring of his thoughts. "And I must stay."

She was right. Harrison bowed his head toward hers. "Promise me you'll be careful, Sophie. If he hurts you, pushes you, or even hints that he might, I want you to stop letting him near you." He kissed her hair again, his lips brushing the top of her ear. Then her temple, then her cheek, and tasted the salt of her tears. When she lifted her face and rose on her toes, the longing he had struggled to bury resurrected. Her fingers clasped behind his neck, and he took her lips in tender passion while his hands memorized the gentle curves of her waist.

Then, cradling the back of her head with his hand, he felt a hairpin between his fingers, and fought the urge to dislodge it, to dislodge all of them. Desire swelled, and the darkness made him far too bold. *We are not man and wife that I may unbind her hair,* he told himself. *We are . . . what, exactly?*

Harrison pressed one final kiss to Sophie's lips before taking a step back, his hands cupping her shoulders. "Sophie," he breathed, "if things were different I would ask your father's permission to court you properly."

"But you can't."

"I want you to know that I would."

"If things were different."

"Yes."

But things were not different. He was an escaped prisoner of war on the run. She was a spy of Richmond. They simply could not be together.

"TROUBLES NEVER come alone, but in battalions."

—SALLIE ANN BROCK, Richmond citizen

"WE HAVE TO BE WATCHFUL and circumspect—wise as serpents—and harmless as doves, for truly the lions are seeking to devour us."

—ELIZABETH VAN LEW, Union agent in Richmond

A BATTALION OF TROUBLES

Chapter Twenty-four

Outside Richmond, Virginia Peninsula
Thursday, February 11, 1864

The baying of the bloodhounds clawed at Harrison's ears. They were getting closer, and so were their handlers, as they bounded between rivers and creeks on this marshy peninsula. He could almost feel their teeth sinking into his cold flesh. Every muscle in his body quivered with tension as he crouched behind an uprooted tree trunk, McDonald beside him. "Go!"

The two men launched out from their hiding place like arrows from their bows. Harrison pumped his legs as hard and fast as he could, deliberately crisscrossing his path with McDonald's to confuse the tracking dogs. The chilled Virginia swamp had long since soaked through the paper-thin soles of Harrison's shoes, and now sucked at his feet. Every breath seared his lungs as he chugged the wintery air, while fire raged within his thighs and calves.

Only when their bodies gave out did Harrison and McDonald

halt their excruciating race and collapse near a mound of stones. Bones bleached white with sun and time poked up from a drift of wet leaves, a reminder of the fierce fighting on this land two years ago that could have ended the war, had the Union won.

"That's the Chickahominy." Panting, McDonald pointed to a river about a hundred yards off. "We've got to cross it to get to Williamsburg, and this here is as good a place as any. Maybe better. But later." He wheezed. "Nightfall."

Harrison nodded his agreement, still struggling to refill his lungs. If the ground were not sodden with slush, he would lie flat on top of it. But if he soaked his clothes, they'd never dry out. It was an invitation pneumonia—or worse—would not refuse.

Finally, night unfurled its ruffled hem, enveloping the peninsula in darkness. Harrison and McDonald grimly stripped off their shirts, trousers, and drawers. Holding his clothes and shoes above his head, Harrison stepped into the river's current after McDonald. Shock knifed through him. The water's icy swirl sloshed against his naked body, up to his armpits as he forced his shaking legs to wade across and reminded himself to breathe.

Teeth chattering violently, Harrison reached the opposite bank and stiffly climbed out of the river onto ground nearly as wet as the river-bed. "We can't sleep on this," he muttered. Snowflakes drifted down, landing on his wet skin as he pulled his clothing back on.

"Nor in this," McDonald said, lifting his face to the white-flecked sky. "Keep going, soldier?"

"Let's go." Harrison fell into step with the major, ignoring his hunger, denying his fatigue, and praying they would not both freeze to death by dawn.

Their slogging footsteps were muffled by the snow. Wind moaned through the pine trees towering above them. As the storm wore on, branches bowed beneath their pristine burdens, occasionally breaking and sending clouds of glitter to the earth.

Beautiful, Harrison mused. *Deadly.* The North Star, their one guiding light, had disappeared behind the snow clouds. His spine tingled with warning that they had lost their way.

"You don't suppose we're headed back to Richmond, do you?" They'd been walking for hours.

"I've been praying against that. But we must travel on, even if we go back to Richmond instead of Williamsburg, or else we'll surely perish."

———

St. John's Church, Richmond, Virginia
Sunday, February 14, 1864

Shivering in her box pew, Sophie Kent stared, unseeing, at the stained glass above the altar, even after the service ended. The broken body of Robert Ford swam in her vision, brighter by far than the Bible scenes lit by the streaming sun. She had visited him in Libby's hospital yesterday and was haunted by it still. Suspecting Ford of complicity in the prison breakout, during which 109 Union officers escaped, the commandant had ordered him whipped nearly to death—five hundred lashes. He bore each one without betraying a single member of the underground. Now Ford lingered at death's door. Sophie bowed her head beneath the weight of deception and suffering and hope deferred.

"Well?" Lawrence prodded. "Are you waiting for the Almighty Himself to dismiss us?"

Looking up, she forced a smile in his direction, shrugging, as if to excuse her dazed expression. As if she had not been begging God for Robert Ford's life, for Harrison's safety—wherever he was—and for Abraham's recovery from the infection that now poisoned his thigh.

"Or are you woolgathering again?"

"Thinking, Lawrence. It's called thinking."

The church bells rang, just as they had the morning the escape had been discovered, and Sophie shuddered. In Richmond, their clear, sonorous tones had long since ceased to be a call to worship or mark of celebration. Now the clamor brought alarm, running feet, and a trickle of hope that the Union might be successful at last.

Lawrence turned his gaze straight ahead, fastened it on the light streaming in through the vibrantly colored plates. "Yes, darling. And there's a lot to think about isn't there? For instance, Oliver Shaw. How interesting that he showed up at your house the night of the breakout. And yet I haven't seen him since. Have you?"

Sophie's skin tingled under his dissecting blue gaze. "No, not since that night." It was the truth. Bella had sent word to a free colored man in the underground network. He came for the Kent house fugitives before dawn and secreted them away to a farm outside the city.

"Hmm." Lawrence seemed to study her then. "The timing, so odd. Don't you think?"

Sophie blinked, as though the connection had never occurred to her. "Oh, I suppose. He did say he'd sell his stories and then be off again to hunt for more news, didn't he?"

"Shame," Lawrence said, stretching his arm behind Sophie's shoulders. "He could have covered this one." His smile was cold and thin.

Virginia Peninsula
Monday, February 15, 1864

"There." Harrison pointed to smoke billowing from a chimney through a sky thick with snow. "So help me God, we are going in."

"Hang it, Caldwell! They're likely looking for fugitives and just itching for some kind of reward!" McDonald's lips were blue, a reflection, Harrison suspected, of his own. Snowflakes rimmed his eyelashes without melting.

They'd covered seventy-five miles by foot, Harrison guessed, tracked by dogs, soldiers, and citizens. Fatigue pulled at him like quicksand, blood crusted his feet, and hunger tore through his middle. "We didn't dig four tunnels with rats running over our faces and sewage oozing around us just to die in some field outside Williamsburg."

"We don't know where we are." McDonald looked at the sky. "You're guessing."

"We're about to find out. Follow my lead."

Harrison trudged up to the door of a modest stone house and knocked, McDonald next to him. When a white woman opened the door wearing indigo-dyed homespun, Harrison affected his best Southern accent.

"Beggin' your pardon, ma'am. But could you spare us some vittles? We just escaped from Yankee custody near Norfolk, and sure did scrape the bottom of our barrels a while back."

Her eyes widened, then misted with apparent sympathy. "Scoot on in here now, and let me see what we can rustle up. How does ham, eggs, hoecake, coffee, and buttermilk sound to you soldiers?"

"Like a whole lot of heaven, don't it, Tibbs?" Harrison elbowed McDonald. "Don't mind Tibbs here. He's a mute. But he sure can pick off them devil Yanks."

"Well, Tibbs, that's all that matters, now, isn't it?" She beamed at him, and Harrison stifled the almost foreign sensation of laughter now bubbling in his chest.

As they ate, their benefactress sat across from them and described exactly where nearby Yankee units were located. "So's you can avoid 'em on your way home."

Harrison grinned at McDonald's stunned expression. "Thank you kindly, ma'am, and much obliged."

By nightfall, they were safely behind Union lines.

———

Kent House, Richmond, Virginia
Tuesday, March 1, 1864

Outside the kitchen house, the pewter sky wept as Bella placed a cool rag on Abraham's fevered brow. Lois and Sophie were in the main house, but Pearl, Emiline, and Rachel all sat at the table, rolling bandages from strips of petticoats and old linens. Terrified country folk had poured into the city yesterday, warning of Union marauders north of Richmond. The tocsin sent five battalions of the home defense brigade rushing to the front, while women and the infirm readied for an onslaught of injured men.

"Won't be long now," Bella whispered, her voice blending with the drumming rain outside. As much as she had wanted to plot their escape from Richmond, Abraham was in no condition for the journey, especially not in this cold, wet weather. This raid—the one Sophie had learned of from Miss Van Lew weeks ago—could be their deliverance.

The Union plan, as understood by the Richmond underground, had been a bold one, to put it mildly, from the start. With fewer than four thousand troops, they intended to attack from the North, free all twelve thousand Union prisoners at Libby and Belle Isle, and together set fire to the city and capture Confederate leaders. *If the Union believes the prisoners strong enough to aid the soldiers, then Harrison hasn't published his story yet.* She trusted he'd at least mailed her letter to her daughter Liberty.

The broken-down condition of the Yankee prisoners wasn't the only thing the Union didn't know. A Rebel clerk named Erasmus Ross had told the underground that Turner had planted kegs of gunpowder in the basement, enough to blow up the prison and all its inhabitants, which he vowed to do rather than let them fall into Yankee hands.

Bella stared out the window now. Flames cracked like whips in the fireplace over the steady breathing of slaves preparing bandages for soldiers who would not come.

And then, thunder. Dishes rattled, windows shivered. Bella looked at Abraham, whose eyelids fluttered open. He locked eyes with her. "Artillery," he rasped. "Mile distant."

Bella paced the cramped quarters of the kitchen house, wringing her hands, listening, waiting.

"You gonna wear out my floor, child, plus you making me dizzy," Pearl said.

Bella eased to the floor again by her husband's side. "Well, Abe? Ready to be shed of this place?"

A smile tugged at his lips. "Been ready for some time."

So had Bella. Daphne's directive to stay until Sophie was all right weighed lightly on her. Sophie seemed to be managing her grief, her household, and her spy work just fine lately. The young woman was stronger, perhaps, than Daphne had realized. That scar on her wrist in the shape of a knife's edge—it could have been from anything, though she never had the nerve to ask. Besides, Bella was so on edge for Abraham, and so lonesome for Liberty and her own freedom, she was light-headed with anticipation. Finally, the end was in sight. *If only we knew what happened to Harrison . . .*

"We've got a wedding to plan when we get home," Bella said, joy rippling pleasantly over her uncertainty.

"Or maybe Liberty's got it all planned out."

"I expect she might." After all, Bella had been gone almost three months, rather than the three weeks she had planned. "In that case, I'll just let her tell me all about it, and get started on a wedding quilt for her and Silas."

Closing her eyes, the booming artillery swept Bella back to Gettysburg, when the fighting last summer had invaded their homes and changed their lives forever. The sounds of battle had terrified then, and now, here in Richmond, it was a symphony of hope. Soon enough, she'd be home again with her family, in a land already healing from its wounds. Perhaps a fresh blanket of snow covered the scarred ground already, and kept any foul vapors locked tight within the frozen earth. Oh, how she longed to go home. To Liberty. To freedom.

Suddenly, Bella turned toward the window. "No." She rose up from the floor and hurried outside into the rain to listen.

The artillery had stopped.

— · —

Cold seeped into Sophie through the cupola glass, and yet she pressed closer, willing the strains of the contest to crescendo.

Footsteps murmured up the stairs, bringing Bella to Sophie's side at the window. "No smoke," Sophie whispered, and sensed Bella deflate.

From every direction, the view was as ordinary as it had ever been. No Rebel troops beating a hasty retreat back into the city. No bluecoats at their heels. Nothing but rain pounded the city. "Another failure." Bella's tone was flat. Spent. "We cannot wait for another raid, another Union debacle. Abraham and I have got to go on our own. Now."

Sophie grabbed Bella's hands, and saw her own apprehension reflecting in Bella's shining brown eyes. She also saw Daphne. "Bella, I beg you, have a care. Abraham isn't well enough." After losing Daphne, she could not bear the thought that now Bella and Abraham would put their lives at risk, as well.

Water streamed in rivulets down the pane behind Bella. "You are not our keeper." But her tone was gentle, sympathetic to Sophie's obvious logic.

"Fischer is gone, and Captain Russell never enters the kitchen house. As long as Abraham remains there, you have nothing to fear."

"We aren't free here. You've been kind as can be, Sophie-girl, but our season here is at its close. We need liberty the way our lungs need air."

A jagged lump shifted sharply in Sophie's throat. "Of course. But if you leave now, you'll never make it."

"Two weeks, then." Bella's voice left no room for argument. "Time enough for Abraham to heal."

"All right." Sophie released a breath. "I'll make arrangements with McNiven and Rowley for March 14."

———

Fortress Monroe, Virginia
Saturday, March 12, 1864

Towel thrown over his shoulder, Harrison Caldwell swirled shaving soap on his face, then carefully drew the razor against his stubble. With thirty-two days between him and his imprisonment, the sharp angles of his cheeks and jaw had softened somewhat, and his muscles had begun to build again with proper nourishment and exercise. Not a day passed that he did not thank God that he'd been one of the lucky ones.

Of the 109 officers who escaped, two drowned crossing the Chickahominy in the wrong place, and forty-eight were recaptured. Colonel Thomas Rose was taken by Rebel soldiers dressed in Union jackets. Harrison could not imagine his devastation as they threw him back into Libby's dungeon.

After Harrison arrived at Fortress Monroe with Union cavalry escort, he spoke with General Butler personally about the prisoner exchange program and conditions at Libby. Then, true to his original intent, he wrote an unparalleled story about Libby Prison and the escape, and sold it, ironically, to the *New York Tribune*. His report, and other eyewitness accounts from other escapees, had prompted a groundswell of Northern outrage over the Rebels' treatment of war prisoners. Under pressure from the public, Congress appointed a Joint Select Committee on the Conduct of the War to investigate conditions in the prisons. At the same time, the United States Sanitary Commission began its own inquiry. Harrison could not have hoped for a better reception.

"Caldwell," an officer called, breaking Harrison's reverie. "Butler's asking for you. He's outside."

Rinsing his razor in the wash basin, Harrison swiped a hand over his smooth face and dried it with his towel before shrugging his shirt on and tucking it into his trousers.

Outside, General Benjamin Butler's small black eyes shone above the heavy bags drooping from his lower eyelids. "How about a walk?"

Though Butler's paunch strained his brass buttons, Harrison suspected the stroll had more to do with Harrison's craving for fresh air than the balding general's need for exercise.

Falling into step beside the bulldog of a man beside him, Harrison inhaled the salty breeze while seagulls squawked over Hampton Roads.

"Still writing stories?" Butler asked.

"I am," Harrison replied. "There are more stories here, among your soldiers, contrabands, and the missionaries teaching them, than there are in Philadelphia. I hope you don't mind me staying on for a bit longer?"

"I don't want you back in Philadelphia. But I don't want you here anymore, either."

Harrison frowned. "Beg pardon?"

"Need you back in Richmond," Butler growled. "As a spy."

His feet froze. "You can't be serious."

"Nobody's looking for you. Besides, who would recognize you there? Other prisoners won't see you. Erasmus Ross is on our side. Even if you see Dick Turner, I'm certain he wouldn't recognize you now. You've lost that gaunt look, you're not spotted with lice—and didn't you tell me even your hair grew back a different color?"

Harrison ran his hand over his head. "But you have spies. Aren't you working Elizabeth Van Lew and her network?"

"I need more. And you have a natural gift for it."

"All due respect, General, but how would you know a thing like that?"

"I learned much from you, remember." He motioned to a nearby park bench, and they sat on it, staring out over the impressive fleet of Union ships harbored in the bay. Down toward the water, two men were loading sick or wounded soldiers onto a horse-drawn railroad car to take them to the hospital.

"You spied when you infiltrated the South to write the Weeping Time story," Butler was saying. "You invented an alias for yourself, Oliver Shaw, that carried you and your colored companion through

Rebel lines to get South, and then through a party with Confederate officers, plus a chance meeting with a Rebel captain the very night of the escape. Your story about being a Rebel prisoner escaped from Norfolk was so convincing a secesh woman directed you to our units." The general paused for breath, stroked his mustache downward. "You see, Caldwell. You have no problem getting the information you want, and using it to your advantage. Do what you do best. Write for a newspaper. Get the information the Union wants and use it to our advantage."

Possibility burned in Harrison's belly as he considered Butler's words. They spelled trouble, sure enough. *And don't I always head for trouble?*

"Aside from your accidental foray into Libby Prison, you've been writing about the war as an observer," Butler said. "It's time to put those keen powers of observation to use in a more direct way for your country. Help end this war."

Colonel Rose's warm handshake and parting words rushed back to Harrison. *You've proven yourself to be one of us—an observer no more. Now onward, to finish the race set before us, yes?* And now this colonel languished in chains, in an absolute misery of rat-infested darkness while Harrison tasted the mist of the sea on his lips. Bella and Abraham were stuck as well, and Sophie . . . Sophie was already risking her life to spy. In Richmond.

"I'll do it."

"Glad to hear it, Mr. Shaw." A rare smirk slanted on General Butler's puffy face. "Your passage is already arranged. That blasted Robert Ould refuses to exchange prisoners with me. But we'll see what happens when I send him six hundred Rebel prisoners of war. With those boys in sight of their homeland and Richmond cheering for their safe return, will he turn them away then? He'd be mobbed for it, or worse. No, he will accept the boys I send him and give us our own in return. Mark it well."

"And I'll be on the ship with them." Harrison nodded. Truly, it was perfect. In the mad rush of prisoners returning home, no one would notice him at all. If they did, they would hail him a hero without a second thought. With a little dirt on his face, and some tattered clothes, he'd fit right in. "When do I leave?"

"Tomorrow."

Chapter Twenty-five

Rocketts Landing, Richmond, Virginia
Sunday, March 13, 1864

The crush of the crowd pressed Sophie against Lawrence as they fought their way down to the docks. The Armory Band filled the air with boisterous patriotic music, and Sophie felt every drumbeat in her chest. Mere moments ago at St. John's Church, the reverend announced that for the first time since last year, Rebel prisoners of war were coming home. Six hundred, to be exact. They waved from two over-packed truce boats now approaching the wharf. It seemed as though half of Richmond had come to Rocketts straight from their church services to greet them.

Shock and nervous hope buzzed through Sophie's veins as she considered that perhaps she was about to reunite with her father. Would she recognize him? Would he, her? How drastically the war had altered each of them!

"He may not be here, you know," Lawrence warned, rationally. Six hundred was nothing compared to the thousands still captive in the North.

She nodded, rather than compete with the noise of the cheering throng. Then, the Armory Band faded, but strains of music still carried on the water.

"They're singing!" a woman shouted, pointing at the decks bristled with soldiers.

Then Sophie heard it, too. *Hurrah, hurrah, for Southern rights, hurrah!* The Rebel soldiers were serenading the crowd. Their joy caught in Sophie's throat. Around her, Richmonders thrust their handkerchiefs and hats in the air, waving them madly. "Hip, hip, hurrah!" they shouted. "Hip, hip, hurrah!" The Army Band struck up the tune of "Dixie," and in one ethereal moment, Sophie was transported to the beginning of the war, when Richmond had been sending their sons to battle, so confident they'd return as victors in less than ninety days. The tears that choked her were bittersweet.

As the vessels loomed larger, shouts of recognition rang from boat to shore and back again. Then the first boat touched. A hush fell over the crowd as the first soldiers disembarked.

"Father!" a child cried out, and Sophie was filled with sudden longing for her own. "I see Father!" The crowd opened a lane for them, and the little girl ran into her father's open arms, clutching a small Confederate flag in one chubby fist.

One by one, the soldiers filed off the boat, some clearly searching for loved ones they did not see, while others fell into embraces they'd surely dreamed of. They were lean, yes, but not hollow like the Libby prisoners, or emaciated like the men of Belle Isle. The crowd onshore swelled and swirled around Sophie as hundreds debarked at the gangway. When her father was not among them, the tide of disappointment threatened to carry her away.

She tugged on Lawrence's arm. "I don't see him," she said. "Let's go."

His arm around her waist, Lawrence guided her to the fringes of the crowd.

A broad hand grasped her arm. Her heart nearly stopped as she turned. "Daddy?" she gasped.

"Hello, Goldilocks." He was thinner, with more grey at his temples than before, but his complexion was hale enough, his eyes bright, and as blue as the Virginia sky in spring.

"Thank God you're all right!" Of course he was. This was the man she had thought of as Zeus throughout her childhood. Sophie threw her arms around his waist, melting into her father like the small child with her flag. Citizens and soldiers surged around them, parting like river around rocks.

"And this young man here? Captain Russell, I presume?"

"A pleasure, and a very great honor, to meet you, sir." Lawrence pumped his hand heartily.

"You've been keeping an eye on my Sophie, have you? I am indebted."

"The pleasure has been mine, I assure you, sir. Refreshments are to be served at Capitol Square by President Davis himself. Would you care to go?"

Preston shook his head. "Thank you, Captain, but there is no place I'd rather be than home at this moment. It's not full of boarders, is it?"

Sophie told him it wasn't.

"Good. Then we'll have room for this one."

Sophie's eyes rounded with confusion. Her gaze skittered from left to right.

And landed on Harrison Caldwell. His brown eyes sent a jolt down her spine.

"Shaw?" Lawrence stepped forward. "What in heaven's name are you doing here?"

"Nice seeing you again, too." Harrison gave Lawrence an easy grin as he shook his hand. "Decided to cover the prisoner exchange from the perspective of the released. Did you know Rooney, General Lee's son, was on that boat? Now that's a story if there ever was one."

"You know each other already? Sophie?" Preston asked, looking as delighted as Sophie was aghast.

Words webbed in her chest.

"How do you do, Miss Kent?" Harrison took up the silence, bowing to her. Sophie marveled at the difference a month of freedom had made in his physique. "We met in November, I believe it was, and I swung around last month but I've been away, otherwise. Chasing leads, and all of that business."

"Quite right, quite right," Preston said. "When I was your age, I did the same. And I had a family at home," he added, as if to justify Harrison's vagabond reporter's lifestyle.

"I do apologize for interrupting such a poignant moment in your family. Russell, how are things at the Ordnance Bureau?" He pulled Lawrence aside, giving Preston and Sophie space to talk.

"Tredegar is desperate for skilled laborers . . ." Lawrence's voice faded as they stepped away.

"I—you—met him on the boat?" Sophie grasped to make sense of it all.

"I did. He's a reporter without a paper." Preston shook his head. "Tough place to be. I told him he could stay with us as long as he's in Richmond. Lodging was impossible to get in Richmond when I left with the army in '62. I imagine it's only gotten worse. But enough of Mr. Shaw! Let me look at my little girl."

Preston's smile wilted as the significance of Sophie's black dress registered in his eyes. It was easier to deny his wife's death when he was away, Sophie guessed. Now he'd have to face home and hearth without Eleanor. He rubbed his hand over his face, and seemed to age ten more years. "Oh, Sophie. You have endured so much. Come, daughter. Let's go home."

Harrison waved them along. "I'm going to Capitol Square with Russell, here. I'll be along later, after you've had some time together."

Sophie took Preston's proffered arm, still barely able to believe he was home at all. Let alone with his new friend and boarder, Oliver Shaw.

––––––

Lawrence Russell eyed Oliver Shaw as they strolled through Capitol Square, chagrined that even though he'd met Sophie's father at the docks, this Marylander was already ahead of him in the first impressions department. Perhaps it wouldn't have bothered him so much if Sophie had not looked so spellbound to see him again. *Unfair,* he chided himself. *She was in shock at seeing her father with almost no warning whatever.* Truthfully, Lawrence was quite surprised himself. He'd begun to wonder if she had a father at Fort Delaware at all, or if that was only a convenient smokescreen. *Like me.*

"Forgive me, Shaw, but just how did you manage to secure a place in Mr. Kent's home before you even got off the boat?" Lawrence was careful to smile as he asked the question.

"Oh yes, isn't that fortunate?" Shaw chuckled. Lawrence didn't. "At the start of the trip I noticed him having trouble reading the fine print of a newspaper, so I simply offered to read it for him. Being a reporter myself, I couldn't help but make commentary on the editorial, and he pegged me as a journalist right away and introduced himself simply as Preston. I went about the ship, interviewing other soldiers. After I'd spoken with several of them, Preston asked me more about myself, and I told him I work independently, hoping to sell my stories. When he heard that, he insisted I stay at his home while in Richmond. He even said he would help me get a staff position at one of the papers if at all possible. As I said. Fortunate."

"Quite. Well. How very satisfactory for you. And for Miss Kent."
"How's that?"

"She has her father back, of course." His eyes narrowed into slits.
"Yes, yes, of course. Sorry, would you excuse me?"

Lawrence watched as Shaw approached Jefferson Davis and introduced himself.

"Well, Mr. Davis, how does it feel to have six hundred soldiers back at long last?" he asked.

"I promised to get them back in the field at once, and that is what I intend to do." The president's response belied his previous role as the U.S. Secretary of War.

"Do you suppose, Mr. President, that they really want to return to hard service after being so long in prison already?"

Davis pointed to three small boys playing on the granite pedestal of the Washington statue, around the knees of Thomas Jefferson, Patrick Henry, and George Mason. "It may seem hard, but even those young lads will have their turn."

"Indeed, sir. And how will you feed the army? I hear it can barely be done."

Lawrence leaned in, eager to hear the answer himself. Davis straightened to regal heights before responding. "I don't see why rats, if fat, are not as good as squirrels. Our boys did eat mule meat at Vicksburg, and nowadays that would be considered a great luxury."

Rats, indeed. Lawrence turned away in disgust.

"Rats?" It was Graham, clerk in the Commissary Department, at Lawrence's side.

"Afraid so. Tell me, now, would this despicable predicament be in spite of or because of Commissary General Northrop?"

Graham scowled, shook his head. "Hard to say. If the cure for our ailing government were pointing fingers, we'd be hearty and hale long ere this day, that much is sure."

"Speaking of—is Hayes still laid out with the grippe?"

"He is. He's got awful aim, too. Revolting." Graham shuddered, jowls quivering. "Say, who's that fellow talking with Davis now? Looks familiar, somehow."

"Oliver Shaw."

Graham frowned. "Not the reporter from Maryland."

"The same."

"Splendid! Think we'll see more of him? He's a great storyteller, that one."

"Quite." Lawrence shaded his eyes as he measured him. He wasn't entirely convinced Shaw's stories were confined to the news. *Baseless.* His head ached with paranoia, had ever since that raid two weeks ago. The timing, if not the size of the Union forces, had been so well-suited, he couldn't shake the suspicion that the Federals had been tipped off from someone inside Richmond. Orders found on the dead Union colonel's body detailed the plan to set all the prisoners free, kill Davis and the cabinet members, and set fire to the city. Completely outside the bounds of civilized warfare. No Union general admitted to giving the orders. The Northern press said they were forged by the Confederacy, but Lawrence didn't believe that. No Southerner did.

At least, no loyal Southerner. The elusive Richmond Underground was growing bigger, stronger, more dangerous all the time. Lawrence scanned the jubilant crowd teeming in Capitol Square. Any one of them could be disloyal. Any one of them could be a spy. His gaze settled on Oliver Shaw only to find that the reporter's assessing gaze was already fastened upon Lawrence.

———

"Just a moment, Daddy. Let me go ask Pearl to make you as fine a feast as we can." *And warn Bella and Abraham to stay out of sight!* Sophie's warm drawl held no hint of the urgency scuttling through her.

"Where's Fischer?" Preston cocked his head, as if listening for the footsteps of his combination steward, butler, manservant.

"Oh! Let me help you." She unfastened the top button of his cloak.

"It's Fischer's job. Where is he? Taking Sunday off? You haven't gotten lax with the staff in my absence, have you?"

Sophie slid the coat off his shoulders and hung it on the hall stand. "I'll tell you about that just as soon as I set Pearl to cooking, all right?" She offered a half smile, then turned to walk away.

"Sophia Virginia. You'll tell me now, young lady." He stalked into the parlor, swiped a finger on the mantel, checking for dust, then sat on the settee. "Sit."

With only a small marble-topped table between them, she lowered herself onto the crimson armchair, her pleated black skirts billowing around her. A brisk breeze swept through the open window, clearing her senses. "I had to dismiss him."

"You what?"

"Dismissed him."

"Whatever for?" His voice boomed, and she glanced at the open windows and imagined the neighbors rushing to theirs.

"He defied my authority." Her words were even and cool, though her neck itched beneath her collar. "He questioned my choices."

"What choices?" Preston spread his hands. "Otto Fischer has been a proven, loyal servant. He knows how I like things done. If he questioned you, is it not possible you needed to reconsider your decisions?"

Sophie bristled. "Daddy. If there's one thing you've taught me, it's that we do not abide rebellion in our help and that's exactly what Fischer displayed. I did not imagine that he was immune to that rule. Does it apply only to the slaves, then? Or does absolute authority belong only to you?"

Preston sat back, eyebrows arched high in his brow. She had stunned him, she could tell. But she wasn't finished. "That was not the only reason, either. Times are hard, Daddy. Flour is at two hundred twenty dollars a barrel, and meal is sixteen dollars a bushel. A pair of secondhand shoes costs almost twenty dollars at auction—more than a month's pay! And this is only the beginning of our basic needs. Dismissing Fischer eased our financial strain, at least in part."

He leaned forward, elbows on his knees. Furrows bracketed his mouth. "Two hundred twenty? Are you sure?"

She nodded. "Prices soar higher every week."

"Where is Fischer now?"

"I don't know. He's no longer my concern. Or yours. Things are not the way you left them."

His gaze slid to her hands, and she realized she had balled her handkerchief in her fist again. Just like her mother.

"You've been forced to grow up in my absence, Sophie. I do not mean to criticize."

Thoughts of Eleanor hung in the air between them, so thickly Sophie felt she would choke on them. Her mourning gown, which she had worn for six months already, a chafing reminder of her death. Would he not even say her mother's name?

"You left us when we needed you most. You left me." Tears bit her eyes, but she blinked them back. "You left Mother."

He tugged at the collar of his shirt. "I doubt she even knew I was gone."

A brittle laugh broke from Sophie's lips. "On the contrary. She asked for you every day. Every hour, some days. I defended you, over and over and over again. I used words like honor and duty, sacrifice and service. I made her believe that you loved her right up until the end, though you were never here when she wanted you."

Preston kneaded the back of his neck, stared at the fraying seams of his shoes. "Well. It's in the past now. And she died well, you said, which is the most important thing."

"I lied." The words were blades, and she thrust them from her.

Preston flinched. *Good.* She wanted him to feel something of the agony she had borne on his behalf, and hers.

"Yes, I wanted to spare you additional pain while you were in prison, rotting and in despair, for all I knew. But now you're home, and whole, when I had to amputate a piece of my heart to survive." She beat her fist to her chest. "It doesn't grow back." Exhilaration flooded her senses as she unleashed the truth upon him. Some secrets were too toxic to bear alone.

And yet he did not ask for details. Did not plead to know her last words, or the expression on her face in death's slumber. *Coward.* "Don't you want to know how it really ended, Daddy? The truth?"

The rims of his eyes grew red. "I do not."

"She was mad. Not just forgetful or prone to headaches and crying spells, but completely, utterly, violently insane, until I feared I would follow her into distraction myself." The words spilled over each other recklessly, like boulders down a mountainside, heedless of their damage, wanting only to find rest at the bottom.

"Stop." His voice was hoarse, but she wouldn't, couldn't, obey.

"Daphne and I took turns not just as nursemaid, but guard, so she would not harm herself or others."

"I beg of you, stop!"

"She should have been in the sanitarium. If you hadn't been so proud about the family name, maybe they could have helped her. Maybe she'd still be alive. But as it was, I was so desperate for it all to end, and so was Mother." Sophie held out her arm and tugged up her sleeve, exposing the thin white line slashed across her wrist. "She—"

"Enough!" Her father's rage sliced the explanation from her lips. He lunged from his seat, grabbed Sophie's shoulders and shook her.

Her words retreated in the face of the wildness staring her down. There was a savage element in Preston's gaze she'd seen only once before, right before Susan disappeared. But he'd never touched Sophie in anger before. Now he raised his hand in readiness to strike her.

"No!" Sophie shouted.

Unable to ignore the sound of Sophie's cry, Abraham crossed the yard from the kitchen house and burst through the back door to search for her attacker. She had harbored both him and Bella for weeks, months. Surely his vow not to enter the main house, as a safeguard for himself, should be broken in order to protect her.

Urged on by masculine instinct, Abraham charged into the parlor, and found himself face-to-face with a white man who was turning redder by the moment.

Sophie lunged for the man's hand, pulling him back, away from

Abraham, abject fear written on her face. "D-Daddy, it's a-all-all right." The stammer proved it wasn't. If this was Sophie's father and he had just been released from prison, Abraham could well imagine his state of mind. Finding a strange colored man in his home was surely a shock, especially given what Sophie had told him about his past.

"Who is this boy? What are you doing in my house?" He picked up a Grecian urn and swung it over his head. The fire in his eyes crackled with hatred and pain—and fear.

Sophie pulled on his upraised arm, but he elbowed her back. She stumbled backward, blood trickling from her lip.

"Get back!" he shouted to her. "In the name of heaven, cease your fighting and rebelling!"

Abraham held out his hands as he would to a stallion not yet broken. "I'm no enemy, sir. I mean you no harm."

"Who is your master?"

"I am my own."

Mr. Kent's eyelids flared, and the lines of his face tensed for battle. In that instant, they were no longer two men in a parlor, but a Confederate soldier defending his home against a Yankee Negro, for surely his Northern accent gave that much away. Abraham scanned the room for a weapon with which to defend himself.

Suddenly, white hot anger ate through Abraham's veins like acid that he should be already sentenced to punishment, without trial or even conversation. Swiping a fire poker from its stand, he thrust it toward Preston's chest, his aim meant for every Rebel soldier who had massacred captured Negro soldiers, for Turner, who had whipped his wife, and for every warden and guard at Libby who had treated the colored prisoners like slaves. Releasing his pent-up rage, Abraham charged the symbol of everything he hated.

Preston parried, stumbled, fumbled, and dropped the vase with a thud on the carpet. His eyes shone with apparent shock. Panic, perhaps. A dark smile curled on Abraham's face, pulling against his teeth.

For once, the colored man has the upper hand. Palms slick with sweat, he gripped his crude lance as he drove nearer his target.

Someone was screaming. As long as it wasn't Bella, Abraham didn't care. Preston tripped on the claw foot of the table, and suddenly he was on the floor, the hollow of his throat pulsing against the tip of Abraham's weapon.

"Please . . ." A whisper. "He's my father."

Abraham flicked a gaze at Sophie, her face as pale as bleached linen, then riveted his attention again on the white man quivering in fear beneath him. "He deserves this."

Then, *You are not a murderer.* His own conscience, fighting to be heard amid the deafening clamor of Abraham's fury. *Do not justify his fear of colored men.* But he wanted to. For moments on end, his muscles tight with anticipation, he wanted to unchain the drive he had collared for months in Libby Prison. To kill an aggressive white man the way white men killed his fellow prisoners. Weren't the captured Negroes fathers, too? Didn't their children mourn their daddies as much as Sophie would, or more?

Vengeance is mine, I will repay. God's words. Not Abraham's.

In a flash of staggering awareness, Abraham threw the fire poker away from himself. As it clattered on the hearth, he dropped to his knees, bowed his head, and shuddered at how close he'd come to committing murder. *Forgive me,* he prayed.

"Daddy, don't!"

A whoosh of air. The crack of the urn shattering upon Abraham's skull. Blazing, throbbing pain.

Darkness.

Chapter Twenty-six

What have you done? Sophie stared at this man, her father, wanting to believe he was an imposter instead. She knew Preston's views on slavery, but she had never—not once—seen him physically harm another human being, regardless of their skin color. But now that he had subdued Abraham, he was a wild bull again, stamping and snorting, as if to dare anyone else to challenge his authority in his own home. The wind lifted Preston's thatch of greying hair from his forehead, and Sophie noticed a scar that hadn't been there before. *Were you beaten at Fort Delaware, the way you beat down Abraham?* But the taste of blood crowded the words from her mouth.

"Do you know this man?" Preston asked her, but her voice had completely left her.

In the next moment, Lois bustled into the parlor, nearly dropping her dusting rags at the sight of Sophie's father, and Abraham on the floor.

"Hello, Lois," Preston said. "Come in, please. The cat's got Sophie's tongue again, and I want you to help me. Who is this boy?"

Dread coiled within Sophie as she sought Lois's eyes, but the woman kept her gaze submissively pinned to the floor.

"Lois," Preston continued. "Your sister, your son, and your daughter are all gone." Esther, whom Sophie could have saved. Joseph, the little boy who was auctioned off before he became a threat to the master who could not abide a colored male in the house. Fran, Susan's maidservant who was sold away when Susan vanished. "I hear that times are tight. I wouldn't be opposed to selling Emiline or Rachel—you choose—for some extra cash. Unless, of course, you tell me who this intruder is."

Sophie could not breathe. *If she tells the truth . . .* yet how could Lois keep silent, when her own daughter would be the cost?

"He—he a blacksmith. Freeman."

"A blacksmith. I see. And just what was he doing here?"

The back door slammed. Footsteps came tumbling through the hall. Bella appeared in the doorway. Stiffened.

"Daphne. Do you know anything about this man here?"

Sophie's heart lodged in her throat as Bella gasped and knelt by her husband.

"Abraham!" She scooped his head onto her lap, dabbed his forehead with the corner of her apron, murmured in his ear.

"Ah. Lovers. I'm sorry, Daphne. Apparently, my daughter did not enforce all of our rules in my absence. But I'm home now, and I will not abide a colored man on the property."

A knock on the front door echoed in the hall. Eager for the interruption, Sophie managed to answer it.

"Hello, darling." Lawrence kissed her cheek. "You look ill! Are you?"

She shook her head as she closed the door behind them both. Lawrence followed the sound of Preston's voice, Sophie behind him.

In the parlor, a stiff spring breeze chilled the sweat beading at Bella's hairline. "A blacksmith, you say?" Captain Russell asked. "Daphne, does he work at Tredegar?"

273

She shook her head.

"But he's free. Yes?"

A nod.

"Where is his pass?"

Bella locked eyes with Sophie. His papers, and Bella's, would be coming in the morning with the men who would spirit them away to freedom, at the cost of six thousand Confederate dollars. But right now, he didn't have one.

"No pass, then? Mr. Kent, according to the law, this man should be sold back into slavery."

Tears streamed down Bella's face as she gripped the husband who was already slipping away from her. "You're a freeman," she muttered. "Free. You're free." As if repeating the truth could prevent him being sold into the slavery he fought against.

"Daddy, no—"

"He was found on your property," the captain continued. "He belongs to you. If you have no use for him here—"

"I don't."

"Daddy, w-wait!"

"You're free." Bella heard nothing else, saw nothing else, but Abraham. Then she saw nothing at all, as darkness numbed the ripping away of her hope.

———

Tredegar Iron Works
Sunday, March 13, 1864

Sooty smells of coal and iron nudged Abraham as much as the jarring of hammers on anvils. Head throbbing, he wondered how he'd gotten to his blacksmith shop in Gettysburg already—and why he wasn't at his house for a spell instead. Had he been ill for the entire journey home from Richmond? *I don't even remember the agents coming for us.* Deeply, he inhaled, too disoriented to indulge in relief just yet.

"Abraham." A man's voice. Unfamiliar. Abraham squinted at him, but the sun streaming in through the window at his back rendered him no more than a silhouette. "They said your name was Abraham. You coming round?"

Pushing himself up on his elbows, Abraham shook his head to clear the haze.

"Good. They also said you were a blacksmith. And Lord knows I have need of that."

Nodding, Abraham looked around as he swung his legs over the side of the cot. The sun-streaked room was filled with them, and the cots were filled with Negroes. *A barracks? Am I with a colored regiment at Camp William Penn?* "Where am I?"

"Home." The man gestured to the doorway, and Abraham followed him outside. "Welcome to Tredegar Iron Works."

Abraham's limbs turned to lead even as knots of defeat ripened in his stomach.

"I'm Joseph R. Anderson, the owner."

"Of Tredegar."

"And of you."

No. Not this. Brick smokestacks loomed all around Abraham, like sentinels over the Confederacy's ironmaker. His spirit railed against them. *If I am made to work here, I might as well be forging the shackles of slavery!*

"But I think you'll find the arrangement very agreeable here. Food and clothing provided, of course. My supervisors don't whip the laborers, except for theft, drinking, card playing, direct disobedience of orders, that sort of thing. I much prefer positive incentives, and so does my workforce. You'll work ten hours per day, and for every day you work beyond the required twenty-four per month, you'll receive seven dollars and fifty cents cash to spend or save as you like."

Anderson's voice droned on as he strolled through the plant,

Abraham following. The massive complex, puffing and screeching between the canal and the James River, boasted a spike mill, rolling mill, locomotive shop, foundry, boring mill, carpenter shop, machine shop, boiler shop, blacksmith shop, brass foundry, armory rolling mill, gun foundry, cartwheel foundry, and more. Three large buildings provided worker housing for slave laborers owned by the ironworks, while white laborers came in daily from their own homes. A hospital offered medical care on the premises. And guards patrolled the perimeter.

"You'll start tomorrow, Abraham." Anderson fixed his intense but not unkind gaze upon him.

Tomorrow. The day he and Bella were to make their escape. Clenching his teeth, Abraham resolved to keep looking for another way out and prayed Bella would leave without him.

Kent House, Richmond, Virginia
Monday, March 14, 1864

"Bella!" Sophie's voice dragged Bella back to wakefulness. "You were supposed to go! Abraham would have wanted you to go home, we don't know when there will be another chance!"

A trace of alarm trickled through Bella as she roused herself from the pallet by the door. In the firelight, Sophie was wild-eyed, her hair rebelling against its braid and spilling over the shoulders of her dressing gown. "I missed it? But I was right here, I would have heard, I would have woken up!"

"It's five o'clock. They should have been here an hour ago. Unless something went awry . . ."

The ladder creaked as Lois climbed down its rungs. Shuffling over, she sank onto her heels, tears glistening in wobbly tracks on her face. "I'm sorry, child. I know you wanted to get home. But my babies ain't never had their taste of freedom yet. Figured it was time they had their turn."

Understanding penetrated into Bella's hazy mind. "The tea."

Lois nodded. "Told you it would help you sleep." She'd laced it with laudanum, and sent Emiline and Rachel with the agents instead. "I lost too many loves. I had to send my girls away to freedom. Missy Sophie, I know you'd never hurt us, but your daddy is another story. I had to do what I could for my girls. They got their whole lives ahead of them."

Bella exhaled and nodded. She knew exactly what it was to send a child away for her own good. Hadn't she done it herself? "I understand." Bella's ache to see Liberty now was nowhere near what Lois's ache must have been for Rachel and Emiline to be free. "Then I guess my place is here, until Abraham can be free with me." The idea of leaving Abraham in bondage would not have set right with her.

Lois nodded, wiped her nose, and went back up the ladder to bed.

Sophie sat on her heels, clearly stunned.

"Listen," Bella said. "As long as we're here in Richmond, we've got work to do. God does not abandon the work of His hands. Now. Dawn's coming soon enough. We best get ready for the day."

Kent House, Richmond, Virginia
Monday, March 14, 1864

Something rippled through Sophie's middle as she swept down the stairs for dinner. After six months of mourning, she had finally shed her stiff, black dresses. Tonight, she wore a lavender taffeta gown with square neckline and triple flounces of lace trimming her three-quarter length sleeves. Nervously, Sophie patted her hair in its chignon at the base of her neck.

Preston, Lawrence, and Harrison rose as she entered the parlor, trying not to think of the horrid scene that had played out there just yesterday afternoon when Abraham was taken away. Madeline Blair had accepted Sophie's invitation to join them for dinner tonight, and her smile now revealed just how delighted she was not to be dining alone. Even though her own two sons were not home yet, she seemed genuinely thrilled that Sophie's father, at least, had returned.

"What a vision," Lawrence said, but it was Harrison who startled her with the tenderness in his gaze. She hadn't had a moment alone with him since he'd arrived at Rocketts yesterday. Questions burned to be asked.

"Shall we?" Preston led the way to the dining room.

Lawrence seated Sophie, then himself, beside her, while Preston did the same for Mrs. Blair. Harrison sent her a smile from across the table, and her blood warmed in response. It was not at all how she'd imagined seeing him again. But then, she hadn't allowed herself to indulge in that sort of fancy at all.

Preston said grace for the meal, and Lois and Bella served the best Pearl could offer on their Wedgewood china: pork and baked beans, sweet potatoes, stewed apples. These days, it was a feast for a conquering hero indeed. Thankfully, her father had recovered from the news that Rachel and Emiline had run away. At least enough for him to engage in pleasant conversation at dinner.

"What do you hear from your boys?" Preston asked Mrs. Blair. "Hard to believe they're all old enough to fight for their country already."

Joel isn't, Sophie thought. *And he certainly isn't old enough to die for it.* But she held her tongue and smiled encouragingly to her favorite neighbor.

Mrs. Blair lifted her chin. "Last I heard, there was a great revival among Lee's boys, and mine. Preaching nearly every night, and baptisms, too. 'Times are hard, but we trust God to bring us through it,' Asher writes. And didn't the psalmist say that 'Blessed is the nation whose God is the Lord'?"

"Indeed, Psalm 33, verse twelve. A great comfort for all of us," Preston said. "How is your youngest getting along?"

"As fine as any of them as far as I can tell. You'll forgive me for being terribly proud of all my boys."

"Now that's a pride that's fitting." Preston raised his glass. "To all our boys in the field, and their mothers at home."

Sophie lifted her glass along with Harrison and Lawrence in admiration of Mrs. Blair's tremendous courage and prayed God would bless her for it.

"Hear, hear," echoed around the table.

Mrs. Blair's face bloomed poppy red, and her hazel eyes glazed with tears. "To our boys, God bless and keep them," she said, and they all drank, though it was only water and not champagne in their goblets.

"Well, I have news of my own," Preston said around a bite of pork. "I visited the *Examiner* office today, and they say they will have me back. I can start tomorrow."

"Don't you need time to rest?" Sophie asked.

"Rest? In a time like this? There's far too much work to be done, and I'm fit enough to do it. Only—my eyesight isn't what it once was. Strained it beyond redemption in those dark cells at Fort Delaware. Which means, I could use a scrivener, of sorts." His eyes gleamed. "What do you say, Goldilocks? You used to want to be writer, if I recall."

"I still do."

"Then come with me. Take notes as I interview my sources, and dictation as I write the stories. It'll be a better education than anything you had in Philadelphia, I wager. I might even let you write a story yourself if you like."

Sophie's fork clattered on her plate. She pressed her napkin to her lips, almost in disbelief. Mastering herself, she smoothed the linen in her lap once more and flashed her father a smile. "I'd love to!"

"Bravo," Harrison said, beaming, and Mrs. Blair murmured her approval.

"Yes. Now Mr. Shaw, I did some digging around for you as well today. But I'm afraid none of the papers are hiring a staff writer these days. I consider myself fortunate to get my former position back."

Harrison nodded, then took a drink of his water. "It's as I expected."

"Perhaps another line of work would suit? You'll be conscripted if you don't find an occupation which exempts you. A clerkship? Richmond is rife with those. Russell, what do you think? Know of any openings?"

Sophie watched a hint of color creep into Lawrence's cheeks. "Not in my bureau, I'm afraid."

"But the War Department," Sophie tried. "Didn't you say this afternoon that Mr. Hayes, in the War Department, had taken so ill he'd decided to recover in the country?"

Lawrence pierced her with his gaze. He cleared his throat. "I did."

"Oh?" Harrison casually cut his meat. "And what is involved with a clerkship?"

"You write correspondence for the Secretary of War," Preston said. "And when mail comes to him from any quarter—whether from a poor country widow or President Davis himself—you read it, then write on the back of the envelope a summary of the contents. Then the Secretary will make a note to indicate how he'd like you to respond. You write the letter, and he signs it."

Harrison's eyebrows raised. "I do believe I could handle that."

"Without a doubt. I'll write you a reference straight away. What do you say, Captain? Will you write one, too? I personally vouch for this fellow, so have no qualms whatever on that account. I'm sure it takes two references to get the job. But we must be quick about it, before someone else vies for the same. Agreed?"

Remarkably, Lawrence did. Sophie's mind whirred. *Does Harrison really intend to stay in Richmond indefinitely? What other aim could he have, if not to spy?* Visions of Spencer Kellogg swaying from the end of his rope assaulted her mind. She may have been able to avoid suspicion thus far, but Harrison—if anyone tried looking into the background of Oliver Shaw, they would come up with precious little, or none at all.

Sophie's appetite fled as worry knotted her stomach. For the rest of the meal, she quietly sipped her water and matched the expressions on the faces around her, though her eyes did not want to shine, and her lips would rather not flatter. *All the world's a stage, And all the men and women merely players . . .*

After dinner, Mrs. Blair kissed Sophie's cheek in farewell and returned to her home, but the evening was not yet over. In the parlor, with both Harrison and her father as the audience, Sophie could scarcely act the part of Lawrence's beloved. How could she pretend to be moved by empty compliments when the man she longed for was in the same room? By the time Preston retired to his chamber, Sophie claimed a headache and bid Lawrence a hasty goodnight. A sigh deflated her as she locked the door after him.

"Sophie."

Face warming immediately to Harrison's voice, she followed him into the library, and he closed the door but for a few inches.

"Harrison, what are you doing?"

He grasped her hands in his and pulled her deeper into the room. "The same as you." Flecks of gold glinted in his shining brown eyes. "We are both perfectly positioned, especially if I get the clerkship in the War Department. But your performance with Lawrence Russell was sorely lacking tonight."

She wriggled free of his grip and dropped her hands into the taffeta folds billowing from her waist. "What?" Her eyes narrowed.

"There it is." Maddeningly, he chuckled. "I could feel that icy blast coming from your direction even from where I was sitting. Did you hear what he said as he stood to leave?"

A bit too chilly in here for my taste. But, "I don't love him." Wetness lined her lashes as she walked away, leaning on the marble mantel above the fireplace. "You already knew that." *You already know who I love.*

"But you must not lose him."

Sophie rounded on him. "I remember a time not so very long ago when you couldn't understand why I was seeing him at all."

"I don't like it. I despise it. But I understand why it must be so. There is a difference." He gentled his tone. "If you continue to be cold toward his affections, he'll grow suspicious of either you or of me. Either way, the result could be disastrous."

"My heart—" She crushed the lace of her neckline beneath her palm. "My heart won't lie. I don't want him." *I want you.* Surely she did not need to say it.

Harrison's resolve faltered as she stepped toward him, the dying fire behind her casting a halo around her golden hair. "He must believe you do. At least, for now. Try."

"How can you ask this of me?"

"Come now, it's simple. If he smiles at you, return it." He grinned, and slowly, her lips curved winsomely.

"Good. When he reaches for you, don't stiffen or pull away." Harrison wrapped his hand around the hollow of her waist, and with only the slightest pressure, she melted toward him, smelling of roses and violet water.

"If he lifts your face to meet his, make him believe you want him to kiss you. Can you do that?" He tipped her chin with his forefinger, and she looked at him with such pleading, his lesson stalled in his tightening chest. Her eyelids drifted closed, her lips parted slightly, and she warmed beneath his touch. Suddenly he was no longer a spy training another, but a man holding a breathtakingly beautiful woman, with no one else around. *Not just any woman. Sophie.*

Quickly, he released her, passed his hand over his jaw. "That's, um, convincing. Well done."

Crimson flooded her cheeks. "I'm not so expert an actress," she whispered.

Harrison lifted the sash on the window and let the cool spring air sweep him back to his good senses. When he turned around, Sophie's hand was on the doorknob.

"Sophie, wait."

She turned, and he could see in her eyes how much he'd hurt her.

"I don't know if this will make things easier or harder, but I can't let you walk away wondering where we stand." He sighed. "Could you come back in the room please?"

She plopped into an armchair and folded her hands in a pool of twilight taffeta.

He sat opposite her. "I hate seeing you with another man. I ache to fold you in my arms and kiss you the way you deserve to be kissed, Sophie. But if I do, I can't imagine sharing you with Russell again, and it won't make playing the part of his lover any easier for you either. And—perhaps it's my mother's training all those years while I lived with her at the boarding school, but I insist on asking your father's permission to court you properly. I won't be content stealing moments in the shadows. Only, the timing isn't right yet."

"How can I pretend to give Lawrence my whole heart when it has belonged to another for more than five years?" Tears glittered in her eyes, and Harrison hated that he had put them there.

Rising again from his chair, he paced the room to keep from taking her in his arms. He studied the giant peonies blooming beneath his tortured tread. "Then I must return to you the larger portion—at least for now—that you may have enough to share with Lawrence. He will know, Sophie. A man knows when he's being lied to by his lover. Already he eyes me with distrust. He must not turn on you as well." He rested his hand on the wing of the chair, and gauged her reaction.

"So." She swallowed, spine ramrod straight, then hit him with her flashing green gaze. "You and I live in the same house. Spy for the same cause. You feed me your intelligence, and I will send it, along with mine, to Elizabeth Van Lew."

"Yes. There will be a time for us later. But for now, we work. For the reunification of the nation, yes, but even more, for Bella and Abraham, Lois and Pearl. For millions of souls in bondage today, and the millions of future generations who will be shackled if the Union fails."

Her face transformed into a mask of firm resolve as she stood.

"Yes. For this, we work. We must not fail."

"We won't." As he bade her good night, electricity charging in the air between them, he prayed it would not take long.

Chapter Twenty-seven

Tredegar Iron Works, Richmond, Virginia
Monday, April 4, 1864

At the end of another ten-hour day, Abraham Jamison mopped the sweat from his face and silently cursed his fate. He should have rejoined his own regiment by now. His hands ached to caress his wife and itched to fire his rifle. Instead, they blistered and calloused around the hammer as he beat out heavy iron bands used to reinforce the breeches of Confederate cannon. *Being in prison was one thing,* he thought, visions of Libby snaking through him. *But being forced to labor for the cause that upholds slavery . . .* Words were simply too weak to match his abhorrence. His only solace was that the materials were of substandard quality. And so was his work—at least, as often as he could get away with it.

Mud cushioned Abraham's footsteps as he left the blacksmith shop jutting into the James River. But the same wind that cooled his sweat-filmed body would dry out the roads soon enough, and the spring's campaigns would begin. Barely suppressing a groan, he squeezed the burn in his right shoulder and circled his arm to loosen the tightness in his muscles. It would take some time to work back up to his previous blacksmithing physique. If he was lucky, however, he'd be long gone before that happened.

Turning his back to the river's smooth opal shine, he lifted his gaze above his fellow laborers coming out of the shops and foundries, and scanned the wooded hills against which the city's spires bristled. They were covered with the lime-green haze of tree branches studded with buds of unopened leaves. His hope was cocooned just as tightly but with little promise of unfurling. Bella was still in Richmond, yet so out of reach she may as well have been in Georgia. Without a pass, she could not come to the iron works, and he was not allowed to leave.

A heavy step announced the approach of another worker. Abraham turned to find John Taylor, a free Negro who worked in the gun foundry, on his way out for the night. "Well, Jamison, does the work suit?" His smile gleamed.

Abraham grunted. "Work's fine. Location, though—" He shook his head. "Not my first choice."

"Mm-hmm. If I didn't have family here, I'd put in for a transfer to one of the furnaces west of here. For the scenery, of course." He winked. "Now that the shipment of corn is here from Georgia, they'll be in blast again and needing hands."

"West of here, you said?" Abraham asked.

"I did. There's a few south of Winchester, one of which is right on the border of West Virginia. Then there's a whole slew of them west of Lynchburg, too. Also within riding distance of freedom."

"Are they not concerned about danger from Union troops?"

Taylor shrugged. "It's been the Rebel cavalry stirring up most of the trouble so far. Those furnaces were in place before the western part of Virginia seceded from us. They may be concerned about Yankees, but the furnaces won't be moved on account of it." He tipped his hat.

Abraham reached out and touched his arm. "Your wife. Does she go to market?"

"She does that. She's the assistant cook for her mistress—leastwise, until I can buy her freedom."

"Do you reckon she'd pass a note to my wife there for me?"

Taylor reckoned she would.

———————

Castle Thunder, Richmond, Virginia
Thursday, April 21, 1864

Spring arrived in Richmond with the fanfare one would expect from a city that did nothing by halves. Cherry trees and dogwoods bloomed pink and white, while live oaks draped moss and shade over streets that never emptied. Roses rambled, wisteria climbed, and azaleas spilled between the iron fence rails marking the officers' residences. All other fences—including the Kents'—had been removed and made into cannon.

At Castle Thunder, however, the only beauty was in the flaming marigold sunset and the river it turned to gold, just below Canal Street. West of Libby Prison, the Castle was the political prison for spies, refractory Confederate soldiers, deserters, and any civilians considered suspicious or disloyal. Inmates were routinely hanged by their thumbs, whipped, and "bucked" with a board threaded between bent knees and elbows.

"There she is." Preston pointed to a woman in man's clothing, being escorted between two of Winder's detectives at the head of a raucous crowd of Negroes and white boys. "Ready? We must get this to the printer straight off for it to go in tomorrow's paper."

Sophie scribbled her pencil over her foolscap pad as Preston dictated the story:

Female Yankee Surgeon.—The female Yankee surgeon captured by our pickets a short time since, in the neighborhood of the army of Tennessee, was received in this city yesterday evening, and sent to the Castle in the charge of a detective. Her appearance on the street in full male costume, with the exception of a gipsey hat, created quite an excitement amongst the idle negroes and boys who followed and surrounded her. She gave her name as Dr. Mary E. Walker, and declared that she had been captured on neutral ground. She was dressed in black pants and black or dark talma or paletot. She was consigned to the female ward of Castle Thunder, there being no accommodations at the Libby for prisoners of her sex.

Sophie looked up, squinting up at the three-story brick structure and tried to imagine what the female ward must be like.

"We must not omit to add that she is ugly and skinny, and apparently above thirty years of age."

She looked at Preston, to see if he was jesting. Mary Walker was frayed at the edges, and in need of a good bath, but certainly not ugly or skinny.

"Write it, please. 'We must not omit to add that she is ugly and skinny—'"

"I remember," she muttered, and added the line to his report. She could not afford to question him.

Preston steered her away from the crowd and set them on the path toward the *Examiner's* office. "Between you and me, Goldilocks, that woman is a mockery to her sex, and an outright spy. There's no such thing as a female surgeon."

Dr. Walker was lucky Preston did not add this to his report, as well. "So you think she's lying."

"Isn't that what spies do best?" His smile sent a shiver down her spine as cardinals trilled above them. "She should hang with the lot of them. Coming from Tennessee, she's probably got more information about our troop strength and positions tucked away in her little head than any of us realize. Can't let that kind of information get North."

Sophie nodded. "Of course not."

A week later, in the privacy of her chamber, secrets swarmed in Sophie's mind. Soldiers marched outside on Franklin Street as they had day and night lately, amassing under General Lee. Her head ached as she encrypted the news she'd gathered into the code of numbers and letters. Bella had managed to communicate with Dr. Mary Walker through the fence around the prison yard while the floors were being swabbed, and extracted the very information Preston Kent was right to fear she had. The woman surgeon was no spy. But her recollections of her journey were valuable, indeed.

Abraham had managed to inform Bella of the critical furnaces near the border with West Virginia. *A Union cavalry raid can destroy equipment and allow for the slave laborers there to escape, inflicting further damage on the Confederate quest for iron.*

Harrison, now firmly in place as a clerk in the War Department, had added his own intelligence. *Longstreet's Corps is joining Lee's army. The Commissary General's estimates for the next six months are for four hundred thousand men.*

By the time Sophie passed the missive to Bella to tuck inside her hollow egg, her hand was cramped and smudged with ink, her heart sore from its own tug-of-war. Deceiving those around her needled her—and for this she was grateful. But the more intelligence she fed Elizabeth Van Lew, the more the war invaded her dreams, just as it had invaded her city.

Once Franklin Street emptied of its soldiers, her feet carried her to Mrs. Blair's doorstep, as they so often did after she coded a message. Knitting for Joel and Asher—for Madeline's hands ached with the change of seasons—calmed her.

Hollywood Cemetery, Richmond, Virginia
Friday, May 13, 1864

For the second time in two weeks, Lawrence Russell stood in dress uniform next to Sophie, again in black, at Hollywood Cemetery. On May 1, President Jefferson and Varina Davis had laid to rest the body of their five-year-old son Joseph, who had fallen to his death from a balcony. Today Confederate General J. E. B. Stuart was buried. Grimly, Lawrence wondered who would be next, and if blue skies and songbirds would mock the Confederacy's losses forever as they did right now.

A knot formed in his gut as Lawrence considered the great men the South had already lost. *Would any of them still be alive if the cannons had not been faulty? If the guns and ammunition had been produced in sufficient supply?* These were questions without answers, but as an officer of the Ordnance Bureau, he could not shove them from his mind. How often had General Lee complained of cannons bursting, how much had he begged for more weapons, and those of better aim?

Lawrence shook his head and cast his gaze toward the James River wending its way lethargically along the south edge of the cemetery. Wind sighed through holly trees and brought the pinch of freshly turned earth to his nose. At least the tocsin did not sound today, as it had so often this month. The Yankees had two hundred thousand in Virginia now. The Rebels, but little over half that number. Whatever control Lawrence once felt over his life and the things he held dear was slipping through his hands like water, leaving a residue of helplessness behind. He despised it.

Instinctively, he reached for Sophie's hand and held it fast. He would not lose her, as he had lost Juliet. Beneath her ostrich-plumed hat, the sun lit her narrowed green eyes—until a shadow covered her face, and they widened in obvious relief.

Shaw. Lawrence studied the reporter-turned-clerk who had just stepped into the ray of light to block it from Sophie's eyes. *Curious fellow, that one.* Congenial, intelligent, and clearly a favorite of Mr.

Kent's, to Lawrence's irritation. But at the last two parties, Lawrence noticed that Shaw either danced with every woman save Sophie or bowed out completely, refusing to dance at all. And yet, he would block an unwanted glare from her face. Or close a window if she shuddered. Or lift the sash at the flutter of her fan. Lawrence had even caught him sending a slave to her with a glass of water if Sophie so much as licked her lips across a crowded room.

And he got nothing in return. *Fool.* It was almost pitiful. Did he yearn for Sophie with unrequited love, or did he just have an over-grown sense of chivalry? *No matter.* Sophie belonged to Lawrence. She confirmed it every time she listened to him share about his woes at the bureau or his concerns about the war. Juliet would have been bored to tears, but Sophie clung to every word he said. Her heart—and her lips—were his alone. As the earth rocked and shuddered beneath his worn-out boots, it was the one thing Lawrence knew to be true.

Slipping his hand into his pocket, his fingers curled around the engagement ring that waited for Sophie's finger. *The ring Juliet rejected.* Lately, the timing hadn't been right for a proposal. But soon it would be. And then he'd have Sophie for the rest of his life.

———

Kent House, Richmond, Virginia
Tuesday, May 31, 1864

Harrison knocked on the doorframe to the library, but when Sophie did not look up, he quietly entered anyway. She was bent over the desk, winding a strand of blonde hair around her left forefinger while her right hand suspended a pencil above a book.

"What are you reading?" he asked as he approached.

She startled, then leaned back in her chair. "Writing," she said. "The question is, what am I writing in the margins of the page—since I save the good paper for the final drafts—and the answer is 'absolutely nothing.'"

"And here I was afraid I was interrupting something." He grinned.

"I only wish you were." She dropped her pencil on the desk.

"Can I help?"

Sophie screwed her lips to one side. "My father said I could write a piece about Castle Thunder. The research alone—"

Harrison nodded. "Staggering. And maybe, you wonder if you can do it justice?"

"Yes. I'm afraid I'll cheapen the truth if I don't tell it right."

"The more important the story, the higher the stakes. The more frightening the prospect of failing. I do understand."

She eyed him, warily.

"Come now, surely you don't believe that writing comes easily all the time, even to me. It's work. But work that is worthy of the effort. May I?" He nodded to the script crowding the columns of printed text.

"Don't poke fun, now." But with a half smile slanted on her face, she offered him her seat, and he took it.

He squinted at her scratches. "Do I need a cipher key for this?"

Color rose in her cheeks, but a rare burst of laughter spilled from her lips, like music. "Allow me." She leaned over his shoulder, an errant curl bobbing beside his cheek, and rested her hand on the back of his chair. Pale green satin hugged and draped the lines of her figure so becomingly he forgot what he was about. *Focus, Caldwell.* He closed his eyes to listen.

". . . and so it proved to many a Confederate soldier, who, lying in the dungeons damp, or crowded into the common pens, for long weeks and months awaiting trial for some violation of army regulation, sickened, and were taken forth—not to the court martial, but to Oakwood Cemetery, where Death was recruiting another great Confederate army." She paused, and his eyes popped open as she straightened, folding her arms in front of the hourglass curve of her waist. "Well?" She grimaced.

"I thought you said you were having trouble with it."

A smile flickered. "Don't you want to slash and scrawl?"

"For old times' sake? My writing style is tighter than yours, but you need not imitate me in order to succeed. You've come into your own, Sophie. You don't need me. You're a fine writer. All you need now is the courage to go after it."

"Based on one paragraph of text?"

Harrison shook his head. "We get the Richmond papers in Philadelphia, too, you know. I read your columns." *And cheered you on.*

She looped her curl behind her ear. "How did you know it was me?"

"John Thornton—the hero of Elizabeth Gaskell's novel *North and South*? You loved that book. I couldn't get you to stop talking about it, along with *Uncle Tom's Cabin*. Remember?" He laughed at the surprise on her face. "Charming tale of social ills, even if it is set in England, and full of romance too. Despite regional differences, a dashing, ambitious man from the North falls in love with a willful, yet beautiful woman from the South. Is that about right?"

Sophie's eyebrow quirked. "It is. Just right." Sunlight sparked off the locket at her throat as she smiled at him.

Harrison stood and tugged at his collar, suddenly hot around his neck. "How are things going with Lawrence?"

Sophie bristled. Harrison might as well have thrown a bucket of cold water over her. She felt drenched with disappointment. Lawrence had so much of her already, why bring him into this one moment? She lifted her chin slightly, deflecting the emotional blow. "Things are going exactly the way you want them to."

His face reddened. "I see. Does he suspect anything?"

"I quite doubt it."

A deeper shade of red. He cleared his throat. "Well. Good, then. I'll feel better about going away."

"Away? Where? When?" Surprise eclipsed her indignation.

"I'm to be ready to march at a moment's notice with the Department Battalion."

She blinked, at a loss. "The what?"

"The clerks. The city is calling out the clerks. They went out once already without me, but now they need every man."

"But I thought you were exempt from service due to your government position!"

"You're not wrong. Exceptions to exemptions have become the general rule, to defend Richmond."

For a mere second, she closed her eyes to master herself. Cannonading and musketry could be heard from all quarters, it seemed, and several times a week as General Grant probed at the capital's defenses. It had not bothered her before now. "Will you fight?" she whispered, her voice gone. "Against the Union?"

Harrison's face hardened into tense lines. "I'll build ditches and fortifications, but I'll not fire against my own country—assuming I even have a weapon at all. Besides, they say we'll not see any fighting, but leave that to the regulars."

But she did not register his last sentence. Instead, another thought seized Sophie, even darker than the first. "They won't hesitate to shoot at you!" *You'll be killed by your own comrades,* she did not say.

"It's only for three weeks."

"It only takes a heartbeat to pull a trigger." Her hands fluttered to her hair, to the locket sticking to her neck, to the folds of her satin skirt, as if they had a nervous disorder all their own. *As if I were my mother.* Panic threatened. She could not become her mother. And Harrison could not die.

"Sophie." Harrison grabbed her hands and steadied her with his piercing brown eyes. He spoke in low tones, the roll of faraway thunder, lest anyone overhear. "Think. I'm being conscripted by a desperate Confederacy. If I refuse to go, I'll end up in Castle Thunder for desertion alone. If they suspect enough to look into my background, if they discover no Oliver Shaw worked at a paper in Baltimore, they'll know I'm a spy. Where does that leave you and your father, for giving me quarter?" She tried to pull away, to be free of the web that entangled them, though it was one of their own making. Harrison pulled her closer, his arms like iron bands around her waist, until her bodice pressed against his linen shirt.

"You'll be marked as accomplices at best, spies at worst," he whispered fiercely. "It will ruin you for Richmond even beyond this blasted war, the way Elizabeth Van Lew is already ruined by ostracism. Your father stands to lose his property, his fortune, his social standing, your inheritance, everything. He'll be tossed into Thunder right along with me, and you'll share a cell with Mary Walker."

"Stop," she gasped, and flattened her hands against his chest, for the images that scrolled through her mind as he spoke left her breathless.

"It's the truth." His tone softened, but he did not release his hold.

"Truth," she repeated, miserably. Some days she felt like she was swimming in lies, treading water in a sea of deception. One day, surely, she would drown in her own secrets.

Harrison slid her hand over his pounding heart and held it there. It beat in time to hers. "It's the truth," he said once more. Their hands blurred together in her vision.

When she lifted her face, he wiped a tear from her cheek before dropping his gaze to her lips. He was her safety net, her life raft, and her guide post. How could she manage to send him away again? Without thinking, Sophie's hands looped behind his neck, her fingertips slipping into his hair above his collar.

"Sophie." His voice was gravelly. "I cannot stand for *this* truth to become one more secret." Nose tinged with pink, he tenderly unhooked her arms from his neck, kissed the tops of her hands, and released them. "I won't do this while you are courted by another, even if it's only a sham. I won't let you give yourself to two men at once. I'll wait for your whole heart instead."

But when Harrison marched away with his battalion two days later, he took Sophie's whole heart with him.

Chapter Twenty-eight

Kent House, Richmond, Virginia
Thursday, June 9, 1864

"It's a nightmare." Lawrence Russell muttered into his tumbler of water and wished for all the world it was whiskey instead. The shots he'd had at the tavern before coming had barely taken the edge off. Sophie calmly rocked in the parlor, a stark contrast to his white-hot fury.

"What happened?" Her voice, a balm to his frayed nerves. She was an angel, in a froth of white muslin, belted with a ribbon of sunshine to match the golden braid circling her head like a halo. *No, she is the goddess Juno. My savior.* For without her support, he'd have come unhinged long ago.

He drew a steadying breath, inhaling the rain-scrubbed breeze drifting through the open window. "Union cavalry raid from West Virginia. Right through the heart of our iron country. They surprised three Tredegar furnaces—*three* of them!" He clanked his tumbler on the marble-topped table and gripped the arms of his chair until his knuckles shone white.

"Oh my."

Lawrence's jaw locked tight. Slowly, he worked it loose, pushing his chin from side to side with his hand. "They got Cloverdale furnace, the South's chief supplier of metal. Grace furnace, which produces cannon iron. And Mount Torry furnace, which Tredegar just purchased in December. All three are nothing but smoldering ruins now."

"How awful. Was anyone hurt?"

"The Confederacy is hurt, my dear, and by extension, thousands of her sons. Tens of thousands. More." Rain drummed outside the parlor, soaking the heat with humidity. Sweat plastering Lawrence's collar to his neck; he unfastened the top two buttons. "We cannot fight without weapons. We cannot make weapons without iron, we can't forge iron without the furnaces, and I'll be hanged if I know how to run or rebuild furnaces when the slave workers all run to the other side with every blasted Union raid!"

He stood and trampled the maple leaf patterned carpet as he paced about the room. "They captured large numbers of draft animals we simply can't replace and destroyed—destroyed, wantonly!—extensive stores of provisions. A criminal waste. The workers will go hungry, the few who didn't run." Lawrence paused in front of the mirror above the fireplace, rubbing the muscles in his jaw again. The bags beneath his eyes were growing heavier with each passing week. And no wonder. "General Grant thrusts at our defenses, probing for chinks. We're short of men. And we're short of ordnance. Just like we've been for the last three bloody—sorry, darling—years. And the administration is so wrapped up in red tape it can scarcely see the scarlet tide of casualties that will soon be rushing in."

Frustration ate a hole in his gut, he was sure of it. He needed a tonic. He needed Sophie. Crossing to her rocker, Lawrence took her hand and helped her stand. But when he folded her in his arms, she stiffened.

"Are you well?" he asked.

"I'm just tired, that's all."

And distant, when he craved her closeness. Cold, when he was so obviously flaming with fury and in need of her—soothing ministrations. In fact, "You really don't seem to be much upset by this latest, monumental setback to our country. Were you listening?"

Her eyes widened innocently. "What? Of course I'm upset! Furnaces ruined, slaves escaped, horses stolen, food destroyed—I heard every word."

"Even worse, then."

Sophie's eyes flashed beneath his scrutinizing gaze, and Juliet's face surged in his mind. Those long bristly lashes, fluttering like a bird's wings. The feigned innocence. "I don't know what you mean." Juliet's words exactly.

No. Not again. Not this, too. Not now. Lawrence chased the biting memories away, forbidding them to undermine his new romance. Sophie was not Juliet. He should not assume too much—no matter how clear the parallels.

"I'm sorry, darling. This was not the conversation I intended to have with you today." These were not the problems he'd planned on facing. It wasn't just Lee's army in need of weapons. In Georgia, General Joe Johnston's army kept falling back toward Atlanta, clamoring for both food and ordnance.

"You're under a great deal of pressure, I know."

"Enormous." He brought her hand to his lips and kissed each of her slender fingers. "We're getting reports from Johnston, in Georgia, that Sherman has 254 pieces of artillery in the field, to his 154. And Rebel shells are unreliable. Many fail to reach their targets at all, while many that do refuse to explode." He cut his voice low, for to speak with anything less than bravado about the Confederacy's godlike generals and soldiers had become tantamount to treason. "If Atlanta falls, which it very well may, Richmond will be the South's sole source of munitions. And now, when we most need Tredegar to increase production and improve performance, we lose three furnaces and a host of labor."

Sophie's green eyes shone like sea glass as she smoothed the worry from his brow, though her own was lined with concern. "You're doing all you can. There are simply too many factors you cannot control."

And there were some things he could. "Marry me."

Sophie's heart turned violently in her chest. "Lawrence, you jest," she whispered, and sank down into her chair, hands shaking in the folds of her billowing white skirt.

"Not at all." He dropped on one knee and pulled a ring from his pocket. "If the world comes crashing down around us, if I have you, I have enough. Be my wife."

She stared at the ring pinched between his fingers. "D-did you already speak with my father?" She was stalling.

"Come now, darling. At your age, you're just shy of spinsterhood. I'd say you can make up your own mind, free of guilt, and he'll be happy enough to have you married off. And as soon as possible, for my sake."

Her lips refused to return his smile. Goosebumps covered her skin. She could not reach for the ring, even as the next step in her deepening deception. Even for the sake of the Union, she could not play this game a moment longer. It was Harrison she wanted, not Lawrence. As much as she was loath to hurt the man kneeling before her, if she accepted his offer now, breaking the engagement later would only inflict greater pain. It was not fair to Lawrence, or to Harrison, not to mention her own shredded heart. Tears welled in Sophie's eyes. But words remained locked in her aching chest. *How does one go about breaking another's heart?*

Lawrence moved to slide the ring on her finger, but she curled her hand into a fist, and held it tight against her waist.

The shock in his wide blue eyes cut through her.

That's how. Her stomach pitched and rolled. "I—I never meant to hurt you." Yet how could this have ended without pain?

"You reject me?"

Sophie rolled her lips between her teeth, her silence her answer. *Please, let it be enough.* She willed Lawrence to leave with his dignity intact.

His eyes narrowed, flickering. "So all this time, it was a game for you? As it was in the beginning, you never stopped playing?" Lawrence was on his feet now, pacing feverishly, rubbing at the muscle bunching in his jaw. "I've been a fool. Again."

She stood. "You're not a fool," she tried. "Dozens of women would rejoice to have even a portion of your affections."

"But not you," he snarled. "I give you my entire heart, offer you my life, my future, after months of courtship and suddenly you're not interested. Why?"

He strode toward her, his chestnut hair falling over his forehead. She stepped back. He caught her wrist in his hand, eyes wild and rimmed with red.

"Let me go." Her blood rushed in her ears.

"Ah, the one thing I want least to do." His lips curled. "But aren't you gone already?"

Nothing she could say would make this better.

"Have you betrayed me, then?" He grabbed her other wrist. Yanking her to himself, he crossed her hands behind his back in a forced embrace, the brass buttons of his jacket marching up and down her bodice. "To whom? Another man. Or another country?" Sophie caught the odor of liquor on his breath. He cinched her tighter, and her fingers tingled, then numbed.

"Captain Russell!" Her voice shook. "Unhand me! You are no gentleman to treat me so harshly. You will not call on me again."

He released her, only to slap her across the mouth, sending her stumbling back into the table and upsetting the glass he'd placed there. "And you are no lady. How dare you do this to me? How dare you?" He moved to strike her again, but she darted from his path.

"You've been drinking. I want you to leave. It's over."

"Ah, so this is my fault, is it? You would blame your disloyalty on me when it is you who have turned coat?"

"Captain Russell. The lady asked you to leave." Bella, standing tall a few feet from him, looking directly into his eyes. Her face a mask of stone.

Lawrence's dark laughter raised the hair on Sophie's arms. "The Negress is giving a Confederate officer an order? Am I completely emasculated then? By war, by women, by slaves?" He shook his head and a pang of pity flitted through Sophie for what he must be feeling. "Your mistress would do well to learn from your loyalty. But my business isn't finished here yet."

Bella stepped closer, muscles taut. "Yes, sir. It is." She did not want to engage with this feral man, but she had a sight more fight in her than Sophie did. The captain and Mr. Kent—not to mention the entire neighborhood—still believed Bella was Daphne, the slave who would not rebel. But Bella knew who she was. And she would not stand by while that girl was beaten, which she believed without a doubt the captain would do. She knew his kind. Could smell the desperation in his sweat. He hungered for control and figured a woman, of all people, ought to give it to him.

Ignoring Bella, Lawrence turned once more to his prey. "When did it happen? How long has that light in your eyes been shining for another?"

He lunged toward Sophie, and Bella threw herself against him, knocking him sideways into the piano. A discordant crash filled the room until he righted himself and turned on Bella, eyes wild. "Do you not know the law?"

She knew the punishment for attacking a white man, according to Richmond courts. But, "'Thou shalt love the Lord thy God with all thy heart, and with all thy soul, and with all thy mind . . . Thou shalt love thy neighbour as thyself. On these two commandments hang *all* the law and the prophets.' I know the law, Captain Russell. The question is, do you?"

"Amen."

Bella rounded on Preston Kent, whose gaze had already moved to Sophie's swollen lip and to the handprints on her wrist.

"This slave struck—"

"You struck my daughter? Left your mark on her?" His voice rattled the windows. "You have five seconds to vacate the property, and if you dare bring Daphne to court"—he extended his arm toward Bella—"I will roast you in the papers until you think you'll never be able to quench the fire. I never want to see you here again."

Lawrence Russell stormed away.

Chapter Twenty-nine

Kent House, Richmond, Virginia
Thursday, June 30, 1864

*A*fter three weeks of digging, building, and marching in stifling heat and sizzling rain, Harrison Caldwell climbed stiffly up the front porch of the Kent House. He shook Preston's hand in greeting before easing into the rocking chair beside him. Crickets chirped and cicadas whirred against the thick summer evening, while tree frogs twanged from the dogwoods.

"Good to have you back, son. See any action?"

"Afraid not. We marched in support of the ironclads as they went down the James, and built four miles of fortifications out to Deep Bottom, near Chaffin's Farm. Hard labor, but no fighting." Harrison leaned back against his rocker and inhaled the scent of wisteria puddling in the air. *A welcome change from the stench of the battalion latrine.*

"Well, you missed the excitement here. None of which had to do with the war."

"Did I?"

"We had a bit of a skirmish of our own. That Lawrence Russell fellow proposed to my Sophie."

"Did he." Harrison looked straight ahead, heart sinking.

"She refused him."

Harrison whipped his head around to face Preston. "Did she?"

Preston clapped him on the back and bellowed in laughter. "What's the matter? Did you leave your entire vocabulary out there in the ditches? What happened to your store of words, Shaw?"

Harrison laughed with him. "Sorry, I—she said no? So it's over?"

Preston nodded. "If I ever see that man come around here again, I'll shoot him myself."

"He hurt her?" Dread coiled in his belly. If anything happened to Sophie, after Harrison had urged her to keep seeing him . . .

"Some. Could have been worse. Much worse."

"Well, sir, if he's out of the picture, I'd like to ask you something." Harrison swallowed, removed his hat. Passed a hand over his unkempt hair, ruing his untidy appearance.

"Permission to court her."

Harrison hesitated. "Is it that obvious?"

"You two were made for each other. And there's no way a man would go out of his way to avoid Sophia Virginia as much as you have lately unless it was a deliberate attempt to extinguish your feelings for her. I just can't figure out why it took Goldilocks so long to figure that out. You're a fine fellow. A man of character, I can tell. Even if you weren't born in Virginia." A smile quirked beneath his mustache.

"So it's all right with you?" Harrison rose, muscles no longer sore. "I may court her, truly?"

"I wish you would. That girl deserves every happiness she can get. But may I make one suggestion?"

"Of course."

"A bath, Mr. Shaw. It goes a long way with women. Trust me."

"You'll feel better with some rest." But Bella was worried for Sophie, even as she said it. She hadn't been eating much lately, not since Harrison had gone away, and even less since she'd refused Captain Russell. Then again, no one ate much anymore, even if their appetites were healthy—not with flour up to $500 a barrel, cornmeal $125 per bushel, and no beef to be found in the city. Bella unfastened the last button of Sophie's day gown and slipped it off her shoulders, holding it so Sophie could step out of it. Next, she untied the tapes at her waist and let the hoops fall to the floor. Layer by layer, Sophie came undone until she could finally don her nightgown. It was only half past eight.

Sophie pressed her hands to her temples, as she always did when her head ached, then plucked out the pins in her hair. "Tell me again what Abraham told you." Her voice was low as she brushed out her hair, and her eyes flashed in the mirror at Bella's reflection.

Bella repeated the news from Tredegar as simply as she knew how. As she did so, she could almost see the gears spinning behind Sophie's eyes as she mentally synthesized this information with what she'd learned from assisting her father with the news.

Finally, Sophie nodded thoughtfully, and plaited her hair in a thick golden braid for the night. "I wish I knew how much of this is helpful," she confessed. Bella, too, had wondered. Weekly, and more often than that, Sophie sent coded messages through Bella and her hollowed eggs to Miss Van Lew, who passed them to Colonel George Sharpe, who'd replaced Butler as the point of contact at Fortress Monroe. Attached to every message was the risk of discovery, for the chance that what they sent was worthwhile.

"At least we know Abraham's information made a difference," Bella offered.

Sophie smiled as she tied a blue silk ribbon at the end of her braid. "That was invaluable, as Captain Russell was so kind to point out." Her smile slipped then. "How are you faring, Bella? With Abraham at Tredegar?"

A sigh feathered her lips. She'd rather be home, with him, with

305

Liberty, and Silas too. Still, "He's not in prison. They feed him, clothe him, and the supervisors do not whip the laborers." *The slaves.* She could not bring herself to frame the words. Could not stomach the fact that her husband was no longer free. "I hear from him regularly. And if he keeps giving us good information like he has, the war will end and we'll all be free."

Sophie tilted her head. "If you wanted to leave sooner, we can try again, you know."

"Won't be long now," Bella said, again, for the hundredth time. "I go with Abraham or not at all." She could not leave him here in bondage, no matter how reasonable Joseph R. Anderson was with his laborers. "Besides, whatever would you do without me?" She smiled, but she was only half jesting. It was Bella who went to market every day and conferred with other colored folks, slave and free, filtering intelligence and delivering it to Sophie. And she was the one who passed the messages to Miss Van Lew's slave at market, too. Robert Ford had escaped North, thank God, and so had a handful of white Unionists. Those who remained shouldered the work, and there was much to do.

"Without you, Bella? I shudder at the thought." Moving to her writing desk, Sophie took out a thin sheet of foolscap and her pencil, and retrieved the cipher from the locket around her neck. "Thank you. I'm turning in early after this. Come back for it in an hour."

"See you then." Bella quietly left the room and glided down the stairs. She left the house from the rear door and ran smack into Harrison Caldwell.

"Bel-Daphne!" Harrison shook his head and smiled apologetically. "How are you?"

Bella couldn't help but smile at the reporter turned spy, even though his original "fool-proof" plan had brought them where neither could have possibly foreseen. "I'm fine, I suppose, but not as fine as Sophie'll be when she sees you."

His eyes sparked as he looked past her toward the house.

"Come on, Romeo." She took his elbow and led him to the kitchen house. "You aren't going to see her like that." She wrinkled her nose.

"Say now, that's the smell of hard work, right there. Laborious, tedious, backbreaking work."

"Defending our Confederacy, no less." She cocked an eyebrow, and he spread his hands.

"You would expect no less from a battalion of pencil-pushing clerks, now would you? We're rather stalwart, as it turns out, though you may not guess it from the circumference of our necks."

Bella laughed. "Well. You'd smell a whole lot prettier if you'd scrub some of that stalwart off your Rebel self."

"Agreed." Fireflies pulsing around him, Harrison pumped his water and carried it to the tub behind the kitchen house to bathe beneath an amethyst sky.

"Ready." Harrison appeared in the doorway to the kitchen house, still slightly flushed from scrubbing. "Will you—ahem—announce me?"

Bella propped her fists on her hips. "I don't know, Mr. Shaw, the hour is getting on. You may just have to wait until morning."

The smile slid from his face. "You wouldn't."

No, she wouldn't. Shaking her head, she led the way back inside the Kent house. "She has a headache."

"Maybe I can make her feel better."

"She's tired. Might be sleeping. And if she is, I will beat you back if I have to. That girl needs rest."

"Spent all day marching in the glare of the sun, did she? After weeks of hard labor?"

Bella swatted his arm, and he bowed in deference.

"If she's sleeping, I'll not disturb her."

"That's right." Bella paused at the bottom of the stairs. "You stay here. I'll send her down if she's awake."

Bella climbed to the second floor and knocked lightly on Sophie's door before pushing it open a crack. "Sophie?"

"Mmm?"

"Still up?"

"Yes, just finishing. Come in." Sophie's muffled voice beckoned.

"You have a visitor," Bella said as she entered. "Unless you want me to turn him away."

Sophie froze. Looked up, eyes wide. "Harrison?"

Bella nodded, and Sophie jumped up, scrambled for the layers she had so recently shed. Quickly, Bella slipped in the room to help her.

In record time, Sophie was back in her drawers and chemise, and laced back into her corset, surrounded by hoops and petticoats, and draped in a fresh, if simple, at-home gown of cornflower blue linen. Cheeks flushed, Sophie's hands flew to her braid.

"It's fine," Bella said. "You're decent, and that boy's been waiting on you."

"I suppose he has something to tell me." Sophie glanced at the message she had almost finished encoding. "I'll encode his information and bring it to you when I'm done, all right?"

"Just fine. He's waiting downstairs. Your father just crossed the street for a front porch visit with Mrs. Blair. You won't be disturbed."

Downstairs, Sophie slipped into the library and Bella fetched Harrison from the parlor where he waited. "Library," she said.

"Thank you."

Bella jabbed her finger on his chest as he rose. "Be good. Or else."

His eyebrows bounced. "I know better than to cross you." He grinned. "And I promise, I'll behave. I won't be long, I just—I just have to see her."

"I know you do." Bella smiled and swept away.

Sophie stared at the half-closed door to the hallway, waiting almost breathlessly. A tapping sounded from the other side, and she bade him come in.

Harrison entered, leaving the door ajar a few inches. Looked up. Arrested her with his gaze.

"You're back," she murmured. Warmth flooded her cheeks at such an inane greeting.

"I am."

As he closed the distance between them, she worried the locket between her thumb and forefinger, and gestured toward the cipher grid she had brought with her to capture his news. "I was just . . . writing . . . Do you have anything to add?"

"I do." He told her of the position and strength of the fortifications he spent weeks building and of the departure of the ironclads from Richmond. Surely, this was exactly what Sharpe would want to learn. His clean linen scent ruffled her concentration. So did the depth of his brown eyes. If she didn't encode the information now, she would surely forget it.

But when Sophie pulled out the chair, Harrison laid his hand on hers. Lifted it. Kissed the ink stain on the right side of her hand. "It'll wait, Sophie," he whispered. "But I can't." Slowly, he laced his fingers through hers. "I heard."

"About Captain Russell?"

He drew her closer, anchoring her against him until she wondered if he could feel her beating heart against his chest. "I spoke with your father."

Already? She drew a deep breath, sure her knees would give way if she were not held fast within his hold. "What did he—"

His lips met hers in silent answer, and she indulged willingly in the kiss she had been waiting for. Eyes closed, she breathed him in, tasting his love for her in the sureness of his embrace. Sophie's hands glided along the muscular curves of his biceps and shoulders before circling his neck with her arms. Firmly, tenderly, his mouth trailed to her cheek, her ear, her neck, and again to her lips. "I love you," he whispered, "and have loved you, for so long . . ."

Warmth spread through her and she melted against him, returning every sweet kiss he offered. "I love you, too," she murmured, and he covered her mouth once more, lingering. In his arms, she was both lost and found. With his left hand firmly on the curve of her waist, Harrison cradled her head with his right, then stroked her hair downward along the length of her braid. A gentle tug, and she felt her hastily tied ribbon come loose in his hand, her braid unraveling. Desire, unfurling.

Until, seized with a sudden sense of impropriety, she wrenched away, though her longing for him was so intense, it startled her. Breathlessly, she twisted her wayward tresses into a loose rope and tossed her braid back over her shoulder.

"Forgive me." Harrison's voice was gravelly. "I should—I ought to—I am overcome."

Sophie nodded, her breath skittering over her lips. Her own heart was full to overflowing. But she would not have their love cheapened with indiscretions and regret. That was Susan's way, not Sophie's. It wasn't Harrison's, either. All those moments he could have kissed her but didn't. His intentions had always been honorable. "Court me," she whispered, "but not temptation."

"Then could you please not be so . . . tempting?" He grinned. "Truly, if you were not so altogether lovely, self-restraint would be a far easier task."

Her cheeks warmed beneath his admiring gaze. She folded her hands behind her back to keep them from wandering behind Harrison's.

Blowing out a sigh, he ran a hand through his hair. "Nonetheless—you are right. I take my leave." Backing away from her, he flashed her a smile, bade her good night, and left the room.

Her ribbon still trailed from his hand.

———

Summer marched by in a cloud of dust to the beat of fife and drum as Richmond remained under siege. The tocsin cried danger, the militia followed, and sounds of battle became as common as shouting at auctions for used shoes. Harrison's battalion ebbed and flowed into the trenches like the tide, and Sophie's heart went with him. Each time he returned, he had new information to supplement what he learned in the War Department. Bella's weekly visits to the market garnered snatches of intelligence as well.

Sophie listened to her sources, digested each report, condensed it into rows of coded text, and sent it on its way. Her head pounded, and her hands had taken to shaking, though she hid that from Mrs. Blair and her father as well as she could. Two more Unionists had fled Richmond. One was cast into Castle Thunder. No one knew who was next.

Whether it favored the Union or the Confederacy, the news from all quarters reeked of suffering. Sherman pummeled Atlanta, while civilians remained inside. At Petersburg, where the Blair boys were stationed, the Union army exploded a mine in Confederate defenses, then spilled into the crater they'd created where they were killed like fish in a barrel. Waiting for word from her sons whittled lines into Mrs. Blair's face.

Just beyond the Blair and Kent parlors, Rebel wounded and Yankee prisoners choked the crowded city, as they had during the summer of 1862. *Was it only two years ago?* Rumors that Union General McClellan was coming to take Richmond had buoyed her with hope then even as the nearby battles turned the city into a charnel house. *Surely, the war is about to end,* she'd said. But her mother, unable to discern the sounds of battle from the echoes haunting her mind, had been rattled, even more than the windows. *The tapping,* she had said of the popping musketry, *it's Esther in the hiding place! You see, she made it North again! I knew she would, I knew it!* She'd been as wrong as the rumors of Union victory. And then Eleanor had hidden in the secret room herself. Rocking, singing, moaning, crying.

Sophie shook her head to dislodge the memories. Dwelling in the past was futile.

The Union is at the gates, she told herself, again. *Surely, the war is about to end.* Sophie only prayed Richmond would not meet Atlanta's fate. And that if it did, it would not be because of her.

Richmond and Danville Depot, Richmond, Virginia
Monday, August 1, 1864

Susan Kent wiped beads of perspiration from her brow and tumbled out of the railway car along with every other miserable refugee. Staggering away from the hissing train after a harrowing journey from Atlanta, a whoosh of steamy, rank-smelling air assaulted her. Dust and grime caked her sweat-glossed skin.

Having no baggage, Susan elbowed her way out of the station yard and inhaled that familiar smell of the James River, over which she had just crossed on the railroad bridge. For better or for worse, she was home.

Not that I recognize it, she thought as she made her way east through the crowd to Cary Street. Strangers of every shade of means, from poverty to extravagant wealth, wore every variety of clothing, and spoke in a tumultuous array of accents. The spicy aroma of tobacco that had once spilled from the riverside factories was replaced with the odors of human confinement: sweat, disease, waste. Susan hiked north to Franklin Street to put their stench behind her.

Shading her eyes against the summer sun, she did not see a single face she knew, and was glad of it. Surely no one would see "the stunning Susan Kent" in hers. Smallpox had seen to that.

Her fingertips fluttered over her face, dipping into the small craters the disease had taken from her body in exchange for her life. Tears of shame bit her eyes. No one could call her a beauty ever again.

Swiping her pockmarked cheeks, Susan slogged up Church Hill through thick, damp air. She was exhausted, famished, filthy, and vexed that she had no idea if she'd be welcomed home. In fact, her father had made it clear she was never to return. She could only hope her reduced condition might invoke the necessary pity. By the time she reached the corner of Twenty-seventh and Franklin Streets, her nerves were buzzing like horseflies.

Susan knocked on the front door and waited to be greeted by Otto Fischer. When the door opened, however, it was as if she was looking at a younger version of herself. Blonde, curly hair. Creamy skin. A figure that would turn heads if she knew how to use it properly. But the eyes were green, like Susan's stepmother, Eleanor, rather than Susan's blue.

"Sophie." Susan tried on a tight smile, and found it ill-fitting.

But Sophie frowned. "May I help you?"

Susan's pride turned inside out. Her pocked skin and gaunt form had rendered her a stranger to her own sister.

Preston came to the door then, placing his hand on Sophie's shoulder. "If you're looking for lodging, ma'am, I'm afraid we're not taking boarders. Good afternoon." He moved to close the door, but she thrust her hand out to stop him.

"Daddy."

His face went pale, his blue eyes narrow. They were Susan's eyes. Surely he could see that, though the rest of her was altered beyond repair.

"Susan?" Sophie looked to Preston. "She's been ill," she whispered.

His cheeks reddened above his beard. "I told you never to come here again, and I meant it. Scars or not. I have but one daughter now, and she's right here." He wrapped his arm around Sophie's shoulders, but Sophie shrugged out of his affection.

"You would not even listen to what she has to say?"

"The time for discussing ended years ago." A scowl slashed his face as he peered over her shoulder. "Where's your husband?"

"The foreign immigrant you forced me to marry right before he moved me away? That one?"

"Is there another?"

Susan snorted. *Well played.* "No. I have no husband." She lifted her left hand to display her ringless finger. "Divorced me after I was ravaged by smallpox." Utterly false. But the truth—that she had already been pregnant with another man's baby when she wed, refused to consummate her marriage, annulled it, and left the baby with Noah to raise—why, that story was far less sympathetic.

Sophie gasped. "I'm so sorry. I thought he was an honorable man."

Honor. A useless quality these days. Still, Susan attempted to appear grieved.

"Please," Sophie said to their father, the one thing they had in common anymore. "She is the prodigal daughter, come home at last!"

Preston faced Susan then. "Prodigal daughter, eh?"

The title chafed and fell to the ground. Susan's only regret was that she was reduced to beg shelter from her father. "I have nothing." She spread her hands. "No means at all by which to support myself."

"You never wanted to support yourself," he hissed. "And you would not have had to if you had obeyed our rules." His gaze shifted to scan the street behind her, and she knew exactly what he was thinking. *Whatever will the neighbors think?* She smirked at his obvious discomfort.

"Tongues will wag, Daddy." And she pushed past him and into the home she had lived in from childhood, when he'd had it built with Eleanor's money, their first house too full of the memory of Susan's deceased mother for Preston's comfort. "Where is Fischer, anyhow?"

A hint of color touched Sophie's cheeks. "No longer employed here."

Susan shrugged, then ambled into the parlor with confidence, as if she were the favored child she had been until Sophie had usurped her. The room was largely the same as when she'd left nine years ago. She'd been a child of nineteen then. Now she was a "ma'am," not a "miss."

". . . can't turn her out onto the street, not with crime and vice now so rampant in Richmond . . ." she heard Sophie say. The girl had a point.

"I don't take up much room."

Preston glowered. "Do you repent of your scandalous ways?"

If Susan knew what was good for her, she should grovel. Instead, she laughed. "'Do you repent?'" she mocked him. "'Do you recant?' Come now, is this the Spanish Inquisition or is this a family? What was it you used to say? 'There's nothing more important than family.' But oh, that's right. What you *meant* to say was, 'There's nothing more important than the family *name*.'"

Sophie stepped backward, twisted her hands together. Susan smirked. "I forgot about that thing you do with your hands when you're uncomfortable. Your mother did that, too. Where is Eleanor, by the way?"

Instantly, Sophie dropped her hands by her sides. Preston glared.

"Dead yet? Yes? Well, in any case, I should think having another family member come home would be welcome."

Preston thrust his finger in Susan's face, and she shrunk back instinctively. "You will *never* replace Eleanor, if that's what you're hinting at. Never. If you want to stay, you may do so as hired help. Earn your keep that way, save up, and be gone."

Susan gasped, genuinely shocked. "Hired help? And I suppose I'd stay in the slave quarters on a pallet in the loft?"

"There happen to be two vacancies. Laundress and scrub maid. Lois and Pearl would be happy to have you."

Susan inhaled sharply, and exhaled indignation like an atmosphere. "I will do no such thing!" Her voice trembled with barely restrained rage. "I will stay in this house with the same privileges as Sophie—"

"You forfeited the right nearly a decade ago."

"I'll stay here as your daughter, your firstborn child, born of your first beloved wife, or I will go out there and survive the only way I know how." She pointed a bony finger toward the street. "As a woman of the night. I may be scarred, but what does that matter in the dark? And I will drag your precious family name through the vilest muck of the slums until neither of you are received by society again." Her words boiled out of her. "Don't think I won't. As you already know, Daddy,

I have a knack for creating scandal. And I've only gotten better at it." Her lips curled with slippery satisfaction.

There now, she thought, quite comfortably. *This* smile was a perfect fit. It felt so good to win.

Chapter Thirty

First Market, Richmond, Virginia
Tuesday, August 2, 1864

*B*eneath the bright and brassy sky, Bella zigzagged between carriages, horses, and piles of manure as she crossed Seventeenth Street on Franklin. She could barely breathe. Tears thickened in her throat as she immersed herself in the morning crowd streaming into the huge brick marketplace. Steaming from the recent rain, the building teemed with threadbare buyers orbiting hard-faced sellers. *Pound of coffee, twenty dollars! Pound of sugar, ten dollars! Two quarts milk, five dollars! Two pounds rice, five dollars! Barrel of flour, four hundred dollars!* Their clamor was nothing compared to Harrison's voice still clanging in her ears.

News from Pennsylvania, he'd told her last night. The lines framing his mouth, his hand on her arm had raised the hair on her neck. *Chambersburg.* Twenty-five miles west of Liberty and Silas in Gettysburg. *Confederate raiders burned the town for failure to pay the Rebels $500,000 in U.S. currency or $100,000 in gold.* The only civilian who died was an elderly Negro, Harrison said. But the citizens were so enraged they killed five Rebel soldiers themselves.

Liberty was fine, Harrison had suggested, though his brown eyes were dark with concern. He was likely right. But danger had come too close. How could the Union have allowed this to happen, little more than a year after the battle of Gettysburg ripped through their lives and homes? Who could say that it wouldn't happen again? *There is no safe place. Not here, not in Pennsylvania.* Sweat itched beneath Bella's head scarf. *All the more reason to bring down the Confederacy from the inside.*

Bella's face hardened with resolve even as she traded a thick stack of Confederate dollars for a quart of white beans, one of new potatoes, and a bushel of cornmeal.

Her errand complete, she pushed her way out of the stalls, and found Edith Taylor with a basket over her arm.

"Good morning, Edith! How is your husband?" John Taylor was the freeman Tredegar employee who, along with his wife, Edith, were the conduits of communication between Abraham and Bella.

"Just fine, just fine." Edith smiled, but did not reach for any note tucked inside her apron pocket.

Bella deflated. "No word from Abraham, then?" It had been weeks.

"And there won't be, neither, I guess."

"What?" Bella's pulse trotted. "Why?"

"John says he's gone. Transferred to Columbia furnace on the border of West Virginny." She dropped her voice as she shifted her market basket to her other arm. "Reckon he'll run? Without you?"

Bella had no idea.

———

Mechanics Hall, Richmond, Virginia
Tuesday, August 2, 1864

Stifling a yawn, Harrison Caldwell bent over his work in the cramped space outside Secretary of War Seddon's office. He was grateful to be out of the trenches, but now he was buried in clerical work following the Departmental Battalion's recent, albeit brief, deployment. Nearby, Richmonders and refugees strolled through Capitol Square before the sun burned off the morning haze. Turning his gaze from the streaked windows of Mechanics Hall, Harrison fought through a haze of his own. The day they returned to the city, the battle of the Crater had been fought at Petersburg, just south of them. That was two days ago, and Harrison's ears were ringing still. The quake of battle yet thrummed in his veins, along with the roar of the fire he imagined he could hear all the way from Chambersburg. *Will this cursed war never end?*

Sighing, he turned his attention to the letter in his hand. It was from Isaac Carrington, the provost marshal of Richmond since General Winder had gone to Georgia to command Andersonville, the prison camp at Camp Sumter. Carrington was also a habeas corpus commissioner, empowered by the War Department to investigate cases of citizens charged with disloyalty and held in Castle Thunder. As such, he sent his reports to Secretary of War Seddon, Harrison's boss.

If the reports did not hold such power over the imprisoned, Harrison would call them laughable. They were mere notes, and not all well-written. Seddon did not require the commissioners to record testimonies, from the imprisoned or witnesses, so no story was complete. They were ordered to report their findings, but given no deadline and no uniform categories of information to collect. There was no requirement that every prisoner be reported on and no penalties for failing to report, lost reports, or inaccurate reports. Commissioners could recommend a prisoner be set free, but their greatest power was in simply not recommending freedom. It was tantamount to a sentence lasting for the duration of the war.

Rubbing his hand over his face, Harrison scanned Carrington's letter now and was relieved to read that Dr. Mary Walker, the Union surgeon imprisoned in April, would be released this month. Sophie would be especially glad of that.

Next, there was a list of prisoners, long overdue, along with the charges. Harrison's brow knitted. Beside one out of every ten names was the simple phrase: Union man. Below the list, more notes from Carrington, this time on the case of one John Miller from Henry County, Virginia. Arrested for saying he wished the Yankees would invade the county, that he would not help the Southern cause, and that he wished every secessionist was hanged. "No case can be made in court for the utterance of the Treasonable language imputed to the prisoner," Carrington wrote. But, he added, "It is inexpedient to allow men who utter such sentiments to go at large during the present crisis."

Dread snaked through Harrison. If Miller would remain in Castle Thunder for his words, what would they do to Harrison if he was discovered? *When,* he corrected himself. *When I'm discovered.* For surely, it was only a matter of time. And he already knew what they would do to him.

Folding the papers into thirds, he slipped them back into their envelope and printed a brief description of the contents for Secretary Seddon on the outside of it. After tossing it into a basket on the corner of his table, he picked up the next piece of correspondence addressed to the Secretary and opened it. Scanned the script. And read it again. Cold alarm coursed through him.

I submit that the person of Sophie Kent, 27th and Franklin Streets, be a subject of investigation on charges of disloyalty. She is a known abolitionist, and favors the Union, as her previous activities at Libby Prison indicate, though she has since ceased. She is a danger to the security of the Confederacy and as such, should be locked away.

Harrison turned the paper over and studied the envelope but could not find a signature. The accusing words were written in bold, slashing strokes. *A man's hand. But who?* Lawrence Russell knew Harrison worked for Seddon. Would he dare send a note across his desk?

Quietly, Harrison folded the charge and stuffed it, along with its envelope, into his trousers pocket, where it burned against his thigh until he went home for the night and watched it burn to ashes.

If it had landed on a different clerk's desk . . . Harrison shuddered. Then a sickening realization hit him in the gut. *Just what do you suppose will happen next time you're called to the trenches?*

———

Kent House, Richmond, Virginia
Wednesday, August 3, 1864

Sophie brushed out her hair for the night and wondered how long Susan would hover over her. Her questions about Eleanor's death had not been welcome. Sophie's answers had been truthful, but brief enough that they raised Susan's eyebrows.

"You've grown into a beautiful woman, Sophie." A smile slithered across her face. "It's all right, I know you can't say the same about me." Her laughter prickled Sophie's skin.

"I'm so sorry you went through all of that."

"Not nearly as sorry as I am."

Sophie set down her brush and began plaiting her hair. Nothing she said to her sister seemed to satisfy.

"Your suitor—Oliver, is it?" She wrinkled her nose. "Not really a masculine name, is it? No matter. He's handsome enough, I suppose. He must be quite a man for Daddy to have him stay here. He told me you weren't taking boarders, remember? He was ready to turn me out straight away. And yet Oliver Shaw is just downstairs, staying in our home as comfortable as you please. Clearly, Daddy is as smitten with him as Oliver is smitten with you."

Sophie's gaze darted to her sister's for a moment, wondering what game she was playing.

"It's adorable. You two must be very happy together. Do you love him?"

"Yes."

"And he loves you?"

"So he says," Sophie murmured, "and I believe him."

"Marvelous. It shows, really. You have nothing to worry about on that account."

Sophie frowned as she tied a ribbon around the end of her braid. "Why should I worry?"

Susan's eyebrows spiked into her pockmarked brow. "You shouldn't! Didn't I just say that? My, what a lovely locket you wear. Here, let me help you take it off for bed."

"No, thank you." Her hand went instinctively to the oval silver pendant that encased Elizabeth's cipher.

"You sleep with your jewelry on? The chain will kink, you know." She clucked her tongue and shook her head, as though she was really concerned.

"It's fine. Do you mind, Susan? I'm exhausted." Spreading open the mosquito net draped over her bed, she climbed inside, tied the linen strips to close the net, and pulled the sheet to her chin.

"It must be a gift then, for you to guard it so carefully. From Oliver? Come now, you can tell me. I'm very good at keeping secrets."

I'm better. "Good night, Susan." And she rolled onto her side, toward the wall.

Kent House, Richmond, Virginia
Monday, August 15, 1864

The front door slammed behind Susan as she stormed out onto the porch, unable to endure the sticky sweetness between Oliver and Sophie. *How had she managed to catch him?* Though she'd never admit as much to her little sister, he was actually quite charming. His lean frame, which everyone had these days, was not skinny by any means, but defined with hard, muscular curves, thanks to his labor in the city's fortifications. To have a man like that wrap his arms around her just once more . . . Susan's face scorched with anger. It would never happen again.

Exhaling her frustration, she leaned against a pillar and looked out over Church Hill. Fireflies blinked their yellow lights, and wind rustled through dogwood and magnolia trees. The shadows agreed with Susan. *This is where I belong. Alone, and in the dark.*

A branch snapped just beyond the porch. She wasn't alone, after all. "Who's there?" She marched down the stairs, in the mood to pick a fight. "Show yourself!"

A man's silhouette came into view. Slowly. Unthreatening. Susan could handle herself with a man, especially in the dark.

"What are you doing here? This is private property, you know." She moved closer to him, joining his shadow beneath the tree.

"Forgive me—do you live here?" he asked.

"Of course I do."

"Are you—family? Your voice sounds so much like Sophie's."

She squinted up at his face, unable to make out his features. *Good.* Then he'd be unable to see her scars.

"I'm her sister, not that I had any say in the matter. Susan. Who are you?"

He removed his hat and bowed to her. A charming gesture. One she'd not been paid in quite some time. "You have a quarrel with her?"

"I might." She crossed her arms. "You still haven't told me who you are."

"Captain Lawrence Russell. Charmed, I'm sure. And if I could see well enough to find your hand, I'd kiss it."

A smile formed on her lips. "Why are you here, Captain Lawrence Russell? Enjoying the show?" Through the window, one could plainly see Oliver and Sophie chatting in the parlor.

"Torturing myself with it, more like. But please, don't tell your father."

She propped her fist on her hip. "Not supposed to be here, then? So you're hiding in the shadows like a common criminal?"

"Sophie rejected my proposal for marriage. Or did she tell you already?"

Susan's jaw dropped. "Recently?"

"Quite. My wounds are still gaping wide open."

"Why, you'd think those two have been courting for a year the way they carry on in there. So in love—it's revolting!"

"You're some sister, if I may say so." She heard, rather than saw, the smile framing his words. And then, a weighted sigh. "I should have known it was Oliver all along. And after I wrote him a recommendation to secure his position as a clerk." This voice was edged with steel.

"Angry, are we?"

"To put it mildly. If it were day, you'd see my face is afire."

Without thinking, she reached out, walked her fingers up his chest, his neck, and laid her hand upon his cheek, her fingers and heel of her palm brushing his neatly trimmed beard. It was warm beneath her touch, but grew hotter still by the moment. Now this was a man. And Sophie had won his affections, as well? Something leapt inside her, a wild longing for pleasure and distraction and—ah yes, Scandal, her very dear friend.

He cleared his throat.

Susan dropped her hand. "Oliver and my sister both hurt you, yes? Why don't we settle the score?"

"How do you propose to do that?"

She snapped her fingers. "Like that."

Lips still burning from Sophie's good night kiss, Harrison poured water into his washbasin and laved it over his face and neck. It failed to quench the fire she kindled within him. If she were not so disciplined and careful with her affections, he'd never survive living in the same house with her with his honor—and hers—intact. As soon as he could do it as Harrison Caldwell, and not as Oliver Shaw, he would wed her and bed her. He was thirty-one years old, for pity's sake. It was high time he had a family. *Heaven help me if this war doesn't end soon.* In the meantime, he splashed more water over his face.

After stripping down to his drawers, he climbed on the bed, tied the mosquito netting closed around it, and tried not to think about tomorrow. The clerks were being called out again, to man the fortifications on the north side of Richmond. Which meant that tomorrow night would be sleepless and taut with tension. Would tomorrow be the day he'd face Yankee guns? Would he be shot by the cause he loved?

Groaning, he pulled his Bible from beneath his pillow and turned to Psalm 31, marked by the blue satin ribbon he'd pulled from Sophie's hair. "For thou art my rock and my fortress; therefore for thy name's sake lead me, and guide me. Pull me out of the net that they have laid privily for me: for thou art my strength. Into thine hand I commit my spirit: thou hast redeemed me, O Lord God of truth. . . . My times are in thy hand."

God of truth, Harrison prayed, *lead me. Guide me.* He closed his Bible and laid it back on the nightstand, but kept Sophie's ribbon in his hand. As he held its fine satin grain between his thumb and forefinger, he recalled how the Lord had brought him this far, through battles, through prison, through a suffocating tunnel—four of them, actually—and led him right back here. Surely He would fulfill His purposes for Harrison, and keep him safe to come back to Sophie once more. *And Lord, keep her safe while I'm gone.*

Slumber overtook him, and he surrendered to its deep. Sophie came to him in his dreams, a vision of golden, silken tenderness, a welcome replacement for ghosts of battlefield dead that had paraded through his mind every night for years past. Where there had been horror and decay, she filled him with hope, joy, and the promise of all things new, whether he was waking or sleeping. He only prayed he did the same for her.

In his dream, her hair spilled over her shoulders in ribbons of sunshine. She was smiling and unashamed, his wife. He took her in his arms and lavished her with kisses. She nibbled his earlobe, her breath hot and sultry on his skin, then returned to his mouth. And bit him.

Harrison wrenched awake, heart racing. "Sophie?" Had she gone mad? He brought his fingers to his lips, and found them warm and swollen from urgent kissing. His gut twisted in shame that the unrestrained passion might not have been a dream. He couldn't see her face in the dark, but her hair tumbled down, tickling his face and shoulders. Just barely, he could see the white mosquito net swaying in the breeze behind her like a wraith. Her ever-present locket gleamed in the moonlight as it dangled from her neck.

Jolting upright, he placed his hands firmly on her waist to push her from him. Shock surged through him as he realized that nothing but her cotton nightgown barred him from her corsetless curves.

"Stop," he whispered. "You're not helping me."

Her fingers swirled through his hair. He caught her wrists, and her pulse throbbed beneath his thumbs as he resolutely pushed her away.

"Don't you want to—"

"Stop!" Of course he wanted to. Whatever she was going to say, he wanted it. But, "I want to honor you more than I want that pleasure, and right now you're making it extremely difficult! Whatever happened to not courting temptation?"

"Changed my mind."

His bare chest warmed from the heat radiating from her body as she leaned in. If he touched her once more, even to move her, he feared his hands would not let her go. She was so close, so willing. And so unrestrained he was completely bewildered. Suppressing a groan, he scrambled from the soft woman in his bed, swiping the mosquito net out of his way. The floor slapped his feet as he landed, grounding him in reality.

"Go." His voice was leaden. "This can never, ever happen again or I'll find some ratty boardinghouse instead." He didn't know if he was strong enough to resist another opportunity to satisfy his flesh. "I love you too much to let this happen. We do things God's way, or not at all." But she had already slipped out the door.

When morning yawned, slow and lazy, Harrison packed for the trenches, his face still burning from the night before. *We'll sort it out when I get back.* A few days away would be time enough to cool down. And to pray about how to proceed. He tossed his Bible into his knapsack, then remembered he'd fallen asleep with Sophie's ribbon in his hand. He looked under the bed, beside it, and in his sheets, but it was nowhere to be found. She must have taken it with her when she left last night. Had he spoken so harshly that she'd withdrawn her love as well?

"CIVILIZATION ADVANCED a century. Justice, truth, humanity were vindicated. Labor was now without manacles, honored and respected. No wonder that the walls of our houses were swaying; the heart of our city a flaming altar, as this mighty work was done. Oh, army of my country, how glorious was your welcome! The wonderful deliverance wrought out for the negro; they feel but cannot tell you, but when eternity shall unknot the records of time, you will see written for them by the Almighty their unpenned stories, then to be read before a listening universe. Bottled are their tears on His ear."

—ELIZABETH VAN LEW, Union agent in Richmond

"WE KNOW IT WOULD not have befallen us without His permission who overruleth all things. We must do our duty as best we can and believe that the inscrutable Providence who permitted our present situation may be preparing us for a more useful and higher destiny, which without this lesson we might neither have retained or appreciated."

—MARY CUSTIS LEE, wife of Gen. Robert E. Lee, speaking of the Confederate defeat

Act Five

THE CURTAIN FALLS

Chapter Thirty-one

Kent House, Richmond, Virginia
Tuesday, August 16, 1864

The hair raised on Sophie's neck as she stared at Bella's reflection in the mirror. "What did you say?"

Seconds ticked inside Bella's pause as she studied the chain on the back of her neck. "The clasp on your locket. It's bent. Like you tried to take it off without unhooking it first. Did you?"

Sophie wheeled around to face her. "No."

"You're sure? You didn't have a message to code last night?"

"No! The last time was four days ago." Was that right? She pressed her fingers to her temples, willing herself to remember. *Troops are taken through the city mostly at night, along with a long train of artillery, with great secrecy in the movements. Mr. Barnes says they go to the Valley to reinforce Early. Seven regiments of infantry in the neighborhood of Deep Bottom. Work is being done to the fortifications on the north side of the city.* "Yes, that's right. It was right before the battle began." The battle that still went on ten miles southeast of Richmond, the noise of which invaded their Franklin Street home.

"I remember that," said Bella. "And I've seen this chain every morning and night since then as I've been helping you in and out of your gowns. I'm telling you, it's different this morning." Their eyes met.

Sophie opened the locket. The cipher was still tucked inside. But that corner of the paper—had it been creased just so before? And there—a smudge of pencil lead she hadn't noticed before. Minuscule. But there. Her heart galloped. She snapped it shut.

"Is it altered? In any way?" Bella's eyes penetrated Sophie's.

"I—I don't know."

"Could Harrison have needed it?"

Sophie frowned. "I doubt it. But—oh! He's leaving today to man the northern fortifications!" The trenches she had named in her coded message.

Wordlessly, she swept down the stairs and into the dining room, where Susan sipped her tea, her hair in a loose braid over her shoulder. "Have you seen Mr. Shaw?"

"Just left."

"Without saying goodbye?" She looked at Bella, whose lined brow confirmed it didn't sound like him.

Susan shrugged. "Would have been awkward, don't you think?"

"Why?"

Her sister cocked her head and smiled fiendishly. Batted her eyelashes like butterfly wings. "Both of us, and him, together?"

Sophie studied her strange demeanor. Then her gaze caught on the cornflower blue ribbon tying Susan's braid. The one Harrison had kept from the night of their impassioned kiss in the library. "Is that—is that mine?" Her mouth was suddenly dry.

"Oh!" Susan flipped the end of her braid like a twitching horse tail. "Why yes, he said it was. But Oliver—I mean Mr. Shaw, pardon me ever so—said it would look better on me. Matches my eyes, you know. Does it? That's what he said."

Sophie felt as though she'd been struck. Bella glowered in the periphery of her vision but did not say a word. Neither did Sophie, having lost her voice completely.

"He also said you're a bit prudish. Apparently you told him not to court temptation?" She clucked her tongue. "Well! Little wonder he gave me such a warm welcome. He's a grown-up man with grown-up urges. Said he was glad to have a woman like me who knew how to take care of them. Now, now, don't go all teary on me." Another sip of her tea.

No. Harrison would never betray her like this. "You're lying."

"Am I? Then how do you explain my having your ribbon? It's only natural that a previously married twenty-eight-year-old would have a few more charms for him than a twenty-four-year-old little maiden like you. Don't concern yourself too much, now. He'll look for you in the daylight." She pointed to the scars on her face. "But if you want to keep him happy in the dark, I can show you what he likes."

St. John's Church, Richmond, Virginia
Sunday, August 21, 1864

After five days of Susan's taunts, countered by Bella's certainty that she was lying, Sophie sat beside her father in the pew and tried to focus on the reverend's sermon.

Impossible. Worry churned in her gut. It wasn't just the thought of Harrison's possible infidelity, but the idea that someone, for some reason, had removed her locket from her neck and replaced it before she woke up. Sophie had not passed her any intelligence for more than a week, so nervous was she about stepping into a trap. But surely, the most important information she could send was nothing more than Elizabeth could have divined herself: that no supplies were being sent to General Early through Richmond anymore, which meant he must subsist or starve.

Beyond that, the intelligence the Federals requested was becoming impossible to detect. Accompanying Preston for his interviews, Sophie had noted that the government was planting false reports to conceal the true movements of Confederate troops. Rumors swirled in the streets like chaff above the threshing floor. After struggling to sift through all the misinformation, Sophie was at a loss for truth, just at the time the Union needed it the most. Lee, Longstreet, Early, Kershaw—their names tangled in her weary mind.

Preston stood, and Sophie realized it was time for the congregation to sing. Rising, she shared a hymnal with her father. She stole a glance at him, and his eyes smiled down at her. *Oh Daddy, if you only knew . . .* Flesh and blood, side by side, but how at odds their heartfelt loyalties. His rich voice blended with Sophie's and bounced off the page back into her ears.

> *Sovereign Ruler of the skies,*
> *Ever gracious, ever wise,*
> *All our times are in thy hand,*
> *All events at thy command.*

Sophie believed it. So did her father. So did Harrison, and Mrs. Blair, and thousands now gathered to worship and beseech the Almighty in churches and in army camps across Virginia. Though Southern soil received its sons, and Southern homes grew lonely, still the faithful came to pray. Sophie blinked back tears as she considered that in this at least, God-fearing souls of Union and Confederate sympathies agreed: *All our times are in thy hand, all events at thy command.*

Harrison Caldwell reached the rear door of St. John's Church just as the service ended. *God of truth, be near.* Five days and nights manning the fortifications had felt like an eternity of tedium. He could not stop thinking about Sophie and her serious lapse of judgment. It had occurred to him under a star-studded sky that if she'd thrown discretion aside in their courtship, she may not be exercising caution in her espionage, either. He'd already caught one accusation. In time, if she didn't control herself, there would be more.

Then he saw her, emerging into the sunshine in a pale pink gown sprigged with roses. Harrison doffed his hat and waited for her and Preston to draw near. The satin bow beneath her chin fluttered in summer's steamy breath, while the wide brim of her straw hat waved languidly. With white-gloved hands she clutched her Bible, and Harrison wondered how this woman could possibly be the same one from the memories seared in his mind.

"Mr. Shaw!" Preston shook Harrison's hand and welcomed him back. Sophie's wide gaze rippled over him before her brim hid her face once more. "You two have some catching up to do. I'll meet you at home."

Harrison fell into step next to Sophie, whose pace seemed brisker than usual. He cleared his throat, unsure of how to breach the chasm so clearly still between them.

Then, "I see you are well."

"Disappointed?" He smiled, but suspected he might be right.

"I don't know what to feel, or think, or say."

Ah, so there it was. The heart of the matter, already. "I'm sorry if I hurt you," he tried. "The night before I left. And by not coming to say goodbye."

She lifted her face then, green eyes sharp in their censure. "Why didn't you?"

Harrison rubbed the back of his neck as they strolled through a lacework of light and shadow. The answer should have been obvious. "Don't you already know?"

"Ashamed of your behavior?"

He frowned. "No. Surprised, bewildered, disoriented, but not ashamed. I followed my own convictions. I stand by that."

A shrill cry burst from Sophie's lips. "Convictions! I can think of another name for it!"

"Such as?"

"I'm too much of a lady to say it, let alone act on it." With shaking hand, she stuffed a strand of hair back behind her ear. "You agreed, *Oliver*," she whispered fiercely, gaze darting left and right.

"Agreed to what? I thought I made myself quite clear. It was you who behaved like Potiphar's wife!"

"Me!"

"Yes, you!"

Sophie's face flamed crimson. "I haven't the slightest what you mean!"

Confusion rooted Harrison to the ground while she stalked on ahead of him. Recovering, he rejoined her. He grabbed for her hand and caught her wrist instead. "Sophie—" He froze. Closed his eyes. For pressing against his thumb, hidden by the edge of her glove, was a distinct cord of scar tissue. He would have noticed it, even in the dark.

But he hadn't.

Relief flooded through him as he locked eyes with his beloved. It wasn't Sophie who had come to him in the night like a tramp after all. But, "She wore your locket. I thought it was you." He kissed the scar on her wrist and enfolded her hand in his. Her eyes flared as he guided her off the main road onto a lesser traveled side street.

"Susan," she whispered. "Bella said the clasp of my locket was bent. She must have taken it from me in my sleep." Suddenly, she reached up and touched his face. "I should have known. Bella told me she was lying, and I believed her, but then you spoke as though something actually did happen between the two of you." Her expression fell. "Oh my. Did you kiss her? Don't lie to me."

"I don't know."

Her eyebrows plunged. "Try."

"I was kissing you in my dream—I may have kissed her, truly, but I vow I thought I was kissing you. It was dark. She only whispered. I couldn't see her face, only felt her hair on my skin, and your locket."

Sophie looked away, cheeks blooming all over again.

"Why would she do that?"

"Because she is Susan." Sophie's tone was suddenly hard. "And she loves to hurt people more than anything else in this world."

"I sent her away, Sophie, as soon as I awoke. Whatever she said, you must believe me."

She nodded, but the lines of her face did not fade. "I do. But—she had the locket."

Breath stilled in his chest. "Did she open it?"

"I don't know. I can't tell." She bit the edge of her lip.

"Has she acted differently toward you since then?"

"Honestly, I have no idea what she knows." Sophie looked haunted by the suspense, but there was nothing he could do. If Susan accused Sophie in writing, could he intercept it? Possibly. If she went to Carrington in person, what then?

Harrison captured her hands in his. "It's going to be all right."

"Another lie, perhaps. But a sweet one."

This, he could not contradict.

A sadness surfaced in her eyes. "Oh, what a tangled web we weave, When first we practice to deceive!"

Harrison smiled at the familiar lines from Walter Scott's epic poem "Marmion," then countered it with two more lines from the same: "Where's the coward that would not dare To fight for such a land?" He brought her hand to his lips and impressed a kiss upon it once more. Together, they headed home.

———

Capitol Square, Richmond, Virginia
Sunday, August 21, 1864

Susan sat on the steps of the Washington Monument, masked by night's darkness, and watched Captain Lawrence Russell thread his way through a messy knot of revelers. It wasn't just his silhouette she recognized, but his commanding gait. *Now here is a man who knows what he's about.*

"Well?" He sat down beside her. "How did it go? Did you break some hearts?"

"I believe I did." She grinned behind the lace veil of her Leghorn straw hat. "Unfortunately, they put themselves back together again. But I sure had a lark trying."

"I'll just bet you did." The flash of moonlight on his teeth sent a delicious ripple through her. That she had not even managed to get one conscious kiss from Oliver Shaw did not need to be said. *Humiliating.*

"And you?" she asked, her voice turning sober. "How's your heart after my sister smashed it?"

Sighing deeply, Lawrence looked out over the square, smelling of sandalwood and tobacco and wool heated from a man's body a long summer day. He stroked his hand over his beard. "Sore. To put it mildly. It would be easier to recover if . . ."

"If you hated her." Calmly, she smoothed the blonde satin bands trimming her white muslin gown. A perfect complement to her perfectly coifed hair.

"Exactly."

She nodded, knowingly. After all, she'd been crushed before, too. Had given herself to a lover who promised to marry her, only to find his child growing in her belly and him already a married man. It had been easy to hate him. It was easy to hate her father for exiling her to a husband she didn't love, just to hasten her away. She hated Noah Becker for being so foolish as to marry her in the first place, and for finding love years later, while she still slept alone. At first she'd even hated Ana, her daughter, for invading her body, but once she pawned the baby off on Noah, that hatred cooled to a comfortable apathy. But she still knew how to hate. Like the disease that had pocked her skin, hatred ate away at her still. It never stopped.

"So Captain, what would help you hate my sister? Would her obvious love of the Negro suffice?"

He rubbed the muscle in his jaw. "I don't hate Negroes. It would have to be something really shocking. Something..."

"Criminal, perhaps?" she guessed.

He whipped to face her, eyes gleaming. "Why? What have you heard? What do you know? Is it treasonous?"

She'd struck a nerve. Lawrence's eagerness to trap her sister startled her, but not unpleasantly. Rather insightful, really. *Ah, so this is the way to your heart.*

"Please." He grasped her gloved hands firmly in his. She bowed her head, lest his penetrating gaze detect the flaws in her complexion despite her net veil. "Please," he said again. "If you have any information, I would be indebted to you."

Just how indebted? She did not ask.

"So do you? Have anything to share?"

Pedestrians and carriages swarmed through the square, the whine of their voices and wheels mingling with the chorus of crickets. Yet Lawrence hung on Susan's every word with a desperate focus.

"I just might." Her lips curved purposefully.

"What?"

"Something mysterious."

"But is it treasonous? I always did wonder about her so-called Christian charity toward Libby Prison. You found evidence of her disloyalty? If I can't have love, I will have justice."

Justice, he called it. "You mean revenge."

Lawrence shrugged. "A rose by any other name, and all of that. Do you have proof or not?"

Susan's eyes narrowed. "She would have known right away it was missing. I'm biding my time, Captain Russell, until I have more tangible evidence. Trust me."

"Trust you?" He laughed darkly, and Susan caught the joke. "I'll trust you to hurt your sister and no further. Lucky for me, that's my aim as well. We'll meet again."

"Of course."

With that, he kissed her hand, making her forget for one slice of a moment how hideous she had become.

What a shame it would be when he no longer needed her.

Chapter Thirty-two

Sophie's stomach burned with secrets. Sherman had taken Atlanta earlier this month. If Richmond fell, surely the war would be over. As hope and possibility increased, so did risk.

Shading her eyes against the sun, she looked out over Church Hill, stubbornly ignoring the pounding headache that had only grown worse with each passing week, and with every message passed. From Harrison: *Eight guns have been sent to Chaffin's Farm . . . Hampton's Cavalry remains on New Market Hill.* From Bella: *Richmond's Fire Brigade was ordered throughout the city, rounding up able-bodied men to be sent to Petersburg.* From John Taylor at Tredegar: *Such a dearth of soft iron, it is said that no more is to be had for the manufacture of heavy ammunition. No iron suitable for making nails or spikes has been on hand for two weeks past.*

Madeline Blair had read Asher's letter from Petersburg to Sophie as well, but Sophie willfully let the words slip through her without weighing them for their value to the North. She refused to use her friend's companionship against her own sons. Now Sophie set her hands to knitting for Asher and Joel as she rocked on the back porch, for Mrs. Blair's hands were knotted with arthritis, and it pained the woman even more to think that come winter, her boys would suffer with cold. Truth be told, Sophie enjoyed the rhythmic work. Somehow it kept her from unraveling.

Wind whispered through linden trees barely tipped with autumn's promise. Summer was ending the same way it had passed its sunburnt months. With strains of battle, and air tinged with smoke and sulfur. With riderless horses with boots reversed in their stirrups, with church bells tolling for the dead, and alarm bells predicting that more would soon be on their way. The clash of war rang in every home, and, Sophie suspected, every heart, as Yankees and Rebels locked and thrashed around Richmond. Union cavalry were destroying food sources in the Valley of Virginia, teaching Rebels, both civilian and military, just how few morsels it took to survive.

Sophie Kent was so tired she could barely coax her needles to knit and purl. Her nerves had been standing on tiptoe for so long they now seemed to collapse. Sifting through rumors, guarding against Susan's prying eyes and questions, and working with her father had all taken their toll. If she could just close her eyes for a moment . . . A refreshingly cool breeze swayed over her face in silent lullaby, urging her to sleep . . .

"Sophie." Harrison's voice pulled her back.

She smiled as she opened her eyes to his handsome, chiseled face, squinting at the sun over his shoulder. "Home from work so early?"

Then she heard it. The tocsin. The church bells. Pealing in frantic alarm.

"Yankees have captured Fort Harrison. They're advancing toward the city. I have to go." His eyes held hers as he helped her up from her rocker. "I wish I didn't."

She shook her head, as if to erase his concern, but fear swam through her. If the Yankees came near enough the fortifications, Harrison would be under fire. Forcing a smile, she tried to chase the shadows from his eyes. "The 'dog-catchers' would send you out for sure. I'll pray for your safe and speedy return."

His gaze shifted, scanning behind and around the porch. "Goodbye then." The hint of a sigh, a lingering kiss, and tight embrace. A whisper in her ear: "Elizabeth Van Lew has been accused. She's under investigation. Watch yourself."

A tremor shot through Sophie's body, and she sagged in his bracing arms. With unspeakable gentleness, he tucked her head against his shoulder, his other arm cinching her waist. Time evaporated as he buried a kiss in her hair.

"Our times are in Your hands, Lord, deliver us . . ." Harrison's voice rasped over the prayer.

The bells of Richmond seemed to scream as he trudged heavily away.

———

Columbia Furnace, Shenandoah Valley, Virginia
Friday, October 7, 1864

Abraham's muscles strained against his scratchy homespun tunic. Heart pumping, he wheeled a load of iron ore up the hill next to the forty-foot-high stone pyramid furnace. After shoveling the ore into the pyramid's mouth, he arched his aching back and indulged in the view.

It was magnificent. Though the area directly around the iron plantation was cleared of timber, the surrounding hills gently rose and fell, draped with forest's bristled mantle. Distant blue and violet ridges backed green slopes dotted here and there with the hint of season's change.

Expelling a sigh, Abraham picked up the handles of his cart and cast one more longing look into the country beyond. He was doing no good for Bella or for the Union from here. Worse, his labor was aiding the enemy. West Virginia beckoned to Abraham. *Oh, to enter those folds of freedom. Oh, for the season of my life to change . . .* There was a time for everything. But his time to escape had not yet come. He was as closely watched here as he'd been at the Richmond works, perhaps even more so. Praying for patience, Abraham descended the hill.

Thunder rumbled from a cloudless azure sky. Abraham jerked his head up. Dropped his handcart. Raced farther up the hill, though roots tripped his eager feet, and scanned the perimeter. *Not thunder. Cavalry.* And this time, the uniforms were blue.

Flying down the hill, Abraham did not feel the rocks shredding his paper-thin soles or the branches switching his arms. As the ground trembled with the approach of hammering hooves, chaos broke out at the furnace. White laborers shouted orders that Negroes did not heed. Mules and oxen stamped and snorted in their pens. And suddenly, mounted Yankees were upon them, with ropes, guns, and torches.

Courage surged in Abraham as he lit out toward the closest Yankee. "Abraham Jamison, 54th Massachusetts. Fought at Wagner under Col. Robert Gould Shaw." He saluted the mounted officer as mayhem churned around them. "Sure would be grateful for a ride."

Wiping the look of surprise from his face, the officer smiled. "Some furlough, Private. Ready to report for duty?"

"Yes, sir."

Reaching down, the officer helped Abraham up onto the back of his horse, then spurred the mount into a gallop.

———

Kent House, Richmond, Virginia
Tuesday, October 18, 1864

Bella rapped her knuckles on Sophie's door. "Thinking about getting up sometime?" The sun was plenty high in the sky. The girl might be worn out from worry for Harrison, but that was no reason to keep abed all day.

She knocked again. Still no answer. "Sophie?" She pushed open the door. A slightly sour odor pinched her nose as she approached the still form on the bed. Dread shivered down her spine.

Slowly, Sophie turned. Her color was high and the shadows beneath her eyes were dark, like bruises. "It's you!" she cried, and reached up to take Bella's hand. Sophie's skin was as hot and dry as a hearth. "Daphne!"

"Sweet Jesus," Bella whispered. "No, Sophie-girl. It's Bella."

Sophie's face knotted. "You're Daphne. And you were sick, and it was my fault. Yes, that's right, I remember now."

A frown rippled Bella's forehead.

"Oh, you're upset with me still. Of course you are. I'm so sorry, Daphne. But you look better now. Are you better?"

Fever talk. *Oh, Lord.* Bella rushed to the washbasin, soaked a cloth with clean water and brought it back to lay on Sophie's brow. "Now you're sick, and it's my turn to take care of you."

The quinine! The bottle she'd brought for Daphne last fall was almost untouched. It had been too late to be of use for her, but surely, for Sophie, it would work. It was early. It had to work.

Bella hurried out of Sophie's chamber, and to the room where Daphne had been ill. She'd left it tucked inside the bureau, and forgotten it there. But certainly the medicine was still potent, being kept from the light of the sun. Hope swelled. She reached inside the bureau for the bottle.

And found nothing. She searched every inch of the room, and the quinine was nowhere to be found.

———

"Sophie, honey?" Susan poked her head inside her sister's bedchamber. "Heard you weren't feeling well, is that right?"

Sophie stirred, but made no other response. *Perfect.* Avoiding all the creaky boards in the floor, Susan stepped to her sister's bedside and pulled the sheet down from her chin. The girl was shivering, but hot to the touch. Susan skimmed her fingers along her neck, in search of the locket and chain.

It wasn't there. *Blast!* She needed it now. Lawrence was growing restless for it, and she feared he'd reached the limit of his patience. After their last meeting, she knew it was useless to string him along any further, though she lived for their nocturnal trysts. She'd hoped that he'd looked forward to them half as much. But Lawrence had become cold, distant. She wasn't getting anywhere. If she could hand him something tangible, perhaps he'd give her something in return. Oh, how she longed for affection.

Boldly, Susan tugged down on the neckline of Sophie's nightgown, searching for the necklace. She had no idea what that little scrap of paper meant, but if it was important enough to keep secret, surely Lawrence would want to have it. Only now, it was nowhere to be found.

Agitation ticked inside her. She moved to the bureau, opened the top drawer, felt inside for the small metal pendant. *Ouch!* She withdrew her fingers. *A paper cut?* She opened the drawer a little wider, carefully pinched a thin stack of papers and withdrew.

What a mess! That was Sophie's handwriting on the pages, but the margins were crowded with undecipherable notes. *What is this?* Susan squinted closer at Sophie's script. The fact that these papers had been hidden was a promising start, at least. Her eyes rounded in surprise as she flipped through one page after another. *Essays? Confessions?* Whatever they were, they were incriminating. Not just antislavery, but anti-secessionist rhetoric blazed forth as the dominant themes. More than enough for Lawrence, she was sure.

Sophie groaned, and Susan hid the papers behind her, backing toward the door.

"Daddy?"

She froze, curious.

Sophie turned onto her back but didn't open her eyes. "Daddy, I miss Susan. Where did she go? I'm so confused."

Obviously. Susan nearly slipped out the door.

Then, "Mother cries all the time. I don't know why . . . you won't let me write to Susan . . . She can behave so wickedly. . . But she's my sister . . . Can't I ever see her again?"

Delirious. Mad with fever. But Susan's face was suddenly damp with tears. Furiously, she swiped at them and scurried down the hall, her precious evidence rustling in her hand.

Kent House, Richmond, Virginia
Friday, October 21, 1864

Bella stared at Susan's pitted face, and felt her own harden with a furied understanding.

"I have something you want, don't I?" Susan held the bottle of quinine in her bony hand. "I can't imagine how you came by it, though, since quinine is scarce as hen's teeth in the South. But this time, I'll lay that aside, since you have something for me. Care to trade?"

Bella narrowed her eyes, while her nostrils flared. "What do you want?"

"The locket. I see the chain around your neck plain as day. You might as well give it up. If you don't, I'll tell my father you tried to steal it, and then he'll send you packing."

"It belongs to Miss Sophie. I'm keeping it safe for her while she's sick. And if I didn't know any better, I'd think you're the one trying to steal from her."

"How can you say such a thing? That was my locket to begin with. I left it here by accident and she adopted it as her own. I only want it back. For sentimental reasons. It's all I have left of my stepmother, God rest her soul."

Bella's lips flattened. Sophie needed that quinine. Without it, the locket would be useless, anyway. Unclasping it from behind her neck,

346

she clenched the chain in her fist, the locket dangling. "Medicine, please." She held out her hand.

Once the quinine was safely in her grip, she passed the locket to Susan's greedy hands and walked away.

Behind her, Susan gasped. "There's nothing in it!"

Bella turned. "Are the images of your father and stepmother not there?"

"No, no, you insolent witch. Something *else*!"

"What?" Bella's eyebrows arched.

"I don't know. Something!"

Bella shrugged, and pivoted away. "I simply don't know what you mean."

But as she tipped the precious medicine between Sophie's lips, unease ripened in her gut. If Susan really wanted to know where the quinine had come from, there was no telling how much she'd be able to pry from Lois or Pearl about Bella's true identity.

Capitol Square, Richmond, Virginia
Saturday, October 22, 1864

"Well?"

Susan bristled at Lawrence Russell's biting tone. "You catch more flies with honey than you do with vinegar." She pouted out of habit, though at this time of night he couldn't make out her face anyway. *Just the way I want it.*

He sighed, rubbing at a muscle in his jaw. "You can have no idea how tired I am of this cat-and-mouse charade. None!"

Susan's chin thrust high in the air. She withdrew Sophie's papers from inside her cloak, and instantly, he was transformed. Spellbound, even. With her.

"Please tell me that's something I can use."

"What if it is?"

347

"I'll be grateful."

"How grateful?"

"Appropriately so." He reached out and took her hand, removed the glove fingertip by fingertip and pressed a whiskery kiss inside her palm. A thrill swept through her like fire through dry brush. She wanted more. And she knew how to get it. Suddenly, not finding the mysterious folded-up paper from inside the locket did not seem so bad.

"I have nine pages here, Lawrence. Each one full to the edges with anti-slavery, anti-secessionist ravings written in Sophie's own hand."

He stretched out his open hand.

"Something for nothing? I don't think so."

A low rumble of laughter told her he caught her meaning. "Hard to believe you and Sophie are related sometimes. But I like your style." He leaned in and swayed his lips against hers, the only part of her face that was free from dimply scars.

Heart prancing with wild delight, she handed him one page, as promised.

He kissed her again, and got another.

And another, and again, until all nine pages were within his hands, and Susan's lips were hot from his kisses. That she'd had to pay for each one mattered not at all. She'd gotten what she wanted from him, as he had from her. Yet somehow, she realized despondently, she felt as empty as a tomb.

The game was over. She'd betrayed her sister. Quietly, she bade him goodbye.

"Not so fast." He grabbed her hand and hooked it through the crook of his elbow. "Let's just see what I paid for, shall we?"

As soon as she realized he was leading her toward the sputtering gaslight, she struggled against his hold. "No tricks, I promise, just let me go." Her voice was remarkably restrained for the alarm whipping through her spirit.

"Why so anxious to be off?" He pulled her into the pool of light, and she turned her head away, shame coursing through her. Thankfully, he only had eyes for the pages she'd given him. "Marvelous," he muttered. "Absolutely marvelous! How did you do it?"

In that thin moment of approval, she forgot herself and looked at him, to see clearly the man she had kissed. He was more handsome than she imagined, and in his eyes, she read joy.

Then horror. He was horrified, by her face.

Mortification gripped her, shook her, paralyzed her.

"Ugh!" he yelled, face twisting in obvious revulsion. People turned to stare. "No wonder you wanted to only meet in the dark!" His words hit her like dung.

Hatred surged into every corner of her being. "How dare you!" she screamed, not caring if her shrill voice caused a stir. It was what she was best at, after all. Susan sprang forward, snatched the papers out of his hands, wheeled around, and ran. No one could humiliate her like that and expect to get away with it. *No one.*

Chapter Thirty-three

Kent House, Richmond, Virginia
Tuesday, October 25, 1864

Six days, Sophie mused as she smoothed out Elizabeth's grid on the writing desk. Her body had been racked by a dangerously high fever for six days, Bella had said. Sophie could not recall a single one of them. Bella had safeguarded the cipher, if not the locket, but the necklace was a small price to pay for the quinine. The medicine that had failed to save Daphne had saved Sophie's life instead.

But there was no time for protracted convalescence. It was time to work. Bella had learned from the Van Lew slaves that the investigation of Elizabeth had ended for lack of hard evidence against her. She was still the funnel through which intelligence reached Sharpe. And Sophie was still one of her main informants. The Confederate Congress was debating whether to conscript and grant freedom to slaves, Bella had told her tonight. The Federals would want to know about it. Sophie dipped the nib of her pen in the inkwell, and suspended it above her paper while she referred to the cipher.

Something was wrong.

She laid down her pen and held the cipher flat with one hand. With her right forefinger, she pinned a letter down onto the grid.

It jumped. Right out of its square.

Astonished, Sophie jerked back, then leaned forward and watched as the lines and circles jumped around on the paper like fleas, one hopping over another. She shook her head, rubbed her eyes, squinted again. The letters wiggled in their boxes, changing shape.

Her gut twisted. Breath shortened. *This can't be happening. I must be dreaming.* But she wasn't. Frantically, she grabbed her Bible and opened to where the psalms should be, searching for comfort, or wisdom, or truth.

She couldn't read a thing. The letters danced on the page in drunken revelry, and would not, could not be tamed. If it were not a holy book she would have thrown it against the wall. She picked up *Les Miserables*, and couldn't read that either. *Great Expectations. North and South.* Soon her floor was littered with open books she could not read. Panic rose, the room spun. *Was this how it began for Mother?* A silver blade flashed in memory's eye. A scream. A slice. An arc of blood. Sophie grabbed the scar on her wrist.

A knock on her door and she jumped.

"Sophie?" Harrison's voice.

She ran to meet him in the doorway, nearly fell upon his neck. Her feet left the floor as he picked her up in a fierce embrace. "Bella said you were so ill," he said. "But the quinine saved you. And I wasn't here for you. If I had lost you . . ."

"But Harrison," she whispered desperately, tears spilling down her cheeks. "I'm losing my mind!"

Days passed, and still she could not read or write. Preston learned of it right away, since it halted her ability to assist him. She read in his eyes and heard in his voice the terror she kept barely contained. In whispered conference with Pearl, he ordered her treatment. She drank whatever was given her, until mercifully, she barely did anything but sleep.

Voices drifted in and out of her consciousness, and every once in a while, she was aware of the pull of a brush through her hair. Hands turning her onto her back. Damp, cold cloths across her forehead—but these she brushed off as quickly as they came, for they felt like the hands of the dead being laid across her skin. Why, why were they here? Had she killed them somehow, though she only ever wanted to stop the bloodletting by helping to end the war? If they were ghosts of Rebel soldiers killed by information she had passed, or of Union soldiers, killed by faulty intelligence she fed them, she should not have been surprised. If losing the ability to read and write was her punishment, Sophie would pray she could accept it. Salty tears slid down to her lips. She did not bother to lick them away.

"More laudanum," Sophie heard her father say from somewhere beyond the fog. "Give her more laudanum. Do not hold back."

"Yes, Massa." An unattached voice.

"I will not stand to lose her the way I lost her mother, do you understand me? If she awakes, give her laudanum!"

Sophie rolled onto her side, grabbed a bedpan, and retched into it. She could not become her mother.

But Daughter, you've already begun.

Eleanor appeared before Sophie as she had at the end, her eerie smile just one more slit on her body among dozens of scabbed-over slashes. *Too much blood,* she'd said. *Bad humors. Let them out, you must let them out.*

"No," Sophie said to the vapor in her mind. But her mother's voice was so loud, she cringed.

Why yes, of course, it's better this way, dear. Now the blood on our hands is our own. The blood on your hands is your own.

Sophie brought her hands to her face and saw curtains of blood flowing from the slits on her wrists. A scream ripped from her throat, wrenching her back to consciousness. Breathless, crying, she wiped her hands on her sheets before daring to look at them. They were dry. She was whole. Just one little scar on her wrist, and that not of her own making. Yes, she was thinking clearly now. She'd only been taking the knife from her mother. It was an accident.

Is that how you saw it, Dear? I'm so glad.

"See how wildly she stares!"

"More laudanum!"

And Sophie drank what they brought to her lips. Her mind retreated from itself, her tortured thoughts buried like a twisted sheet beneath a thickly padded quilt. Voices seemed shrouded in bolts of batting. Meaning was severed from their sound.

Eventually, words worked their way through the batting. "How are you today?"

"I am mad," she would reply without looking at the one who hovered near. How odd, that she should feel so calm.

Across the parlor from Susan, Preston's cigar smoke puffed from behind the newspaper he held in front of his face, though surely his eyes were too weak to read it. With a stab, she wondered if he was deliberately ignoring her.

Nearly two weeks had passed since Susan had snatched the evidence of Sophie's disloyalty from the greedy hands of Lawrence Russell. It burned within her possession, still, as she carefully considered her next move. If she showed it to her father, would it drive a wedge between him and Sophie? Or would he condemn Susan as a conniving, bitter woman bent on spreading malicious lies out of spite? Susan had feared it would be the latter.

No matter. With Sophie ill, she need not take the risk of exposing her. By the simple process of elimination, her father's affections must turn toward Susan once again. Sheer loneliness—or at least nostalgia—

ought to soften him at least a trifle toward her. *And it wouldn't hurt anyone if I were to file down my edges, too.*

She cleared her throat. "Daddy, may I read that to you? Save on your eyes when you can."

He peered at her over the top of his paper, then set it aside with a sigh. "I wasn't really reading, anyway."

Susan screwed her lips to the side. "Thinking about Sophie?"

He grunted, and she prickled.

"She's not coming back, you know." Her mind was clearly gone, even if Susan was the only one who could admit it. Right now, Madeline Blair was upstairs reading to her, though the girl had been unresponsive all day.

Preston shifted on the settee and turned his tired gaze to the fire wavering behind its grate.

Sophie's going the way of her mother, I suppose. She had more sense to say it aloud. From what the servants had told Susan, Eleanor had gone stark raving mad and now it was her daughter's turn. Her father must be haunted by it.

"We used to be close," she said. "You used to love me. But you weren't there for me when I needed you the most."

His eyes met hers. "What are you talking about? You were the one who flaunted yourself about with reckless abandon, virtually begging for scandal and vice."

"No. Not as a child. I needed you with me after Mother died, but you left me alone with the servants while you chased the news."

"Only for days, or weeks at a time."

"An eternity to a child."

"To provide for you!"

To run away from your pain! She shook her head, breathed deeply, tried desperately to tame her tongue. "Other reporters stayed close to home, you could have too. I needed you." Her lips trembled. "I never stopped."

Surprise registered in his eyes. "Susan, I'm sorry if you felt left behind as a child. But certainly now as a grown woman you can understand that I did what I had to do. Besides, if I hadn't left Richmond to cover stories elsewhere, I never would have met and married Eleanor and had Sophie."

"What a shame that would have been." The poisonous words flicked out from Susan's lips before she could stop them. Heat blazed beneath the collar of her gown. Would her stepmother trump her still, even from the grave? Would her half sister be uppermost in his heart, even from the clutches of insanity?

Preston's eyes threw daggers across the room. "Regardless of your feelings toward your late stepmother, it was her fortune that built this house and kept you in the lifestyle you always felt so entitled to. In fact, it keeps us going still, while the rest of Richmond staggers about in rags!"

He was missing the point entirely. "I'm your daughter."

"Don't you remember? You decided not to be when you refused to live under my authority so many years ago. It was you, Susan, who turned from me." He rose and slowly, stiffly covered the space between them. "And still, you're not truly home."

Susan stood to meet his misty gaze. "What can you mean? I'm right here!"

"Your body is, my dear. But not your heart."

"You speak in riddles," she said. But a thaw crept over her at the sound of "my dear" on his lips.

His shoulders sagged. "Oh, Susan. You are so very hard."

"Sophie is nearly gone," she tried again, bewildered. "I'm the only family you've got."

"I have no one." He wiped his hand over his beard and leaned against the doorway before half turning back to her. "I'm leaving in the morning."

"What? Now?"

"Sophie doesn't know whether I'm here or not. Besides, newspaper editors are no longer exempt from service. I'm going to serve with the local troops defending Richmond."

"But—your heart!" It was a miracle he'd survived combat at Gettysburg with his condition.

"My heart is not your concern," he rasped. "It never was."

Susan stared at his broad back as he walked away, tears welling in her eyes. But as his footsteps faded, another set quietly took their place.

"Susan, honey?"

Susan jerked at the touch of Mrs. Blair's arm around her shoulders. She sank down onto the sofa, and Mrs. Blair sank with her. "You were listening?"

The older woman sighed. "I couldn't help but overhear a little." She offered an embroidered handkerchief, and Susan took it. "I see your hurt, and I know you're prickly as a porcupine because of it. Now, I'm not your mother, God rest her, and I don't pretend to be. But I'm *a* mother, and I do believe it would do us both some good if I could spread a little mothering over you."

Susan shrugged. "I don't need a mother."

Mrs. Blair held her tight. "And yet you need your father."

Susan opened her mouth, but Mrs. Blair held up her hand to stop her. "Dry your eyes, honey, but you let me do the talking for just a spell. I can see that you've suffered mightily, and my guess is that some of it's your own doing, and some of it isn't. You've got bitterness written all over you. Now you think it's your daddy's job to make you happy again, but you're wrong. Each of us is in charge of our own happiness. We can't wait for someone else—anyone else—to hand it to us."

"But I'm his *daughter* and he doesn't even—"

"You have a lot to say. But have you once said the words your daddy is longing to hear?"

Susan squinted at her. *What business of Madeline Blair's was it anyway?*

"Apologize, honey."

She huffed. "Like the prodigal son. Is that the idea?" *Father, I have sinned against heaven, and in thy sight . . .* The parable trailed through Susan's mind.

"Your daddy is just waiting to love you if you would only make things right."

Grunting, Susan wiped her nose. Shook her head. "He isn't. It's Sophie he loves, not me."

A sad smile softened Mrs. Blair's face. "Sounds like you need to ask the Almighty for help."

"Help with what?"

"Ask Him to help you know the right thing to do—and then ask Him to help you do it. One without the other is no good, you know."

Susan closed her eyes to keep from glaring at her neighbor. Then, coolly, "You must be very tired, Mrs. Blair. I understand you have a cat waiting for you at home." A twinge of guilt shot through her. What a cruel thing to say to a woman with a husband and two sons in the grave, and two more sons dodging death every day.

Mrs. Blair kissed Susan's pockmarked cheek. "Good night, then. And Susan—pray."

But Susan had forgotten how.

Kent House, Richmond, Virginia
Monday, November 9, 1864

"Pearl. I can do that." Bella bade the older woman sit down. The poor woman had been brewing tea and cooking what scant supplies she had for Sophie until she teetered toward collapse. Gratitude written on her face, Pearl slid onto the bench with a heavy sigh.

"Was it like this when Eleanor started going?" Bella dared to ask, not sure if she wanted the answer.

"Seems like," said Pearl, yawning. "It was bad. Tell you that much. Fits, and then nothing, just lying around like the dead, then fits again. . . . And she saw things. People. She'd talk to them."

"Sophie saw all that happen to her mother?"

"Saw it? She spent her best years trying to pull her out of it. We

357

followed the doctor's orders precisely, just like we're doing now."

Bella frowned. "Has a doctor seen Sophie?"

"Nah. He saw Missus Eleanor, though, and it's the same thing, just a different soul. Massa remembers what to do."

Carefully, Bella poured boiling water into a cup and added a wire basket of tea leaves. "Like this?"

"That's right. Then you add the laudanum. It's right there."

"Laudanum," Bella repeated. "That's made from opium, isn't it?" She'd seen enough opium at Gettysburg to last her a lifetime.

"Believe it is, baby." Pearl stretched her arms over her head and yawned again. "We got lucky with this one. Opium and laudanum so scarce you can't hardly find it anywhere in the South these days. But we had a store set by for the Missus from years ago. Otherwise, Missy would be up a creek."

"So you've been adding laudanum to her drinks every day?"

"Oh, yes, more than once a day. Whenever she'll take it. That's Massa's orders."

Bella rounded on her, eyes wide. "She's overdosed! It's hurting her!" She'd watched both the Confederate surgeon and her own future son-in-law unwittingly do the same in Gettysburg. "The drug starts out innocently enough, an escape from pain. But use it too much, it'll make you crazy. Kill you, even."

"What? *Make* you crazy? Massa says it's supposed to *fix* the crazy!"

"Did it work on Missus Eleanor?" she asked pointedly.

"No, baby, she a bad case. Real bad case."

Bella cocked her head. *Of course she was.* "The laudanum stops now."

"Massa ordered it!"

"Well, Mr. Kent isn't here." He and Harrison were both out with their battalions, somewhere outside the city.

Pearl clucked her tongue and shuddered. "He gonna be vexed when he comes back and sees Missy not getting her medicine."

"He'll be thrilled when he comes home and finds that Missy doesn't need it."

Kent House, Richmond, Virginia
Thursday, November 17, 1864

Bone-tired, chilled, and stiff, Harrison Caldwell arrived back at the Kent House wrapped in dread. He could only guess as to whether there had been any change in Sophie's condition. When he'd kissed her goodbye, she hadn't even known he was there. She probably didn't realize he'd been gone at all. *Or that the world turns—and the war rages—without her.*

In truth, being away had been a reprieve. He was helpless to improve her condition, and he could not stand by and watch her slip from him. Releasing a pent-up sigh, he let himself in with the key and latched the door behind him.

Voices drifted down the hall to him. *Callers? At this hour?* He was in no mood to be congenial. Then another thought struck him. Were they here because Sophie had taken a turn for the worse?

Heedless of his unkempt appearance, he rushed into the parlor, and then the library. Two heads were bowed together over a book. One a mass of thick black hair, and one piled high with light. Sophie looked up. Her smile trembled as she rose.

"Welcome home, darling."

In the next instant, he swept her into his arms and rained kisses upon her face before releasing her, suddenly mindful of the mud and slush on his clothes. "I prayed for you. Are you well?"

She was thin, he noticed. Thinner than usual. But her eyes were bright, not vapid. She was dressed and standing, and—"Reading?"

Her smile slipped.

"She's doing fine," Bella answered for her, rising.

"How euphemistic." A half smile twisted on her face. "The fever—

the one I can't remember—was too high, is my guess. Something snapped in my brain, and I can't make sense of the letters. They just look like random marks to me. So Bella is helping me to memorize the shapes of whole words, not just letters. When Susan isn't around, anyway." Susan still believed Bella was Daphne, an illiterate slave. "Maybe one day it'll come back to me just like that." She snapped her fingers. "But if I don't relearn how to read and write I'll go cra—I mean, I will be very frustrated and sad. Words are my life. Or they were before I met you."

Harrison smiled at her compliment, even as he ached with sympathy. She lost the capacity for the written language? How very, very hard. "We'll get through this."

"Goldilocks?" Preston Kent walked into the library, apparently having just got in from home guard duty himself. In an instant, he folded Sophie into his embrace. "You're going to be fine. Just fine."

"Daddy, you're home?" Susan called from the hallway, then appeared in the doorway. In a flash, her face darkened and her lips cinched tighter than a miser's purse as she watched Preston and Sophie's reunion. "Welcome back," she said coldly. "To both of you." She turned and stormed away.

Chapter Thirty-four

Spotswood Hotel, Richmond, Virginia
Monday, January 2, 1865

*T*he thick envelope grew damp in Susan's hand. Heels clicking down the stairs, she carried it through swarms of government workers and civilians to the Confederate Post Office in the basement of the Spotswood. Rumors and news whirled in the air along with cheap perfume and the smell of wool in need of laundering. Susan had no taste for any of it.

She had tried winning back her father's affections and had failed. Truth be told, she hated that his acceptance of her was so important. But against her wishes, her happiness now hung upon it. And clearly, it could not be had as long as Sophie was his darling—which she was more than ever now that they almost lost her. His heart was not big enough for both his daughters. *Never was.* It was Susan's turn to be loved.

She didn't need to pray, as Mrs. Blair had suggested, to know her next move. The only course left was to deliver it directly to the War Department herself. Susan simply couldn't risk her father hating her even more for accusing his "Goldilocks" of disloyalty. Nor could she risk being seen at Mechanics Hall in person. Tongues would wag. Her betrayal of her sister might eclipse Sophie's betrayal of the South in Preston's mind. One never could tell about fathers.

It is the right thing to do, Susan told herself as she stuffed the envelope into the slot for outgoing mail. *For the South.*

Mechanics Hall, Richmond, Virginia
Friday, January 6, 1865

Harrison rubbed his eyes and tried again to focus on the correspondence in front of him. There had been a rash of accusations against Unionists lately, and he had been on high alert for further mentions of Sophie. Rather than allowing her fever-induced disability to end her activities in espionage, she had simply enlisted Bella's help in coding the messages. She was just as much at risk as she ever was. All of them were.

"Shaw." A fellow clerk named Ainsley ambled over to his desk and spread some papers before him. The edges were curled, and they were creased down the middle, and they were absolutely crammed with script, some of which was crossed out by what looked to be an editor's pen. "What do you make of this?"

Harrison frowned. "Did this just come in the mail?"

"Yes it did. But the envelope was already open. Any note of explanation or instructions there may have been must have fallen out in transit. Can you make out what it says? It's so smudged."

"Let's see here." He began reading aloud, and then stopped abruptly.

"Something wrong?"

Harrison squinted. Swallowed. Marshalled his wits. "It's just hard to decipher with these editor proofing marks all over it."

"But you used to be a newspaper man, right? So you ought to be just fine. Right?"

"Mm-hmm. You'd think, wouldn't you?" Especially since they were written in his own hand. These were Sophie's first attempts at journalism, written six, seven years ago. But the themes were still relevant today. Unfortunately, here in Richmond, both Sophie and Harrison came down on the wrong side of the debate. Harrison's jaw clamped. There, in the corner of the page, was scrawled *S. Kent, Philadelphia Female Boarding School.* He would not lose her again. He could not stomach the thought of her being thrown in prison.

"All right." Ainsley interrupted Harrison. "What about that right there?" He pointed to a large chunk of text where Harrison had rewritten the conclusion of Sophie's article. "Can you read that for me?"

The text was in block letters, easy enough for anyone to discern, Harrison thought. Still, he obliged.

"I see. And now, can you read this?" Ainsley slid an envelope from Harrison's "done" basket right under his nose. Pointed to the handwriting. "Because I'd sure as anything think that if you can read one, you can read the other. Am I right or am I right?"

He knew. Harrison's mind whirred. Ainsley knew that Harrison had written those things, which was certainly his ticket to Castle Thunder. But he didn't seem concerned with the identity of S. Kent. Paired with the city of Philadelphia as it was, it was unlikely Ainsley would make the mental leap that a citizen of Richmond was the writer. Harrison was the only person in question.

He aimed to keep it that way. If he was put in Castle Thunder, those papers would be filed and promptly lost, for there simply was no uniform system for keeping track of Unionist inmates. The evidence against Sophie would just . . . disappear. She'd be safe, as long as he sacrificed himself on her behalf. Yes, he'd be in prison, but he'd done it before. He could do it again. Besides, he'd never been in Castle Thunder before. When he got out, he'd write a report about it. As much as he wanted to tell Sophie goodbye, and warn her to watch her step, the last thing he wanted was to lead any detectives straight to her house. The nagging thought that he would no longer be able to intercept additional accusations of her wormed through his middle. *Lord, let this one be the last.*

"Shaw." Ainsley prodded quietly.

Harrison swallowed and raked his fingers through his hair, relishing the absence of lice. "Ready when you are."

———

Sophie reeled. "No," she whispered.

The waning afternoon light struggled through the doorway around Preston as he shut the door behind him. "I'm as shocked and disappointed as you are, my dear. But I saw him being brought to Castle Thunder under guard myself this afternoon." Preston's ashen face confirmed it was no falsehood.

"What charge?" She braced herself. *Spies hang.*

"Disloyalty," Preston said. "Something about anti-slavery, anti-secession views." He shrugged out of his cloak and hung it on the hall stand, along with his hat.

"That's all?"

"It's enough. They found it in writing, I learned. Sophie, I'm sorry. It's a strict law, but necessary in these times. Richmond crawls with those who would destroy us from within our own capital. Not every Unionist is a spy, but you can bet your bottom shinplaster that every spy is a Unionist."

Passing between the statues of Mars and Venus, she followed him down the hall and into the library where he sat in his favorite leather armchair. "But Oliver worked in the War Department! He helped build the fortifications around Richmond and manned them himself! What other loyalty do they demand?" *What proof do they have?* She dared not ask.

Shaking his head, Preston pinched tobacco from a paper bag and tamped it down into the bowl of his pipe. "I don't agree with every law, but I abide by each one of them, and so should you. As much as I hate to admit it, Oliver Shaw may have more sinister designs on the Confederacy than we imagine. I know nothing of his family, after all. I was far too impetuous in inviting him to board with us. And allowing him to court you." He poked a thin stick of kindling into the fire and lit his pipe with it. Smoke puffed from his mouth and billowed above his head, filling the library with its redolent scent. "We gave him quarter. I nearly gave him my daughter, for pity's sake. If he's so cunning he fooled the both of us, there's no limit to the damage he may have done. He worked in the War Department with sensitive materials every day!"

"Daddy, you're speculating. It seems his only crime was having an opinion."

Preston shook his head, cradling his pipe in his hand, then chewed the stem once more. "I must atone. Let the clerks have the trenches, and let those who can read and write do the reporting. My eyesight may be weak, but I'm not colorblind. I can spot a blue coat as well as anyone. And I sure as heck can pull a trigger."

"What are you—"

"I'm going to the front with my old regiment, the 21st Virginia. You can tell Mrs. Blair I'll look out for her sons while I'm there. If Petersburg falls, so will Richmond. That's the place for me."

Tears pooled in Sophie's eyes. "Must you go?" Would he leave her now, when Harrison had just been taken from her, as well?

"Tomorrow. I'm doing this for you, to preserve our way of life. You'll stay away from Thunder. Understand?"

She did.

In a daze, she left the room and dragged heavily up the stairs.

"Did someone die?" Susan, waiting at the top.

"Oliver's been thrown into Castle Thunder, and Daddy's going to the front."

Hesitation ballooned in the space between the sisters, where Sophie had expected a snide remark instead. "Oliver? Why?"

"Someone found something he wrote, and called it disloyal."

But what? She pressed her hands to her temples and tried to focus. Harrison was far too cautious and intelligent to put anything incriminating in writing! What on earth could anyone possibly find here, where Harrison had no history at all?

Oh no. Heart thudding, Sophie brushed past her sister and into her chamber, pushing the door shut behind her. Hurrying to her bureau, she yanked open the top drawer. Slid her hand beneath the liner. And found nothing. Her trembling hands were empty. Had the articles she'd saved for sentiment condemned the man she loved to prison?

"Looking for something?"

Sophie jerked her head up, and met Susan's piercing blue gaze in the doorway.

"So am I." Slowly, smiling, Susan turned away and sashayed down the stairs humming "Dixie."

Day melted into night, and night seeped into day, over and over, until two tenuous weeks trickled by. Until one day in late January, Susan dropped the newspaper on the dining room table next to Sophie's modest breakfast.

"Friends of yours?" she sneered. Sleet slashed the windows at her back, blurring frost-encrusted trees bending beneath their crystal weight.

Apprehension barbed as Sophie set down her cup of coffee and squinted at the tiny columns, but the letters flipped and dipped impossibly. Forehead aching with concentration, she pinned each word to the paper as she tried to make it out.

"Oh, that's right. You forgot how to read." Susan snatched the paper from her and cleared her throat, while heat singed Sophie's cheeks. "Allow me. 'The public will be gratified to know that on January 20, Rebel authorities struck simultaneous blows at the secret Unionists, which resulted in the arrests of F. W. E. Lohmann, John Hancock, James

Duke and his sons Moses, Thomas, and William, all Richmond residents, as well as Isaac Silver and John H. Timberlake of Spotsylvania County.'"

Sophie's palms grew damp. *Eight men? In one day?*

"'They now all reside in Castle Thunder. The editor of this paper would congratulate the detectives on this work if only it were not so tardy. One would hope more arrests of this nature will be made' . . . et cetera. So many, all at once." Susan's bright words echoed Sophie's considerably dimmer sentiments. "I do wonder who will be next. Perhaps a woman."

It wasn't. On January 23, Samuel Ruth, the colored railroad superintendent who aided in the escape of Dr. Caleb Lansing and other Yankees, was arrested with the same charge: disloyalty. Ten Union agents now languished in Castle Thunder, including Harrison.

Who is left? Abby Green, Lucy Rice, and Robert Ford, the former hostler for Warden Turner, had all fled North months ago. Elizabeth Van Lew had survived her own investigation, and her former slave Mary Bowser was still serving in the Confederate White House. William Rowley the farmer, Thomas McNiven the baker, Erasmus Ross the clerk at Libby Prison, Sophie and Bella—all of them were still active. Likely, there were more that even Sophie was not aware of. But surely it was only a matter of time until one of them—or more—disappeared as well.

Castle Thunder, Richmond, Virginia
Friday, February 3, 1865

Winter's frosty breath penetrated the clothing Harrison had been wearing ever since his arrest. The fog's chill was a small price to pay, however, for a breath of fresh, if damp, air. Given no soap or water with which to bathe, and being confined to small rooms, the inmates at Castle Thunder quickly ripened with their own stench. It had been three weeks since the prison had last turned its inmates into the yard so the prison floors could be washed.

Briskly, Harrison walked laps around the fenced-in prison yard, beneath a bleak, colorless sky. His pace slowed in embarrassingly short order, however. *Little wonder.* He'd been surviving on half a loaf of corn bread a day, which was either rock-hard or alive with worms.

"Watch it!" A swarthy fellow shouted, and Harrison jerked his head up just in time to avoid walking right into another prisoner.

"I beg your pardon." Harrison skirted the man, and kept going, paying closer attention this time to his surroundings. There were hundreds of prisoners at Castle Thunder. Unionists, Confederate deserters and stragglers, Union deserters, and overflow convicts from the local jails. Gentlemen whose only crime lay in their opinions mingled with hardened criminals. Likely, there were Rebel spies among them, too. It was a far cry from the camaraderie he'd enjoyed with the officers at Libby.

Stuffing his hands in his pockets, he paced the perimeter in silence. Even his tread was muffled by the fog.

Then, "Don't I know you, Freckles?"

Harrison glanced up, surprised to find the prisoner in blue addressing him. *Union deserter.* And he looked familiar. "Sorry, no." He kept walking.

A hand on his arm whipped Harrison around again. "I think I do. My name's Milo. And yours is . . ."

"Oliver Shaw."

Milo tilted his head, squinting. "Nah. Doesn't suit. But I remember you. That unmistakable hair. Your freckles. Your Northern accent."

"You must have me confused. This is my first stay here at Castle Thunder. Excuse me."

"Why? Got someplace better to be?" Milo smirked, greasy hair falling down into his eyes.

Harrison grinned with an air of nonchalance he did not feel.

"Don't we all?" Laughter rippled through a small knot of men now gathering around them.

Milo snapped his fingers. "Fortress Monroe. Right? It would have been . . . almost a year ago. You came in half-starved, stayed with us a while—heck, you interviewed me! That's it, you were writing stories, right after you wrote the one about escaping from Libby Prison. But your name isn't Oliver Shaw. Say, what are you in here for?"

"Why, I'm innocent. Just like the rest of you." This time, no one laughed. Harrison's gaze skittered across the crowd. Several pairs of eyes burned through the fog and bore into his.

"You're not a soldier, are you?" Milo blathered on, right on Harrison's heels as he walked away. Would his questions never cease? Sweat prickled beneath Harrison's collar as he eyed the guards on the edges of the yard.

"And neither are you," he parried. If Milo revealed Harrison's true identity—"Crying shame deserting one army didn't ingratiate you with the other."

"You're not a Southerner. You were imprisoned once before, came to Monroe, and yet here you are again. If you're not a deserter, then—"

Harrison wheeled on Milo, plowed his fist into his jaw. Milo returned with a hard punch to his gut, igniting the fighting instinct Harrison had tamped down since the impetuous days of his fatherless youth. Harrison raised his fists, and so did Milo. Their breath suspended in clouds between them as they orbited one another. Prisoners gathered round, cheering for some excitement.

A sly grin snaked across Milo's face. "What? Don't want anyone else to know you're a—"

Lightning fast, Harrison lashed out against the bridge of his nose, felt it crack beneath his knuckles. Blood streaming into his mouth, Milo doubled over and barreled into Harrison's middle, knocking him to the thawing ground, flat on his back.

"Stop!" called a guard, but Harrison only fought harder. If Milo told a guard what he thought he knew, it could be his end.

Footsteps rattled the platform at the top of the fence as two guards came running toward them. With ice-cold slush soaking through his back, Harrison grabbed Milo's shirt, yanked him forward and plowed the crown of his head into Milo's already broken nose. He slumped, and Harrison scrambled out from beneath him—right into the wrenching grip of the guards.

"What happened?" one of them asked. "Union loyalist couldn't handle a little teasing from a Union deserter?"

Light-headed, Harrison braced himself as they escorted him to the bricked section of the prison yard reserved for punishment. Before he understood what was happening, they had lashed his arms beneath his knees, pulled up his shirt from the waist, and were thrashing his bare back with a broad leather strap.

That night, Harrison Caldwell begged sleep to cover him, engulf him, take him away from this place. Today's tête-à-tête with Milo had been far too revealing. So much so, he wondered if the wheels had already been set in motion to now charge him with espionage. Certainly Milo would talk with anyone who would listen.

Doubt stung Harrison as much as the welts on his skin. If they knew he was a spy, would they think to investigate Sophie? Did his presence here actually endanger her more? Weariness ached in his bones as pain throbbed across his back.

Trapping a groan in his chest, Harrison winced as he rolled to his other side on the floor, his bones poking into the hardwood no matter which way he turned. His clothes had not yet dried out from being soaked, and he imagined they wouldn't before he caught pneumonia. *Lord,* he began to pray, but for the first time in memory, he could not find the right words. As his eyes drifted closed, Psalm 31 washed over him: *Pull me out of the net that they have laid privily for me: for thou art my strength. Into thine hand I commit my spirit: thou hast redeemed me, O Lord God of truth . . . I will be glad and rejoice in thy mercy: for thou hast considered my trouble; thou hast known my soul in adversities; And hast not shut me up into the hand of the enemy: thou hast set my feet in a large room.*

A loud snore from somewhere in the tightly packed room jerked Harrison, and his lips quirked in a smile at the heavenly thought of a large room. Finally he fell into a fitful sleep with these verses echoing in his spirit: *My times are in thy hand: deliver me from the hand of mine enemies, and from them that persecute me . . . Be of good courage, and he shall strengthen your heart, all ye that hope in the Lord.*

Reluctantly, morning came, and with it, a stern-faced guard. "Shaw."

Harrison rubbed his eyes, grateful, at least, that his real name had not yet been discovered. "Yes."

"You're being moved today."

Suddenly, he was wide awake. "Have I been acquitted?" Audacious hope. Still, he'd heard that Samuel Ruth had been honorably discharged from Thunder, thanks to habeas corpus Commissioner Sydney Baxter. Harrison had filed Baxter's reports himself at the War Department! Surely the goodwill Harrison had established with the commissioner—

"Acquitted?" The guard laughed. "Sentenced, is more like it."

Harrison felt the blood drain from his face as a noose loomed in his mind. He swallowed the bile backing up in his throat. *So Milo had gotten through after all.* "What hour?"

"Twelve noon."

Harrison bowed his head, prayed for the strength to die nobly for his country, and for another to take his place in Sophie's life to bring her the happiness she deserved.

"That is, assuming the train is on time."

"Train?" Harrison's thoughts chugged to keep up.

"We need more space, and you need a lesson in Confederate patriotism. You're going to the front, soldier. God knows the ranks have room for you there."

Chapter Thirty-five

Richmond and Petersburg Depot, Richmond, Virginia
Saturday, February 4, 1865

*A*bove the train station, snow eddied like cotton fluff against a sky of the palest blue silk. Nose and cheeks pinched with cold, Sophie carefully trod across the rutted, ice-enameled yard, hugging two parcels to her deep green velvet cloak.

"Headed to Petersburg?" she asked the conductor as soon as she reached the platform.

"That's a fact. No room for civilians on this train, though."

"Oh no, I'm not going. These are for our soldiers there." Her father in the 21st Virginia, and Joel and Asher Blair in their own regiment. One of the packages was from their mother, who was now abed with a racking cough. "Have you room for these parcels?" The Confederate Post Office below Spotswood was a disaster. The food she and Mrs. Blair packed to supplement the men's rations would certainly spoil before it reached them if they had chosen that route.

The conductor nodded, rolling his handlebar mustache between his forefinger and thumb. "That car there, if you'll just set them inside the door." He pointed. "It'll reach them right quick."

Sophie nodded her thanks, the ostrich plume of her hat dipping into her view, and threaded through a crowd of women who were hoping for news from the front. Snowflakes flecked their shabby hats and tattered hems. *Should we evacuate? Do they need more food? Are our boys in want? I've not got much food left but I'll look for more jewelry to give the Treasury if it will help . . .* Everyone suffered now, soldiers and civilians. They were starving for food and hope and assurance that the slain had not fallen in vain. Famine and suspense were shadows over Richmond that even the sun could not chase away.

After feeding the boxes to the yawning boxcar, Sophie turned— and froze. For there, working his way through the snow-spotted women, was Harrison, a guard at his elbow. A pulpy, purple bruise swallowed his right eye, and his cheekbones pushed against his pale skin. But it was him—alive, and free of Castle Thunder.

The guard addressed the conductor, pointing to Harrison, then to the train, and Sophie slowly walked toward them, the thin layer of snow muting her steps until she was close enough to touch him if she would but reach out. She didn't.

He raised his gaze to meet hers, and his hard brown eyes instantly flashed with recognition, betraying his shock at her presence. The guard and conductor raised their voices in a debate Sophie could not register, providing a covering for precious few whispered words.

"Going somewhere?" he asked. His words, so casual. His eyes, deadly intent.

Sophie shook her head. "Sending a parcel to Daddy, at the front."

Harrison cocked his eyebrow. "Maybe I'll see him there."

"You're not—going—to fight?"

"So to speak."

Tears sprang to her eyes as their conversation from months ago washed over her with crushing force. *I'll not fire against my own country,* he'd said. *They won't hesitate to shoot at you!* Her own words resurrected. She buried them in her throat. They had only seconds left, surely.

"Listen." He turned his body, so they were shoulder to shoulder, as mere strangers in the crowd. "You have business with Samuel Ruth. He waits for your call at his office."

Sophie understood. The railroad superintendent was free again, and ready to pass on valuable intelligence. Through Sophie. So many others in the network were still imprisoned, or in hiding.

"Do not hesitate," Harrison muttered, barely moving his lips. "No matter what." He glanced at her, and his meaning thudded to the bottom of her stomach like a boulder. Their intelligence of Rebel movements, plans, and troop strength would no longer just endanger Lee's army. It would put Harrison's life in peril too, even more so than her father's and Mrs. Blair's sons. Native Virginians had no trouble defending themselves against the Union. Harrison, however, was caught on the wrong side of the line.

Sophie's breath shortened. How could she continue the work?

"You must carry on. Follow your convictions, no matter the cost."

"Promise you'll come back to me," she whispered desperately.

The ghost of a smile flickered on his lips. "I promise I'll try."

She shook her head. "Say you'll return." *Please, I beg you.*

"I don't know if it's true. I will not lie to you." Without looking at her, he entwined his cool fingers with hers, their hands hidden in the velvet folds of her skirts. "Our times are in His hands, Sophie. Courage."

Soon, the train hissed and shrieked toward war with Harrison aboard. The snow thickened in the widening space between them, blotting him from view.

By mid-March, courage was a rare commodity in all of Richmond. Sherman had captured and burned Columbia, South Carolina, and days after Abraham Lincoln was inaugurated for his second term, Sheridan scattered the remainder of General Early's army in Virginia, cutting off the remaining source of food for the hundred thousand hungry in Richmond.

Red flags fluttered outside houses along Clay Street, announcing the owners were auctioneering their furniture, or renting to the highest bidder. The price of flour spiked to $1200 a barrel. Confederate currency plummeted to $107 Confederate dollars for a single dollar in gold. Boxes and machinery were steadily dispatched down the Danville railroad. Tredegar shut down, and sent unfinished munitions via the James River canal toward Lynchburg. Lee was so desperate for men that the Confederate Congress finally passed a resolution allowing black men to take up arms for the South, a move that alienated many Southerners even further from the government. All of this, the Union military wanted to know. All of this Sophie told them, through Bella, her scribe and conduit to Elizabeth Van Lew. None of it gave Sophie pause. She had no reason to wonder if the intelligence would bring harm to the two men she loved.

And then, one bright, wind-whipped day, she did.

"Fort Stedman, you said?" Sophie sat across from the desk of Samuel Ruth in his office on Eighth Street and Broad. Outside, beneath a snapping Rebel flag, the Richmond, Fredericksburg, and Potomac train screeched to a halt on its Broad Street tracks.

"I'm sure of it." Mr. Ruth's deep voice rumbled. "It's a Union-held fort along the siege line just outside of Petersburg. Gordon means to storm it as soon as the roads dry out."

Gordon. The 21st Virginia was under his command. Her father would be in that fight. Sophie closed her eyes against threatening tears.

"If Fort Stedman falls to the Rebels, they could break the siege," Mr. Ruth predicted. "The Union must be warned, post haste. Miss Kent."

She opened her eyes.

"We could win. Petersburg is the key to Richmond. If it falls, so will Richmond, and thus, the entire Confederacy. The war could end, soon. But not if we lose Fort Stedman."

Do not hesitate. No matter the cost.

Sophie nodded, both to Mr. Ruth, and to Harrison's haunting voice. "I understand." But would the cost of her convictions be her father?

Capitol Square, Richmond, Virginia
Wednesday, March 22, 1865

The faint scent of a coming spring feathered Bella's face as her heart beat in time with the fife and drum. The lawns of Capitol Square churned to mud beneath the feet of thousands who had come to watch this historic event. Just nine days after Congress approved enlisting black soldiers, the first three companies proudly paraded here in their new uniforms.

Bella scanned the faces around her, and did not find much pride among them. Curiosity, perhaps. In some cases, disgust.

"Ridiculous affair," a voice near Bella said. "Arming Negroes as soldiers elevates them above slavery. The government undermines the very foundation of the country. Besides, it's too late for these men to do any good for Lee anyhow." Bella prayed the woman was right.

"They're as good as free now," a Negro woman on Bella's other side murmured. "As soon as they do their duty, they'll be free."

And if the North wins, you'll all be free. Bella watched the colored troops strutting through the square, and visions of Abraham in his crisp blue uniform swam in her mind. She had no idea what had become of him. *Surely he could have sent a message somehow, couldn't he?* Maybe he couldn't. Maybe something had happened to him—or maybe he'd escaped to West Virginia, leaving her in Richmond alone. *After I came here for him more than a year ago!* Wildly, her emotions swung and struggled, until she could not determine which was uppermost. Fear? Dismay? Resentment? She closed her eyes, and saw his face again. *Longing.* Yes, that was it. She ached for her husband, no matter what kept them apart.

Bella's eyes popped open, and she re-focused on what was in front of her. *Wishing never did anybody any good anyhow.* She would put one foot in front of the other, just like those marching troops stomping in time to their martial music. God would forgive her if she did not match their springing steps. Fatigue and uncertainty shackled her. She was so weary. *Fear thou not; for I am with thee: be not dismayed; for I am thy God: I will strengthen thee; yea, I will help thee.* Unshed tears ached in her throat. The verses that bloomed in her spirit now were the same words that had bolstered her in Gettysburg during and after that battle. *Lord,* she prayed. *Abraham may be gone, but You're right here beside me. And 'who shall separate us from the love of Christ? Shall tribulation, or distress, or persecution, or famine, or nakedness, or peril, or sword?' No. We are more than conquerors through him that loved us.*

As the troops filed out of the square, the crowd dispersed. Bella headed east, toward home.

About a block outside of Capitol Square, Bella was surprised to see Susan Kent among those strolling along the sidewalk not ten yards in front of her. She was even more surprised when Susan veered from the path toward home, and toward the city's densest concentration of brothels.

She wouldn't. But the girl's scars were obviously more than skin-deep. *Would she?* Bella pursed her lips. Prostitution was not the answer. Quietly, she followed Susan until they were in an alley three blocks east of Capitol Square, where the ground was littered with scattered hay and horse manure from nearby livery stables, and women bared themselves shamelessly in picture windows, enticing a steady stream of customers.

Susan paused, her veiled gaze turned toward a bawdy house, and Bella's skin crawled as though vermin already crept over it. She could keep silent no longer.

"Miss Kent."

Susan startled, then turned, eyes wide behind the netting draped from the brim of her hat. "Daphne?"

Bella closed the distance between them. "Miss Kent, whatever problem you're chewing on, this here isn't going to wash it away." She jerked her head toward the prostitutes in the window. "This is no solution for you."

"And how would you know that?"

"You've got an emptiness inside you, I can see that. But this will only make the hole grow bigger, Miss Kent. What you're craving won't be fulfilled this way. It's wrong."

Susan smiled. "Haven't you noticed? 'Wrong' seems to be my specialty. At least according to my father."

"Don't prove him right, now. You go down this road, you may never come back. You'll die empty, alone, and young. You won't last five years before disease will riddle you and take your life."

"Riddled." Susan snorted. "I've already been riddled with disease, you fool. Can you not see the bullet holes in my skin?"

"You still have a life to live."

Susan shook her head defiantly. "What life? The only life I ever wanted to live is dead. If it wasn't ruined with my own scandal, it was buried along with this sorry Confederacy. No man will have me. My own father hates me."

"But do you hate yourself? That's the only reason I can think of that would have you throwing yourself away like this."

Susan hated being invisible. She wanted to belong to someone, even if only for a few moments. She was desperate to feel wanted, on any level, since she could never be loved the way her ex-husband loved his Caitlin, and the way Oliver Shaw loved Sophie. But even beyond that, she needed an income. Susan couldn't—she wouldn't—stay at her father's house forever. She just needed a little something to help her get started somewhere else . . .

Daphne was still talking. "You have a roof over your head, and as much food as anyone else in this starving town. You don't need to do this to survive."

Susan narrowed her eyes at her sister's maidservant. Never in her life had a slave spoken to her in this manner. Her chin was up, her gaze meeting Susan's directly. Why, she even used proper English grammar! Worse, she spoke to Susan as though she were her equal. But she wasn't. Where on earth did she get these airs? This slave was preaching to Susan with as much boldness as Mrs. Blair had so many months ago, and a few times since—and with as much success. *None.*

"And Sophie doesn't hate you, and neither does your father, not deep down," Daphne was saying.

Sophie. Not Miss Sophie. The nerve. "No? How do you know? Did he ever say anything about me when I was gone? Wonder aloud where I was, how I fared?"

"Perhaps not in words, but he was clearly distraught."

"When? Right after I left?"

A hesitation. "Of course." Her eyes shifted.

"Daphne." Susan smiled. "You were purchased at the Weeping Time in 1859 from Pierce Butler's lot of slaves. Correct?"

A frown flickered over her brow. But, "Yes."

Susan looped her arm through the slave's, held her snugly. "I left Richmond in 1857. How would you know my father's emotional state two years before you joined our household?"

A lump bobbed in her throat. "Miss Sophie told me."

"Sophie couldn't know that either. She was in boarding school in Philadelphia. You're lying to me. Why?"

Bella tried to pull away from Susan, but Susan only held on tighter. Whatever game this was, it certainly seemed as though Susan had the upper hand. Control tasted so delicious. "Lois and Pearl mentioned you used to work in the Big House down on St. Simon's Island. Tell me, when you set the table, how many forks and spoons and knives went to each place setting?"

"Is this a test?"

"Only if you fail it."

She did. Susan squeezed the slave's arm tighter. "You're not Daphne at all, are you?"

"Who else would I be?"

"Who is your master?"

Her brown eyes smoldered, unblinking, as the wind teased coils of hair from beneath her head scarf. "God alone."

The words barbed Susan. "Do you mean to say you're free? Then what on earth are you doing in our—" Stunned with comprehension, Susan stopped. There could be only one reason for a free colored woman to pose as a slave in the Confederate capital. "You're a spy!" she hissed.

The woman's eyes went dark. Her jaw set.

Yes, it all made sense now. The quinine she'd used for Sophie could only have been gotten from the North. The locket she'd worn around her neck and the strange paper she'd spirited away from it. If Sophie wasn't an outright accomplice, her sympathy toward the plight of slaves had made her vulnerable to giving quarter to this colored spy. Sophie would not question this woman's activities, no one would notice her comings and goings. Slaves could hide in plain sight. No one paid them any mind unless they misbehaved. They were—*invisible. Like me.*

"Come on now, you're talking crazy. Let's get you on home."

No. Susan would never share her home with the likes of this colored woman again. She was not Sophie's maidservant at all. *Which means Sophie doesn't own her.*

Across the alley, a door opened in a brick establishment sandwiched between a brothel and a stable. When a burly man emerged, Susan scanned the four-story building from which he came. The windows were barred. It was a slave jail. She seized upon the opportunity, hailing him over.

"Are you a slave trader?" she asked, and immediately, the woman posing as Bella tried to break free. The man caught her in the same instant, wrenching her wrists behind her back.

"Robert Lumpkin. Best in town. What have you got for me here?"

"Her pass is forged," Susan began. "She's pretending to be a different slave. I have reason to believe she's a spy."

"That a fact?" His breath smelled of tobacco and cheap whiskey. He looked her up and down. "Show me your teeth, girl."

She refused.

"She's got all her teeth. She's strong and healthy, but you see, she's a spy."

Lumpkin cleared his throat. "You sure about that? Got proof?"

"Well, I—I'm just sure of it, that's all! Can't you take a lady's word over a Negro's?"

"Thing is, spies go to Castle Thunder, even the colored ones. Whether they're slave or free, colored spies go to Thunder. And the wardens don't pay them that turns 'em in, neither. I pay." He raised his eyebrows. "This here's a fine chattel. As handsome as they come, light-complected, and if she's strong and healthy like you say she is, she'll fetch a hefty sum. So I leave it to you. Try and take her to Thunder on your own, or let me take her off your hands right now, and you get a nice wad of cash in return."

Cash. Money of her own, without selling her body in this filthy alley. It wouldn't last forever, but it would buy her time. Without so much as a glance at the groaning colored woman beside her, Susan nodded her head. "Deal."

Sophie paced the naked floor of her bedchamber, her rugs having been sent with her father, along with all the spare blankets in the house, to provide warmth for his threadbare regiment. Samuel Ruth's intelligence ricocheted in her mind, shredding her gossamer-thin peace of mind to tatters. *Gordon's divisions . . . Fort Stedman . . . Petersburg . . . Richmond . . . as soon as the roads dry out . . .* She pressed her hands to her temples, but it did not quiet the clanging in her mind.

If the Union was ready for an attack, it would mean slaughter for

Gordon's anemic division. For her father. *The war could end . . .* But would the intelligence that brought down the Confederacy kill her father as well? *And must it be by my own hand?*

The clock ticked away the silence, refusing to bow to her indecision. It marched steadily along, like the thousands and thousands of troops that had tramped along Franklin Street in front of her home in the last four years. How many more men would Davis send to war?

In a swish of green silk, Sophie swept out onto her second-story balcony and looked out over the city. Church steeples still gleamed and the river still sparkled, but between them, Richmond was worn out and used up. Stately iron fences that had once helped order the neighborhoods had been melted and cast into cannon. Weeds sprouted from cracked sidewalks, doors swung crazily on broken hinges, gaslights no longer illumined the night, and paint peeled and flaked from even the finest buildings. The city's resources simply would not stretch to fix the broken, and the men who could make repairs were all in the army—or the grave.

Almost every family grieved loss. Cemeteries crawled with dark figures as women draped in mourning visited their departed sons, husbands, fathers, brothers, sweethearts. Famine carved their figures. Care lined their faces like the ruts in the roads.

The roads were drying out.

If the war was to end anytime soon, the time to act was now. The price Sophie might pay was no greater than what tens of thousands had already offered up: the lives of those they held most dear. Beloved men—and their starving families and ruined homes—would be sacrificed on the altar of "country" until this dreadful war would end. *It has to end.*

Knuckles white on the balustrade, Sophie bowed her head beneath enormous, invisible weight. Tears bathed her cheeks. *Are you mightier than God, that the fate of the nations rests in your hands?* Her conscience pricked. Of course she wasn't. She inhaled deeply, and could almost taste the brackish scent of the James below. She would follow her convictions, and trust God for the outcome. She did not need to open her Bible to recall the words of Psalm 46. *He maketh wars to cease unto the end of the earth; he breaketh the bow, and cutteth the spear in sunder; he burneth the chariot in the fire. Be still, and know that I am God . . .*

Sophie raised her head, wiped the tears from her face. *Lord,* she prayed. *You are the Alpha and Omega. The Beginning and the End. Please, I beg you, end this terrible war.* Boldly, she requested protection for her father and for Harrison, for Asher and Joel Blair, and for Abraham, wherever they were.

With the March breeze wafting in around her, she returned to her chamber and waited for Bella.

Only Bella didn't come. Two trips to the kitchen house an hour apart only confirmed she was still gone. With Lois and Pearl's assurance that they'd send Bella to her as soon as she returned, Sophie wandered back into her room, needled with anxiety.

Sophie had already waited long enough to pass the intelligence about Fort Stedman's imminent attack. But without Bella . . . She locked the door, then pulled the cipher from between the pages of her Bible. The faded scrawl defied her. Sixes flopped to nines and back again. The letter "b" flipped to "d." The letter "n" grew a hump to become an "m," and "w" halved itself into a "v." *Impossible!* She'd never be able to code anything without Bella's help. The wrong letter and number combinations could alter the entire meaning, or render it completely meaningless. She'd have to write it without the code.

Bedposts moaned on the floor as Sophie shoved the bed away from the wall. Crouching, she peeled a curling strip of rose-patterned wallpaper, exposing another patch of bare plaster. For months this had been their only paper. She prayed the scrap that now trembled in her hands would be the last piece conscripted into service.

Pressing the paper flat with one hand, Sophie carefully guided her pencil across the glue-stained surface. After reaching the end of one painstaking sentence in plain English, she sat back and studied the letters. Dismay pummeled her. The words shifted shapes before her eyes.

Had she written them correctly at all? Why, she could barely read the marks her hand had made! Frustration boiling in her breast, she tore off the sentence, ripped it and dropped the shreds into the chamber pot.

Gong! The grandfather clock struck a blow against Sophie's spirit. *Gong! Gong!* Time was running out! *Gong! Gong! Gong!* Desperately, Sophie turned to the window. *Gong!* The Van Lew mansion was but four blocks away. *Gong!* Clouds shuttered the moonlight. *Gong! Gong!*

Finally, the chiming ceased. *Ten o'clock.* Perhaps not too late for a caller, if she hurried. Lips pressed together, Sophie hastened down the stairs and out the back door.

By the time she returned from her clandestine errand, her heart needed to be coaxed to sleep over the span of the next hour. Only after the clock resounded its twelve strokes did she finally surrender to slumber.

But slumber brought no peace. In her dreams, she soared like Icarus above the horror unfolding below. The sulfur breath of battle rose in a thick yellow blanket, blocking the sun. Muskets popped, cannon boomed, and strong men screamed like schoolgirls. Blood mingled with the last patches of snow, until the ground was corded and puddled with pink. Frantically, Sophie swooped down among the unraveling men, searching for her father among the fallen. Then she saw him, slumped over a fence he hadn't cleared. Flying to him, she turned him over.

But it was Harrison who stared vacantly back at her. With a cry, she captured him to her bosom, and tried to fly away to safety. But her wings, like those of Icarus, had melted away from the heat of battle. She could no more save him than she'd been able to end the war.

————

Susan had barely finished her morning cup of coffee when a knock pulled her to the front hall. Out of habit, she patted her hair and pinched her cheeks before opening the door.

Mrs. Blair stood before her, pale and drawn. "They're gone." Strands of brown hair fluttered listlessly in the breeze.

"What? Mrs. Blair?" Sophie approached from behind, a frightful, wrinkled mess in yesterday's gown. Why, it looked as though she had slept in that frock!

"Come in." Susan shut the door behind her as the older woman shuffled inside.

"Gone," she said again. "Eunice. Dorcas. Timothy. Simon. All my servants just—disappeared! After being part of our family for more than twenty years!"

"Oh my heavens," Sophie whispered, and led Mrs. Blair into the parlor to sit. It was the third time slaves ran away from a Church Hill home this year. All over the city, it was the same story. One that Susan had planned to use to her advantage—but could not have dreamed it would be this easy.

Lines formed between Mrs. Blair's eyebrows. "Oh, whatever will become of them now?"

Susan looked pointedly at Sophie, waiting for her to make some remark about the slaves finally being free, and how wondrous that was for God's whole wide world. But she didn't.

"We raised our servants up properly in our home, teaching them the Bible and how to pray—which is more than those abolitionists can say they've done for the African race! Just what will become of all these Negroes suddenly bursting upon their freedom? Where will they live, if not with their masters? Who will give them clothing and food whenever they need it, or nurse them back to health if they are ill?" She covered her face with her hands and wept.

Sophie murmured something in Mrs. Blair's ear that Susan couldn't hear. Her arm wrapped around Mrs. Blair's shaking shoulders and held her fast, though Sophie was an abolitionist herself. How very odd.

"They don't even know their letters!" Mrs. Blair cried. "How do they expect to fend for themselves when they don't even know how to read!"

Susan stepped closer, seizing the opening. "Are you sure? Sometimes servants will surprise you. Or perhaps, they ran off with someone better equipped to guide them. Someone who can read."

Sophie met her gaze, her eyes so rimmed with red Susan wondered if she had slept at all. She frowned. "Did—did Daphne ever come home last night? Do you know?"

Susan swallowed. "I was going to tell you. She ran off, too."

Mrs. Blair's gaze swiveled between Susan and Sophie.

"What—what do you mean?"

"I mean she's gone. She saw an opportunity to strike out for her freedom—or perhaps to be a Moses to her own little band of runaways—and she took it."

Sophie pushed up off the sofa, twisted her hands together as she paced the room. "But why would she do that? Are you sure? Maybe she's in trouble . . ."

"Trouble? What kind of trouble could she possibly be in, unless it's the kind she causes herself? Besides, she confessed in her own hand. Now do tell me, Sophie, since when did Kent slaves know how to read and write?" It was a gamble, of course. But Susan suspected that spies would have to know their letters to be effective. "I would have brought it for you to read, but I knew that would be useless, so I didn't bother."

Mrs. Blair rose and grasped Sophie's hands. "Your servant knew her letters? Do you think—would she have tempted mine to run with her?"

Sophie dropped her gaze to the floor. "I don't know what to think."

Chapter Thirty-six

Outside Fort Stedman, east of Petersburg, Virginia
Saturday, March 25, 1865, 4:00 a.m.

*B*eneath a moonless sky of thick black ink, Harrison
Caldwell pulsed with suspense. In the nearby woods, tree frogs trilled,
while damp smells of thawed soil and last year's rotten leaves tweaked
his nose. His tattered homespun uniform chafed both his body and his
mind. *I will not fire upon my country.*

A twig snapped beneath his bare foot as Harrison advanced with
hordes of Rebel soldiers similarly shod, save precious few with shoes.
Their objective: Fort Stedman, and Batteries X and XI, which flanked
it on the North and South sides. If the Confederates could capture this
fort and its artillery, they'd move north and south along Union lines
to clear neighboring fortifications. This would make way for the main
attack, which would lead to the main Union supply base of City Point,
which also happened to be Grant's headquarters. Almost half of Lee's
infantry—nearly twenty thousand men—had been ordered to the

fight. Rebel success right here, right now, could break the Union siege on Petersburg, and prolong the war indefinitely.

The battle also promised to bring Harrison close enough to desert into Union lines.

Harrison bumped into the soldier in front of him, halted, and tugged his slouch hat forward on his head. *So the games begin.* His palms grew slick against the rifle he shouldered. Ahead of him, cloaked in predawn darkness, parties of Rebel sharpshooters and engineers masqueraded as deserting soldiers. Faint Southern drawls probed toward Yankee pickets in as fine a piece of play-acting as Harrison had ever paid to see.

Then, dimly, shouts. Grunts. What Harrison could not hear, he could certainly imagine: fists striking flesh, and rifle butts slamming foes, desperation strengthening each war-weary Rebel. The stomach-turning surprise of Yankee pickets realizing they'd been expertly fooled. The sharpshooters and engineers had overwhelmed the Union pickets without firing any shots to give themselves away. Harrison's nerves pulled as tight as his muscles as the thwack of axes against obstructions clapped his ears.

Now Harrison and the infantry that enveloped him advanced. Ahead of them, if the plan held, three groups of men swarmed the Union works to capture Battery X and Fort Stedman.

Time's measured march collapsed as Harrison charged blindly ahead on calloused soles among men possessed. Suddenly, the earth shuddered as Union twelve-pounders blasted canister shot, their flashes illuminating the fight. The cannons' wind blew Harrison's hat from his head, while the roar drowned every other sound. Their position revealed, the Yankee cannoneers were silenced after only a dozen rounds, as the Rebels threw them over the works and into the ditch. Only then could Harrison hear the shrieks of those who'd been in the artillery's path.

Harrison rushed forward. *If I can just get close enough . . .* Progress slowed as he and a mass of Rebels breached the perimeter of sharpened rails, and came before the moat directly in front of the fort. Above Harrison, muzzles sparked as Union defenders poured leaden rain straight down on the attackers.

Sweat slicked down Harrison's chest and back as men moaned in fear, or pain, around him. Soldiers who had endured four years of privation and battle died in a moat, at the hands of an enemy they could not see, for a cause that they could not win. The living stumbled and scrambled over those who fell, searching frantically for a place to get into the fort.

Finally, an opening was found, and Confederates streamed into the fort, bringing bedlam with them. Yankees and Rebels locked together like hissing copperheads, writhing in their rough and tumble fight. Muskets flashed, steel clanged, and cannons roared back to life at the hands of the Confederates.

Out of nowhere, a fist pummeled Harrison in the jaw, and he wheeled toward his invisible opponent. "I'm for the Union!" he said. Another blow split his lip like overripe fruit, and a trickle of blood warmed his chin.

"That a fact? Just like all these other Johnnies here, eh?"

With a thud, Billy Yank's fist blasted Harrison's stomach, and he doubled over as the pain spread throughout his middle. In the next moment, as he spun out of reach, he realized what he should have predicted all along: the advance teams of Rebels who had posed as deserters made a mockery of Harrison's truth. No Union soldier would believe him now. Worse, they wouldn't want to.

Within minutes, the Confederates won Fort Stedman. Stunned, Harrison watched as Yankees double-quicked back to the Confederate works as prisoners. *The ten-month siege of Petersburg is breaking.* Acid burned from his stomach to his throat. *How long will the war go on now?*

Sometime after the sun rose—had an hour passed, or two?—punishing fire blasted down upon Confederate-held Fort Stedman. Between the earthshaking explosions, Rebel scouts burst into the fort with reports of a Union line forming a semicircle around them a mile and a half in length. When Gordon ordered the Rebels to hightail it for safety back in Petersburg, Harrison read heartbreak in their shaggy, gaunt faces, defeat in their quivering frames, even as he scrambled pell-mell among them to get clear of the coming fire. The battle was turning.

Federal infantry massed behind them, charging with repeating rifles and bayonets. Then artillery's furious thunder filled the air as though the heavens were colliding. Shells shrieked above the Rebels re-treating past the moat and *chevaux de frise*. One hundred fifty yards of open space gaped between Harrison and the Confederate side. Unless, of course, he surrendered.

I could do it, Harrison thought. After all, Union victory would be hard to celebrate from the grave. One after another, several Rebs about-faced, hands in the air, rather than cross that yawning distance. Others pushed past him, fleeing toward safety like madmen, while older or convalescent soldiers labored in their wake through the smoking, lead-ridden field.

Harrison squinted into the sun as he turned toward the Yankees. Southerners scuttled past him. Recognition seized him.

No.

Harrison wheeled west again, his gaze following the form of Preston Kent. *Why is he here? Why not in the local troops instead, away from the fray?* Questions exploded in his mind as he watched Sophie's father push forward. Lead arced through the sky above Preston, while musket fire rattled behind Harrison. Fifty yards in, Preston stumbled at the edge of a smoldering crater made by a cannonball, righted himself, and charged ahead, darting around fallen soldiers, more holes, and shells that had yet to detonate.

Halfway to safety, the soldier twenty feet from Preston was ripped apart by a cannonball as though he were made of cornhusks. For an instant, Harrison lost sight of Preston.

Where is he? Harrison sifted through the dashing figures until—*oh no. Not now.*

Preston had stopped running. His hand clutched over his chest, he staggered, dropped to his knees. Collapsed. *He has no business being out here!* If his heart did not fail him completely, it was only a matter of time until a bullet or shell stopped its beating.

Soldiers rushed by Preston on both sides. Not one of them slowed to spirit the older man away. *They think he's already gone.*

Deliver me, deliver us, Harrison prayed, and launched into the deafening fray. The sulfurous fog of gunpowder choked him as he distanced himself from the country he loved to save a man fighting for a cause he despised. None of that mattered now. *Hang on, Preston!* If Harrison had any power at all to save him, he would not let Sophie's father die today.

Seconds ticked by as Harrison dodged death and disfigurement on his way to Preston. Sweat stung his eyes and spilled down his back between his shoulder blades. Blood and Virginia clay stained his bare feet crimson. Charred earth and grass burned his soles.

Finally, he skidded to Preston's crumpled form. His face was ashen but still he breathed. "I've got you!" Harrison shouted though his voice couldn't be heard. "Come on!" With Preston's arm around Harrison's neck, he bore up under him, cinched his waist with an iron-tight grip, and half-guided, half-dragged the man forward. *We'll never make it.* Harrison silenced the voice with prayer. *Please God. Please.*

Miraculously, another soldier heaved up under Preston's other arm. He and Harrison clasped wrists to form a hammock for Preston. As soon as the older man slumped into it, feet off the ground, they charged forward. Harrison's hair rippled from the wind of crashing shells and flying bullets.

Twenty-five yards to go.

Twenty.

Fifteen yards.

Thirty feet, twenty-five feet, twenty—

Oof! Harrison's knee buckled beneath him as fire seared through his ankle. *Hang it all!* He'd wrenched it tripping into a smoking hole.

Minié balls plowed into the earth beside him, spraying his face with dirt. Seeing at once what had happened, the Good Samaritan Johnny hoisted Preston over his shoulder and scurried the rest of the way. Harrison limped behind them. They were seconds away from safety.

Then an explosion blasted through the dimness of Harrison's hearing, lifted his body on a wave of air and shrapnel and dirt. He floated on the dirty yellow cloud of gun smoke then, with hell just below him and heaven above. Blood oozed from his nose and ears. *Into thine hand I commit my spirit . . .*

Chapter Thirty-seven

St. John's Church, Richmond, Virginia
Sunday, April 2, 1865

*A*lone in her pew at St. John's Church, Sophie's mind wandered far from the sermon. Bella was still missing. Susan's story that she'd run away hadn't convinced her, although Sophie's inquiries into every slave jail in Richmond failed to turn her up. Her father had been sent home from the front a week ago with a heart so weak he had kept to his bed ever since, but with the stunning news that Harrison had been injured somewhere between the lines of blue and grey. *How severely? Did he live? Where is he now? Will he recover?* But Preston had no answers. Her nightmare had become reality.

Suppressing a groan, Sophie bowed her head beneath crushing guilt and prayed once more for God to redeem this agonizing mess.

Footsteps whispered on the carpeted aisle. She looked up in time to see a messenger hand the reverend a note in the middle of his sermon before scurrying back out of the church. The reverend's shoulders sagged.

"Brethren," he began, though most of the congregants by now were women and children. "Trying times are before us. General Lee has been defeated outside Petersburg. The Yankees will likely push through to Richmond, but remember that God is with us in the storm as well as in the calm." He raised his voice to be heard above the gasps and murmurs gaining strength. "We may never meet again. Go quietly to your homes, and whatever may be in store for us, let us not forget that we are Christian men and women, and may the protection of the Father, the Son, and Holy Ghost be with you all."

The church service was over.

"Rumor," said a woman as soon as they exited the building. "Like so many before. You'll see, we'll be fine."

But Mrs. Blair tugged at Sophie's elbow. "If Richmond is under threat, my boys will be coming back home now. I won't have them coming back to an empty house." As the woman scurried off, neither she nor Sophie acknowledged they might have already been killed at Petersburg. It was too horrible a thought to entertain, especially now that they were so close to the end of the war, for surely that's what this was.

Wasn't it? Doubt and hope vied for Sophie's heart. She had to know for certain.

Daffodils nodded beneath budding dogwoods and magnolias as Sophie's violet silk hem skimmed the sidewalks. News came first through the Spotswood Hotel on the western fringe of Capitol Square. That's where she would go.

By the time she crossed the dozen blocks, ash swirled in the air around the Washington statue as government officials burned piles of documents. Lawrence Russell was among them, though he had aged so much she barely recognized him.

"Captain Russell!" Desperate for reliable news, Sophie hurried to his side. "What's happening?"

Sweat from the fire's heat trickled down his haggard face. "Lee's lines were penetrated. Petersburg has fallen. Richmond is next." Flames danced in his blazing blue eyes. "Happy?"

A spark leapt to her skirt, and she swatted it away with her white-gloved hand, backing away from the fire.

Captain Russell chuckled darkly. "Yes, Miss Kent, run away from this little fire. Before the day is over, it will run after you. It's poetic, really. You played with fire, and now you'll be burned by it."

"What do I do?" she whispered, more to herself than anyone else.

"Go home and wait, of course. I'm getting out of here. Mark my words. Richmond will burn, and no one here will save it."

The rest of the afternoon was a frenzied haze. Rumors were swapped, modified, and finally, confirmed. The government would evacuate Richmond immediately. The citizens were on their own.

The banks all opened at two o'clock though it was a Sunday, and patrons thronged to withdraw their life savings, as diminished as they had become. As Sophie walked back toward Church Hill in a daze, the streets gradually filled with men waving farewell to families that had boarded them, wagons and carriages teetering with boxes and trunks, slaves carrying bundles on their heads toward the Richmond & Danville depot. Prison guards and bureaucrats joined columns of refugees headed for the canal towpath that led west to Lynchburg.

When she finally arrived home, Sophie shook with suspense. *Richmond will burn*, Captain Russell had said. *And no one here will save it.*

———

Lumpkin's Slave Jail, Richmond, Virginia
Sunday, April 2, 1865

Iron shackles locked coldly over Bella's wrists. When another ring snapped around her neck, chaining her to a string of forty-nine other dark-skinned souls, she nearly retched on Robert Lumpkin's shoes.

Every jangle clawed at her heart. Never in her life had she felt so much like cattle.

"Git! Try anything along the way and I'll have your hide."

Chains clanked and feet shuffled as the coffle moved out into the alley.

"You know where we're going?" Bella murmured to the woman in front of her. "Auction?" *What else could it possibly be?*

The woman merely shrugged. "Don't know nothin' about that."

A gust of wind brought the smell of smoke from the direction of Capitol Square, three blocks west. *Something's going on.*

As soon as they turned out of the alley and into the street, the coffle was swallowed up in a thick stream of white folks and their slaves, pushing carts and mules, carrying bundles and toting trunks. Bella only had to listen for a moment to understand. *Richmond is evacuating. The Yankees are coming, at last.* She would be free. All of them would be.

Hope burst into bloom, then wilted just as fast. Lumpkin aimed to preserve his property. If Bella's guess was right, he was taking them farther south, where they would remain in bondage at least long enough for him to recoup his investment.

Bella gritted her teeth as she shuffled among the crowd, anger and humiliation licking through her veins. *Lord God,* she prayed. *Show Yourself. Your Word says I am more than a conqueror through You, but you see these chains. Break them.* Her faith felt just as shackled.

An hour later, they were at the Richmond & Danville train station, along with hundreds of anxious ladies still in their shabby Sunday best. Home Guard soldiers patrolled the depot, holding back anyone without a pass from the Secretary of War.

"Now see here," Lumpkin shouted at one of them. "We are getting on this train!"

"Fifty-one people? Have you a pass?"

"Since when does a white man need a pass to get on a train around here?" Lumpkin bellowed.

"Since right now. I have one train for Treasury employees, one for the quartermaster and other officials, another with telegraph operators and crewmen, and one for the president and his department heads. Nongovernment personnel get nowhere without a pass!"

Their voices rose in a useless shouting match. At length, Lumpkin ceded. Red-faced and trembling with rage, he jerked the coffle to turn them around, and herded them back to the jail.

Mayo's Bridge, Richmond, Virginia
Monday, April 3, 1865, 4:00 a.m.

Revulsion turned Lawrence Russell's stomach as he guided his mount through the riotous streets of Richmond. *These people don't deserve the Confederate capital anyway.* The gas lines having been cut, looters held paper torches aloft as they mobbed warehouses and stores for whatever they could carry away. The commissary near Mayo's Bridge was thrown open, and a growing crowd attacked barrels of flour and meal, sacks of sugar, and slabs of bacon. Legal plunder quickly slid into illegal, as mobs fanned into the lower city, looting shops and private homes at will.

The scent of alcohol burned Lawrence's nose as the gutters flowed freely with liquor, in accordance with City Council's orders to destroy it before the Yankees could get it. Barrels of whiskey had been axed open, bottles of gin and brandy shattered on the sidewalks. Up and down the street, kegs were poured out, and casks and cases smashed. Lawrence's nose wrinkled in disgust as his horse stepped around men and women scooping liquor into their hats, or their boots, or their mouths. *Animals.* And yet, what he wouldn't give for just one civilized shot of whiskey himself.

His horse skittered sideways when a drunken soldier from one of the local troops stumbled into it.

"Ach. Pardon me."

That German accent. The spectacles. Lawrence squinted at the man's sloppy smile. "Fischer? Otto Fischer?"

"Pardon, officer, but my superior released us and said we could do whatever we wanted. Go home, go south, go drink . . ."

So Fischer had been caught in the conscription net when Congress raised the age limit. "It's me. Lawrence Russell. I used to court Sophie Kent, remember?"

Fischer flinched as though he'd been struck. "Snake, that one. Too many secrets," he hissed.

Lawrence dismounted, held the bridle firmly, and pumped Fischer's hand.

The Kents' former steward swiped a hand over his hair and swallowed. He'd grown even thinner than Lawrence had remembered him, but that was no surprise these days. "You getting out of here, then, Captain?" His speech was only slightly slurred.

"Indeed, straightaway in fact." *Before they set fire to the bridges.* "And you? What are your plans?"

Fischer shook his head. "No plans. I'm old and I'm tired. Tired of starting over in a new world. Coming from Germany to America was difficult enough. If the South falls and the slaves are freed, it will be a new world all over again. One in which I cannot imagine living. I'm a house servant, Captain Russell. If I must compete with millions of Negroes for a job—ach! Even without my livelihood in jeopardy, it simply goes against the laws of nature. The South will no longer be my home, and I'll not set a foot in the North. So you see, Captain, why I drink tonight."

Lawrence saw very clearly. "What are you going to do about it?"

"Do? What can I do? What is there to do?"

A dark smile curled Lawrence's lips. "I'll let you in on a secret. Sophie Kent is rabidly disloyal. Perhaps even a spy. Only I lost the evidence to convict her."

Fischer's eyes rounded. "I knew she was up to something! I knew it!"

"'Course you did. Did you know that she is much to blame for Richmond's loss? With the government evacuating, she's getting away with it completely, too."

It was enough. Swinging back up into his saddle, Lawrence bid the bitter conscript farewell, and galloped over Mayo's Bridge, away from the wreckage, and toward establishing a new Confederate government in Danville. He had no time to chase after revenge. But Otto Fischer did.

———

A deafening explosion rocked Sophie right out of her bed. Scrambling up from the floor, she ran out onto her balcony and gripped the balustrade as she looked toward the river. A huge volume of smoke like an illuminated balloon shot high into the air. Another blast shook the house from cupola to foundation, and then another, shattering the windows facing the James. Shells arced and burst through the sky like fireworks. The glares from the explosions were as bright as the noonday sun.

Susan burst into Sophie's room. "What is it? What's happening? Are the Yankees bombarding us again?" She shook with terror. "Not another Atlanta . . ." she cried.

"It's not Yankees. Look." Sophie beckoned her out onto the balcony, with a warning not to step on the broken glass. "Three Confederate warships were anchored in the James River."

"I don't see them. Are they under all that smoke?"

"Not anymore. The Confederates blew them up rather than allow the Yankees to use them and the cannons and ammunition they held."

"So they're really coming," Susan said.

"The Rebels certainly think so." Sophie's ears still rung from the blast. *Oh no.* "The ships." All of them docked at the wharf caught fire. Then a row of tobacco warehouses on the waterfront went up next. Soon wind whipped the flames into such a frenzy that Sophie could hear their roar even from Church Hill.

Then the bright sound of breaking glass. But all these windows had already shattered from the blast. "Do you hear that?" Sophie asked Susan.

She nodded.

"Let's check on Daddy."

Susan led the way with her candle, and Sophie followed her downstairs, where Preston had convalesced in the spare room ever since his return.

"Daddy?" Sophie called.

"Daddy isn't here now, is he?"

Sophie wheeled toward the voice as its owner stepped into the hallway. Susan cried out.

"Fischer?"

Were it not for the candle's flare reflecting off his spectacles, he would be a mere shadow.

My shadow? Memory flickered.

"I told you your house would burn."

"No," Sophie gasped, comprehension now blazing within her. She stepped backwards. Susan's shaking hands wrapped around her shoulders.

"Yankee lover, all alone, You're still made of flesh and bone. Daddy's gone and Mommy's dead, Turn your aid to Rebs instead." A smile smeared his face, and the blood froze in Sophie's veins. "Remember that? I'll bet you remember this: Big houses still burn. Watch yours!" Fischer held up two sloshing pails reeking of alcohol.

———

"Giddyup!" Harrison kicked his heels into his mount and charged across Mayo's Bridge from the south side, whipping past a stream of Rebel soldiers. No one seemed to care that he'd deserted the Southern army. Order and law had evacuated along with the Confederate government.

"Heading the wrong way!" a soldier called to him in passing.

Leaning into the gallop, he thundered ahead, crackling fire loud in his ears from behind him as the bridge went up in flames. The railroad bridges to the west and east were already collapsing in fiery chunks into the James, which hissed with steam.

Harrison's head ached with his recent concussion as he urged his horse toward the burning city. To the east, dense yellow smoke billowed above Rocketts Landing and the Navy Yard, and tobacco warehouses lining Canal Street burst with light and flame. To the west, the Confederate arsenal exploded with a deafening roar.

At last, the bridge spit Harrison into the inferno engulfing the lower city. The streets were lined with flames and the telltale odor of burning alcohol. He wheeled his horse east, but the leaping flames were too much for the beast to take. Quickly, Harrison peeled off his shirt, tied it over the horse's eyes, and kicked him once again.

Heat washed over Harrison in undulating waves. Sheets of fire leapt from window to window, and from warehouse to bank to hotel. Not a single alarm sounded. No one even tried to contain the blaze. *Please God, stay the flames.*

———

Susan stood shoulder to shoulder with Sophie in the library. Otto Fischer reeked as much as the whiskey he poured on the floorboards, threw at the bookcases and sloshed over the brocade curtains.

"F—Fi—Fischer!" Sophie sputtered like the candle in Susan's hand. He wasn't just draped in shadows, he was made of them.

He looked up, and noticed Susan for the first time. Clearly, he hadn't expected to see her. "Susan? What is this grotesque mask you wear? Whatever happened to that creamy, silken skin of yours?"

"Otto Fischer, how dare you?" Her father stood in the doorway, pale as a ghost. He stepped forward, looking every bit as tall and imposing as the father Susan had always remembered. "You would burn me and my daughters in our beds?" Susan wondered if her ears played tricks on her. It sounded as though her father was interceding for her right along with Sophie.

"Haven't you heard? There is no law tonight. It's vigilante justice."

"Justice! You think you're here to mete out justice? Like Nat

401

Turner?" Preston hunched his shoulders forward, clutched at his chest.

"Wait." Fischer held out his hands. "You don't know the whole story. The fall of the Confederacy is no accident, you know."

Preston grunted in obvious pain. "You have ten seconds to get off my property or I'll kill you myself—there being no law tonight."

But Susan's father could barely remain on his feet.

"I came here tonight looking for a spy. Did you know you've been quartering one in your house?"

Sophie's hand twitched inside Susan's, and Susan saw with crystal clarity that she had brought this upon herself, and upon her little sister and father. All of her grasping after Preston's attention—her accusations of Sophie—her stubborn refusal to apologize, or even to pray . . . It had all led to this moment. Harm would come. But Susan would not escape it, either. Guilt coated her like the sweat now filming her skin. *God . . . forgive me!*

"You're lying," Preston snarled at Fischer. "Leave!" Every word clearly cost him. Susan wrapped her arm around her father's waist for fear he would collapse. Sophie supported him from the other side.

But Fischer stood his ground. "In good time." He held an unlit match aloft. "But I leave you with the gift of truth. The spy in your midst is—"

"Right here."

Sophie jumped at the sound of Harrison's voice.

"Are you all right?" he asked, though his own body was slick with sweat and stained with soot.

"Oliver?" Preston said.

"Actually, my name is Harrison Caldwell."

Sophie held her breath as Preston cast his dissecting gaze on Harrison. "You were a spy?" He turned to her. "Sophie—?"

Tears spilled down her cheeks in answer, and she felt his knees give way. She and Susan guided him to a chair before he collapsed. "You knew," he whispered. "Did you help him? Did you spy for the Union, too?"

It was killing him. Sophie's betrayal would finish his limping heart. "I'll always be your girl." She smiled through her tears.

"It was you!" Fischer pulled a revolver from his belt, aimed it at Harrison. "Spies hang, you know. But in this case, a bullet will do."

"Fischer," Preston panted, head bowed, utterly defeated. "It's over. All of it. Gone. Go home."

"Home? I have no home." The hammer clicked back on the gun.

Suddenly, an explosion rocked the house with a force so monumental, it could only mean the fire had reached the arsenal. More explosions followed, one after another, knocking them all to the whiskey-soaked floor. Fischer's gun was shaken loose from his sweaty grip. He scrambled after it.

"Harrison!" Sophie screamed, but her voice was lost in the never-ending roar as hundreds of railcars full of ammunition detonated, their reverberations spreading throughout the city in terrible, mind-numbing waves.

The room jarred again, and Harrison lunged at Fischer. The floor pitched and yawed and still they wrestled like drunken sailors aboard their ship.

Susan dropped her candle.

Within moments, the tiny burning wick had sent fire across the alcohol-soaked floor. Crackling orange puddles spread toward Harrison and Fischer while flames leaped up the drapes. Fischer scrambled to his feet and ran out the door shouting, "I told you your house would burn!"

"Water!" Harrison shouted as he hefted Preston out of the chair. Sophie and Susan launched out the back door and ran to the pump.

Lois and Pearl came quaking from the kitchen house.

"Fire inside," Sophie shouted, barely able to hear her own voice past the ringing in her ears. The slave women ducked back into the kitchen house and returned with pots and pails to carry water.

Harrison helped Preston into the slave quarters, then dashed back outside. "Don't come near the fire," he told them as Susan pumped. Sophie dunked a rag in the water and handed it to him. "Leave the pails in the hallway, or if that's too hot, or the smoke is too thick, just leave them on the back porch . . ." After tying the wet rag over his nose and mouth, he swiped the bucket from under the spout and ran inside with it.

Beneath a sky that boiled with smoke from a city going up in flames, the women took turns pumping as fast and hard as they could, and carried the sloshing pails into the house. Water splashed the hem of Sophie's billowing nightgown, and blisters budded on her palms. *Please God,* Sophie prayed as her hair whipped into her eyes. *Please,* she said again, over and over.

Until finally, Harrison emerged from the house, his chest streaked with soot and smoke. Coughing to clear his lungs, he tugged the rag loose and wiped it over his face. "Fire's out."

Sophie dropped her pails, and the cool water splashed over her feet. Shaking with relief, she walked toward him. In three long strides, he spanned the distance between them and captured her in his arms, pressed her tightly against his bare chest.

"It's all right now," he whispered, the heat of the fire radiating from his skin. "It's over. I'm not leaving you again."

Chapter Thirty-eight

Lumpkin's Slave Jail, Richmond, Virginia
Monday, April 3, 1865

*W*ake up, wake up!"

Bella jolted awake after getting barely any sleep at all, and immediately leapt to her feet. The door to her jail cell had been swung wide open. She followed her fellow inmates as they burst into the light of day, charred though it was, to find Union soldiers hurrying to put out the fires. So the Yankees had come after all.

Slavery chain done broke at last! Broke at last! Broke at last! Slavery chain done broke at last! Gonna praise God 'til I die!

The song of her fellow inmates filtered through her shock. Bella lifted her hands to the sky and closed her eyes, tears streaming down her face, and joined her voice to theirs. "Slavery chain done broke at last! Gonna praise God 'til I die!"

She opened her eyes and turned north toward Broad Street, where United States Colored Troops, 28th regiment, marched west in smart formation. Colored Richmonders lined the street, cheering their liberators with shouts and song.

"Jesus has opened the way," called one.

"We been waiting on you," called another.

Some of them asked after relatives who had fled north. *Have you seen a man named Moses? He has a scar above his eyebrow. A woman named Liz, with a space between her two front teeth?* After their emancipation, reuniting with their families seemed foremost in their minds. It was certainly foremost in Bella's. She would find Sophie in good time, but for now, she had other business to attend to.

The soldiers were too disciplined to break rank and answer their questions at the moment.

Once they arrived at Camp Lee, however, the colored troops stacked their arms and eagerly shook the hands of those who had followed them. Bella swelled with pride that the colored regiment should be conquering heroes in the rubble of the Confederate capital. She clasped each hand she could reach, and could not resist asking about her husband.

"Abraham Jamison?" she said. "He was in the 54th Massachusetts, fought at Fort Wagner, but then was captured and imprisoned at Libby. Last I knew he was working in a furnace in western Virginia . . . Abraham Jamison," she said again and again as she went down the line.

The next hand she shook did not let her go. "Bella."

For a moment, words abandoned her.

Abraham pulled her against his muscled chest in a fierce embrace. "Thank God you're all right!"

Tears spilled down her cheeks. "Abe! You fought for Richmond?"

He pulled back to look at her, and she rejoiced that his handsome face was no longer gaunt and defeated. "I fought for you. I fought for all of us."

She touched his face, to make sure she wasn't dreaming. "You did it, Love. You won. All of them are free at last. I'm so proud of y—"

Abraham covered her lips with a kiss that took her breath away.

As Bella melted into the strong arms of her husband, the cheers of the unshackled rang joyfully in her ears. *Thank You, God*, she prayed. *More than conquerors indeed.*

Kent House, Richmond, Virginia
Monday, April 3, 1865

Sophie stood back as Susan fluffed the pillows behind Preston's back, unsure if he even wanted Sophie around. His world, and his heart, had crumbled.

"Sophie," he said.

She stepped to his side.

"Bring Oli—Harrison, too."

Susan stepped into the hall, and in moments, Harrison took her place at Preston's side.

"Harrison Caldwell." Preston's voice was weak. "Caldwell? Was your mother Christine?"

"The very same."

"She was Mother's best friend from Philadelphia," Sophie added.

Preston grunted. "Then she would be pleased."

"But you aren't," she whispered.

"I am old. And tired. And in mourning for the Confederacy. But—" He sighed heavily. "If it were not for Harrison here, I'd be buried right along with it. You saved my life, though I was your enemy."

"You were never the enemy," Harrison said.

Preston's brow wrinkled. "But weren't you a spy for the Union? Weren't both of you spying for the Yankees?"

Sophie bowed her head. "I followed my convictions, Daddy. And so did Harrison. But I'll always be your—one of your girls." She turned to Susan, who was waiting quietly against the wall, and smiled.

"I'm done fighting. It's over." Preston peered up at Harrison. "You are truly a newspaperman?"

"Yes, sir. And I truly love your daughter."

"I know you do. Otherwise, you wouldn't have saved me. Twice. Thank you for that. Now be off with you. I'm sure you have plans to make. Susan can keep me company."

Sophie kissed her father's brow, and Harrison shook his hand before they took their leave, and Susan resumed her post.

Susan sat next to her father and held his hand, coals burning in her gut. But if he could forgive Sophie for what she did for the Yankees, then perhaps . . . *No more stalling,* she told herself. *God help me.* "Daddy."

He looked at her with hooded eyes.

She licked her lips. Swallowed. "Forgive me. I've sinned against God, and you." Tears coursed down her cheeks as the words finally broke from her lips.

His own composure crumbled as he pulled her down into an embrace, and she sobbed onto his chest. Preston laid his hand on her hair. "Forgiven. And if I have wronged you, if my shortcomings harmed you, I ask your forgiveness, too, before it is too late."

"What?" She pulled back to search his face.

"Do you forgive?" His eyelids fluttered.

"Yes but Daddy—too late for what?"

Preston sighed deeply. "Perhaps it is right that I should die along with the Confederacy."

"No. No! You can't die, not now, not when I've just truly come home to you again!"

"Daughter." He held her hand, but weakly. "I see you. I love you. But I don't have the heart to keep up with this changing world." The corner of his lips turned up as he thumped his chest.

Susan's spirit rebelled. He couldn't leave her now. If not for her sake, then— "You have a granddaughter."

He turned his head, opened his eyes, frowning. "You're a mother?"

She shrugged, and more tears spilled from her eyes. "Only technically."

"Noah Becker's girl?"

Susan hesitated before nodding. "Yes. Noah is the best father that girl could ever hope to have."

Confusion furrowed his brow. "I thought you said he abandoned you after your illness. Yet he's a good father?"

She pressed her lips together for a moment. "I lied. We annulled the marriage early on, and I was only too happy to be shed of them both. I would not presume to take Analiese from him for the world." He frowned, but she kept going. "Forgive me. Noah's family is in Germany still. I'm sure she'd love to meet you, her only living grandparent this side of the ocean."

"What is she—eight or nine years old now?"

"Yes. Brown hair, and blue eyes like yours. Exactly the same shade."

"Where?"

"I left her in Atlanta." Inwardly, Susan cringed at the memory of their parting. "She's in the care of a very capable governess. I'm sure life is better for them now that I'm not there—you know how I can make a person miserable. But you should meet your granddaughter, as soon as the railroads are repaired." *Please God, let it be something for him to live for . . .*

"Will you find her for me?"

Susan almost laughed with relief. "I'll do my best. I promise."

"Oh pardon me."

Susan turned, and found a gaunt, bearded soldier dripping with rags in the doorway. But there was something about his eyes . . .

He cleared his throat. "Susan? I mean, Miss Kent? Mr. Kent? It's me. Asher Blair. Mother is home tending Joel's minor wounds, but she sent me over to check on you. I saw your servant in the yard and she told me I might as well come on in . . . I don't mean to intrude, I just—is there anything I can do for you?"

Preston reached out his hand. "Son, you have done more than

one man should ever require of another. Thank you for your service. Welcome home."

Asher's eyes crinkled in his weathered face.

"And Mr. Blair," Susan added. "Tell your mother I prayed, and came all the way home."

"That I will." He bowed to her. "I trust she'll know what that means?"

Susan nodded. "Yes. Now go to her. We're all so very glad you and Joel are home, too."

Harrison enveloped Sophie's hand in his own as they sat on the front porch swing. The smell of the charred library followed them, but it only mingled with the odor of the burned city. Earlier, they had watched from the balcony as Yankee soldiers and cavalry had streamed into Richmond and raised the Stars and Stripes over the smoldering capital once more. But Sophie had seen enough of war to last quite a while. A lifetime, she supposed.

"I have something for you." A smile toyed with the corner of Harrison's lips as he withdrew a single book from his pocket. The burnished corners curled back, but the pages remained intact. "It's *North and South*."

"It survived!" Sophie hugged it to her chest. "But you know I can't read it."

"You will. You'll learn to read and write again. I'll make it my personal mission." He winked. "In the meantime, I'll read to you, and when you want to write a story, I will be your pen. You have a marvelous story to tell, Sophie, and no one can tell it but you."

"What about you? Think of all you've seen and done! The prisons, the war department, the battles . . ."

"My story begins and ends with you. If you'll let it." A lump shifted in his throat. "Sophie, would you do me the honor of being my wife?"

Sophie's breath caught in her chest as he wrapped his arms around her, his rich brown eyes drawing her in. Her body warmed to him as

410

though he still wore the heat of the fire. "We'll stay here if you want and help rebuild the city. Or we can return to Philadelphia. Either way, let's do it together. Let's write our own happily ever after. One that will rival any in your novels. I have no ring to give you just yet, but I will. And what I have is already yours. My devotion. My heart. My life."

"Yes," she whispered through her tears, and he wiped them away with his thumbs. As Sophie gave her lips to the only man she ever wanted, *North and South* fell away.

The End

Epilogue

Chicago, Illinois
Friday, September 20, 1889

"Four tickets, please."

"That'll be two dollars."

Bella Jamison watched in wonder as Harrison paid money to get back inside Libby Prison. The building had been dismantled in Richmond brick by brick and timber by timber, carefully catalogued, and reconstructed here on Chicago's Wabash Street as the Libby Prison War Museum. Even as the brass band outside hailed its grand opening, a shudder passed through Bella as a quarter of a century peeled away. One glance at Sophie Caldwell, beside her, suggested she felt the same way.

Abraham stood tall next to Bella, still striking in his Union blue uniform though grey frosted his hair. Bella could only guess at the riot of emotion and memory unleashing inside him. He'd been a soldier, a prisoner, and a slave during the course of the war. Now, not only was he both veteran and victor, but he was a full citizen of the United States. The service of U. S. Colored Troops must have helped convince Congress to ratify the Fourteenth Amendment granting blacks citizenship.

Returning from the ticket booth, Harrison handed tickets to each of them, and to Sophie and Bella, colorful booklets with *Libby Prison War Museum Catalogue* splashed across their covers. "One for each couple. There. Do we look like proper tourists now?" Faint lines fanned from the corners of his eyes, and Bella marveled that this man, both hardened and softened by war, was the ambitious scalawag of a reporter she'd first met in Gettysburg. A lifetime ago. She was sixty years old now, and Abraham sixty-five. She ached with arthritis, and Abraham suffered rheumatism, but they still had each other, and more.

Silas's mother had moved into Liberty Inn as a southern refugee after Atlanta fell. After she died a few years ago, Abraham and Bella sold their Washington Street home and moved into Liberty Inn, surrounded by Liberty and Silas and their four beautiful girls.

"After you." With one arm spread toward the doorway, Harrison rested his other hand on the small of Sophie's back just above her navy satin bustle and nodded to Abraham. Enveloping Bella's hand in his, Abraham led them into the Prisoners Reception Room, the Caldwells filing in behind them.

As the group shuffled with the crowd throughout the first floor, Bella bent over relic after relic from the war. Journals kept and trinkets carved from bones by various Libby inmates. Photos of emaciated Libby and Belle Isle prisoners upon their release. An 1863 recruiting poster for colored troops captioned, "Come and Join Us, Brothers." The table upon which General Grant wrote out the terms of surrender at Appomattox Court House, Virginia, in 1865. A portion of the bloodstained pillow that held Abraham Lincoln's head as he died, just days later. An orange and red Ku Klux Klan flag dated 1866, depicting a dragon breathing out the Latin motto *Quod Semper, Quod Ubique, Quo Ab omnibus.*

Tears stung Bella's eyes as she tightened her grip on Abraham's hand. *So much suffering. So much hatred still poisoning the nation.* Shaking her head, she fixed her attention on Abraham instead, and on Sophie and Harrison, who had risked so much for others' freedom.

"Generations of slavery turned those folks against us." Abraham's voice rumbled low in his chest. "It'll take generations more for our country to heal up. But we're on our way now, aren't we?"

"Yes, Love." Bella squeezed his calloused blacksmith hand. "Thank you."

"Pardon me, sir." A black woman touched Abraham's sleeve. "You fought for me. Thank you. Thank you for what you done. You won for me."

Modestly, Abraham accepted her thanks, his shoulders straightening.

"Proud to be on your arm, you know," Bella told him.

A lump shifted in his throat. "I've always been proud you've been by my side. Through everything. If I never told you before."

Bella nodded, heart full, and thanked God once more for the family He'd set her in—and that her twin had not died in vain.

Upstairs, in a room labeled the Chickamauga Room, Harrison's gait slowed noticeably. He no longer peered into glass cases, but gazed at the rafters overhead. The windows. The spittle-stained planks below his polished shoes.

Until, "There." He pointed at a patch of floor. "That was mine." A profound stillness settled over his face as he held his hat over his heart, his gaze fixed to the spot. Respectfully, Abraham did the same, though the black prisoners' experience in the cellar had been left out completely from the catalogue. Bella and Sophie lowered their heads in reverence.

"Whatcha lookin' at? Somebody die there on that spot or somethin'?" A tow-headed boy elbowed into their circle.

Sophie's heart constricted as a smile cracked Harrison's somber composure. "In a manner of speaking, my boy. Yes." He caught Sophie's eyes, and understanding arced between them. Libby Prison had been the place where Christine Caldwell's prayers for her son were answered. No doubt she would have been thrilled that her grandchildren Elizabeth and Robert, now in college, were steadfast in their faith, too.

"I beg your pardon, sir." One of the uniformed guides approached Harrison. "Does this spot mean something to you?"

"I slept here, if you could call it that, for two months before the breakout. Spoon style, of course. And we all flopped at once, on command." A chuckle rumbled in his chest.

"Do you mean—you were a prisoner here? And you escaped in the mass breakout in February 1864?"

"I did." He didn't mention he helped dig the tunnels himself.

"Splendid! An honor to have you here today, sir." The guide pumped Harrison's right hand. "We're making brass plates to mark the prisoners' spots. Would you mind terribly, if I had your name, rank, regiment, and time you were here?"

"Harrison Caldwell, reporter, not a soldier. November 30, 1863, to February 9, 1864."

Both dates sent ripples down Sophie's spine.

"I don't believe it."

Sophie turned toward the voice. A cry of recognition escaped her as she grasped the hands of Dr. Caleb Lansing, and his stunning wife, Charlotte, dressed in the latest Paris fashions of Charles Worth. "I should have known you'd both come, too!"

"Of course!" Charlotte embraced Sophie almost as tightly as she had the first time they met, at the Lansings' wedding. *Thank you,* Charlotte had whispered into Sophie's ear then. *Thank you for my husband. Thank you.*

"Harrison, good fellow, how's business in Philadelphia?" Dr. Lansing's grey eyes glinted.

"Chugging along, thanks to some unforgettable stories not of my own making."

"Such as your wife's." Dr. Lansing smiled at Sophie, and a blush crept up her cheeks.

"Wait a minute." The guide interrupted. "Harrison Caldwell, the Philadelphia publisher? And you, ma'am, can you be Sophia Caldwell? The famous author?"

Heads turned.

Sophie smiled. "I don't know about 'famous.'"

"Yes." Harrison draped his arm around her shoulders. "The answer is yes, she is the famous author I was only too fortunate to publish. Have you read her work?" Harrison asked the guide.

"My wife has every one of her books, from her wartime reminiscences to her novels!" He shook Harrison's and Sophie's hands enthusiastically. "Say, you can settle an argument for us, Mrs. Caldwell, if you'd be so kind."

"What's that?" She smiled.

"Whatever happened to your sister, Susan, and your father, after the war ended? It wasn't clear by the end of your reminiscences."

Sophie nodded. "It wasn't clear to any of us then, either. But Susan was true to her word, and helped locate Analiese and Noah Becker some time after the war. By then, he had remarried and had settled in Iowa. Susan and my father and I went out to meet them together, and not long after that my father's heart finally failed him. It was almost like he was waiting to meet Ana first."

"I'm sorry to hear that." The guide shifted awkwardly. "And Susan? What's her story?"

Sophie glanced at Harrison and chuckled. "Long and somewhat complicated. But she did end up marrying Asher Blair, and they lived in the house she and I grew up in, very near his mother. I believe she's staying out of trouble these days."

The guide rocked back on his heels. "Any children?"

"No."

"Another great mystery solved. Splendid. My wife will be amazed I now have the missing pieces to that puzzle. You know, she has quite a collection of war stories about women—nurses, spies, soldiers. I believe you published most of them yourself, isn't that right, Mr. Caldwell? That was quite a gamble."

"To publish women authors? Their stories needed to be told, and they were the only ones who could tell them right. It made perfect sense at the time. Still does."

"You mean you're rich!"

Harrison laughed. "Not by half, but we get along fine." Portions of the publishing profits were sent to the beneficiary of the authors' choice, from Soldiers Orphans Homes to female nursing schools to the American Missionary Association, which trained Negroes as teachers. Rachel and Emiline, former Kent household slaves, had graduated from the Hampton Normal School in Virginia, which was chartered by the AMA, and now taught their own high school classes of Negro students.

"Sophie Caldwell?" A woman appeared at her elbow, offering her Libby Prison catalogue. "Would you sign this for me? I'd love to have your autograph!" Sophie agreed, carefully concentrated on her script, and handed the catalogue back.

"Thank you so much! But this verse you wrote below your name. Psalm 31:24. What does it say?"

In the span of just a few grateful heartbeats, Sophie drank in the sight of Harrison, Bella, Abraham, Dr. Lansing, and Charlotte, here in Libby Prison. Caitlin, Noah, and Analiese Becker surged in her mind's eye as well. Sophie and Harrison would visit them in Iowa again after their brief stay here in Chicago. Her throat tightened as she considered the sum of their sacrifices, which were outweighed only by the staggering sum of their faith and courage.

"Be of good courage and he shall strengthen your heart, all ye that hope in the Lord."

The History
behind the Story

Spy of Richmond grew out of my interest in the historical figure of Elizabeth Van Lew, the wealthy, Richmond-born, Philadelphia-educated woman whose love for the Union and hatred of slavery set her on a path toward espionage. US General Grant later called Miss Van Lew his most valuable spy in Richmond. Truly, she was a spy mistress, with several other lesser known men and women doing the dangerous work of gathering intelligence before feeding it to her. Sophie Kent is a fictional character, but her background, attitudes, and activities reflect those of young women in Miss Van Lew's spy ring.

Harrison Caldwell, and Bella and Abraham Jamison are completely fictional characters, but represent the experiences of real people in their situations. Some reporters were thrown into military prisons. Unionists were imprisoned in Castle Thunder and then put on the frontlines. A few Northern wives came to Richmond to be near their imprisoned husbands. At least one black woman, Mary Bowser (aka Mary Jane Richards), gave up her freedom to return to Richmond and spy for Elizabeth Van Lew, her former owner. Bowser served as a slave in the White House of the Confederacy. Black US soldiers fought without pay until Congress passed a law in June 1864 to give them equal pay to whites. About twenty black US troops were held in Libby's cellar, and black slaves were put to work at Tredegar, as well as in labor battalions. The citizenship they all longed for came in the Fourteenth Amendment to the Constitution, ratified in July 1868.

The fever-induced dyslexia Sophie suffered would not be understood until the following century. Laudanum was often taken by women to treat various ailments without knowledge of the negative effects of addiction and overdose.

Sophie's assistance helping Dr. Caleb Lansing escape was inspired by the historical event of fifteen-year-old Josephine Holmes doing the same for Libby prisoner John R. McCullough, assistant surgeon for the 1st Wisconsin infantry. McCullough then put General Benjamin Butler in touch with Elizabeth Van Lew, which prompted her to organize her spy network. Other characters in this novel who were actually spies in her network include: Thomas McNiven, William Rowley, Erasmus Ross, Lucy Rice, and Abby Green. Samuel Ruth had his own network of spies, which overlapped Van Lew's, and he really did supply critical intelligence about Fort Stedman in March 1865.

Spy of Richmond is peppered with historical events and figures. Joseph Wheelan and his book *Libby Prison Breakout* were an enormous help as I portrayed life for both white and black prisoners, as well as the four tunnels that were dug and the breakout itself. The *Libby Chronicle* was a real creation of the prisoners, and so were the classes the officers taught each other during captivity. Historical figures from Libby include the Confederate Dr. Wilkes, Warden Dick Turner, Turner's hostler Robert Ford, clerk Erasmus Ross, "Old Ben," "The General," and the two chief engineers of the breakout: Colonel Thomas Rose and Major A. G. Hamilton. Two months after Colonel Rose was recaptured in February 1864, he was paroled, and served in Sherman's army in Georgia until Atlanta fell and later sent to Tennessee. He made the military his career even after the war, and died after his retirement. His grave lies in Arlington National Cemetery. Junius Browne and Albert Richardson were real reporters from the *New York Tribune* who had been held at Libby for months before being transferred elsewhere.

In chapter 16, Robert Ould's note about Harrison Caldwell is text from a note Ould wrote to a Confederate colonel about Browne and Richardson. The scene in which Erasmus Ross inexplicably allows Abraham Jamison to escape was inspired by records of Ross doing exactly that, though for white prisoners.

Other historical figures portrayed or mentioned in the novel are General John H. Winder, Spencer Kellogg Brown, Commissary General Northrop, Confederate Secretary of War James Seddon, Chief of the Ordnance Bureau Josiah Gorgas, Confederate President Jefferson and Varina Davis, Rebel spies Rose O'Neal Greenhow and Belle Boyd, Dr. Mary Edwards Walker, Confederate Prisoner Exchange Officer Robert Ould, US General Benjamin Butler, Tredegar Iron Works owner Joseph R. Anderson, and slave dealer Robert Lumpkin.

The evacuation fires of April 2, 1865, destroyed twenty blocks of lower Richmond. An estimated twenty civilians died due to either the fires or the lawless rioting. Tredegar Iron Works, however, survived, and now houses the American Civil War Center. Visitors to Richmond may also visit Saint John's Episcopal Church, Hollywood Cemetery, Chimborazo Medical Museum, the White House of the Confederacy, and the Museum of the Confederacy. Only a plaque marks the site of Elizabeth Van Lew's mansion. After the war, she was shunned by most of Richmond for her pivotal role as a spy, and after serving as Postmaster of Richmond for eight years, withdrew into her home until she died in poverty in 1900. Her grave can be found in Shockoe Cemetery, along with a boulder whose bronze plate reads: *Elizabeth L. Van Lew 1818—1900. She risked everything that is dear to man—friends—fortune—comfort—health—life itself—all for the one absorbing desire of her heart—that slavery might be abolished and the Union preserved. This boulder from the Capitol Hill in Boston is a tribute from Massachusetts friends.*

In the 1880s, Chicago businessmen purchased the former Libby Prison, dismantled it, shipped it by rail to Chicago, and rebuilt it with thousands of Civil War artifacts inside, including those mentioned in the epilogue. The Libby Prison War Museum opened September 20, 1889, and attracted more than 250,000 visitors during the first year, including veterans who'd once been imprisoned at Libby. The museum was razed ten years later.

Descendants of Civil War veterans from the North and the South dedicated a plaque in 1980 at the prison site in Richmond, the only evidence that Libby Prison once stood there.

In post–Civil War America, women of both North and South published more than ever before as their memoirs captured the public's attention. After four long years of hardship, women told their tales of nursing, soldiering, spying, organizing aid societies and commissions, and simply surviving the unthinkable. They were heroines behind the lines.

Primary source material, photos, and other resources may be found at www.heroinesbehindthelines.com.

Selected Bibliography

Ash, Stephen V. *The Black Experience in the Civil War South*. Dulles, Virginia: Potomac Books, 2013.

Bearss, Edwin and Bryce Suderow. *The Petersburg Campaign: The Western Front Battles*. El Dorado Hills, California: Savas Beatie, 2014.

Brown, Spencer Kellogg. *Spencer Kellogg Brown, His Life in Kansas and His Death as a Spy, 1842–1863*. New York, New York: D. Appleton and Company, 1903.

Carlson, Peter. *Junius and Albert's Adventures in the Confederacy*. New York, New York: PublicAffairs, 2013.

Coski, Ruth Ann. *The White House of the Confederacy: A Pictorial Tour*. Richmond, Virginia: The Museum of the Confederacy, 2012.

Dew, Charles B. *Ironmaker to the Confederacy: Joseph R. Anderson and the Tredegar Iron Works*. Richmond, Virginia: Library of Virginia, 1999. First edition, Yale University Press, 1966.

Furgurson, Ernest B. *Ashes of Glory: Richmond at War*. New York, New York: Alfred A. Knopf, 1996.

Glazier, Willard W. *The Capture, the Prison Pen, and the Escape*.

Hartford, Connecticut: H. E. Goodwin, 1867.

Jones, John Beauchamp. *A Rebel War Clerk's Diary at the Confederate States Capital.* Philadelphia, Pennsylvania: J. B. Lippincott & Co., 1866.

Lankford, Nelson. *Richmond Burning: The Last Days of the Confederate Capital.* New York, New York: Viking, 2002.

Lee, Richard M. *General Lee's City.* McLean, Virginia: EPM Publications, Inc., 1987.

Massey, Mary Elizabeth. *Ersatz in the Confederacy: Shortages and Substitutions on the Southern Home Front.* Columbia, South Carolina: University of South Carolina Press, 1952.

Neely, Mark E. *Southern Rights: Political Prisoners and the Myth of Confederate Constitutionalism.* Charlottesville, Virginia: University of Virginia Press, 1999.

Pinkerton, Allan. *The Spy of the Rebellion.* New York, New York: G. W. Carleton & Co., 1883.

Putnam, Sallie B. *Richmond During the War.* New York, New York: G. W. Carleton & Co. Publishers, 1867.

Ryan, David D., ed. *A Yankee Spy in Richmond.* Mechanicsburg, Pennsylvania: Stackpole Books, 1996.

Thomas, Emory M. *The Confederate State of Richmond: A Biography of the Capital.* Baton Rouge, Louisiana: Louisiana State University Press, 1971.

Trammell, Jack. *The Richmond Slave Trade: The Economic Backbone of the Old Dominion.* Charleston, South Carolina: The History Press, 2012.

Varon, Elizabeth R. *Southern Lady, Yankee Spy: The True Story of Elizabeth Van Lew.* Oxford, England: Oxford University Press, 2003.

Wheelan, Joseph. *Libby Prison Breakout.* New York, New York: PublicAffairs, 2010.

Wixson, Neal E. *From Civility to Survival: Richmond Ladies During the Civil War.* Bloomington, Indiana: iUniverse, 2012.

Discussion Guide

1. In the prologue, Sophie's father considers her differing opinion on slavery as a personal betrayal. When have you seen a difference of opinion cause a family rift? Was there a way to avoid it?

2. For years, Sophie set aside her own goals to keep the peace with her father and care for her mother. What is an appropriate balance of taking care of family and pursuing one's goals today?

3. Mr. Kent asks, "What's more important than family?" How would you answer that question?

4. For months, Sophie kept the manner of her mother's death secret from her father in order to protect him. Is this type of deception justified? Why or why not?

5. Dr. Caleb Lansing tells Sophie, "We must work as hard as we can at what we've been called to do, and leave the outcome up to God." When have you found this to be true in your own life?

6. Before his capture, Abraham Jamison fought for the Union army without pay, rather than accept half pay as a black soldier. He

fought to prove black people were equal to whites and deserved citizenship, at great hardship to both himself and his hungry wife. Can you think of a cause for which you would sacrifice great personal comfort?

7. After Sophie met with Dr. Lansing in the morgue, she felt so drastically altered by her actions she wondered if others could tell that she had changed. When have your actions changed you?

8. Harrison Caldwell's plans for a quick sojourn in Richmond are drastically altered upon his arrest. Share a time when your plans were dramatically changed. How did you handle it?

9. While in Libby Prison, Harrison muses that his own ambition caused his capture. When do you think a person's ambition can cause him or her harm? Can ambition hold us captive? How?

10. Sophie uses Captain Lawrence Russell first for protection, then as a source of intelligence. In what ways do we use people for our own benefit today?

11. Even though Sophie's parents and half sister are not physically present in the first two acts of the book, memories of all three of them influence Sophie. How does your family affect you, even when they aren't around?

12. Throughout Harrison's time in Richmond, he refers to Psalm 31:15, which says, "My times are in thy hand." Read all of Psalm 31. Which parts resonate most with you?

13. When Harrison is thrown into Libby Prison, he recalls the proverb, "Beware of what you wish for." When have you received something you thought you wanted, only to realize it wasn't what you expected?

14. Sophie cherishes old drafts of her articles full of Harrison's corrections. What corrections or advice do you cherish now that was difficult to hear at first?

15. When Harrison crawls through a tomb-like tunnel in order to emerge in freedom, he tells himself, "This is not a grave. It is rebirth." How does this parallel to a spiritual journey?

16. Sophie's fear of following her mother toward insanity haunted her. How do you keep your fears from controlling you?

17. In Richmond, Bella reminds herself, "I am not a slave." When Abraham is about to be sold away, she tells him, "You're free. You're free." How does what we believe about ourselves affect us?

18. Sophie's father orders laudanum to be given to her to help heal her, without understanding that the overdose would harm her mind and body. How do we sometimes try to help ourselves and others with something that could actually harm us?

19. Abraham hates helping the Confederacy by working for Tredegar Iron Works but doing so gives him information valuable to the Union. When has God used a trial in your own life in a surprising way?

20. Harrison encourages Sophie, and ultimately other war survivors, to tell their stories. Why is it important both for those sharing, and for those of us who hear?

Acknowledgments

$\mathcal{I}$ owe a debt of gratitude and appreciation to:

Moody Publishers/River North Fiction, for their dedication to bringing this series to life.

My agent, Tim Beals of Credo Communications, for his enduring support.

My husband, Rob, and children, Elsa and Ethan, for being far more supportive and understanding than I have any right to expect, for the four years it has taken me to research, write, and edit this entire series. My heart can barely contain the love I have for each of you. Rob, you are my happily ever after.

My parents, Peter and Pixie Falck, for watching the kids and bringing me food when I'm too busy to even have an appetite. Also, Dad, your help capturing and ordering my ideas during the outlining stage was indispensable.

Kelly Sizemore, Library of Virginia; Joseph Wheelan, author of *Libby Prison Breakout*; L. Paige Newman, Virginia Historical Society; John Deeben, National Archives; author Karen A. Chase, Church

Hill Association; friends and fellow historical writers Cass Wessel and Peter Leavell; and the staff at Chimborazo Hospital Medical Museum, the Museum of the Confederacy (both in Richmond, Virginia); the Casemate Museum (Fort Monroe, Virginia), and the Siege Museum (Petersburg, Virginia) for contributing to my research.

A host of friends for help with child care: Teresa Carr, Melissa DeFord, Kris Ertl, Kristin Coulson, Amy Lanser, and Jacqueline Thompson.

Darci McVay, for bringing meals to my family, unsolicited, but appreciated more than you know.

Above all, I thank the Lord for granting me the opportunity to tell these stories, for inspiration, and for sustaining me and my family during the years it took to bring them to life. If there is anything good between these pages, it's only because of Him.

About the Author

Jocelyn Green is an award-winning author of multiple fiction and nonfiction works, including *Faith Deployed: Daily Encouragement for Military Wives*, and *The 5 Love Languages Military Edition*, which she cowrote with Dr. Gary Chapman. Her first novel in the Heroines Behind the Lines series, *Wedded to War*, was a Christy Award finalist, and the gold medal winner in historical fiction from the Military Writers Society of America. A native Northerner, she and her Southern-born-and-bred husband live in Cedar Falls, Iowa, with their two children. Her goal with every book is to inspire faith and courage in her readers. Visit her at www.jocelyngreen.com.

MORE FROM
THE HEROINES BEHIND
THE LINES SERIES

978-0-8024-0576-0   978-0-8024-0577-7   978-0-8024-0578-4

river north

Thank you! We are honored that you took the time out of your busy schedule to read this book. If you enjoyed what you read, would you consider sharing the message with others?

- Write a review online at amazon.com, bn.com, goodreads.com, cbd.com.

- Recommend this book to friends in your book club, workplace, church, school, classes, or small group.

- Go to facebook.com/RiverNorthFiction, "like" the page, and post a comment as to what you enjoyed the most.

- Mention this book in a Facebook post, Twitter update, Pinterest pin, or a blog post.

- Pick up a copy for someone you know who would be encouraged by this message.

- Subscribe to our newsletter for information on upcoming titles, inside information on discounts and promotions, and learn more about your favorite authors at RiverNorthFiction.com.

midday connection

Discover a safe place to authentically process life's journey on **Midday Connection**, hosted by Anita Lustrea and Melinda Schmidt. This live radio program is designed to encourage women with a focus on growing the whole person: body, mind, and soul. You'll grow toward spiritual freedom and personal transformation as you learn who God is and who He created us to be.

www.middayconnection.org

MOODY Radio™

*From the Word **to Life***